Shattered Stone

The Stone Mage Series
Book 2

Amelia G. Sides

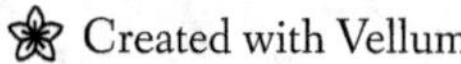 Created with Vellum

For my father, Larry, who never said a book was too hard for me growing up.
Learning to read and plow through his collection of fantasy and science fiction shaped my life.
Thank you, Dad.

Part One

Arden

Chapter 1

Escaping the Capital

Beryl sat thinking, curled in her cloak, waiting for her promised rescue to appear. Argent pressed against her side, his bulk a wall of heat against the chill of the cell. Rune curled in her arms, a faint purr vibrating the small grey tabby's body as he projected strength and love along their bond.

She sat trying to concentrate on the feel of the animals' fur and not the press of the surrounding darkness, the chill clammy stone of her prison cell. She didn't dare try to cast a light rune; so far the guards had ignored the fact that they were guarding a mage, but they could bind her magic with rune infused cuffs. She couldn't even risk trying to pick the locks and get out on her own. She owed Darius too much to run.

No one had bothered her since the late night meeting with her now former Master, Darius. She hadn't been surprised to learn that he was the leader of the King's spy network or that he'd asked her to join it as a ghost. If it meant that she and her bond mates would survive, she would do whatever he asked of her. Argent lay across the small pack he'd left her, hiding it from view in case the guards checked the cell. Beryl stroked the massive hunting hound's wiry grey and black coat with one hand, trying to get him to relax into sleep; they would need all the strength they had for the coming days.

The entire castle had to know the tale of her supposed treachery by now. While she sat in a cell, the true attacker, Delorean, was out plotting his next move. The healers had dealt with the burns that covered her chest, arms, and hands, leaving her with tender but mostly healed skin, but she still was head to toe bruises and magical exhaustion. Her bond mates were uninjured beyond the stress and exhaustion they all shared, but they all needed the time to recover from the medical backlash.

When the spell overloaded, exploding the wall of the ballroom, she redirected the blast outward, into the garden, instead of inward toward the crowded room of dignitaries there for the presentation of the child prince, James. Argent herded everyone but the guards, chasing him away from the wall before it exploded. Thankfully, so few people were injured beyond a few cuts and bruises. Beryl had staggered from the wall, collapsing in exhaustion only to wake up in a cell.

"Sleep," She told her bond mates, *"I'll keep watch,"* A general swell of agreement filled the bond for a moment before it settled back into the gentle hum at the back of her mind. Reaching out, she mentally touched each animal, checking on them before she settled back against the wall behind her, waiting.

Kuro, her third bond mate, was roosting in a tree close to the castle, already asleep and waiting on the dawn. The Shiro, a sea hawk, had been a steady presence of rage at the back of Beryl's mind since she woke from the blast. The bird had tried to keep track of the Man who hurt her bonded but hadn't seen him since the attack on the castle. If he was hiding in the castle or town, she could not see him.

Beryl tried to sooth the bird to little effect; it didn't matter in the end. Delorean hadn't been seen during the attack, and he wasn't thought to be a mage. Only someone with magic could have caused the explosion, making her the prime suspect. Servants had seen her and her bond mates bolting through the halls toward the garden where the disaster happened, pointing every finger her way.

This was twice now that he had escaped capture after harming her, once when she was a child and now again as an adult. Until the curse he placed on her was broken, she couldn't even name her attacker and no one would believe her since he was not a mage. There was nothing she could do about it beyond try to prevent him from further harming those around her. She would have to be more vigilant.

The last two years with Darius had been amazing. She'd learned magic she'd only dreamed about, lived in the palace as an apprentice, and now she'd lost everything. She'd escaped from her uncle, started making a life for herself, and now everything was in ashes all over again.

A cloaked figure eased the cell door open on greased hinges a few hours before dawn, gesturing for her to follow. Grabbing her pack she scooped Rune up onto her shoulder heading out the cell door with Argent padding silently behind. The figure guided them through dark, silent halls and servant corridors using the light from a small mage light orb mostly shielded by a piece of leather.

Disoriented from the dark hallways and rush, Beryl almost fell when her guide made a sudden stop in front of a heavy wooden door. Pulling the door open just enough to slide through, the guide exited, gesturing her through a moment later. Two sturdy brown horses waited tied to a bush in a small wood about a mile from the gate, it was obvious that Flox wasn't one of them. A part of her heart hurt for having to leave her horse, but the entire town knew what he looked like after them going on so many message runs for the castle.

She took the reins handed to her and mounted, barely making sure Rune was secured in a pouch on the saddle before they were off at a trot. It forced Kuro to wait and fly once the sun rose, catching up with them as she could. They rode without pause, cantering on the better stretches of the back roads they traveled on.

They rode all day, only stopping to water the horses or walk for brief stretches to keep the horses from foundering or overheating. Her guide did not speak beyond terse commands, and Beryl did not bother to ask questions. She spent the small negligible amount of time they stopped every hour caring for Argent. Large dogs were not built to travel long distances, and she was hard pressed to keep him from overheating or falling behind. She called for a halt once on the first day to bind Argent's feet in leather strips to stop them from tearing. She doubted her horse would consent to carry the large dog, but the animal continued to push himself to keep the pace their guide set without complaint.

It was dark by the time they came to a town on the fourth day. Kuro had flown ahead and sent back images of a sea town snug atop black cliffs of dark stone and browning grass. She dashed any hope of their journey ending there as they went straight through town and to the docks. They took away the horses and showed her to a cabin. Kuro refused to come down, instead intending to follow the ship or rest in the rigging. Once Beryl and her bond mates were in the cabin, her guide set a pack next to hers and headed toward the door.

"Lord Darius wishes you luck. The Captain will show you to the next leg of your journey. I don't know where you're going but I wish you luck," it was the most the man had said the entire trip. He'd been silent except for the occasional command to camp or mount when a rest break was over. He gave her a small nod of encouragement before shutting the cabin door behind him. Soon after, the cries of the sailors and rattle of tack showed that the ship was casting off.

Three days later she stood on the rail enjoying the wind and spray batting against her face, her brown braid blown back to thump against her back. Captain Harris was a stern man when shouting orders to his crew, but smiled as he told stories of the other passengers and cargoes he had transported over the years. She was masquerading as his niece, who was traveling to visit family.

Rune roamed the ship hunting mice and rats while Argent kept Beryl company on the deck or in the cabin. The sailors had noticed the Shiro following the ship and even riding the rigging at night or in calm weather, but took it as a wonderful omen, making the sign of Ruth whenever the sea hawk was seen. The bird herself was happy to be back at sea. She sent images of whales and schools of fish across the bond. Argent was seasick and spent most of his time hunkered as low to the deck as he could get, still trying to recover his strength from the four day march. The bond seemed to both help and hinder with his sickness as the others felt his misery and shared in his pain, but they could share a small bit of their strength and well-being with him.

They were headed to Saint Bart's, a medium-sized harbor town that did a brisk trade in wood and cloth. From there she was headed to an inn to spend the night. The contact would know her and would reveal themselves when and where it was safe.

If they didn't contact her by nightfall of the second day, she was to leave and find somewhere isolated and safe to stay before contacting Darius by message stone. The pack left by her guide contained more trail food and basic clothes that she could use if she had to travel alone. A small purse had been in the pack Darius had supplied. It should be enough to get a few days' food and lodging if she needed it.

She spent most of her time on the ship warding the cabins and masts of the ship along with making several message stones for Captain Harris that would send slips of paper attached to the stones back to Darius' receiving circle in the Capitol. The crew was wary of her, both for being the Captain's niece and for being a mage, however they warmed up to her when she warded things for them. Most of the crew now had jackets with runes against stains and water-proofing runes stitched into the lining to keep them warm and dry out at sea.

She'd just have to wait and see what the rest of her trip sent her. She was too indebted to Darius to abandon his cause now. Beryl spent the afternoon combining the contents of her two packs into one and readying the two dresses the Captain had given her for tomor-row. She would need to look like a respectable lady going to visit her family and not a mage with three bond mates and a price on her head.

The spy network that Darius controlled seemed to be massive. Captain Harris showed her the small rune for listening that was tattooed on his wrist, hidden by a leather cuff he wore. All the Listeners had them. It had become a thing of fashion for the middle class and some upper to get tattoos of runes for luck or a skill they wanted. While a rune for listening was strange to many, when most wanted runes for wealth or good fortune, it would be overlooked and hidden from those who didn't know the true meaning. If she passed her training, she would receive a small rune of her own, except as a mage they could imbue hers with magic and act as an enhancer to her powers of hearing and memory.

At dinner that night, Captain Harris spent most of the meal in silence, occasionally giving her advice on how to deal with unfamiliar people in town or who she could ask for help that owed him or the Listeners a favor if she ran into trouble. She was already nervous about heading out on her own with no actual destination. She knew if the contact did not come tomorrow, she would have to find some-where isolated to hide out until she could contact Darius. She would stick to the coast and find an isolated cabin that was not being used. She had promised Kuro that they would live by the sea after all, and there was no reason not to start now.

The next morning she dressed in the full-length gown of pale blue that Captain Harris had provided. It was last year's fashion and large but still something a down on their luck middle to upper class merchant family might wear. The gown was high-necked and long-sleeved, covering her scars and mage jewelry. Wearing her grey cloak and gloves, she looked the part of a demure merchant's daughter. They hid Rune under the flap of her pack. The Captain also gifted her with an old but serviceable carpet bag into which she had moved her knives and a few other things to make the pack lighter and give Rune more room.

"I've arranged a cart to take you to the inn once we dock." Captain

Harris said accepting the cup of tea she poured for him with a murmur of thanks. "You should be safe enough at Last Hope Harbor until your message arrives."

"Thank you, Captain." Beryl said with a sigh, giving Rune a piece of the tea cookie she'd been crumbling.

"I'm not saying it will be easy, Miss, you're wanted by the crown and that makes just being in public a hazard. Thankfully, while the population has heard of the attack on the capital by a rogue mage, I doubt they knew many details or what you look like."

"I'll stay out of sight when I can." Beryl said with a sigh, "I'm used to blending in from traveling with my Uncle, it shouldn't be too different from hiding from people hoping to catch a young girl or mage to beat up."

"Sadly, you're right." He sighed, setting his cup down with a frown, "The innkeeper at Last Hope is Rosaria, a smart woman who knows how to keep silent about her guests. She'll make sure you're not harassed in the inn, but outside you're on your own."

"I'll be careful." She promised not sure how she should feel with the fatherly concern from the Captain, she hadn't had someone who wanted to keep her safe since she was a small child.

The next day they docked and were shown to a small but clean room at the back of the second floor. Rosaria was a boisterous woman who cackled with laughter at her own jokes, especially the ones about using Argent to keep the men away. The Captain came by to make sure she was settled before heading on his way. The ship headed out that afternoon on the evening tide. She would meet up with her guide sometime the next day.

She did not want to risk being outed as a mage, so she kept mostly to the inn. She bought a supply of dried beef from the cook that she and her bond mates could all eat by saying it was a treat for Argent. It should last them almost a week if they were sparing with it.

The next day it was almost dinner before she met her contact. She was sitting at a table near the wall eating a bowl of soup while slipping Argent scraps of bread when a woman walked up to their table.

"Do you mind if I sit?" she asked. She was wearing a plain yellow dress that would have fit on any middle-class lady or merchant's wife in town. Brown hair and brown eyes added to the ordinariness that coated the woman.

"No, please have a seat." The woman slid a folded sheet of paper across the table, flashing the rune for listening sat on the underside of her wrist. "Don't open it here. You must make the next leg of your journey alone, I'm afraid. Consider this your first test. You'll often work alone and without guidance. Once you reach your destination, you'll receive more directions." With a wry grin, she stood. "Ruth's blessing and Bain's forgetfulness," She said, leaving the table and heading out the door.

Beryl finished her soup, paid and went to her room to pack. She would leave at first light. Once in her room she went over the papers, a map, and instructions with Rune and Argent looking over her shoulder. Kuro was still at the shipyards. Once they left, she would fly out and meet them. The map was a crude drawing of roads and landmarks with handwritten instructions of when to turn and which town she was heading for.

The ultimate stop was at a place called Crone's Bluff, a compact town farther down the coast. From there they directed her to a lonely road that seemed to go nowhere, coming to a stop in the middle of a stand of trees and hills. It relieved her she'd gotten Richard to teach their entire group basic map reading.

The realization that Richard and Salendra and all her other friends at the castle thought she was either still in the dungeon or escaped and run away made her chest ache. If they thought she'd run away, then they thought she'd tried to hurt the castle, because why would she run if she were innocent?

It was too much to think of. That part of her life was over now. She was no longer Master Darius's Apprentice and friend of Richard and Salendra. Now she was a rogue mage and a spy in training for the crown. She couldn't let herself be swayed into a stupid action by homesickness. If she died, her bond mates would die. If someone injured them, she would feel the pain like it was her own. They had to take care of each other. She couldn't make rash decisions when all their lives might hang on the balance of her judgment.

Showing them the map from the packet, she drew the route out in her mind. Animals no matter how magical did not always understand the need for things like maps or books. It would be a group decision. She could take the route marked and stick to the roads or they could go through the backcountry and side roads which might take longer and be a rougher hike. One would be easier on all their feet, but the other would be safer. They all agreed they would be more comfortable off the road. They could travel together without one or more of them being forced to hide. From the look of the map, it would be several days to reach Crone's Bluff.

Chapter 2

First Test

In the morning Beryl left the room before dawn, the Inn's common room was empty except for a sleeping stable boy by the fire as she slipped out the back door. She wore her blue dress and cloak over her work pants and tunic in case they were seen. She was just a woman out taking her dog for an early walk.

Once they made it out of town, they paused in a clump of trees for her to remove the dress and pack it, she'd hidden her pack at the edge of town the night before. She buckled argent into his armor and Beryl pulled on her daggers and arm guard. The armor would draw attention, but it also could save their lives if they attacked them.

The first two days they hurried through the forests that lined the road, they walked until it was too dark to see, using Argent and Rune's senses to find good campsites to spend the night. Kuro would fly back to the road once a day to make sure they were heading the right direction. Beryl was confident in her map skills, but it never hurt to double check.

The next two days of the trek were a miserable march through the woods and fields in pounding rain. On the third day, they came to a roaring stream that they had to backtrack upstream until they came to a better place to cross. Kuro sat hunched, miserable on Argent or Beryl's shoulder, shaking the water from her head and neck in a shower of droplets every few minutes; she hated being barred from the sky.

It was almost full dark when they lucked out in finding a small cave to spend the night in. Beryl risked a small fire to warm everyone and dry her clothes. She spent most of the night huddled next to the fire, trying to keep her fingers warm while she oiled Argent's armor and her arm guards. Dressing the next morning in damp clothes they exited the cave to find the rain had slowed to a misty drizzle that floated on the slight breeze, coating hair and skin with a light beading of water but not soaking, thank Ruth.

Just before reaching Crone's Bluff, they headed back toward the road. The road leading to the woods looked small enough that they could miss it if they weren't careful, so they would come in through the town. The rain stopped that morning, changing into a heavy mist as they were coming across farmers' fields on the way into town.

Crone's Bluff looked like a rough town. Sitting on the edge of a bluff with a middle sized harbor below it, the dirty streets ran in no particular order or direction. Houses with broken windows and crooked shutters sat next to painted whore houses with the wares parading along the muddy street or leaning out windows scantily dressed. There had been a poor district in the capital city, but it was nothing like this. There was a sharp edge of desperation to every person who wandered the streets.

Beryl walked along head high, not letting her eyes linger too long on anyone place or thing. She forced herself to walk with a purpose but not hurry. She was someone who knew where she was going and was used to the town, which was what she was trying to project, anyway. The sight of Argent in his armor pacing beside her silenced all but the most ardent of hawkers.

She ignored the shouts of services, goods, and downright junk being offered on either side of her and headed for the center of town. The map said she was to take the left road of the three leading away for the town square; however, it left off four side roads. She had Kuro get a view of the roads leading away from the square from the air. One branched off and rejoined the main road out of town, while another dead ended in a warehouse district near the harbor. The last two roads both headed into the nearby woods.

Fixing the map in her mind, she overlaid it with the two remaining roads. The one on the right matched the shape on the map the best, so they headed down that one. She had barely taken a step in that direction when she glimpsed a shape following them. Without a second thought, they turned away and started down the one that would take them to the main road.

They would circle around and lose their tail first. It could be another member of the Listeners or it could be a local thug trying to catch a stranger unaware, but it was the third option that had her shaping spells against the pebbles she'd picked up as they walked. The follower could also be someone from the army who wanted to turn them in.

The small stones warmed against her hands as she pushed runes for sleep and forgetfulness into them. A word and a hard toss would have her attacker asleep where he lay, but there was no guarantee he was the only one. As long as he was there, the others she wasn't aware of wouldn't suspect anything, if there were others. It was enough to make your head spin.

The man shadowed her until she was almost out of town and then slid back into the gathering darkness as the sun set. She went farther out of town before circling back to the road she needed. She was about to step onto it when her chest went tight. With a soft gasp, she stepped away from the road, sucking in a deeper breath as the tightness eased. She never understood the tightness that would seize her, but she knew it meant that there was danger or a very important decision needed to be made. Whenever she ignored the feeling, it would last for a moment or two before passing, but it never turned out good. She'd take what warnings she could and act on them if it kept her bond mates safe.

Glancing at Argent, she crouched and examined the road. For a dirt road that went nowhere, there had been a lot of traffic on it. A wagon had cut deep ruts through the mud, and boots had trampled the leaves and grass into the mire. She couldn't sense any magic or spells, but it did not mean they couldn't be there. Skirting the road, they slid into the woods. Using every bit of wilderness training she had, Beryl ghosted from tree to tree. Slipping away from the road and deeper into the woods, she slogged her way to where the map directed, the center of the forest.

Only Argent's sudden warning stopped her from stepping on the trip wire hidden among the leaves. It was a simple wire rabbit snare, but it still could have twisted her ankle and hurt Rune or Argent. After that they found some kind of trap every few yards, some of them deadly, like the hanging deadfall full of wooden spikes rigged to fall and crush a person against a handy tree. Beryl was the one who spotted the sentries posted along the road, some hidden in well camouflaged perches high in the trees while others walked the road in plain sight. Trusting her mud covered cloak and brown pants to hide her, she slid past each on her belly, crawling through the leaf litter when there was no brush to hide in.

She moved at a slow trot when she could, crouching when there was cover, and freezing at the slightest sound. Whoever the guards were, they were good. They didn't talk or play cards while they waited; they watched in the focused, sweeping manner of men at war, taking in every detail. The one outstanding thing this told her was that this was not a house of rabble thieves, this was an army. It meant that the guards would have a steady rotation and schedule to keep from getting too tired and missing something, a pattern that she could follow and avoid if she was lucky.

She eased forward as they neared the clearing. She felt her jaw drop as the building came into focus. It was a mansion built like it wanted to be a castle. Made of enormous blocks of grey stone and rising to four floors, its two towers overlooking the clearing and nearby woods. The faint crash of waves meant that the cliffs were not too far beyond the stand of trees on the other side of the mansion.

It had grown dark as she wove her way deeper into the forest. In another half hour it would be pitch black, and with the clouds Beryl doubted Kuro could stay aloft. Birds can't fly when then can't see where to land; Kuro landed in a tree not too far from them, settling into wait until dawn.

Beryl left her pack hidden under the same tree buried in leaves, loading her pockets with spell stones and a few other surprises that might help. If she got out all right, she could get her pack and Kuro on the way out. She crept her way forward, Troche had trained her well, she thought, pushing the familiar pang of grief back with well-worn practice. She probably would always miss the quick tongued thief, but now wasn't the time for remembrances.

It tempted her to step out and simple let them catch her, but after all, this was a test and a test set for a future spy at that. As much as she disliked it, if she was supposed to act like a spy, she would expect them to want her to break into the Mansion and get to an inner room for her meeting. Some small part of her acknowledged that this would hurt as she slid into a crouch waiting for the last guard to pass by, in the flickering light of his lantern she threw herself in a crouching sprint toward the stone wall that made up the right side of the castle.

Crouching in a triangle of darkness with Argent plastered against her side, she waited for the next guard to move on before sliding along the wall to the first dark window. It was locked, and she did not want to risk using a spell to unlock it; she wasn't being tested on her magical ability. Moving on, they paused when Rune sent that he had found a way in. It was a narrow window that a large adult would have trouble squeezing through. It was rare that she could use her small size to her advantage she mused, extending her mage sight over the stone, almost nothing was warded.

The entire building sat on a strong well of natural magic, but the stones were with no warding beyond a small one to keep water from leaking in from the stones on the lower floors. She climbed up to the top window as Argent went after Rune, looking for a bigger entrance he could use. If they did not find one, he would head to the woods while Rune caught up with Beryl.

The window spat her out into a pantry filled with sacks of grain and flour. Stifling a sneeze, she stepped up to the door and stood listening for any sound beyond her breathing. After one hundred heartbeats of nothing, she pulled the door inward, peeking through the crack. The hallway beyond was lit every dozen feet by a lantern bolted to the wall on an iron hook. Sliding along the wall, she slipped from one pool of darkness to another.

The sound of footsteps had her moving faster. She slipped into a side door that showed a winding stair just before the guard walked past. With boots that loud, she wouldn't miss the guards at least. Argent and Rune found a loose door that Rune slipped through and clicked the lock for Argent to enter. They were both on their way to her within moments, but she sent them out exploring instead. No one would blink at a cat in a dark hall. Argent might cause a commotion, but they could pass him off as the master of the house's dog. Now, if she was a spy, where would she want to go?

All the stories always had the items being stolen in the center of the castle or in the remote dungeons; she didn't want to crawl around the dungeons unless she had to, Troche had taken her through the sewers a few times and that was more than enough. So first choice was the center of the castle, maybe the master's office or chambers. The stories always had someone sneaking into the castle to steal documents. She mentally scolded Brennan, the castle librarian, for getting her reading so many novels where a valiant knight had to fight his way into the evil villain's castle. Now all she needed was a mage or ghost to jump out and scare everyone, and it would be just like the books.

The stone wall of the mansion gave way to wood paneling and tapestry hangings the deeper she went. She crept through rooms with rich velvet couches and floors covered in old carpets that sucked the sound from her steps. The last door opened into another stone hallway. Moving as silently as she could, she drifted toward the next door at the end of the hall. They made this one of a heavy red wood. The faint sound of voices murmured from somewhere behind it. So she had found the people. Now what?

Without warning, a hand grabbed her wrist while another covered her mouth with a cloth. She heard Rune hiss and attack someone who cursed as Argent came barreling their way, a bass growl making the world seem to vibrate. The room slid to grey mist as she pressed a sleep spelled stone against her attacker. The cloth fell away from her face, but the cloying sweet stench stayed in her nose and mouth as she sagged against one wall. Grey mist rose and filled her vision, pulling her down into sleep.

* * *

She woke with an aching head and foul mouth in a bed so soft it felt like lying on pillows or feathers. Someone cleared their throat, causing her to bolt out of the covers only to grab her head to make sure it was still on with a groan. The voice chuckled and someone sat on the edge of the bed.

"Here, I am sure you head's killing you. The sleep dust will do that, I'm afraid." Cracking open one eye she took in the man seated next to her holding out a glass of what looked like water.

"Who are you?" she asked. She could feel her bond mates sleeping somewhere, Kuro was agitated, but she also was on a perch in the dark somewhere but at least no pain was coming across the bonds between them.

"Ah, right to the chase I see." He said, extending the water again. "First a drink, nothing in it, I swear." He said taking a sip before handing it to her. After she had taken a small sip of the water, she looked at him, waiting for him to answer her original question.

He was a middle-aged man with dark brown hair sprinkled with grey, cut in a brief clip about an inch long. He was dressed like the master of the house in clothes cut to fit with a fine vest of velvet and a gold watch chain hanging from one pocket. His blue eyes twinkled with suppressed mirth as he watched her. His hands were not stained with ink but showed the calluses of one used to doing heavy work or using a sword. This was a soldier pretending to be a lord. As she continued to watch him, he gave a small grin.

"Very well, to business, you were sent here to find your next trainer, and you have found him." He pulled the cuff back from his wrist, exposing the blue listener rune to the light.

"My name is Baron Sarnes, but you may call me William while we are among fellow members. We know you as Mage and your bond mates are Rune, Argent, and Kuro. They sent you to me by your Master, Darius, to receive training so we can send you to a foreign court to receive training from the court mages. They gave you a map with no directions on what to do once you got here." He broke off with a grin, shaking his finger at her.

"I can tell you, that you're not the first to break into the castle, but you are one of the first to lose so many of our watchers on the road. You were spotted in Crone's Bluff and we received a warning that you were on your way from the good Captain but you disappeared in the time between. You were seen in the town square of Crone's Bluff about to head down toward the woods before you turned away and continued down the road toward the next town," he gave her a small nod of approval at the deception.

"You were not seen on the road coming to the house or in the surrounding courtyard. In fact, you were not seen at all until you came to the door of the room I was in, having a meeting with a member of my watch. Beyond well done for a beginner, added to that you did not use magic that we can tell beyond the sleep spell you cast on one guard when he was attacking you." He moved to the chair next to the bed.

"Your cat scratched up my men rather badly before he was sleep dusted, as did the dog. Your bird by that point was attacking the windows, and we got a paltry amount of sleep dust on it and get it down and hooded. They injured none of them, have no fear." He said raising his hands to stop her unvoiced question.

"In avoiding my watchers, you showed that you know how to travel unseen if you need to. You also could uphold a part small as it was, the act of the merchant's niece. You avoided my men on watch and got into a guarded building. You didn't attack anyone until they threatened you, you do not understand how hard that is to learn and it's a lesson we can skip," he said with a sigh. "The fundamental lessons I believe you'll need are ones on court manners and on how to maintain your cover. With your curse, you'll be able to count on most of the people who see you in passing or meet you once or twice to forget who we introduced you as."

The curse had been the bane of her existence for too long for her to be happy to embrace it. She had been nothing more than the adolescent daughter of a local mage when she chased after a cat one evening and was attacked. She remembered the man attempting some spell, covering her body in lines of blood that he had taken by driving a dagger through her palms. He went insane at the failure of the spell, slashing and stabbing at her before he cast one final spell, her curse.

In the following days they merged the curse into the healing, twisting its nature. No one could remember any details she spoke of the attack or her attacker, dismissing them as irrelevant. Somehow her name was included in the spell, most people forgetting within moments after she told them. She had been going by the title Mage since she went to live with her uncle.

The Baron rose and began pacing, "We have quite a lot to do, my dear."

"Sir, if I may..." He waved her on, continuing to pace. "No one has said what I would do, only that I would learn magic at other courts. No one has said where I'm going or what I can expect."

"It is coming, my dear. You'll be spending week training in the customs of the different courts so you'll be able to converse with any dignitaries from one of them without a misstep. While you're doing that, you'll also be learning how to dress, eat, walk, dance, and act like you belong in the royal courts. If they think you belong, then they'll say things and do things around you they would never say in front of a stranger and that's what all this training is for. To find out the rumors and plots that are brewing in the other courts so it prepares us for any eventuality," he stated, his face grave.

"We're the first line of defense for the Crown, Mage. The ones who warn the King of impending danger. We're the ones who carry the messages that could cause a war if they were intercepted. We're the ones who fight the unseen battles before they can ever set foot on our shores." That said, his face fell into a slight smile. "Now there are clothes in the cabinet for you. You have the rest of the day to care for your animals and learn the layout of the house in the sunlight this time. In the morning we train at dawn. I will have a late lunch brought in for you and your animals brought in; until the morrow, my dear." He said throwing in a courtly bow as he exited the room.

Sliding to the edge of the bed, Beryl finished the glass of water before sitting it on the bedside table. She was wearing a clean tunic and someone had gotten off the worst of the mud, but her hair was still in its mud covered braid. That would take a good hour of bathing to clean and untangle.

Wincing at the tight braid pulling on her scalp, she went to the dresser and opened it to see what they had left her to wear. The dresser had a little of everything, from a ball gown to a man's suit like the one Baron Sarnes was wearing. Everything looked like it would be close to her size. Figuring she might as well be comfortable, she pulled down one pair of pants and a loose men's shirt in deep blue. Opening doors she found the bath and happily got cleaned and dressed after soaking in the tub and washing her hair.

When she emerged Argent was snoring on the hearthrug and Kuro sat hooded on a wooden perch with her beak burrowed into her chest feathers. Rune lay on the bed watching her with drug glazed eyes. Hurrying to him, she drew runes for healing and poison removal, hoping that it would help with getting over the sleep dust, whatever it was. A moment later Rune lost the glazed look to his eyes and sat up, giving his usual grating cry. Beryl scooped him up and cuddled him for a moment before moving to do the same for Argent.

Moving to the perch, she called out for Kuro softly so as not to startle the bird. Once she raised her head and cocked it at Beryl, she carefully removed the hood and stays that had tied the bird to the perch. Beryl then cast the same runes on the bird as she had on the others, but of the three Kuro was the most alert. She was also the angriest. Beryl listened to the bird rant as she hunted down her boots and her pack. The four bond mates shared what they could remember of the last night and the attack. Kuro was rather smug that she was the last to fall. Beryl smiled at this, murmuring how they all knew she was the fiercest of the four.

There was a knock on the door and a woman dressed as a servant brought in a tray of food. A bowl of stew with bread and a cup of ale sat next to a small bowl of minced cooked chicken and another of raw red meat. Argent was given a bowl of scraps of meat and cooked vegetables sat next to him. The servant did the last part fast, clearly afraid of the enormous dog. Beryl thanked her as she curtsied, eying the yawning monster and left.

Beryl pulled on her arm guard and glove and got Kuro, setting her on the wooden rail at the foot of the bed, feeding her scraps of meat while she ate her stew. Rune ate his bowl of chicken from the tray. They all felt much better afterwards and set off and explore the house as the Baron had suggested.

Pulling on her leather coat, she set Kuro on her shoulder and opened the door for the others. There were no windows, but she guessed that they were on one of the upper floors of the building. She had seen no bedrooms on the first floor.

They explored the house, finding empty dining halls, galleries, and a ballroom along with more bedrooms. The doors off the stairs for the top two floors were locked, and she did not open them. None of the servants or the cooks she encountered in the kitchens or rooms spoke to her, so she remained silent.

When she found a door that lead outside, she moved Kuro to her fist and went out, walking around the house, nodding to the guards as she passed them. A group of guards stood to the back side of the house doing sword exercises and practicing archery. At Kuro's urging she released the bird to explore, before beginning her stretches to warm her arms, legs and back.

Argent had found a scent and was tracking it down. Seeing the soldiers stopping to watch, he bounded to Rune and scooped him up in his maw to the resounding gasps of his audience. Beryl gave a sigh as she bopped him lightly on the head, stopped his prancing and held out a hand. With a wuffling sigh, he opened his mouth and let the cat climb out. Beryl pulled out a handkerchief and wiped the worst of the dog's slobber off of Rune before setting him down with a last pat to his small striped head.

"You two have to stop doing that." She said in exasperation. "One day you will do it wrong and swallow or hurt him, Argent." Laughter from the troops greeted this statement. She ignored them and picked a tree as her target. Pulling off her coat and rolling up her sleeves, she moved into place. Squaring her stance, she began throwing daggers into the tree. When she had thrown all but her two long daggers, she retrieved them from the target and started all over again at a greater distance from the last starting point.

Rune curled up on top of her discarded coat and was trying to bathe the dog spit out of his coat keeping a running commentary about silly dogs and ungrateful bond mates that messed up his fur across the bond. Argent ignored this and went back to tracking the pine martin he had scented earlier. Kuro sent them images of the bluffs behind the house as the sea threw itself onto the rocks in plumes of white spray that glittered in the evening light. Beryl had increased her distance from the target twice before they approached her.

"You're Mage I take it?" the soldier asked.

"I am." She said, taking in the older man before her. His hair was a peppered black and silver with dark brown or black eyes that refused to be revealed by the dying light. He wore the same uniform as the other soldiers, a collection of leather and brown or black cloth, armor, and straps with no indicator of rank in sight.

"My name is Lorrik. I'm the Baron's Captain of the Guard. I'll be helping to train you in weapons, tracking and evasion. You know how to throw dagger at a fixed target. How are you at moving targets?" He gestured toward one of her daggers with a raised eyebrow, and she handed it to him.

"I have trained little against moving targets, Captain. I was learning the basics of staff and short sword fighting when I had to leave the capital. I can use a bow and a sling well but never got to moving targets on these either beyond hunting rabbits or wood doves. Dorn focused on hand to hand fighting with and without daggers and throwing daggers. I was to learn how to make my own daggers later this spring."

The reminder she had lost her trainer and the respect of Dorn, hurt. He thought her guilty and regretted ever having trained her. Pushing the thought away, she focused back on the Captain in time to accept back her dagger. He watched her with unreadable eyes before nodding to himself.

"Tomorrow at dawn you'll meet up with my guard and go through the sword and staff drills with us. You'll do this every morning. When you are done with your lessons inside for the day, you will meet me back here and we'll work on your archery and other skills that you may need. Understood?"

"Yes, sir. Is it all right if I join your basic drills now?"

"Get a practice sword and join the line. Have you ever worked in a group formation?"

"No, sir."

"Well, you'll learn it quickly enough. It's useful when working with troops or using a shield. We will teach you both. Go get your sword."

"Yes, sir."

Hours later, she trudged to her room with every muscle protesting. She swore the shield and sword handed her had been switched at some point and filled with led by the end of the practice. Her hands were screaming. She'd never had to use them that hard since she'd the attack when she was a child.

In her room, she pulled off her muddied boots and began peeling her gloves off. The skin on at least two of her scars on both of her hands was torn and bloody. The left was the worst. She watched blood pool in the lines and grooves of her palm as she traced healing and cleansing runes along each wound. If she had to be outside at dawn each day, then she would need to wake up even earlier than that to stretch and work her muscles so that this would not happen every day. With a soft glow, the wounds closed to thin pink lines. A fresh wave of exhaustion hit her as the spell ended. Healing was the one thing that always exhausted her.

Young healers had to be watched, so they didn't overextend themselves and keep healing patient after patient till they bled their life away with their magic. Steeling herself, she quickly healed the other hand, slumping as she finished. Forcing herself up, she got ready for bed.

She had missed dinner and with her schedule she would be hard pressed to make every meal as it was. Digging in her pack, she pulled out a chunk of nuts and grain that was covered in honey. Breaking a piece off, she sucked on the sweet mass of it while she groaned her way through her nightly stretches and exercises. She barely made it to the bed before she was asleep.

Argent woke her while it was still dark the next morning. Her muscles had stiffened in the night and she hobbled around lighting candles and getting dressed before doing her stretches and heading to find something to eat for her bond mates at least. If they worked as hard today as they did yesterday at the drill, she wouldn't be able to eat breakfast until after without fearing that she would throw it up with a misplaced blow or just from the heat.

After practice, she cleaned up and went to the Baron's office to see what the rest of her training would comprise. He looked up from conversing with a woman wearing a high fashion and expensive looking gown, fanning herself with a feathered fan while delicately sipping from a small crystal glass.

"Ah, Mage, please come in. May I introduce Madame Duve? She will assist me in your training."

"Plain looking thing, is she not?" The Madame said, taking in Beryl's pants and tunic. "From now on every time you come here you are to be attired as if you are about to see a King or Queen at court or to visit a member of the royal house." She raised a hand to stop Beryl from speaking when she opened her mouth to ask a question. "I know you don't have the suitable clothes at the moment, but that will be taken care of. For now, please have a seat and remove your gloves. We will work on how to serve tea. Ideally you would have a servant pour the first cups, but it is a thing of courtesy to refill yours and your guest's cup yourself should they need it."

Beryl whirled her jacket off, removing Rune from the pocket to the soft chuckles of the Baron. Laying her coat over a footstool, she slid into the wicker chair being offered. Pulling at the fingertips of her gloves, she removed them and tucked them into a pocket. One of her scars had reopened in the afternoon session of training, leaving a smear of blood running across the top of her hand. She heard the Baron shift as it revealed her hands, while the Madame let out a gasp of horror.

"What in the world have you done to her, William? Has that Captain of the Guard taken to corporal punishments?"

"Madame, no one here did anything." Beryl interrupted with a sigh, "I injured my hands when I was a child. I reopened one of my scars while I was in sword practice. It doesn't even hurt." Beryl tried to placate the woman.

"My dear, you don't understand. In some courts it is fashionable to wear gloves but to many they consider it rude. You would insult your hosts if you came wearing gloves." She frowned. Reaching out, she examined one of Beryl's hands. "At least the scars are limited to the palm. We can place you in half gloves or even lace gloves, and no one would say too much. Is there anything else I need to know about? Peg leg perhaps?" She asked snidely.

Beryl rolled back one sleeve to the elbow, exposing the metal cuffs on her wrists and opened her shirt collar, showing the choker that completed the set and exposing the scars the twisted up her arms and the edge of one next to her collarbone.

"How far do the scars go?" Madame Duve asked in a shaky voice.

"They go up my arms to the shoulder, across my chest and back, and down my upper legs." Beryl said, eyes watching the woman's reaction. Madame Duve swallowed thickly before nodding and getting up. Speaking rapidly, she stood and edged toward the door.

"I'll go get Megan to do your measurements. By the end of the week we will have you a set of gowns to take to court with you that will work for most of the courts. We will have to make them high necked and long-sleeved, which aren't the current fashion in most courts, but as a mage you won't be expected to keep with fashion. We expect mages to be eccentric so we will have to make that work for us." At this she whisked through the door like she was escaping a torture session.

"I'm sorry," the Baron said, a soft burr of accent coming to his words coming to stand next to the Madame's abandoned chair, "Lily isn't used to dealing with pain and doesn't handle it well. She's a titled noble whose husband was one of us. She never knew of his involvement with the crown until he disappeared on a mission. We never knew what became of him, and she became insistent in her need to help during her grief. She's still a fixture in several courts and will be one presenting you at small court functions when you're ready to get your new name and background out into circulation."

"The courts can be brutal if you take one step out of turn. You will be under extra scrutiny since you're from another country and being a mage, they will pump you for information on recent spells and defenses that your country is using. The last thing other courts want to share is their knowledge or information about their own defenses, which is why you will have to get them to become comfortable around you." He took a seat and gestured for her to serve the tea.

"You'll be learning the culture and court etiquette for three countries. There's a chance that you'll visit all three, but it's small. If you're successful and nothing untoward happens, then you may stay at one court for several years, it all depends on you and the court's stability. The first court you will be presented at is Orlean. King Laron is aging, and the country is at peace right now, but there have been rumors of unrest in the other nobles and royal family members that we need confirmed. You'll be taking lessons in the language and culture for the rest of your stay here and learning who's who in each of the courts. Fumbling a noble's name is enough to get you relegated to the bottom of the social heap for the rest of your stay at court."

"So I will play the part of a visiting court mage?"

"A minor one, yes, we have several others working as soldiers or ladies-in-waiting, but we haven't been able to get anything other than vague rumors of unrest. Whatever's going on, its deep within the royal and noble families, and they're not talking to outsiders about it. We're hoping by passing you off as a minor noble who's also a mage we'll be able to get some clearer information."

Two weeks later she sat in a full ball gown, gloved in lace with hair pinned and face rouged, trying to take minuscule bites of the heavily spiced stew. The people of Orlean seemed to enjoy spicy dishes. Argent heaved a sigh at her feet; he wouldn't be eating any table scraps while they were at court. Kuro and Rune sat on another chair, watching the proceedings with interest.

Madame Duve pronounced her manners well enough, even if she wasn't a natural dancer or enjoyed wearing gowns that weighed more than she did. The only thing driving her crazy was the talk at the table. Several others had been invited, and they talked of the politics or latest events of the realm. Beryl struggled to pull the innuendos apart that underlay every comment.

She was slowly becoming able to think fast enough on her feet to respond to any comment thrown her way even if she was not part of the original conversation. They spent a day in the ballroom learning how to circulate among the guests and listen in on conversations without letting others hear what you were saying themselves. She barely could remember the ranks each person was representing while keeping the conversation going.

Unsurprisingly, she could keep up with the men's conversations of hunting and horsemanship much better than those of the women's parties and sorties. She struggled with discussions on local gossip and scandal and those on fashion. Since she was already an accomplished rider, they taught her how to ride sidesaddle and to drive one of the small carts sometimes used at hunts by the ladies of court.

The training made her days a bizarre dichotomy. Before dawn she woke and did her stretches before heading to sword practice dressed in a loose belted tunic, slacks, and boots. After practice, she ate breakfast and went to get dressed. Once in a gown and presentable, she went to the dining hall to recite royal birth lines while dancing patterns to one side of the table. At each lunch and dinner, she dined on some impossible to eat a dish that only locals knew how to eat correctly.

Heading up to change after dinner, she went back outside afterwards to practice archery, sling, and dagger work until it was too dark to see. Then they put away the weapons and went on bizarre games of tag, ghosting through the woods or house with the goal of sneaking in and removing a specific object or having to fight their way out of the house in pairs. If you lost your partner or didn't make it out, you had to do extra practice and run laps around the parameter the next morning.

She was learning the trade of a thief, how to break into houses, to pick pockets, to pass notes without being seen and take things without others seeing her do so. She'd learned much of it already from Troche and knew his lessons had put her ahead of the others she worked with. Her time in Cardu with the thief's guild was serving her well in her new role.

Lorrik loved her spell stones and lamented over not being able to make and use something similar himself. He had her practice with arrows that had cloth bags for tips. When the bag hit, it would do no damage but released a burst of powder around the target. If you filled them with sleep dust, you could knock out a target and bring them back to base however the trick was unreliable, if there was any breeze the dust would blow away and be of no use. She learned how they made the sleep dust and was shown the various other toxins and poisons that could be used and their effects so she could recognize them if someone tried to use them against her.

In a week she was being presented at Madame Duve's country house as one of her many nieces. From there they would travel by boat to Orlean and then to the capital, Paxton, where she would stay with another Listener member while they established their residence in town. If she managed it, she was to stay in the palace, but it was up to her to get an invitation to stay and study with the court mages. Sending a prayer to Ruth that all would go as needed, she turned her attention back to the light conversation going on around her.

She sent a note to Darius' receiving table using one of her spelled stones saying she was safe and receiving training but didn't name anyone or say where she was. He sent back a note saying that to cover her flight they announced that she had been exiled from the country. However, the general rumor was that she had killed herself in a fit of remorse over the attack on the castle. She supposed it was better than everyone thinking she had fled the castle, confirming her guilt.

A week later she was in a carriage headed to the country home of Madame Duve with more luggage than she had ever had in her life. Beryl insisted on keeping a shoulder bag with her most useful possessions in it, even if it. She was too used to having to abandon everything after years of living with Jared to trust that her luggage would make it anywhere without mishap.

She sent what she didn't want discovered to her hiding place in the mountains of the town where her parents used to live using her transport spell. It mainly comprised her apprenticeship apparel, the distinctive greatcoats they knew her for wearing, the bulk of her weapons that she could not wear in a dress, and Argent's armor, which was too well known.

She was sorry to be leaving her great coats behind. The spells woven into them had sustained her during her flight and the journey here. She wouldn't take anything of her own with her. They would replace all the clothing and gear. She would even have to craft new daggers and spell stones. Nothing from her previous life would follow her in to this fresh one.

Argent would travel as a common pet, while Rune would stay in whatever house she wound up in. They planned to use Rune and Kuro to explore the city once they settled in, since she could not travel much without scrutiny. She would get a slight amount of reprieve since she was a mage and was expected to have to go to the library and work on spells and such. The entire game would change once she reached Orlean, but for now she would do her best to blend in.

Chapter 3

Masks & Manners

Beryl fought to keep the polite smile on her face. The party had been in full swing since early that afternoon, and it was approaching midnight. Kuro and Rune were upstairs asleep while Argent had given up and lay sprawled before one fireplace, dozing. The crowded rooms had thinned, and the guests were slowly leaving except for those who wanted to drink themselves into oblivion before their carriages could arrive, disgusting.

Such a drunkard, Lord Randall, seemed determined to extol her ears with every line of every play he had been to see that season currently trapped her. At least he wouldn't remember her tomorrow, between the drink and her curse the most he would remember would be a pleasant party where he met the Madame Duval's niece, a minor mage who was just coming out in society.

That was all that most would remember. She rather hoped no one remembered her new name. It was embarrassing just to think of it. They could name her anything and they picked Eglantine? She shared a long suffering look with Lord Randall's footman as she escorted the Lord to the door and stood for a moment giving a few last goodbyes and courtesies to the last guests as they staggered out.

"You did rather well, Eglantine." Lady Duval said with a sniff, "Come, let's retire to the salon and discuss how the night went."

Beryl suppressed a sigh and followed, fighting to keep her head up and her steps small. She was still not used to wearing such restrictive clothing. While beautiful, the pale blue of the gown suited her fair skin, the tight lacing and wide skirts meant that they constantly forced her to watch where she stepped. She had tripped more than once while she was practicing for the dinner. Sitting in the indicated chair by the fire, she spread her skirts as she tapped at the bond she shared with Argent.

"Wake up, slumbering beast. I'm in the salon if you want to get a late-night snack."

A mental yawn and incoherent grumble greeted her summons, but a moment later, Argent lumbered through the door and ambled to her chair. He gaped a massive yawn at the room before sitting by her chair, leaning so his head rested against her shoulder, watching as Madame Duval accepted a cup of tea from a servant.

"If I give you a biscuit, you have to promise not to drool on my dress." Beryl informed him.

"Do I get a biscuit too?" Rune asked, slipping into the room and quick footing his way to her chair. He leapt up to the arm of the chair and balanced there, head cocked.

"Yes, but you know Madame Duval doesn't want you getting things on the dresses either." she said taking her cup with a small and thank you.

"May I also have a few biscuits for my bond mates?" she asked before the servant left.

He gave a grimace but nodded and left to retrieve them. Madame Duval's servants had been with her for many years, and most shared her disgust for animals of any kind. A moment later he returned with a small plate of biscuits she took with a thank you and a smile.

Setting the plate on a side table, she gestured her bond mates to the hearth next to her before handing out the treats. She would need to remember to find some small treat for Kuro tomorrow, luckily she did not like biscuits or sweets like the other two, she was fond of the occasional piece of fruit or nuts, and maybe she would try to find some blueberries or something at the market.

"You handled yourself well tonight, Eglantine," she said, ignoring Beryl's wince. She insisted on calling her Eglantine to get her used to the name. "We'll hold a few more parties over the rest of the month to continue to introduce you to society, however there will be a minor change of plans." Drawing a small letter from her sleeve and flicking it open. "At the end of the month you will head to the border alone, you'll meet with your Master and the two of you will investigate some unusual occurrences there before going to Orlean." she said handing over the message.

Beryl fought with the cipher for a moment before picking out the random phrases. There wasn't much else to the message. She was to travel to the border on her own and meet Darius in a modest town called, Hastings. They would investigate the border before she continued alone to the coast and to Orlean.

That left her with three more weeks of parties and dinners at least, Argent gave a long-suffering sigh at this. Beryl smothered a smile and cast a fond eye on her bond mate. He was the only one allowed to be out in the open with her while she was Eglantine. Her other bond mates could only be around if she was alone or out of town. None of them liked the arrangement, but they didn't have a choice. It was too well known that the traitor mage who was killed in Arden had three bond mates, an enormous dog, cat, and bird.

"What are your plans for the morrow, niece?" Madame Duval asked, sipping at her tea. Beryl, no, Eglantine obediently picked up her cup and took a sip, suppressing a sigh.

"I hoped to go to the market and to visit the local Library or a few bookstores. I would like to pick up a few things for the voyage next month."

The Madame nodded approval, and they continued to chat about the party and who she needed to remember for a few more minutes before they excused her for bed. Beryl and her two bond mates trooped up the stairs to her rooms. There her maid took her hair down from its elaborate braids and helped her out of the fitted dress before disappearing with the used linens. She'd disabused the poor girl of the need for constant tending, she knew how to dress herself and draw a bath as needed.

Once they were back alone Beryl stretched her reach across the bond to check on her last bond mate, Kuro. The Shiro slept on, ignoring the other three bond mates from her position in a tree that stood behind the house. That done, she slipped into bed; Argent eyed the small bed with another sigh before settling himself on the rug.

She reached down and scratched behind his ears for a moment until his leg twitched in delight before murmuring a soft goodnight. Rune curled on the pillow next to her head, his cold feet slipping under her shoulder and his nose against the back of her neck. The next morning she would continue her investigation in town and hope they simply allowed her hand the entire matter over to the Madame before she left.

* * *

Eglantine smiled politely as she wandered the shops, Rune hidden in the small carpet bag she was carrying while Argent and Kuro watched from a distance, wandering a meandering path of their own. Kuro hunted the marshes and wharves around town while Agent padded down back alleys and the lanes. The only method to their wandering was to be near crowds or places where people would stop to talk. Beryl had been assigned to gather what gossip she could in the town and alert Madame Duve to any concerning rumors.

So far it was making out to be a deathly boring week. Beryl had heard far more than she ever wanted to know about the rising costs of spun wool and lace while wandering the shops this morning and the last few mornings. She made her way toward the town center, intending to get lunch at one of the many street vendors that lined the bustling market.

A man in black robes was shouting out at the passersby, gesturing and ranting in fury. Many of the people passing made the sign of Ruth with one hand as they passed, like they were trying to avert some evil from sticking to them. Beryl couldn't get close enough to hear over the murmurs of the crowd. The man was not near any shops or carts, and no polite society was listening. Several children and burly dock workers heckled him as they ate a quick lunch in the square from the many carts selling hand held pies and such. His robe was stained with rotten fruit and the surrounding ground was spotted with clumps of horse dung and fragments of rotten vegetables. He was not being well received, whatever he was preaching.

"I can go listen." Rune insisted, shifting inside her shoulder bag.

"Don't let anyone see you. Be careful." Beryl murmured, leaning against a shop for a moment so that Rune could make his escape.

She wandered the shop, which was selling ribbons and lace for dresses, stopping to finger a thin blue velvet ribbon as she felt along her connection to her bond mates. She followed along with the small cat as he worked his way through the crowd, darting from one small opening in the crowd to the next. He came to rest next to a stack of boxes to one side of the gathering crowd. Many of the men jeered and shouted at the man while others simply watched, faces blank or twisted in anger.

"Only when you repent and reject the ways of Magic and Mage, can you understand how corrupt their methods are. Aedus, god of the purifying fire, asks us to give up the ways of magic and embrace a pure existence. Magic will be purged from the lands by the fire of Aedus! Aedus asks only that you reject the false gods and come to his worship to be purified. Those that follow Aedus will be spared his vengeance when the time comes. Repent before the flames consume you!" a black gem glinted at his neck, the very air around him seeming to pull at her magic like the voids Darius had sent her to investigate outside of the capital.

Beryl shivered, listening as the man continued to denounce magic and its users, calling for them to be purified from the earth along with all those who didn't worship Aedus. The crowd gathering around him getting rougher, drunken sailors and dock workers shouting slurs and throwing stones.

"Come back, we need to see what Madame Duve knows of this." Beryl urged as several men began brawling to one side of the square.

The watch would arrive soon if things didn't quiet down. Rune quickly left his hiding spot, and they met in a small side alleyway. Beryl scooped him back up into her arms as they moved away from the sounds of fighting behind them. Argent hurried back to the house while Kuro tracked the escalating fight from above.

Beryl hurried to the house, ducking in the back to make sure Argent was safe. They sat watching through Kuro's eyes as the fight got larger and larger. The watch tried to break up the mob, but it only served in directing them to more destruction. By nightfall, when Kuro had to return, parts of the market district were on fire. Madame Duve had been fielding messages and runners all afternoon as the Watchers reported in. Beryl added what she could to the reports from what Kuro could see, but most of it was simply listing the worst of the damage and where the primary group of the mob was as the day progressed.

"The followers of Aedus are becoming a problem." Madame Duve said unhappily, flipping through the reports that littered the surrounding table. "Several smaller towns have launched attacks on the mages living among them. One older mage was burned at the stake, another beaten almost to the point of disfigurement. The healers are uncertain if he will live or not. Arden has always been tolerant of those who wished to follow other gods, but the King will have to act decisively if this violence will be stemmed."

Beryl frowned but didn't interrupt as the older woman began listing out what the various watchers in town's duties would be. She sat on the floor next to the fire, curled around Rune with Argent a solid weight against one hip and Kuro on her shoulder. If mages were being attacked as abominations than those with bond mates would be even easier to single out. They would have to be even more careful about town and once they started the journey north.

"Practice." Argent murmured across the bond, rubbing his head against Beryl's ankle.

"Practice? Practice in what, defense?" Beryl asked, reaching out to rub at his ear that always seemed to need a scratch.

"Practice acting normal, like other animals. We learn how to blend in with the other cats and dogs." the dog said, rumbling unhappily as he shifted to lean harder against his mage.

"It can help." Rune put in stubbornly, still resentful that they often saw him as the weak link in the bond with his small size. He would learn to seem normal if it kept his bond mates safe.

That decided they settled in to listen to Madame Duve's plans and how she handled the issues that were presented to her. Many would seem like some minor error or problem until the older woman began asking pointed questions, showing just how far-reaching each issue was. Beryl could see these management skills coming in handy later when she was sent to the Orlean courts, but for now the exchanges just left her exhausted and aching to have something to do.

There was little that Beryl could do in town beyond continuing to listen for rumors about town since she was leaving in a few weeks. It would give others the task of infiltrating several groups of Aedus' followers. They needed more information before they could see just how dangerous this new religion was or if this was only the work of a few fanatics.

Chapter 4

Investigating the Border

Three weeks later...

Beryl gave a grin as the cart hit another bump. They were on their way and there wasn't a party goer or expensive dress in sight. She'd spent the last three weeks having more lessons on etiquette and dance lessons from Madame Duval, along with parties where she was forced to circulate and discuss the latest fashions or popular books and plays with various Lords and Ladies. They had spent her days tracking down random rumors and bits of gossip about town as she circulated through shops and markets.

She was too happy to even complain about the tight breast band she was wearing. Masquerading as a boy traveling with his dog was much easier than explaining why a young woman was traveling alone. She wore a worn suit and had her hair piled up under a cap. She hitched a ride with a farmer that was headed to one of the small forts near the border.

It had snowed nonstop since they left and she cuddled Rune against her side inside her coat; he had not stopped complaining about the cold since they left the house. Argent wasn't enjoying it either. Beryl cut down an old sweater to cover his chest and front legs, but the ice and snow still cut his feet and built up between his toes. He sat curled around her, half under a blanket that was wrapped around both of them.

Kuro was flying; she was fine with the weather except for the occasional complaint about not being able to see very far because of the snowfall. Beryl had brought extra food because of the cold, but even that supply was dwindling. She would need to buy more at the next stop or trap small animals, which would be hard in this weather. Kuro showed her contempt for that idea by wheeling into a dive and snatching up a mouse to feast on. She could feed herself fine.

Another week of nonstop travel and four days of cart rides interspaced with walking and she was at Fort Brume, right on the edge of the border. She had received a note at Hastings to continue on to the Fort. Soldiers sat around the ragged fort working on armor or cleaning weapons, chopped wood, or slumped in corners asleep. All had injuries. All of those awake and about moved like they were exhausted.

Most of her trek had been through melting slush or frozen ground covered in ruts and holes, making it exhausting and very slow going. It might be spring in the rest of the country, but here in the northern mountains winter still ruled. She pushed them the last few days of walking since they had found no carts heading to the fort. They were all exhausted from the cold, the constant wetness and chill sapped their energy.

Beryl tugged at the muffler she had wrapped around her face and neck, fighting with the ice covered material and wincing as it exposed her wind chapped skin to the air. Tugging off a glove with her teeth, she ignored the numb fingers as she dug for the letter she needed. The soldier manning the gate watched her with raw cheeks and lips. Ice had formed in his mustache and hair, framing bloody cracked lips that grimaced as he worked off his own gloves to accept the letter.

"I'm here to meet Master Darius, he's expecting me," she said, blowing on her hands and fighting the urge to stomp some feeling back into her feet, Kuro rode one shoulder shivering. Argent gave a soft whine and leaned against her leg, his head low.

"Come here, boy, let me check your feet," she whispered. He raised one paw for her to inspect. The ice between his pads was red with blood. "Bain's balls, we need to get you warm. You can't keep going out on the ice if your feet are like this."

"Here, you can go on in, the Mage is in the Chapel, straight back, you can't miss it," he eyed Argent with a tired gaze, "try wrapping his feet in leather and rabbit fur, the sled dogs they use up around here in the winter use some kind of leather boot. You could ask Aaron, the tracker, he would know more about it."

"Thanks, I will. It sounds like we will be here for a while." Beryl said with a sigh, giving Argent's ears a rub before she straightened and headed toward the chapel, its stone spire rising above the rest of the compound.

Inside they directed her past the main chapel, which had been converted to an infirmary filled with the wounded and dying. They led her down a back hall to what must have been the priest's quarters by a young soldier who left as soon as she knocked. Darius stood around a table spread with books and maps along with several others. He glanced up as she entered before breaking into a smile.

"Ah, Mage, come in, come in. Wonderful timing; let me introduce you to everyone. This is Captain Rogers, Staff Sergeant Michaels, and Duke Laston." He said gesturing to the men around the table.

"Pleasure to meet you all," she said with a slight bow. "Excuse me a moment."

Turning, she sat Kuro on the back of a chair near the fire before pulling out Rune and plunking him on the seat of the same chair. She stripped the wet wool from Argent, kneeling to rubbing him down with a rag, getting the rest of the ice off his coat and muzzle before letting him slump next to the fire. A muttered, "Well, I never," rang out behind her as the other men shifted where they stood watching her work.

She dug out some rather frozen hunks of meat from her pack and passed them out before turning back to the rather indignant men watching her. Darius chuckled and gestured her to the table. She ignored how the Duke blustered to one side and stripped out of her coat, hat, and sweater, making the Sergeant choke down a gasp when he realized she was a woman.

"I take it you're one of Master Darius' contacts?" the Captain asked as she rolled up her sleeves, eying her scars and flicking from her to the animals and back.

"Mage is one of my contacts and a Mage in her own right. She is here to assist me in researching these dead areas. If it is a hostile mage causing them, then they're somehow able to effect most of Arden. Mage has investigated other incidents for me up and down the coast, and they are all the same. Either we have a rogue mage who is traveling all over the country, several rogue mages, or we have a mage able to attack areas of land and drain them of their magic from a distance. None are a situation the King will let stand," he gestured for the Captain to continue.

The Duke interrupted, "Surely a proper mage would be of more use? A mere woman will be of little use here in the mountains, while there is still so much snow still on the ground."

"Sir," The Captain tried to interrupt, but the Duke continued over him.

"And Mage, what kind of name is that? I like to know who I am working with, Master Darius, this is most trying." The Duke blustered frowning at the group at large.

"I'm called Mage, Duke Laston. I go by no other name. You may call me what you wish, and I won't take offense from it. I'm here to assist Master Darius and I'll be out of your way as soon that task is completed." Beryl said flatly.

Before the Duke could draw himself up to continue, the Captain stepped in, "Sir, if I may interrupt, there is an urgent matter that I could use your expertise in." he said, deftly drawing the man out of the room while stroking his ego with gentle complements to how organized the fort was running since he'd arrived.

Once they were gone Beryl gave a soft snort, "Maybe I should get diplomacy lessons from the Captain," she murmured, blinking at the shut door, the Staff Sergeant muffled a laugh, changing it into a credible cough after Darius gave his a stern look.

"Some lessons in diplomacy and tact would serve you well." Darius chided, gesturing her back to the table and to the enormous map covering it with circles of red outlined in a starburst pattern. "As you can see, the magically drained areas are more prevalent in the North. Whoever is causing this seems to concentrate on the border more and more. With the levels of snowfall this winter we could miss sites, the melt has started however it could be months before we find the rest; the pattern suggests that the epicenter for the sites is about forty miles farther north, across the border. I want you to scout around the area and investigate a few of the closer sites before heading upriver toward the epicenter." Darius said, gesturing to the map before them.

"Mage, I'll be entrusting the investigation to you. For today you're to get your bond mates and yourself back into top condition. The next few days we will scout the sites close to the fort and planning out your trip past the border. I know you're used to working alone, but I would like to you to have at least one other tracking with you."

Beryl nodded, eying her exhausted bond mates; they'd fallen asleep as soon as they lay down. She was just as tired. The last two days of their trip had been a head down slog through thickening snow. If the snowfall continued, the roads would be impossible in a day. Tracking to sites off the major roads would be brutal.

"Sergeant, can you show Mage to a room or bed she can use? We'll see to the rest of the details tomorrow once everyone is rested."

"This way if you please;" Beryl roused her bond mates, placing Kuro on her arm and Rune in a pocket to the soft chuckle of the sergeant. They showed her to a barracks style room with six beds in rows.

"Sorry about slotting you in with the soldiers, but there are no actual rooms available. Even the Captain and his officers are sleeping out in halls."

"It's fine; trust me, I've had worse. As long as they don't mind having a few animals under foot we'll be fine," she said, placing Rune on the pillow and letting Kuro hop down to roost on the head of the bed. They would all need extra food and water in the morning, but even she was just too bone tired and chilled even now to want to eat.

"Thank you, Sergeant," she said chiding Argent up onto the bed next to her so she could rub some healing balm into his feet and bandage any that had open wounds.

The next morning, habit had her up and out of bed at dawn with the rest of the soldiers. She shuffled with the rest to the chow line, wheedling an extra bowl from the cook for her bond mates. Returning to the barracks, she chided them awake and made sure each had some water and meat before letting them go back to sleep. Rune was the only one up to any activity, slipping out of bed and off to explore the barracks. Beryl ran through her exercises with a handful of soldiers, watching with half their attention as they mended clothes or cleaned leather. When she began the weapons exercises, she felt their gaze sharpen but ignored it.

Finishing a mock hand to hand fight with stabs to groin, throat and eye, she relaxed into a basic fighting stance. She had been working on using wind magics while in a trance since she went to visit Valerian and her apprentice and was slowly integrating the technique for viewing things farther away into her slow stretches and movements. Her friends in Cardu had said that she looked like she was dancing in slow motion when she practiced. She forced thoughts of the past and friends they had forced her to abandon out of her mind. It wouldn't do any good to dwell on what she couldn't change, and it continued to wreck her concentration at the worst time. Besides, they probably thought she was guilty of trying to destroy the castle like everyone else and had been hanged as a spy and traitor to the crown.

With a sigh, she cleared her mind and started the sequence again, slowly drawing her magic to the fore as she did. Once her mind was still, she slowly expanded her awareness, letting her body move through the slow patterns of movement as she rose above the fortress, like a hawk riding a thermal. She committed the layout of the fort to memory and swung outward in ever-widening circles as she surveyed the surrounding area.

The dead spots pulled at her mage sight like black whirlpools, sucking at her magic and strength. They were much stronger and larger here than the ones she had investigated at the capitol. She swooped and slid back into her own skin with a snap. She forced herself to complete the last motions of the pattern she was on before letting herself return to the opening stance and opening her eyes. The soldiers watched as she roused her bond mates and gathered her cloak and gloves.

"Do you want to go outside while I look around?" She asked across the bond, watching with a fond smile as Argent stretched and yawned.

"Too early." Kuro murmured, tucking her head back under a wing. It was much too early in the day to be hunting, the tired bird decided.

Argent lumbered to his feet and followed her out long enough to take care of his full bladder before heading back to steal her bed for a few more hours. Beryl gave a slight smile at the images coming from Rune; he had found the attics of the chapel and was happily hunting mice, a soft stream of almost gleeful humming coming across the bond as he stalked his prey. She needed to make sure they all got more rest and food. She could see Argent's ribs underlying the muscle of his chest, and Kuro weighed less than when they had lived at the capitol going lean.

Beryl wandered the compound, eying the wards on the stockade walls and various buildings. Most were the standard fare, meant to prevent fire and to help hold the timbers together if anything struck or damaged them. She sighed, cataloging what she could get done. Her gear was in decent condition and she would be well equipped once her clothes from yesterday were dry.

She wasn't used to being idle; there was always something to work on or do, research for Darius or learning a new trick of the spy trade. With another sigh, she began casting about for the Staff Sergeant she had met yesterday. Asking a soldier carrying supplies to the kitchens, they directed her to the infirmary.

Staff Sergeant Michaels stood talking to one healer; most of the beds were occupied. Many of the soldiers had head wounds or missing limbs, there were just some things that not even magic could heal. She let her mage sight run along the spells wrapped around each patient, slowly being pulled into the soldier's body as the energy of the spell fed their own depleted healing abilities.

Healing was a delicate balancing act, push the healing too far, and the patient's body would rebound into intense exhaustion which could undo all the work the healer had just done. No magic came without a price, either the patient paid in energy or the healer did. The rate of burnout for healing mages was high, they saw most as cold and unfeeling since it often forced them to turn injured patients away to save their own strength for those who needed it. Herbs and non-magical methods much as possible with magic being left as a last resort. The only reason most of the soldiers here in the infirmary were being treated with minor spells was because a Healer Mage was based at the fort.

The Healers guild and temples protected their members fiercely, most traveled with a weapon trained companion anytime they left the temple. They treated traveling mages with the Mage Council the same; they traveled with a small group of soldiers when they left the capital. Magic was too valuable a resource to be left open to attack. The easiest time to attack a mage or healer was after a massive spell was complete, while they were still drained of magic and energy.

She approached Staff Sergeant Michaels once he turned away

from where he was speaking to a healer. He looked worn and tired even this early in the morning. The entire fort had an air of exhaustion that pervaded the very wood and stone they built it with.

"Staff Sergeant Michaels, I was hoping to speak with you if you have a moment."

"What can I help you with, Mage? Your bond mates are settling in?"

"They're well, thank you. I was hoping to help around the fort. I know I have the day off, but I've never been one to sit around idle." She said with a wry smile.

"We can use the help. Where do your strengths lay? I know most mage's specialize in one or two areas," he trailed off, uncomfortable with discussing magic. The more she traveled the more she was exposed to the prejudices against magic that were becoming more common outside of the capital, as least the Captain was trying to understand.

"I know some basic healing spells and runes. I can spell bandages and close minor wounds. I work in stone and metal. I can forge arrowheads and was learning to craft daggers. I can spell weapons as others forge them for strength and sharpness. I can ward walls and buildings against damage and fire."

"Well, we always have use of more bandages. If you could help with the healers today, I'm sure they would appreciate it. If you have time while you're here to work in the forge or to ward the fort, I would be grateful. We appreciate anything you can do to help protect the men under my command."

"I'll do my best, sir."

"See that you do. You'll want to talk to Healer Mage Mara. She's in the back room treating a patient but once she's finished, she'll be able to direct you."

"Thank you, Staff Sergeant."

She spent the morning stitching runes for healing and purification into roll after roll of bandages for the injured and soon to be injured. Healer Mage Mara was one of the rare mages who dedicated themselves to the Healers of Ruth and learned no other branches of magic. She was an older woman with a long braid of silver hair that coiled down her back.

Beryl realized why most of the soldiers had been so accommodating about her bond mates once she saw Mara's bond mate. A red and black fox called Bax that paced his way from bed to bed, checking on their patients. Rune spent most of the afternoon shadowing Bax to learn how he tested the strength of each healing spell and the health of each patient. Argent sat and watched as Beryl worked on the pile of bandages while Kuro spent the afternoon outside hunting the voles that were venturing out with the thaw.

That night they showed her back to the meeting room with Staff Sergeant Michaels, Master Darius, and another man. They introduced her to the tracker, Aaron, who would work with her for the rest of her time at the fort. Taking a seat, she waited as the rest of the group were served a thick meaty stew and bread, making sure Argent and Rune had a bowl to share. Kuro was in the barracks sleeping off her feast earlier in the day.

Darius started the meeting once everyone was finished with their meal. They went over the plans for the rest of the week, marking out which sites Beryl and Aaron would visit before they headed toward the sites were on the other side of the border. He wanted to move cautiously so they would view several of the local sites before they moved on. Master Darius would head back to the Capitol in the morning and they would correspond with any discoveries by messenger stone.

Beryl shivered to remember the last site drained of magic that she had visited, several hundred yards of forest where nothing survived, centered on a space that had been burned to ash and rock. Nothing in the forest had survived the removal of its natural magic and no animals ventured into the area, leaving the bodies to rot unmolested. The voids here in the North were different but Aaron refused to explain, saying she would see soon enough.

Once the meeting was over Beryl retired to the barracks to ready her gear for the next morning. She sat oiling her bond mate's collars and Argent's harness once her own weapons were cared for and ready. Several soldiers sat on their own beds caring for their own gear or playing a card game with one or two others.

"Heading out tomorrow, Mage?" One of her neighbors asked as he settled on his own bed to repair a torn tunic that was worn under armor.

"Yes, I should be in and out of the fort for a while." She said with a nod, keeping her eyes on her work.

"I'd keep an eye out. There are some nasty beasts wandering around, wolves and bears scavenging for anything they can get. Between them and the raiders, it's dangerous to be out once the sun goes down."

"Thanks for the warning. We'll be careful." Beryl said with a small grin, setting Rune's collar down and starting on Argent's.

"Do yours go around collared? I know Healer Mara's fox doesn't wear one." The man asked, frowning at the gems on each collar and her jeweled cuffs and belt. "Keep the displays of wealth quiet. We have a lot of conscripts this far north working off debts and minor offenses."

"I'll keep an eye out, but I doubt they'll try to steal mage gems. The ones on their collars were made for their protection, anyway. They heal some injuries and shield them from some spells if they're attacked."

"Sensible in a war zone like this, I'm surprise we haven't had a night raid yet since you got here, maybe you brought in some luck for us when you arrived." He offered with a grin.

"We can only hope." She said with a laugh. "Do the raiders attack often?"

"Every few nights, keeps us on our toes." He said with a grin, pulling out oil and a whetstone to sharpen his dagger. "Most of the bandits around here are farmers who fell on terrible times, but these new raiders are organized. Someone had the coin to hire mercenaries and to outfit them with excellent weapons. We're dug in tight here and it will take more than some mercs to oust us, but the outlying farms and hamlet around us are free game. We send the refugees that survive the attacks south but many refuse to leave."

"Would your family leave if they were attacked?"

"I would hope my wife would be smart enough to do so, but it's hard to say. We've worked hard to keep the farm back home. It would be hard to walk away from it."

"That must be nice." Beryl murmured, she hadn't had a real home since she was a child.

Her Uncle Jared had traveled constantly, using her abilities where he could to make the money he drank or gambled away. She had hoped Cardu would have become a home, but after barely a year of study under Master Darius, she was exiled and branded a traitor. She doubted Arden would ever be home again.

The next morning she ate a quick breakfast of oatmeal before gathering her pack and heading to meet Aaron at the blacksmith's forge. He wanted to make sure her weapons were in good shape before they headed out. It surprised her to see a white and black spotted hound sitting next to his feet.

"Mage, good timing; this is Blue, my partner in crime, the best tracking dog I've ever worked with," he said gesturing to the dog. "He wears boots when we're going out across the ice and I want to get your bond mate set up, they'll protect his feet while we track. Let me know if he has any trouble with them, I had to guess on the size," he said, giving her a handful of leather.

Each soft leather pouch was lined with rabbit fur and made to be laced up. Beryl quickly sorted out the boots and Argent sat down to allow her to fit them on his enormous feet. Watching him getting used to them, stepping high as he fought against the added weight made all the bond mates smile as the dog grumbled across the bond.

Aaron and Beryl quickly went through what gear they each were carrying and let the blacksmith check her knives and short sword. They hoped to visit two of the drained sites that day before heading back to the fort so they were keeping their gear light. Gathering everything back into their packs, they started out while it was still early.

Beryl tried to ignore the unhappy mutters and gestures to Ruth or Bain from some passing soldiers as they eyed her bond mates. While most of the soldiers seemed indifferent to her presence, others avoided her. Many commoners had issues with Bond Mates. They simply were too intelligent to be true animals and were seen as a corruption of nature by many. She was glad Rune hid in her hood, while a soldier wouldn't risk injury lashing out at Argent; the small cat was a much easier target.

Unless they lived in a large city, few commoners had ever met a mage or seen magic done beyond the showy tricks of light and fire that were done at carnivals and festivals. Most distrusted mages since they lived and worked mainly with other mages or the upper class. Beryl had been chased out of a few tiny villages when she was traveling with her Uncle but had rarely seen the level of disgust and hatred some soldiers expressed, walking wide to avoid coming near any of them. Luckily, while many disliked or distrusted magic, few will act upon it. None had dared to confront any of them so far, preferring to watch from a distance.

It was a strange dichotomy; the people were more than willing to be healed, but they saw any other magic as corrupt. A new religion had been slowly growing, rejecting the worship of the many gods, and blamed magic on everything from crop failure to adultery. They followed the god Aedus, denying the existence of any other god.

It wasn't a powerful group yet, but some followers had sent petitions to the King to ban the use of magic. They had attacked several mages while traveling or in small towns where the following was gaining momentum. The King punished those responsible after they admitted their guilt proudly, announcing themselves as a follower of Aedus, the one veritable god.

The religion or cult as it seemed to be professed to purify the follower of the corruptive magics practiced by mages. It preached that by following its edicts and declaring themselves to Aedus, it would spare them the scourge coming to wipe out all magic users. Most Gods followed in Arden were benevolent, and while they gave out gifts to their chosen, they rarely punished those who spoke against them or went against their followers' beliefs. Aedus' followers believed he was a holy embodiment of the purifying fire that would descend to remove the nonbelievers.

Her supposed attack on the monarchy was an example for just how deranged magic users were by the followers of Aedus. Once she traveled to Orlean, she would use that belief to get in contact with the various dissenting groups and courtiers of Orlean that would hope to use a bitter, exiled mage against her home country.

The first site they headed out to visit was barely an hour's walk from the fort. This site was small, a roughly circular patch of dead and blackened grass and shrub. Again, like the area near the capitol, it burned the center of the circle until the ground fused into flakes and splinters of black glass. Beryl quickly collected samples to examine back at the fort and they headed to the next site, a massive void of dead trees almost half a day's march away. It would be late when they returned to the fort.

Beryl and her bond mates traveled in silence. They were all subdued; none of them liked the draining feel of being near the areas devoid of magic. The trees and foliage near the center were burnt and the thick smell of smoke and death clung to them as they moved on. No animals moved in the area, having fled from the unnatural void. Someone or something had drained the natural magic that lived in the plants and earth within the circle of damage. The empty, broken land seemed to suck at the magic at the edges of the hole, trying to even out the way magic filled the area.

She suspected that the man who had attacked her as a child had something to do with the attacks while she was still at the capitol, and her friend Brennan helped her research in the massive vaults of the Mage's library housed under the castle. They discovered that for over ten years before her attack there had been a few children a year from families known for having magical abilities who stopped showing any signs of magic. It had stripped them of their magic just as they had drained the ground, turning up after a few hours missing with cuts on their arms and hands and no memory of the missing hours. She'd been meant to be one of those children, and somehow the spell had failed, and somehow she'd survived when they left her for dead.

The next void is horrible. Dead trees, blackened with the heat from the spell extended as far as they can see. A fine ash covers that ground and clings to their clothes and feet as they slowly make their way toward the center of the site. They pass the corpses of birds, fox, and deer, all left to rot where they lay, and untouched by any animals.

Towards the center of the circle of destruction it felled the trees, forcing them to scramble through the dead branches and trunks to reach the circle of burnt stone and earth in the middle. This time there was a difference, however; the ground is hacked and scarred like someone took a pickaxe to it, prying out lumps and shards of black glass and crystals. Beryl gathered a sample of the rock and soil to send to Darius. Maybe there was something different to be found this time.

They began the slow trek back to the fort, their path taking them through a tiny village that had been abandoned. The place was deserted and utterly devoid of life, reminding Beryl too strongly of the voids. The bones of animals slaughtered in the attacks littered the minor road they followed. Broken pieces of cart and burnt-out buildings were all that was left.

She wandered through the destroyed town, trying to ignore the exhaustion and depression that sapped at her strength. This place was dead, stripped of both life and magic. She could almost feel the void leaching the magic and strength from her bones. Her bond mates felt as drained to her as she did. It was hard to remember the reason they were drudging through icy slush, ash, and mud when just being around the voids made you feel hollow and alone.

"So, what brings a mage this far out into the northern wastes?" Aaron asked, taking a drink from his flask before offering it to Beryl. She took a sip of the harsh liquor before handing the small flask back, ignoring his grin at her lack of reaction to the potent drink, she'd had worse traveling with her Uncle.

"I was Master Darius' apprentice for about a year. When he asked me to come, I came," she said with a shrug. The news of the attack on the capitol had not reached most of the soldiers in the North, and few if any had connected the forgettable mage with the one who was exiled from Arden. Most considered her dead anyway, the exile being just a cover for the hushed up execution.

"Surely it cannot be as simple as that?" The tracker said with a grin. "A Mage of your skill and youth would be sought after by half the lads I know back home. How are you up here instead of working a healing hall or being a town mage?"

"Maybe not all women are well suited for hearth and home duty?" She offered, rubbing at Argent's head with one hand. "My parents died while I was still young, and I travelled constantly once I moved to my Uncle's care. I guess I came to enjoy the traveling. Anyway, can you see someone taking a rebellious mage, giant dog, cat, and sea hawk into their home?"

"Most families would overlook such things hoping to get Mage blood into the line." The older man pointed out, settling one hip against a lone remaining fence post while he watched his dog Blue wander the blackened remnants of the village.

"And they would be more than willing to treat said mage like dirt for not being a proper lady in their house. They would have me closeted away in some backroom being a broodmare for the family line barely allowed to speak to my own children, much less the rest of the family." Beryl pointed out, picking up a small ash stained doll that had somehow survived the destruction.

"Surely it's not always that bad?"

"Maybe not, but I'm happy as I am. I need not be married to serve my country and King." She said with a sigh, setting the doll back among the rubble. There was no one here or at the fort who would love such an object any more.

"You never know, you might find some winsome soldier to sweep you off your feet yet." Aaron offered with a smirk, sipping at his flask one last time before he put it up.

"Playing matchmaker, Tracker Aaron?" Beryl asked, smirking right back at the man, making him laugh in delight.

"Nothing so much as that, Lass;" The gruff man said with a chuckle. "I just know that lonely soldiers try their luck with every woman who comes their way. It would be easier for you if they knew you were already taken."

"I doubt anyone would bother me between my being a mage and having Argent with me most of the time. If that's not deterrent enough, then perhaps we can arrange for me to take part in a weapons practice one morning."

"Even the most level-headed soldier can ignore such things when it comes to matters of the flesh, Lass." He pointed out, his face going grim.

"Do you think so little of your own sex?"

"More like I've seen too much in my years on the border, more than any man would want. Men do things in times of war that they would never resort to if they were at home, Lass. I wouldn't want to see you hurt because one man was looking for a moment's release."

"I can defend myself, Tracker Aaron, as can my bond mates. We watch out for each other and won't let the others come to harm. I'm well protected, I can assure you."

"I may just be a man seeing a woman his daughter's age and hoping he can keep her as safe as he would keep her. I won't swaddle you in cotton blankets and lock you away, but I can't help but feel that a woman like my daughter should never be in such a place."

"I hope your daughter never has to go through many of the things that have plagued my life. I fight for the same reason as you, Aaron. To make sure that she never has to."

"Aye, that is the truth of the matter. Very well, Mage." He asked, donning his pack and adjusting the straps, "Shall we continue on? If we step up the pace a bit, we can get back before dark."

"Take the lead, Tracker. We'll follow at your pace."

"As you will, Mage." Aaron said with a grin before striding away whistling for Blue. Beryl gave Argent a last pat before scooping up Rune and turning to follow at a brisk pace.

Chapter 5

Fort Brume

Beryl and Aaron would leave the fort in a week to travel upriver to where Darius believed the epicenter of the disturbances was located. Tracking the locations of the voids and their size showed a strange pattern, almost like someone was traveling up and down the coastal roads from the capital to the northern border of Arden, leaving these voids where ever they stopped for a few days. They littered a spot several days' journey north. Beryl did not dare look too closely at the central site during her scrying sessions, since there were rumors of several mages being used by the raiders.

With the lack of trust in magic most of the soldiers were showing, Beryl wasn't comfortable performing large wardings on the fort if it wasn't necessary. The timber walls surrounding the fort were already well reinforced with both stone and magic. She could feel the familiar press of Darius' magic in the logs of most of the buildings as well, leaving her with little to work on.

It took half a day of working in the forge without complaint before she they allowed her to do anything more than chop wood or pump the bellows. She spent the next two days working with the blacksmith to forge and spell arrowheads for the soldiers. It was hot work even in the chilly spring air, leaving Beryl covered in a slick of sweat and streaks of ash from the forge at the end of each day.

There were few opportunities to clean up in private, and the fort seemed to live under a constant layer of rank smell. Beryl did her best with washing what clothes she could and cleaning up with damp clothes while the barracks were deserted. There were no separate baths and few females beyond the healers who ate and slept in a separate wing.

Rune, Argent, and Kuro wandered as they would about the fort, trying to stay out of the way of the soldiers and workers. The melting ice and snow left a thick layer of churned mud along most of the fort. What had been a firm path just days ago was turning into a sodden bog. They tasked several soldiers with clearing the worst of the slop and adding gravel to the most used paths; it became a punishment detail for the disorderly.

That night at dinner, Beryl sat with several soldiers who were friends with the tracker. Aaron regaled the table with tales of the mishaps he had endured while working for the army or traveling as a trapper in his youth. Most of the soldiers she worked with were veterans of the last campaign; the newer recruits seemed to take extra pains to avoid her, which was galling since they were close to the same age. They watched her with distrusting eyes and took pains to avoid where she worked or ate.

Beryl spent the weeks after her arrival assisting with the injured, repairing what damage she could help with and strengthening wards. Most of the soldiers continued to avoid her, but they at least tolerated her while she worked. She'd gotten too used to having friends and people she enjoyed working with while living in Cardu. She had to remind herself that she'd had worse insults and propositions made while she traveled with her Uncle but somehow the words still hurt.

She bore it, as she always had, pushing her anger and frustration in to her work. The fort would be well warded by the time they headed up river to the epicenter of the voids. She'd noticed the lingering glances and open stares since she arrived at the Fort. Most were the hostile glares she was used to, but many were more like the leering looks she'd gotten in taverns and among the drunken gamblers her Uncle fleeced for a living.

She finished her shift at the forge and grinned to feel the delight of Argent and Kuro playing at the river's edge just outside the fort. They'd been scouting the small dock and barge landing for the coming trip and now were sunning themselves after a lucky catch of a rabbit they'd shared. Argent was enjoying his river cleaned fur drying in the sun and it made her wish for the same. Deciding she started back to the barracks, stripping out of her sweat soaked coat and over shirt as she entered.

Skinning down to her underclothes, she started washing up in the basin to one side since the room was empty. She'd just dumped a pitcher of water over her head and started washing her hair when a hand jerked her back against a hard chest. The pitcher fell from her grasp to shatter, shards spraying her legs and feet, water slicking her skin and soaking her undershirt and breast band.

"Let go of me!" She said feeling her bond mates rushing towards the barracks, Argent was too far away to make it before Rune and she didn't want the small cat injured in the fight.

"I come back to find such a tempting thing next to my bunk, who am I to refuse." He said smelling at her neck even as she twisted in his grasp, kicking with bare feet at his boot and leather covered legs.

"Let go, I'm warning you." She snarled, wishing for her weapons or even a hairpin to stab him with as she thrashed as much as she could pressed against the cabinet and wall.

"Such a tease, you know you want it." He said pawing at her chest while he wrenched her arm behind her back; she threw her head back, making him curse and slam her forward into the wall, blood sliding from his nose.

"You will regret that." He snapped, pushing a leg between her thighs and ripping at her shirt.

"No more than you." She snarled twisting and slamming a hand against his chest releasing the first spell that came to mind, throwing him across the room just as the door slammed open and several soldiers poured in taking in her disheveled state.

"You bitch!" her attacker snarled, climbing to his feet.

"What's going on in here?" Captain Rogers barked, storming into the room.

"The bitch spelled me with something, threw me across the room!"

"Only after you tried to attack me!" Beryl snapped, "And if I'm a bitch, then you're a whore's son for all the manners you seem to know!"

"Enough! Barton, take Simmons to the healers and keep him under guard."

"She bewitched me, sir!" Simmons protested even as another soldier pulled him the rest of the way up and started leading him out.

"I'll get your story after they have looked you over. Move, Soldier!" He snapped, moving further into the room and turning his sharp gaze to Beryl, "Are you injured?"

"Scrapes and bruises." She said catching up her pack and pulling out clothes, he at least turned his back, most of the others watched as she dressed.

"Is what he said true, you spelled him?"

"I was washing my hair when he attacked me. I threw him across the room with a spell when he refused to release me. He's lucky I was unarmed or I would have done worse." She snapped moving to grab Rune as he scrambled into the room growling under his breath.

"Your other animals are out?" he asked, glancing around like Argent would spring out from under one bed.

"They went to the river, they should be back soon." She said snatching up her weapons harness and buckling on her knives. They wouldn't be out of her reach for the rest of her stay if she had anything to say about it.

"Then if you're ready, we can step outside to meet them before we go to the healers. I want you looked over, I know you say you're uninjured, but if this goes to trial there must be documentation."

"Very well, lead the way, Captain Rogers." She bit out fighting with her temper.

Healer Mara gestured Beryl over to a bed near the back wall when they entered, Argent taking up watch near the foot of the bed while Kuro settled herself on the rack used to hold sheets and bandages to one side. Rune refused to leave her side, sitting leaning against his bonded mage while they checked her over. She was declared fine except for a few painful bruises from the soldier's harsh grip on her wrist and shoulders.

"I know you want to get back to work, but I need you to stay the night." Mara said, pressing the younger woman back down against the bed with a firm hand.

"I have tasks to complete, it's barely after noon." Beryl protested.

"Have you eaten?" Mara asked, watching the mage with sharp eyes.

"I had breakfast." She snapped knowing she sounded mulish, but she couldn't imagine being forced to sit and wait. An itch to run burned beneath her skin, chanting that she needed to move.

"And yet it is two hours past the noon break. You will sit there and eat while I speak with the Captain. After that we will see if you're allowed to go back to your work."

"But I'm not injured," she said, fidgeting in place.

"Then you can at least take the noon break you were supposed to take earlier. Not everyone will watch others work themselves to the bone, sit and eat." She said taking a tray from a passing soldier and dropping it into Beryl's lap.

"Mage Mara,"

"No, eat and I will speak with you when I return." She snapped, "Or I will spell you to the bed like the unruly soldier you seem to imitate."

"Very well," Beryl said with a sigh, giving Rune a bite of chicken.

It upset all of her bond mates that they hadn't been there when she needed them. She shared out the meal between the four of them, listening to their distress and guilt. She tried to sooth them but none of them were happy that she'd even been lightly injured and scared. Her own nerves weren't helping rile them all up.

"I'm fine, please don't worry so. " She murmured with a groan, tugging Argent up onto the bed against her legs while Rune took her lap and Kuro one shoulder.

"Someone injured you." Rune said with a sigh, flopping over her lap to present his stomach to be stroked.

"We were not there to protect you. I would have torn his throat out. " Argent put in, a growl rumbling deep in his chest, his fur still bristling in agitation and anger.

"Or pecked out his eyes. " Kuro said in agreement, giving a shriek that made heads turn around the room.

"Hush, those with real wounds need their rest. I'm bruised, not broken," She said stroking each of them. *"Next time you can bite and claw my attacker all you like, but I can fight for myself if needed."*

It was almost dinnertime before they called her to a meeting with Captain Rogers, Staff Sergeant Michaels, Mage Darius, and a pair of guards monitoring Private Simmons. She ignored Darius gesturing her to a chair and moved to stand near the fire so she could lean against the solid bulk of Argent and keep him further from Simmons.

"Thank you for coming, Mage." Darius said with a nod, "I see that I've returned just in time. Are we ready to proceed?"

"I believe so." Captain Rogers said with a frown gaze sliding over Private Simmons, "We heard a commotion in the barracks and they called me to investigate. Upon entering, I found Private Simmons across the room from the woman called Mage. He claimed that she had used magic against him without provocation. I dismissed Private Simmons to the healer's hall and checked on the mage. She was in a state of undress. She claimed that Private Simmons had attacked her while she was bathing and she used magic to throw him across the room when he refused to release her."

"She was asking for it," the Simmons spat, "she's not the innocent here, girl traveling alone, how else would she pay her way?"

"Innocent or not, she clearly rejected your advances." Staff Sergeant Michaels snapped.

"Gentleman, no matter the reasons, a mage of Arden has been attacked. That is not a slight charge, however I would like this dealt with. We do not have time to delay our work and a trial could be months away." Darius said giving Beryl an apologetic look that she ignored. She was a rogue mage exiled from her own country and considered executed by most of the population; there wasn't ever a chance of anything going to trial, no matter the name she was living under.

"What are you suggesting?" Captain Rogers asked, watching the two mages.

"Let the man be punished for his deeds, Mage will leave the fort in a few days and I'm needed back at the capital. Things will go back to normal once we have removed the temptation of a female form."

"Perhaps, but we have several female healers here. I don't need them getting assaulted because we passed this incident over." The Captain said with a sigh, "Duke Laston rode out to return to his lands further south for the winter so we can deal with this as a military matter."

"What about you, Mage? How would you want the man punished?" Staff Sergeant Michaels asked.

"It doesn't matter what I want. We are at war and they need every soldier. Punish him how you like." She said fighting against her own anger and the flood of animosity across the bonds, "I just advise you to keep him away from me and my bond mates. Animals won't show the same restraint I did if he approaches me again."

"Are you certain?"

"Yes, I leave to scout further north for several weeks in two days. If he doesn't bother me for the brief span, I will let the matter go." She said with a bitter smile. She wanted to see the man punished, but it would only make things harder for everyone and expose her as the mage everyone thought dead. She had to make sure she wasn't caught unprepared ever again.

Chapter 6

Captain Marshal

Captain Charles Marshall rubbed at the bruised and split skin along his knuckles. This was the third brawl he had gotten into defending the young Mage he'd found and brought to the city. He refused to think she tried to attack the King, that she was a traitor. The memory of her face, full of terror in the marketplace or strained and exhausted after a vision filled his dreams at night. That was why he was sitting here waiting on a private meeting with the King. He had to know the truth.

They had declared her a traitor to the crown and exiled from the country. Many of the people in town believed that she had been killed or died while in prison, but there was no proof to any of the rumors. They denounced her as a whole by the Mage's Council and all her work as discarded or destroyed. Her former year mates dismissed her as a fraud, not even a true mage except for a small group of silent supporters who had been her friends.

Her former Master, royal adviser Lord Darius, had done nothing to prove her innocence, nor had the King. Even the Queen was silent on the matter, forbidding her servants to discuss the matter in her presence even though Beryl had been present for the birth of the young prince at the Queen's request. It seemed no one would step up and support the young woman who had arrived at the Capitol hoping to become a Royal Mage like her father before her.

The Captain surged to his feet as King James swept into the room, subsiding to his seat once the King was settled, gesturing for the rest of the servants to go. He sat and watched his Captain of the Guard for several long moments until the door shut behind the last person, leaving them alone.

"How is it the Captain of my Guard is getting into tavern brawls like a common reprobate?" King James asked, looking over the worn man before him.

"My King, I know my behavior has not been fitting of my station; however, that does not mean that I can ignore it when others are blaming an innocent woman." Captain Marshal said firmly.

"So you believe that the young Mage was innocent of the charges?"

"I do, sir. I was the one who brought her to the castle, and I have spoken several times with her since. My old Captain, Durn, your former Captain of the Guard vouched for her character and trained her himself in basic combat skills. Your own Adviser, Master Mage Darius, took her under his wing as an apprentice. I cannot see her tricking so many, my King. I refuse to believe the rumors and lies floating around the castle. Mage would not have harmed herself or her bond mates, nor would she harm the castle or the Prince."

The King watched him for a moment before nodding. "What we speak of will not leave this room, am I understood?"

"Of course; I will swear whatever oath you need of me."

"An oath is unnecessary, we know our Mage is not guilty." King James said, meeting Charles' eyes with palpable regret.

"But, sir;" he sputtered in shock, "Why would you let this continue? They curse her name in the streets!"

"It is necessary. She is still a citizen of ours and is doing a valuable service for Arden. I must ask that you stop in your attempts to redeem her. Once her work is complete, she will return, but for now things must stay as they are."

"I will do what I can, but I've never been a man for subterfuge and lies." He said hating how helpless he felt. He was a man of action and all he could see was a friend being beaten down by everyone around him.

"That is all I can ask of you, Captain. You should speak to the Mage Librarian Brennan; she has been to speak with myself or Master Darius every week since the attack pleading for Mage's return." The King sighed others of her loyal friends had sent letters and offered to gather money for her release.

"Is Brennan aware of Mage's current circumstance?"

"Not at present and I must ask that if you inform her of it you do so with the utmost discretion."

"Of course, sir."

"Go now and get those bruises seen to, Captain Marshal. It would not do for the King's Captain of the Guard to be seen injured."

"Thank you, sir." Charles said with a sigh, bowing a last time before leaving the King to his work.

Leaving the healer's hall two hours later, Captain Marshal made his way to the other side of the castle where the Mage's Library was housed. At the very least, he could put the Mage Librarian's fears to rest before he went back to the barracks. He entered the library and was directed to a desk in the back of the main hall. It struck him dumb for a moment at the sight before him.

The Mage Librarian Brennan was beautiful, tall with long blonde hair and a small owl perched on one shoulder. She wore a thin chain choker with three amber beads that pulsed with some inner light drawing the eye. She was working on an enormous volume bound in leather that she was casting a long chain of glowing runes along the spine of the book. He waited until she finished her spell before he stepped up to her desk; the owl giving a soft twittering hoot as he approached.

"Pardon the interruption, but are you Mage Brennan?" he asked, keeping his voice low, not wanting their conversation to be overheard.

"Yes, is there something I can help you with?" the woman asked, the owl twisting to get a better look at the soldier visiting his bond mate.

"I'm Charles Marshall, a Captain of the King's Guard. I hoped to speak with you about Mage." He said wincing when her expression went blank, "I understand that you were friends?"

"You knew Mage?" She asked with a frown before a slight smile broke over her face, "Of course, she spoke of you a few times. You were the Captain who brought her to the Capital."

"Yes, I was hoping you would have a few moments to spare." He said hesitating since he didn't want to discuss this in the open library.

"Let me just put a few things away. Perhaps we can walk? There is a small garden close to the Library."

"That would be wonderful, thank you." He said with clear relief, tension draining from his shoulders, making the owl twitter in amusement. They strolled chatting about inconsequential things, such as introducing him to Timon, her owl, and her work in the library until they reached a far corner of the garden.

"I take it you don't believe Mage is guilty of attacking the presentation of Prince James?" she asked, watching his reaction.

"No, and I have it on good authority that she is innocent." He said smiling at the surprised look she gave him.

"You know this for certain?" she pressed, leaning forward, Timon flaring his wings to keep his balance.

"Yes, but I cannot say much more. She was accused and exiled, but she is well and I hope eventually will be absolved on all the accused crimes. The King asked me to inform you since nothing can be seen coming from him."

"That is wonderful news. I was so worried when the rumors started that she had died in prison. I knew she never would have attacked the Prince, she was there for the birth!"

"I was on a supply run to the northern border at the time and didn't return until the week before the presentation. I saw her for a moment in town; it was like she had seen Bain himself, pale and shaken, but she ran off before I could reach her. I didn't have time to see her again before the attack." He said with a frown of regret and guilt.

"She claimed that she was trying to protect the castle and those present at the presentation from someone else, someone who attacked the castle's wards." She said with a frown.

"Perhaps she was. I have not known her to lie." Charles said with a sigh.

"That settles it; we'll just have to be here to welcome her back once they prove her innocent." Brennan said with a determined nod.

"As easy as that?" He asked, grinning at the optimistic woman.

"Believing in your friends is the easiest or hardest thing most people ever do. We just might have to work harder at it than most." She said fiercely, drawing a bark of laughter out of the stoic Captain.

"That we will, might I call on you again, Mage Brennan? I have a feeling that we will both need all the friends we can get in the coming days."

"I would like that, Captain." She said with a smile, taking his arm and letting him lead her back to the castle.

Chapter 7

Tracking

Beryl crawled toward the edge, stopping next to where Aaron lay watching the compound below them. They had been tracking the voids, piecing together a pattern for the last two weeks. At the center of the disturbances miles into the Northern Mountains was a massive army encampment. Its sprawling desolation made the Fort look like a tiny village.

"How many soldiers?" She asked, keeping her voice low even though they were still a respectful distance from the encampment. She clutched a spelled stone in one hand uselessly watching the tiny dots of practicing soldiers in formation. Nothing she could spell or cast would protect her or her home from a force this large.

"Thousands," Aaron said. "More than enough to wipe out the Fort and the next five or more after it if they followed the border. None of the forts have many troops during the winter since few will brave the snow-filled mountain passes. I want to know how they've been hiding the traffic to and from a camp this big; we should have noticed it months ago."

"Why would they even attack? Arden has no sizable towns in the North; its power is on the coast and sea."

"They can harry the border all spring, summer and fall before returning to the mountains for the winter with their spoils. It's what the raiders here have always done, but with a force this big they can move down the border and hit the northern coastal towns."

"We don't have a quarter of the troops to match them, do we? The King would have to strip the coastal forts to match this many. How did we not hear of this sooner?"

"To amass an army this big, all the raiders would have to join forces. Even that doesn't seem like it would be enough. The Northern Warriors horde their gold for burial, to hire this many mercenaries would have taken every coin they had."

"Maybe it's a combination of both. They are promising mercenaries the gold recovered in the war and pulling in the raider's clans with promises of land?"

"Rowle, of the Clan Red Hand, was chosen to lead the raider Clans two summers ago. If this is his doing, he certainly moves fast. Can that bird of yours tell you what it sees?"

"Yes, or I can see through her eyes." Beryl murmured, most of her attention focused on what the bird and her other bond mates were sending. Argent and Rune noted the patterns that resembled how groups of animals would move, while Kuro pointed out where the soldiers' presence was thin or lacking.

"Good, we will need a map of the compound. We've never got a spy into the northern clans. Everyone is related to everyone else, much like at a royal court, but they give the privilege of serving the clans to cousins and such. You have to be a blood relative to even get entrance into the compounds. With this many mercenaries, we might stand a chance of slipping someone in."

"If there's somewhere I could hide nearby, I might get three spies into the compound." Beryl offered with a grin, pulling out of the bond enough to watch the tracker's expression.

"How?" He demanded, disbelief plain in his eyes.

"I might not pull off being a mercenary, but no one looks twice at a stray cat or dog in a compound this big." Aaron eyed the small cat nestled in the small of her back with uncertainty.

"Rune can take care of himself." She defended the gray tabby that stood as tall as he could, fluffing his tail in agitation. "Even if Rune didn't go, Kuro and Argent would blend in fine."

"Let's get the map of the compound roughed out and then we can find somewhere to set up an extended camp. If the animals are our spies than we'll need a suitable place to retreat to and one they can sneak back to us unnoticed if needed."

"Very well, lead the way." Beryl said with a grin.

* * *

They nestled their last camp on of the high cliffs to the East side of the compound. It had been harder to find an excellent base camp than they thought. The area was riddled with large and small voids, leaving large stretches of forest and plains land dead and burned, uninhabitable.

"I can't use wind magic to scout with other mages nearby. If the sorcerers the captured raiders have been talking about are here, they might notice." Beryl said with a sigh. "Really, we should use as minor magic as possible. They shouldn't be able to see the bond so we can still see into the compound and communicate, but unless we're attacked, I'd rather leave the spells out."

"Sensible. I know little about magic. I take it having a spell cast in one area would highlight that section to a mage?"

"Only if they're looking for it, but we have no way of knowing if they are or not without using magic to check which they would sense."

"Damned to Bain if we do or don't. All right then, no magic until we have a good lock on the magic users in the compound and what their abilities are."

"Agreed," Beryl said with a sigh, this would limit most of her abilities if they got spotted or if one of her bonded got into trouble.

Kuro had the easiest assignment of the group; she had to monitor the town from above, spiraling in and around the compound as she hunted. Argent and Rune's job was harder, they had to play at being a stray. Beryl insisted on them each continuing to wear their collars, but otherwise they went in with no protection or armor, trying to look like strays or wandering pets.

Kuro circled above the compound much as she had been doing the last few days, only stopping to hunt. They were constantly updating the map of the compound as sections of troops were moved. Once they had an excellent picture of the layout and how the troops moved, they would send it on to Darius and the King.

Rune slid from shadow to shadow as he worked his way farther into the compound, hiding in baskets and in carts when he could. He watched as lengthy lines of boots tromped down the road in unison, heading toward the practice area. He sneezed out the reek of leather, sweat, and dust that rose in their wake and moved to the next tent.

Argent snarled at a nearby stray, glad that the mutt backed down and moved on, leaving the larger dog to settle against the canvas side of the tent. It was hot in the sun, but this spot meant that he could hear the soldiers talking amongst themselves as they gathered their gear. It also let Beryl and Aaron figure out the rotation that the guards in that section took, adding the information to the messages they sent back to the fort with Kuro or by message stone to Darius and the other Watchers.

The troops were packing up for a move, a massive line of wagons being loaded with supplies and weapons. While the King was sending more troops north, it would be weeks before they arrived, far too late if the army moved in the next few days. These were not the undisciplined troops that had been attacking the fort on and off for the last year.

The soldiers would overwhelm the tired troops at the Fort and continue on into Arden. They needed to know what the actual aim was here because overrunning the handful of forts and small civilian towns that struggled to survive in the North would not be a worthy prize for any warlord. Whatever they were doing, it was not meant to stop here in the northern borders of Arden.

* * *

They had spotted Rowle the Red Hand rallying the troops, but most of the actual orders seemed to come from the sorcerer's tents and the main tower near the center of camp. The Horde leader left the tents in a temper every evening, but he was putting their orders into practice and commanding the largest group of warriors the northern lands had seen in living memory. They tracked his progress about the camps but so far he stayed with his troops encouraging their progress at the training grounds.

Rune slid through the shadows, ignoring the soft murmurs of encouragement and caution from his bond mates. None of the others could get into the tented pavilions that held the chief and his sorcerers. The troops were full of rumors about the pale foreigners that were magic users who the warlord, Rowle, was paying to ensure his victory. The soldiers and mercenaries spoke of unnatural cold that consumed a room when the sorcerers entered and how they had made examples of several men who had tried to desert, leaving them broken drooling shells that died later that night.

Beryl's voice was hoarse from explaining what was happening through the bond to Aaron. The tracker moved around her as she abandoned her body in favor of seeing through the other animal's eyes as they moved about the compound. They had been hiding in plain sight for three days now, and the information they had gathered was invaluable.

Once a day, Beryl trekked back several miles away from the camp with Aaron to send their messages on to Darius, the King's spymaster. They weren't able to receive anything back without a fixed receiving circle like the one in Darius' office in the Capitol, but they could keep the King and his advisors updated on the situation. So far they could stay hidden from the patrolling guards and troops that milled through the area, but they couldn't stay indefinitely, they only had enough food for another week before it would force them to head back to Fort Brume.

Beryl collapsed from her tailor seat, gasping for breath as the feeling of hands grabbing Rune rang along the bond like a blow. The cat's rage and panic slashed at them as he bit and scratched at leather clad hands. Argent gave voice to a howl that rang over the compound, Kuro screamed from her perch in the forest before launching herself back into the air despite the descending dusk. They whined in unison as rough hands shoved the small cat into a sack.

The bag was moving, disorienting and stomach turning as it swung with the man's stride. It seemed only a few moments before they dumped the bag onto a table and voices rang loud in the cat's ears. He sorted out his feet and guessing which side of the bag was the opening he prepared to pounce as someone walked on heavy boots to the table. Magic burned along his body, freezing his muscles and leaving him thrashing only in his mind as a hand opened the bag and pulled his stiff form out.

"I know you can hear me, Mage." a man's voice said hissed as he stroked along Rune's back. "If you want your bond mate back, come and get him."

Beryl scrambled at the ground, fighting her way to her feet. She knew that voice; it had haunted her dreams for the many years since they attacked her. She had finally placed a name to her childhood attacker when he arrived at the capitol to attend the presentation of the King and Queen's infant son.

Reginald Delorean was a minor nobleman of no genuine power or name. He was not a mage, nor did he serve at any lofty position in Arden. Delorean had left a trail of broken children stripped of their magic as he traveled the country until something went wrong when he tried to take Beryl's magic. He changed tactics then. He was the one draining the magic from his surroundings, causing the voids. It had to be him. And now he wanted to finish what he had started with

Beryl, stripping her of her magic. She was not a child any longer, she would not go down without a fight.

"Mage, what's going on? Where are you going?" Aaron asked as she started packing a light bag with supplies, strapping on her weapons and filling her pockets with spelled stones.

"They captured Rune. I have to go get him."

"Ruth, bless us. How can I help?" He asked, packing up the camp.

"Tell Darius that it's Delorean. He'll understand. Have Mara send a message stone to Darius. I taught her how to do the spell."

"I should be here to help you. What if you need to fight your way out?"

"He knows I'm here. I could walk right into camp and they would take me straight to him." Beryl said with a bitter smile, most of her attention on her bond mates. "I will wait until it's almost dark before heading in. We already know the guard shifts and how to do it."

"All the more reason for me to head in with you; you need someone at your back."

"I can't leave without Rune. I can't leave him and if everything goes wrong, you can at least let the King know what is happening so he can send other Mages here to help. Go, Aaron. Please."

"I don't like this, Lass. You're walking into a snake pit and offering your arm to Bain."

"I doubt Bain has anything to do with this, Aaron. I doubt any of the Gods do."

"It's a three-day trek to get here, but alone I can do it in two, maybe less. If we haven't heard from you in four days, I will try to rally the troops to come get you, but it's no guarantee they'll come."

"It's fine, Aaron. I'm already a ghost to most of the people who know me."

"Let me at least know your name, Lass. Mage is not a proper name to offer the dead."

"My name is Beryl." She said with a slight smile, touched that the tracker wanted to know even if he would forget within the hour thanks to the curse twisted into her scars.

"It's a pleasure to meet you, Beryl. I hope you and your bond mates can meet me again."

"As do I, Aaron. Ruth, light your way."

"And yours, Beryl." He said, pulling the small woman into a quick hug before he shouldered his pack, heading off at a steady jog.

Beryl would leave most of her things where they lay, only taking weapons and a few supplies that might come in handy. She emptied everything into the grass and started packing what she figured would be useful. It was a small enough stack of things.

The knife flashed before Rune's eyes before it bit into one shoulder, drawing a crimson line of pain down one frozen limb. Beryl fell to her knees a half mile or so from the compound with a cry of pain as she watched through her bond mate's eyes.

"Much too slow, Mage; for every hour you dally your bond mate will suffer another injury."

Beryl surged back to her feet, panting as she made her way through the tall grass that edged the compound, Argent moving from behind a supply cart to join her. Beryl pulled out the dog's armor and strapped it into place on the enormous dog, turning his already menacing form into a deadly weapon. Kuro had perched on a tall tent pole and was watching who came and went from the building where Rune was being held.

The sorcerers lived and worked in a stone building with two small towers. Rune was being held in the northernmost tower, somewhere near the top. There would not be a way to sneak in. All the entrances were watched and there was only one way to the top of the tower.

Readying herself Beryl forced herself to crawl through the fighting positions as she called her magic forward. She didn't want to ride the winds to view the camp this time, instead she pushed and pulled at the natural eddies, stirring them up and driving them faster. Half an hour later the storm struck the compound with heavy winds, lightning, and sheets of rain turning visibility to nothing.

She made her slow way into the camp, Argent meeting her and

guiding her to the tower through the driving rain. She could have walked it alone, the line of her bond to Rune tugging her forward to her injured bond mate like a lodestone. Sleep spelled stones took out the few guards braving the weather while Argent took down the guard at the tower door, letting Beryl spell him unconscious.

"So, this is Delorean's lost one," The mage said with a sneer petting at the cat in his arms while watching Beryl and Argent drip onto his floors, "I'm not impressed, I was expecting something more than a half-drowned rat."

"You know, Delorean? Where is he?" she asked, shifting into the room, eyes darting for things she could use. There was little. The mage stood before a small alter holding Rune over the stone slab like he was to be sacrificed, the cat stiff and still in his hands.

"If you dog comes any closer, a broken leg will be the least of its problems." He said eyeing the large dog that was circling along the wall and tightening his grip on the small cat.

"He won't." Beryl said, wincing as the pain radiating through the bond intensified, mentally ordering Argent to back off. "What do you want with us?"

"I want you to take your place at the altar." He said gesturing to the stone table between them with a look her teachers had reserved for the utterly moronic questions put to them.

"And Delorean, is he one of your members?" she pressed, hoping to get more information and drag things out.

"He's one of our Lord's more favored members; He's left me with this most delicious task, I shall enjoy reporting your defeat to him and our Lord." The man said with a sniff, so Delorean wasn't here, she'd misheard or he'd already left the camp.

"You're one of the anti-magic followers?" Beryl asked pulling out a spelled stone and palming it, fingering the rune cut into its surface, "Why would you want to stop magic users, you're a mage!"

"Only those Lord Aedus judges as worthy may wield the magic we reap."

"Magic you steal from children! Is Aedus that much of a coward?"

she spat wincing as his hands tightened in anger making Rune whimper across the bond.

"Only you cowardly mages, binding yourselves to mindless animals. You are nothing but animals yourselves. Aedus will burn the earth until you profaners are nothing but ash."

"What do I have to do to get Rune back?" she asked fighting to keep her face and voice full of panic, Madame Duve would have approved she thought, she could feel Kuro circling the tower in the growing storm screaming her rage to the skies.

"I'll let your precious animal go if you complete the ritual Delorean started." He said with a smile, gesturing to the waiting altar and the pile of dark crystals before him that sat like a void to her magical senses, sucking the magic from anything near them.

"That would kill my bond mates." She told them, her voice ragged, desperately trying to think of a way out for her bond mates. They refused to leave her behind, however she pressed them.

"They aren't my concern and you'll survive it." He said with an uncaring shrug, petting at her bonded with a parody of care. "Cut your hand on the knife and give your blood to the altar, the crystals will do the rest."

"Release Rune first, he can't do anything to hurt you and I'm here, I'll take his place." She said trying to look small and miserable. It wasn't hard.

"Fine, step forward," he said, grinning when she approached.

He cast Rune to the side, ignoring Beryl's cry of shock, snatching her wrist as she tried to lunge and catch him and dragging her to the waiting altar. Argent lunged and caught the cat still locked in his immobility, carrying him to the wall next to the door. Beryl twisted in his grasp, the thick stone between them preventing her from doing much as the larger man dragged her flush against the altar, her free hand slapping down against the stone as she struggled. She could feel the crystals pulling at her life force and magic from where her hand sat against the altar.

Panic and pain bounced back and forth along the bond as one

palm was slashed open by the grinning mage. Argent growled thunderously while keeping himself between Rune and the man who'd hurt him. Kuro raged, her anger leaving Beryl gasping as the bond expanded, magical power building. Each bond mate pushed energy across the bond, throwing everything to their bonded, hoping to tip the balance as the first drops of blood hit the black crystals, which pulsed with an ominous red glow as they siphoned away the magic within.

He slapped her bloody palm against the stone, forcing her to keep it there. She lashed out with the other hand, grappling for the knife. He cursed as her nails scored his skin but avoided the spelled stone she tried to press against his exposed arm, knocking it out of her grasp. She dug at the tendons in his wrist forcing him to drop the blade but the sucking pull of the stone was weakening her, she could feel her magic draining away.

The gems on her cuffs and the collars of her bond mates blazed as they fought against the pull of the void crystals. Magic built as it was pushed and pulled between them. The man chuckled in her ear as the pressure built, grinding her hand against the stone to keep the blood flowing, her vision greying as the energy bleed from her.

With a crash, Kuro burst through the tower window, slamming into the man with a shriek. He flailed backwards with a cry, releasing Beryl. She swept the crystals off the altar, sending them to the floor where they shattered, releasing the energies they'd absorbed in streaks of lightning, arcing through the room in a blaze of light.

Suddenly it was over, Beryl lay blinking on the ground watching where the mage had fallen, his neck at an angle no one could survive. Argent picked up Rune and brought him over, Beryl reversing the spell keeping him immobile she patted him over but beyond the broken leg he seemed okay. She glanced around, looking for Kuro. Something was missing, and she didn't see the hawk. Had she flown back out the window?

She tried to trace the bond, but she couldn't feel the bird. There was a hole in her mind where she should have been crowing triumphantly over her victory. She spotted the limp bundle of feathers when a gust of wind pushed a blast of rain into the room, shifting a limp wing. Beryl threw herself forward, crawling when her body refused to propel her faster. The bird lay limp and rain soaked wings and talons bloody from her assault on the window and man.

"Kuro?" she whimpered carefully stroking along the soft downy chest.

The bird remained still. No croons of affection, or shrieks of triumph, or cries of anger came from her beak and there never would be again. Her brave bird had given herself completely to the fight as she had done everything, breaking bones in her dive through the window to save her bond mates. Beryl wept as she gathered the soft limp body into her arms. The storm screamed outside, building in intensity.

Scooping up Rune as well, she made her slow way out into the storm. Somehow they made it back to camp, where they waited for Aaron to return. In a daze, she splinted Rune's leg and cleaned Kuro. The storm had destroyed the enemy camp, leaving the fighters trying to gather their destroyed gear and supplies.

Beryl wept as she removed the bird's collar and buried the too light form the next morning. Kuro had been a force of angry and courage; the shallow grave did not do her justice. Three days later Aaron returned with the army only a few days behind his squad. He kept watch while she huddled with her bond mates, mourning their lost piece.

Chapter 8

Exile

"**A**re you certain you're ready?" Baron Sarnes asked, watching the mage before him carefully packing her belongings.

"I need to be moving," Beryl said with a sigh, "I can't hide away forever."

"That doesn't mean you can't take the time to mourn your loss."

"If I leave now, I can say... they killed her when I was exiled. It's the perfect cover, and it allows me to be myself instead of trying to play a part." She said forcing herself to release the bracelet that had been her bond mate's collar.

"I'm not saying it's not a wonderful plan, I just worry for you. I feel you are throwing yourself into danger out of grief. I've lost too many soldiers to the recklessness that loss can cause; I'd rather not lose another."

"It's not recklessness, Baron." She said with a sigh, dropping into a chair and hugging Argent to her when he paced over and leaned his colossal head against her chest. "I feel like I'm suffocating, I need air."

"Orlean is not a court to be uncertain in; you need to have your wits about you."

"You and Lady Duve have trained me well, I'll be fine."

"I won't try to stop you, Mage; I just wish I could send someone to watch your back. The courts are deadly in their own right. I feel like I'm sending you from the fire to the blacksmith's anvil."

"And the anvil forges the stronger weapons with the hammer's blows." She offered with a tired smile, "I'll be fine."

"A letter arrived for you," He said handing over the cream envelope, "the carriage leaves at dawn tomorrow so you need to be finished packing before dinner tonight so we can have you baggage ready in the morning."

"I'll be ready, Baron."

"I'll see you at dinner, Mage. Master Rune, Master Argent." He said with a smile, giving the three of them a courtly bow.

She glanced over the things she'd left behind and stood to continue packing, stuffing her leather coats and weapons in one bag. Going as herself at least meant she could take whatever she wanted with her. Beryl gave Argent a last pat and stroked Rune where he was seated next to her bag; she wasn't sure what she'd have done without them there to keep her going.

She'd stayed in the healer's tents while the battle raged against Aedus' army. Huddled against her bond mates, she'd listened to the muted sounds of battle and the moans of the injured as they were brought in. They had routed the army with the mages, the Northern Tribes dispersing and the leader Red Hand being forced into a retreat into the northern mountains across the border.

Her brave Shiro was gone and her mind reached for her missing bond mate repeatedly. Kuro's collar sat against one wrist next to her jeweled cuff, and she had no intention of taking it off. The smooth jade stone sat cool against her skin, its magic stripped, leaving the stone empty and waiting to be refilled. The missing bond was a hole in her mind that nothing seemed to fill, but she couldn't let herself sink back into despondency, Rune and Argent needed her to keep moving. Kuro would have tried to argue with her to keep training and working. The bird had always been one to rage at inactivity.

She finished packing the last bag and laid out her outfit for the morning. She'd be traveling as Eglantine again until she reached Orlean. There had been several incidents of attacks on mage's or their families in the months she was in the North. The King had recalled all the mages he could to Cardu to ensure their safety for now, but riots continued to break out in the larger cities as the push back again magic continued to grow.

Opening her letter, she smiled faintly to see it was from Darius. He had at least looked deeper into Delorean and reported that his house was found empty and abandoned. Darius would keep watch for the man, but for now had no leads to follow. He wished her luck on her journey and offered any support she needed before she left Arden.

Several of Aedus' followers had been captured during attempted attacks on local mages around Arden, but all had died within hours of being captured, poisoned, or hanging themselves in their cells. The only lead they had was that each had worn a black crystal similar to those found in the voids on a throng around their necks. It made little sense that they'd even been able to attack and injure several mages, killing two. Mages were banned from using magic to attack others, but it was allowed in defense and yet none of the attackers had been injured by magic.

She would just have to be extra vigilant while traveling. At least in Orlean there were no rumors of Aedus having a following in the country. His worship didn't appear to have made it across the ocean yet, and Beryl could only hope it stayed that way. What Aedus was offering would tempt to many mages or even the general populations used to being seen as second-class citizens compared to the mage elite.

The government held absolute control over a mage's life in most countries. They were removed from their families at a young age and trained by older mage's indoctrinating them to the expected lifestyle. The government decided where they lived or worked and it could move them about as the monarchy decided without notice. All mages swore a magical oath to their country's leader, forcing them to comply with their demands or be stripped of their magic, Beryl hadn't made that oath yet since her education was interrupted making her a rogue mage.

She was one of the few mages who'd left their apprenticeship early without having their magic bound or a loyalty vow forced. She'd never be forced to choose between her magic or her way of life like the other mages, and she knew others would see the changes Aedus was offering to get out of those vows. Magic needed to be controlled but to have every action and decision in your life controlled by your occupation left many looking for a way out.

Even working as a spy, she'd had little control over things. She'd understood later why Darius had let everyone assume she was dead, cutting off her former friends and supporters. It gave her an advantage as a spy since no one would look for a dead mage however once word got out that she was alive in Orlean she would be branded as a traitor to Arden all over again.

Even her connections to Darius and the Queen hadn't been enough to keep her free and safe after the attack on the castle, she'd been the only one anyone could blame and the city had been frothing with rage. She'd had her supporters and could have pressed for a hearing, but Darius suspected several of the Mage's Counsel members were accepting bribes or were working for their own interests that didn't include protecting the country. She would have just gone to prison, anyway. At least this way she could do more than a rogue mage or spy than as a student in Cardu.

Once she was out of the country she'd be forced to rely on the local contacts for news, not even her messenger stones could travel that far and messages were often intercepted or reviewed before they left the country unless they could be given to a reliable person to sneak out and deliver in person. She'd thought she was alone the last few months since her exile, but once she left Arden, she would be on her own. Argent bumped his head against her hip, and she forced a slight smile to her lips. No, never alone with Argent and Rune by her side.

Part Two

Orlean

Chapter 9

Arriving in Orlean

Beryl looked over the bustling port with a tired sigh. The busy crush of people made her exhausted just looking over the waiting turmoil. The area was a sea of moving color, freight, and people dodging through the crowded lanes. She forced her head up and strode down the pier toward the waiting market, Argent striding at her side and Rune on her shoulder, hidden by her hood.

They made their slow way through the crowded docks and market while she tried to remember the exact instructions they had given her to meet their escort. They would stay in the palace itself as a guest of the royal family instead of with the local Count, who was a member of the Listeners like they'd planned. Once word got out that a mage exiled from Arden was visiting Orlean, she'd been invited to the palace and such an invitation couldn't be refused.

She struggled to keep her wits about her and an eye out for danger as they walked, but her mind wasn't up to the task. It surprised her to see only a handful of beggars and pickpockets in the sizable crowd. Her friends from the thieves' guild in Cardu would have loved a market this crowded. All she wanted to do since Kuro's death was sleep, draped in the warmth and closeness of her remaining bond mates. The world seemed muted around her, and she just didn't have the energy to care about much of anything. She was only forcing herself through the motions because of Rune and Argent, she couldn't lose them.

"Madame Marcian?" a porter asked when she reached the waiting cabs lining the curb.

"Yes?" she replied, digging her fingers into Argent's fur to remind him to be polite as the horses shifted at his low growl. Both of her bond mates had been over protective since the start of their journey.

"His royal highness, Prince Zyon has sent a coach for your use. It would please me to convey you to the palace at your earliest convenience." He said with a polite middle height bow to someone of a rank above him who wasn't royalty.

"The prince honors me," She said with a polite smile as the man's eyes widened as Rune slid out of her hood to peer at the horses and back into the market, "I would be happy to accept transport to the palace."

"This way, Madame," he said gesturing her towards one coach that was given a hair more space than the surrounding others thanks to the royal seals decorating the doors and the plumed horses.

She let Argent climb in first, his ungainly progress making the driver cough back a laugh as the entire carriage shook. Beryl gave him a small amused smile as he handed her into the carriage and secured the door behind them. The large dog's moments of clumsiness were gaining all of them friends, even in other countries. She glanced out the window and tried not to sigh, she could already see the spread of the gossip running across the marketplace as a single traveling woman without an escort in the company of a large dog was met by a royal coach and whisked away to the palace. They would be to talk of the town for weeks to come.

It was a lengthy ride and she could only hope that her trunks would arrive undisturbed. From here on out her every action would be scrutinized and gossiped over so she needed to pay attention, she thought with a sigh, petting Argent when he rested his head in her lap, Rune purring softly against her neck. Tonight she would have her first audience with the royal family before the ball the next week that would introduce her to Orlean society.

She had the names of several merchants around town and a few servants willing to pass on messages or keep an ear out for gossip, but her primary contact for the Listeners would be Count Malouel, a minor noble of the Court. She could only hope he reached her before her first audience with the Royal family. Originally she'd planned to stay at his estate instead of in the palace, but you couldn't refuse a royal offer.

* * *

"Mistress Marcian, welcome to the palace. There are messages waiting for you." One attendant said with a bow as they showed her into a suite of rooms in the North wing of the palace, "I've left them on the desk. May I take your coat?"

"Thank you." Beryl said with a tired smile handing over her coat, "May I ask your name?"

"I am Bertrand, Mistress, and will be at your service during the day for anything you might need during your stay. My brother, Rand, will take over at night should you need anything after the tenth bell."

"Thank you, would it be possible to get some water for my bond mates?" she asked, pulling off her gloves and setting them on the table with her small handbag.

"I shall see to it myself. Will they need food?" he asked, glancing at Argent as he wandered past without twitching a muscle.

"No, they will eat with me later at the dinner."

"I shall make sure accommodations are made for them while you are staying at the palace." He said with a quick bow, gesturing the women waiting behind him in.

"Good afternoon, Mistress;" An older maid said stepping forward eying Argent with a wary look as he wandered by chasing a scent, "they have assigned us as your personal attendants during your stay at the palace. We will assist you with your dressing, keep the rooms ready for your use, and assist you with any needs you may have."

"Thank you," Beryl said with a nod stroking a hand along Argent's back as he passed to one side, "please don't mind Argent, as long as you have no ill intentions towards me he'll be gentle as a lamb."

"The dog and cat don't fight?" One of the younger women asked timidly, earning a glare from the spokesperson of the group.

"No, they're bound to each other; they can't hurt each other without hurting themselves." Beryl said with a shrug, moving towards the desk and its waiting stack of letters. "Can you tell me when I need to be ready for dinner tonight? Also, what are your names, please?"

"Dinner will begin at the seventh evening bell, however it is polite to gather by the fifth bell to socialize before dinner." The older woman said with a sniff gesturing towards a clock on the desk, "I am Viand, the Head Maid of this wing, Adela and Margot will return in two hours to help you dress if you don't need our assistance in unpacking?"

"No, I should be fine. Thank you for your help," Beryl said with a tight smile, ready for them to leave.

As soon as the door closed behind the last servant, the smile fell from her face. With a sigh she started sorting through the letters. Several were from the various courtiers she'd wanted to gain an acquaintance with since they were among the more powerful members. Most were polite invitations for tea, small parties, and a few balls in the coming weeks.

"The trunks are in here, but not your bags from the ship. Argent said, sending her a mental picture of several trunks lining one wall of the bedroom.

"The rooms reek of things, stinking flowers and powders." Rune complained, jumping up and butting his head against her chin before he continued on his patrol of their new domain.

"These are rooms meant for female royal guests," Beryl said with a sigh, *"They were from the make ups some women use. We will see how the court is tonight, I might have to use them if everyone else is."*

There was a knock on the door and a porter brought in her last trunk and bags from the ship while another brought two wide dishes full of water. She tipped the porter with a few coins and took one bowl, setting it in the bedroom while the other stayed near the desk. Once they were alone again she unpacked, Rune helping sort through what had been touched by others. They had rifled through all the trunks but her smaller bags seemed untouched, nothing seemed to be missing from any of the bags or trunks.

"They looked but took nothing, why?" Rune asked, sneezing as he pulled his head out from under a shirt.

"They're curious about us, much the same way we are about them." Beryl said with a shrug.

"They should have asked first." Argent growled, jumping up on to the high bed with a thump that made the entire frame shake.

"Careful." Beryl said with a slight grin, *"I doubt they built with extra-large lap dogs in mind."*

"Which are you wearing?" Rune asked, poking at the dresses she was laying out.

"What do you think? Like they expect or the way we want to dress?" she asked laying out two options as the rest went into the wardrobe to one side, one was a sturdy grey material that she could have worn about town on errands but with silk inserts and lace accents to dress it up, the other was a green silk gown that cost more than she'd made in a year while traveling with her uncle.

"Do we want to be the hunter or the prey?" Argent asked, snorting when she dropped one of the many hats Madame Duve had packed on his head.

"I don't like being prey," Beryl said with a sigh, *"but they might expect it of us. We are far from home and those who could help, they might expect us to run from the wolves."*

"Even prey can turn and bite." Argent muttered, watching Beryl pace with a wuffling sigh of his own. Neither of the animals understood the way humans ranked each other and the differing customs depending on the rank. The pack leader and those who protected the

pack made sense, but the fawning hangers on who did nothing to help would have been cast off in the wilds.

"But wolves can show their belly or turn and bite, we could be both." Rune said, licking at one paw as he thought, *"Cats know when to run and regroup so they live to hunt another day."*

"Tonight we will act as they expect, we can always bite later." Beryl said with a frown putting up the grey dress. She hated not knowing how the surrounding people would react; it left her on edge, waiting for the next blow to fall.

"Do we have to play dumb animals?" Argent asked with a slight whine. Neither of them enjoyed pretending to be what they weren't, ordinary beasts. "Playing *didn't keep us safe before."*

"If they don't expect it of you, they can't plan for it either. If things go wrong, I want you to have every advantage." Beryl said setting her things to the side and going to take a quick bath and wash her hair.

Rune kept up a ranting commentary on how much the various potions she was using on her hair stunk and how loud the clicks of her boots were on the stone floor. Beryl ignored it, knowing they were all on edge now that their task was starting. She dug out a bag of dried meat strips and gave them each one to gnaw on while she started drying and curling her hair. She should have called for her maids to come help, but she wanted the time to prepare herself for the dinner to come.

It wasn't until Rune started sarcastically responding to her mental hellos and how do you do's that she recited that she gave up with a laugh. They'd all practiced enough, now they would just have to hope everything went as planned. She was just stepping into her low dress boots when the maids returned, the younger ones cooing over her hair and the dress.

"Next time call for us, Miss. We'll help you bathe and dress, both of us are well trained in how to do the current fashions and hair styles." Margot said shyly.

"Later, perhaps we can try a few of the new styles but for now I'd like to stick with what I know." Beryl said with a polite smile as she dusted a bit of power on her cheeks and applied a light pink lip stain.

"The fashion right now is for heavy powder and dark lips, Miss." Adela said, looking concerned as Beryl ignored the heavier foundation and dark colors.

"Then I'll stand out all the more," Beryl said, picking up the small green hat and pinning it into place on her curled hair.

Beryl thought it looked ridiculous, but it was what had been in style when she left Arden. Her hair curled into long ringlets that cascaded down her back while the black lace of the gown covered her from neck to palm, the green silk bodice and skirt flared as she stood and strode to the bed to collect her shawl and Rune. Argent slid from the bed and padded over, making the maids scatter from where they'd been trying to persuade her to wear more scent.

"The heavy scents are in fashion, Miss." Adela murmured when she ignored the offered selection of perfumes, looking disappointed.

"I never wear scent if I can help it, my bond mates dislike it." Beryl said with a tight smile, "Is there somewhere I could wait until they announce dinner?"

"You could walk the gardens near the palace if you like; there are a few herb and flower gardens near this wing." Margot offered, "One of the palace runners can show you the way if you wish."

"I do, thank you." Beryl said with a relieved smile, "I'll also need somewhere my bond mates can relieve themselves nearby, if not I need a tray of dirt or grass they can use in the rooms."

"I must ask." Margot said, looking faintly disgusted that she'd have to be dealing with animal bowel habits.

"I would appreciate it," She said suppressing a smile as she gathered up a few compact things she wanted with her into a tiny silk pouch since her normal leather satchel wouldn't be proper, "come, Argent. Let's go for a walk."

The gardens were deserted except for a handful of workers trimming and neatening up the borders of ornamental hedges and cleverly trimmed trees meant to look like various shapes and animals.

They wandered the gravel paths keeping the palace in sight while they all enjoyed the fresh air, weeks on board a ship and with no actual time to move since they'd arrived it was nice to stretch and move as they wished. Beryl settled onto a bench and watched her bond mates play. It had been too long since they'd felt like it.

"They look like they're enjoying themselves." An amused voice said to her left snapping Beryl out of her circling thoughts, she glanced up to see an elegantly dressed woman with thick waves of grey streaked brown hair cascading down her back ornamented with golden ribbons and small bells that chimed faintly as she moved accenting her golden skin.

"We've been traveling too much, they're happy to be off the ship." Beryl said with a polite smile, "Would you like to sit?"

"Only if I'm not interrupting," She said with a wry smile offering a hand, "I'm Lady Cerise Bonheur; it's a pleasure to meet you."

"Mage Beryl Marcian," Beryl said, clasping the offered hand in a light hold, "however everyone calls me Mage."

"I knew you were a foreign visitor, but I didn't realize you were the exiled Mage. I may have to steal you for my companion tonight; everyone would reel from the shock of such an association." She said with a wicked grin.

"Are you aiming to shock the older nobility or just the population in general?" Beryl asked with a slight grin of her own. She loved tweaking the nose of judgmental traditionalists.

"Does it matter?" Cerise asked with a laugh, "They will be offended no matter what I do. If you're not aware, I have a bit of reputation for going against the normal conventions and traditions. I'm the widow of a local noble who refused to retire to my country estate to mourn his passing for the rest of my days. Instead, I hold massive parties with only the best entertainments and most educated guests."

"So they talk bad about you in public, but secretly everyone is vying for an invitation?" Beryl asked with a grin and a raised eyebrow.

"Exactly, I'm the toast of the town and couldn't be more hated, it's marvelous." The older woman said, clasping her hands and leaning back with a gleeful laugh. "Now, tell me about yourself. What are your plans while you're visiting or is this a permanent move?"

"I'm not sure of anything at the moment," Beryl said with a soft laugh. It was refreshing to meet someone so willing to toss aside social conventions, "I'm surprised the royal family invited me to stay at the palace."

"Why would they not? You're a powerful mage who is in exile from your home country; they're hoping to use that power for themselves, or to at least get you to use it for Orlean. They will wine and dine you for months if you let them. Take advantage of it while you can, my friend."

"Royal favor rarely stays." Beryl said gathering up Rune into her arms when he wandered by with Argent, "I just want a bit of quiet for a while."

"You've come to the wrong court if you wish quiet, I'm afraid. Did you lose much in your exile?" she asked, pulling out a small case and lighting an herbal cigarette with a match.

"Why do you ask?" Beryl asked, not liking that how easily the other woman was reading her.

"You seem sad for someone visiting an unfamiliar country, most come full of energy and vitriol spitting curses at the ones who cast them away. You look like you're in mourning." She said gently, watching the younger woman with understanding eyes.

"It's that obvious?" Beryl asked, fighting back the well of tears that always seemed on the edge of tumbling forward.

"Only for those who've lost someone dear to them, I've lost two children, one in childbirth and one while barely walking, and now my husband. You look like I felt those first few years," she said, stroking a fingertip along Rune's head before covering one of Beryl's hands with her own. "Who have you lost, child?"

"When we bond with an animal it becomes part of us," Beryl said unsure why she felt compelled to be honest with the older woman, "it's rare to bond with one, much less three but Kuro was the other in our quartet. We lost her months ago now, but the wound still feels like it happened yesterday."

"This happened during your exile?" she asked, continuing at Beryl's nod, "Then you haven't even had time to grieve, you poor thing."

"I've wept until I don't have the tears, Lady Bonheur; I'm just trying to breathe at the moment." She said giving Argent a hug when he ambled over to lean against her, tail thumping the ground.

"Well, you will have plenty of distractions here at court. Keep your wits about you, child. The nobility can be vicious when they think you might deny them their fun or the power they're seeking."

"I'm aware, Lady Bonheur. I will be careful." She agreed, taking a deep breath and forcing herself to slip on the polite mask that all Madame Duve's lessons had drilled into place.

"Call me Cerise, dear. Come, it's time for dinner and we don't want to be late." She said firmly standing and waiting while Beryl settled Rune cradled in one arm, "We shall be the talk of the night, my dear. I hope you're ready for it. Tell me now and I'll find someone else to dangle before the snobs."

"No, I will cause a stir no matter what I do; I might as well enjoy it." Beryl said forcing her head up and a small polite smile in place.

"That's the spirit, I'll introduce you as we go and give you the gossip on the pompous traditionalists, but let me know if you need me to steer you toward a quiet corner."

Lady Bonheur guided them through the halls to a large entryway full of mingling nobility as they waited to be announced by the Herald and seated in the dining room. She guided her deftly along the marble floor, making introductions and sharing gossip about several of the louder groups enjoying the refreshments and the small group of musicians playing to one side. Beryl took in the various fashions and tried to decide just what some of the women around her were trying to enhance, green cheek powers and ruffled bodices seemed to be the style of the day.

"The fashions are much more varied than I'm used to," Beryl

murmured during a momentary lull, "Cardu was more interested in training us than introducing the mages to international fashions. The maids seemed to think heavy makeup and scents were in fashion."

"Oh, they are. Most of the women here could be hunted on the scent of their perfume alone however the heavy makeups have to be specific. Take Lady Veyron's dark lips and the mask like paint. I doubt she's even able to blink." Cerise said with a sniff.

"Are the fashions influenced by anyone specific?" Beryl asked glancing around at the shifting groups, not seeing anyone seeming to stand out.

"The current fashions are being put into play by the Prince's daughter, Noemi. She's very fond of heavy scents and powders, her face as pale as possible. You at least already have the pale complexion and can get away without the heavy makeup. I'm rather hoping her fashions change once she comes of age. Her mother favored the heavy scents, however."

"What of Prince Zyon? I've heard little of his influence on the court."

"The Prince has been taking over for King Laron with his failing health. I heard the King won't be in attendance this evening, I'm sure it will be what most will talk about tonight. The Prince is the next in line and the hope is that he will marry soon after taking the throne given the death of his wife is nine years past now, may her soul rest."

"Is there anyone I should avoid?" Beryl asked, glancing over the shifting throng with a polite indifferent expression firmly wedged in place.

"Well, the Liege of Corson over in the corner embarrassed the Prince at his last hunting party and has been shunned from most of the events. He's a nasty drunk and ruined a horse. The Prince wasn't amused." She murmured discreetly, gesturing to a sour looking man slouched in a corner by himself.

"The Prince cares for his horses?"

"He cares that things aren't damaged out of carelessness. He is serious about his sport, but few women will ride with him since he leads the field and the hunts can last all day. Sometimes they even go on for hours no matter the weather. Only the young and fit can keep up with him at the chase. Do you hunt?"

"Argent can't keep up with a fast moving hunt, but he enjoys hunting."

"Argent?" she asked, frowning in confusion.

"My bond mate, Argent, was one of the King of Arden's hunting hounds." Beryl said, reaching out to rub his ears for a moment with her free hand.

"Ah, I'm sorry, I never asked their names," Cerise said with a frown, glancing at the dog wandering at their side, "and the cat?"

"Rune, a most curious tabby, I bonded with him after I arrived in Cardu."

"That's right, mages in Arden study at the capital, Cardu. Did you enjoy your time there, the capital had its social distractions, does it not?" She said glancing around to see who they were near.

"I rarely got to attend any of the social events I was there to study. They apprentice young mages to a Master Mage and spend several years moving up the ranks. Will there be any mages here tonight?" Beryl asked, not liking how the woman was avoiding the topic of magic and its practitioners.

"No, there isn't a court mage right now. The last, Mage Lorene, passed away last year and hasn't been replaced. Several local mages of the minor nobility have been vying for the position, and you'll meet them at the next ball. I'm afraid I know nothing of magic so I can't say who to watch out for in that group." She blurted with a nervous laugh.

"If it's anything like Arden, then it will be the most popular candidates." Beryl said filing away the information for later, she'd need to sound the local mages out for any possible rebellion, "I'm afraid I saw little of the town on the way in. We came straight from the ship to the palace. Are there any good markets?"

Cerise raised an eyebrow at the blatant change of topic, but she let it go. They kept to harmless conversation until dinner was announced and everyone started moving towards the doors to one side. They would be seated next to each other since they were entering together, Cerise assured her but they would enter alone, each being announced separately. She gave Beryl a last pat on the arm in encouragement before stepping forward to be announced.

"Lady Bonheur of Gervais!" the Grand Marshal announced as they escorted Cerise out of the room on the arm of a uniformed guard. Another guard arrived and looked at Argent dubiously, but offered his arm to Beryl without comment. She took her place and gave the waiting Grand Marshal a smile as he approached.

"Madame?" he prompted, glancing over the group with a frown.

"Mage Beryl Marcian of Arden, known as Mage and her bond mates Rune and Argent." She said with a tight smile, wondering if he'd announce her name before her curse stripped it from his memory.

"Madame, do you wish me to announce both yourself and your... companions?"

"If you wish to," Beryl said forcing the smile to stay on her face. She was ready to leave and she hadn't even seen the royal family yet; it would be an interminable night.

She strode forward once the Grand Marshal moved, all but dragging her guide from his parade rest next to her. Argent jauntily kept pace next to her while Rune sat up slightly, riding her shoulder and watching the room that was laid out before them. She strode down a wide staircase that deposited them at the foot of the massive table filling the room with the royal family watching over everything from an elevated platform to one side.

"Presenting Mage of Arden and her bond mates," the Grand Marshal announced her as she was guided past Lady Bonheur and toward the tables on the platform, she kept the smile on her face but she could see the confusion on Lady Bonheur's as she was lead to the inner circle of tables.

She was shown to an empty chair only a few seats down from the Prince and his daughter, a large pillow and silver food dishes resting to one side, clearly for Argent. Beryl gave a deep curtsy to the Prince before accepting the chair being held out. She'd need to explain her curse at least slightly so that the Grand Marshal wasn't punished for his misstep, she thought with a mental sigh.

"Up or down?" She asked Rune while Argent investigated the pillow and dishes.

"Up, staying with you." Rune murmured, shifting so he was laying across her shoulders behind her neck where he'd be most out of the way but still able to see everyone at the table.

"I see the rumors of your name are at least partly true? Have you given it up in exile?" The Prince asked, giving her a sharp smile.

"My name is Beryl Marcian, your royal highness, however a curse I received as a child prevents anyone I tell from remembering that fact." Beryl said fighting to keep her tone light as she took in the Prince and his daughter. His pictures had not shown the sharp analyzing gaze or the adolescent daughter's casual arrogant mask.

"Yet, you go by Mage?" he asked sipping at his goblet which seemed to be a sign for the waiting staff to pour drinks along the table.

"Yes, your royal highness, the curse makes people forget my name, but titles seem to stay."

"How interesting," He murmured, gesturing for the waiting staff to serve. "Have you had much of our cuisine, Mistress Mage?"

"Only a few of the stews," She said smiling her thanks to the servant who set a bowl of clear broth before her while another filled her goblet with a herb laced water. "I'm looking forward to trying other dishes."

"Stews are for the winter, I believe you will enjoy the courses planned for tonight. Are you against eating meat? Noemi is against its consumption for moral reasons." He said favoring his daughter with a frown as he took a spoonful of broth only to earn an exasperated look. Clearly it was something they'd argued over often.

"No, your royal highness, I eat meat." She said keeping her expression blank as she sipped at the bone broth, hoping the next course was something she could share with Rune.

"Your dog is a hunting hound, is he not?" he asked, taking a sip of his soup before pushing the dish aside.

"Yes, your royal highness," She said taking a sip of the herbed water and waving away the offer of wine from the waiting attendant.

"Do you hunt?" He asked, toying with his meal while the others ate.

"Yes, I've joined several mounted boar hunts and hunted smaller game on foot with my bond mates. I regretted having to leave my horse behind."

"That is a shame; a fine mount is scarce at times. You're welcome to use one from our stable during a hunt or use one horse here on the grounds if you wish to ride."

"Thank you, your royal highness, I'm sure my bond mates would like the chance to get outdoors after our lengthy journey." She said with a smile, sipping at the lukewarm soup and trying to identify the herbs used while Rune was listening to the conversations happening around them.

"The cat comes with you riding?" The prince asked, clearly shocked as he looked at her in surprise.

"We are rarely separate, your royal highness." She said with a strained smile as the dishes were removed and a small salad replaced the soup. "Rune rides with me in a coat pocket or an open saddlebag; if we're riding gently, he rides on my shoulder much as he is now."

"How interesting," one man to her side murmured with a smile, "what do you hope to see while you're visiting our fine country? The countryside is very fine at the moment."

"I'm hoping to study," Beryl said with a polite smile at the man, "the use of magic here is supposed to be more varied than in Arden and I'd like to learn the techniques myself but I wouldn't be against seeing some of the countryside during my stay. I've grown used to staying busy."

"General Leon is correct, the countryside is quite fine this time of year for both hunting and sightseeing. You should see some of the gardens before the summer heat sets in, perhaps one of the royal estates?" A woman to their left said with a smile for the princess, "The grounds at Alexandria are at their peak right now."

"Do you think we could visit Alexandria, Papa?" Princess Noemi asked softly, not looking at her father; she clearly expected to be denied.

"Thank you, Madame Morisot," The prince said giving the woman a curt nod before turning back to his daughter, "the grounds are quite fine at the Alexandria estate, perhaps we will visit in a few weeks if the weather holds. It might be nice to have a change of scenery. We might even stay until time to leave for the summer palace."

"I would enjoy it." The young princess said neutrally, which earned her a small nod of acknowledgment from her father.

The talk turned to Madame Morisot's rose garden as they brought the next course out, thin slices of lamb with baby roasted vegetables in bright shades of red and purple. Beryl slipped a few bites of meat to Rune but hoped there would be more food available when they got back to their rooms for the animals. The meat was too heavily spiced for her to trust them eating it safely. She wasn't able to comment on much, but she made herself memorize the names and who was discussing what topic over the course of the meal.

"Do you fly hawks?" the prince asked idly over the last few bites of dessert.

"No," Beryl said shortly, fighting back the anger bubbling in her chest.

"Our reports had you hunting with a hawk or eagle? It surprised me to see you without one in your baggage. Were you forced to abandon it as well?" General Leon asked while idly toying with his desert.

"No; I was bonded to a Shiro, a sea hawk." Beryl forced out, knowing her voice was clipped and harsh, "She died before I left the country."

"I apologize," The prince said with a frown, eyes flickering over the table, "I take it your bond mates are more than just animals?"

"No, they are still animals but they're bound to me. They can be useful when casting magic." She forced out, hating that they forced her to hide how amazing her bonded were.

"And this broken bond pains you?" the prince pressed, watching how she reached up to press Rune that much closer, like that would ease the hurt.

"Yes, it pains me." She said unable to stop the small broken laugh that followed. "Doesn't the loss of a pet pain the owner?"

"Can it be replaced?" Noemi asked softly before glancing at her father in regret at intruding on his conversation.

"No, a bond once broken can't be repaired or replaced." Beryl said eyes on her plate as she forced her mask in place turning to the General and asking about his duties with wet eyes.

The rest of the dinner conversation was stilted, and it relieved her when they were released. She ignored the conversations around her and the idling nobles who watched as she strode from the room, Rune clasped against her chest, his deep rumbling purr the only thing keeping her together. She bolted through the halls at a brisk walk, Argent at her heels, knowing she'd cause even more of a scene if she ran.

She barely made it back to her rooms before the tears were falling. She kept thinking she was starting to get over her grief, only to find the wound ripped open yet again by some casual word or slight. She ordered the maids out and locked the doors and ignored their knocks. She stripped out of the finery, pulling on a thin sleep shirt, and curling together in the too enormous bed crying herself into troubled dreams.

Chapter 10

The Palace

The next morning she looked pale and worn, but she ignored the comments of her maids, pulling on her comfortable grey dress and her worn boots. They didn't have to put in an appearance until that night, and she intended to spend the day working. The palace library was supposed to be very fine, and she was stuck on the palace grounds until she got in touch with Count Malouel or borrowed a small carriage or horse.

They strolled the gardens for a while letting Argent and Rune stretch their legs and take care of their bathroom needs however the grounds were deserted this early, a soft fog shrouding them from sight as they walked the long way around to the next wing and the library it housed. Hem wet and muddy as Argent's paws, she pressed a quick spell to both of them to keep the mud outside once they reached the door. The servant who opened it for them twitched at the magic but didn't seem openly disturbed.

"Would you need directions to anywhere specific, Madame?" He asked, eyes widening as Rune jumped into her arms and took his spot on her shoulder.

"I'm headed to the library." She said observing his reaction, noting that while he'd balked at the magic, he didn't show any nervousness about interacting with her overall surprise at the open use of magic, not that it was used, perhaps.

"This way, Madame." He said with a blank expression as he guided her down the hall and two halls over before bowing her through the last door.

The library was massive, and it took her a while to figure out how things were organized given they wrote everything in the Orlean language. She'd been speaking only Orlean by the time she left Arden, but she still tripped up on the occasional word or phrasing. The section on magical spells and theory was small, but it kept her occupied for most of the day. She'd taken notes on several spells she would like to try that seemed to mirror things she'd learned in Arden but used a different method for casting.

While Arden used runes and gems to contain and power spells, Orlean seemed to rely on spoken words and gestures to control the magical power of a casting. It was hard to picture many of the motions from the scant diagrams and pictures available, she'd have to get one of the local mages to demonstrate.

She'd noticed wards of varying strength throughout the halls and entryways, but no lines of controlling runes marked the placement. Replacing the last book, she roused her napping bond mates and headed towards the gardens. The fog had burned off, leaving the weather cool with a brisk wind pushing ominous clouds across the sky; they would receive rain sometime later today.

Changing for lunch she reviewed the small stack of invitations that had arrived. She'd turned heads by being seated at the royal table last night. Most of the more fashionable or the social elite had invited her to various evening parties, and there was a note from Lady Bonheur inviting her to tea the next morning. She sent a tentative acceptance and set the rest of the letters aside to be addressed later that night once she knew how the rest of the day went.

Lunch was a much more informal event however she was still seated at the royal table, if somewhat further down than she had been the night before. She was seated next to an older Mage who watched her take her seat with superior disdain and an outright look of disgust at Rune before ignoring her for the rest of the meal. Beryl took it in stride, making polite conversation with the woman on her left, despairing of finding a competent dress maker before the start of the masquerade season in the coming weeks.

"May I pet your dog?" a youthful voice piped at her elbow once they had served the main course.

"Of course," Beryl agreed with a smile, watching as the child and a small group of waiting young aristocrats fawned over the gentle giant in their midst.

"He's very gentle for such a large animal." The woman on her left said following the cautious approach of her daughter, Argent holding still while she rubbed one ear before giving her wrist a quick lick.

"Thank you, he's a wonderful dog." Beryl said with a smile, "Your daughter is very gentle with him which I appreciate, some children don't realize that animals don't like to have things thrust at them or to be petted roughly."

"What's his name?" The girl asked, coming away from the group to cling to her mother's skirts.

"Celeste," The mother said with a fond smile and sigh, prying her hands from the now rumbled material and holding her gently to her side.

"The dog is called Argent." Beryl said, petting Rune while the tables were being set for the waiting crowd.

"And the cat?" Celeste asked, watching Rune with enormous eyes.

"Rune," Beryl said with a smile as Rune climbed down so that the child could reach to gently pet his head with a featherlight touch.

"Father doesn't care for animals, so we don't have any at home. How are you able to bring them with you to lunch? I've never seen animals in the palace before unless you count the peacocks and they are pretty, but you can't pet them." Celeste said all in one rushed breath, ignoring the gentle squeeze from her mother, hoping to temper her.

"I bound them to me by magic, where I go, so do they." Beryl said with a tight smile, "Even in the palace."

"Wow." Celeste said, eyes going wide, "You do magic?"

"Yes, I'm Mage Marcian, but you can call me Mage, most people do." She said as the dessert, chilled sorbet and fruit, was placed before them.

Celeste and the rest of the children returned to their seats for dessert and Argent came forward to lean his enormous head against her shoulder while watching the others take in the massive dog at the table with looks of surprise and, for many, disgust. The mage on her right pushed his plate away and stood, giving her a pinched, hard look before striding off in anger. Beryl kept her head up and ignored the hushed conversations that Rune and Argent were tracking, talking to Celeste's mother about the upcoming ball that Madame Bonheur was rumored to be holding at the end of the month.

She spent the rest of the day reading in the library before taking a late dinner in her rooms. Her absence at the royal table would be noted, but she wanted more time alone to practice some of what she was reading. She was certain the magic of Orlean related to her own, since the runes used in Arden could be spoken and written to cause an effect. They were more stable if drawn or carved and the spells more powerful, but a minor spell like lighting a candle could be done as easily with a word and gesture as with touching a carved rune on a candle holder.

She locked her rooms and set Argent and Rune to keep watch while she changed into a pair of men's loose pants and a tunic. Beryl needed to move if she would ride the winds. She hadn't attempted this since Kuro's death and kept fumbling the opening movements with her first few tries, tears filling her eyes.

Finally, the motions flowed as she moved through each position, letting her mind drift as she moved through the blocks and strikes. The air in the room felt wrong after so long practicing outside with the feel of the winds moving against her body. She waited until she'd gone through the entire set of moves twice before reaching with her mind and magic for the winds high above her.

This time there was no hawk flying high above them to latch on to, and she tumbled and flailed before she controlled her assent on the shifting currents. Below her the palace lay flung out before her like a string of jewels, magic lighting up some sections, but most of the hallways and gardens were untouched. She'd expected the palace to be much like the one in Arden, coated with magical protections however only certain sections seemed to be spelled. Most of the walls and rooms were untouched. Only the rooms the royal family used and the libraries for the Mages seemed to be protected. She had to be missing something.

She traveled in ever wider circles, yet the voids she'd encountered in Arden were missing. There was a faint pull to her magic in a few places similar to the voids, but the complete devastation was missing. She returned slowly to herself, finishing the last few motions out of habit before moving back to the bed and sprawling next to her bond mates.

"What do you think? There are no voids here." She asked, fiddling with a tassel on one pillow while she tried to picture where the slight pulls against her magic had been centered.

"They are hiding in Arden they took what they wanted, perhaps here they are more careful." Argent offered, licking at his massive paws absently.

"Do they know we are hunting?" Rune asked, stretching and moving off the bed to survey the room and sniff at a few enticing scents he had yet to identify.

"They have to with the death of the mage in the northern mountains. Baron Sarnes said the attacks in the towns throughout Arden haven't stopped. The poor and those who haven't worked with mages are more and more against the use of magic. They are even petitioning the court to remove those appointed out in the smaller towns. Some are leaving anyway since they are getting attacked whenever they leave

their homes." Beryl said with a frown, *"The public are attacking the mages supposed to be helping them. The only ones who aren't being harassed are those attached to the Healers or a temple."*

"They aren't attacking people here." Rune said with a meow, *"They aren't comfortable with magic, but no one is spitting on us like you saw with your uncle."*

"That's in the palace," Beryl pointed out, rolling to her feet and changing into a sleep shirt, *"The palace servants and courtiers could never treat us like that so openly. They dislike having you with me at meals, that means the popular and wealthy mages dislike bond mates here."*

"We knew that we were a curiosity coming from the docks, but no one attacked us." Argent said with a deep sigh.

"We need to get out of the palace and see how the rest of society treats mages. Maybe Lady Bonheur can help us lose the royal escort we're sure to have tomorrow." Beryl said, curling under the covers and letting Argent drape himself over her feet while Rune claimed a pillow near her head.

* * *

The next morning she had breakfast in her rooms before requesting a carriage and dressing for her tea with Lady Bonheur. Her two maids fussed over her hair and she let them arrange it in a spill of curls to one side while a small hat was pinned in place. She wore one of her more subtle gowns, a soft sea blue linen and white lace with a grey leather coat and gloves, something an upper-class merchant's wife would wear out or a minor noble would dress up with a display of jewels. Instead of jewelry, she wore her mage cuffs, choker, and belt, noting the unease that made Adela and Margot fumble as they cleaned up her makeup table and bedroom while she finished her preparations. No, the servants were afraid of mages. She'd have to look into that further.

The carriage waiting for them was thankfully one of the larger traps meant for four or more. Argent took up the entire bench across from her, the horses shying as he clamored on board and into place. She would need to see about finding a carriage horse and trap that she could drive herself if she stayed past the summer. Maybe an older hunting horse that was also trained to drive a small trap would work since they would be used to the hunting hounds and working dogs being about. Everything depended on how her mission went, so far she was seeing little that would should be reported back to Arden. She needed to see underneath all the glittering smiles and pretty clothes, and that was proving harder than she'd imagined. Orlean hid its darkness deep.

The ride to Lady Bonheur's estate was quiet, Beryl tried to send out her magic to sense her surroundings, but the rocking of the carriage kept jolting her out of her scans. Finally she gave up and enjoyed the time spent with her bond mates, contentment flowing back and forth across their bonds as they cuddled, uncaring of the fur left covering the fine material of her dress. The countryside they crossed was left wild even when they entered the Bonheur lands.

"Mistress Mage, a pleasure to see you!" Cerise called out as Beryl stepped from the carriage.

"A pleasure to be here." Beryl said with a laugh as Cerise drew her in for a kiss to one cheek like a doting grandmother.

"Come, we have much to discuss. You are the talk of the town, my dear." She said leading them into the house while the servants dealt with the carriage.

"You have a lovely home, Cerise." Beryl said taking in the changing styles and decorations as she was led deeper into the house and to a back sunroom.

"I've lived in this house since I was eighteen," Cerise said, nodding for the maid to serve the tea, "my husband bought it as part of our marriage agreement. I've redone most of the rooms since then. You should have seen it, elegant and ever so formal, and every room was some shade of blue or grey, boring."

"Well, I approve of the changes." Beryl said taking a cup and nibbling at a sliver of sandwich while Argent gulped his first bite down and gave Cerise a mournful look, making her laugh.

"Do they eat meat?" Cerise asked, waving over another servant and sending off for bowls for the two animals.

"Thank you, most people don't think of them." Beryl said sipping at the sweetened rose mint tea.

"You care for them, so I must as well since you are my guest." She said taking up her own cup, "Now, what parties are you planning to attend? You've arrive in the busiest season with the Masquerade starting soon."

"Yes, I will need to buy some gowns if there are balls the entire season." Beryl said with a frown, "I have several invitations for the rest of the week and my wardrobe is already looking too small."

"We will have to go into town, my tailor can squeeze you in if we go tomorrow." Cerise offered while nibbling at a piece of fruit.

"That would be wonderful, I'm afraid I'm a bit out of my depth with gowns. Most of the time I dress more for comfort or movement then for any fashion."

"Well, you've done well so far," Cerise said with a smile, "you've kept to the edges of polite fashion without being so far off that anyone can call you on it. Considering you're from Arden, you'll be allowed some time to adjust to the local fashions before the society vipers attack you openly."

"They're already talking behind my back, I'd rather it be to my face." Beryl snorted, "I came to Orlean to study, yet everyone seems determined to get me to spend all my time at parties."

"You must make some friends at my party. Many of the local scholars and philosophers will be in attendance. I'm afraid I can't help much with the magical community; that was never a forte of mine."

"The libraries at the Palace are extensive, I've enjoyed the small time I've stolen away there." Beryl said as a servant brought in dishes of chopped meat and water for her bond mates. Rune jumped down to investigate and declaring them free of poisons or drugs, settled in to nibble while Argent munched through his portion before settling next to the wall where he would be out of the way, half hidden by several large plants. It also lets him listen to the distant chatter of the maids as they passed in the hall.

The afternoon went easily and Beryl was back on her way to the Palace in time to catch dinner with the other nobles. She was placed further down this time and ate, listening to the surrounding chatter without contributing. The others seemed willing enough to talk around her, while Argent lay to one side on the pillow waiting for him. Rune slipped away and wandered the palace.

Beryl kept a light touch on him through the bond even as dinner concluded and they walked back to the gardens near their rooms before heading inside. No one they passed tried to talk to them, and the servants were silent as they passed. She sat down and scheduled out the rest of the week, sending out letters of acceptance or refusal to several more invitations that had arrived before changing and settling in to read before bed.

Rune came in late, showing them the narrow servant's stairs and hallways that ran between most of the rooms. It made a perfect hiding place for him to eavesdrop on the other guests and servants. They decided he would scout the palace for rumors while Argent stayed to guard Beryl, just in case. The large dog hated that he couldn't scout as well, but while they could overlook a small cat, a dog the size of a pony wouldn't be.

The next morning Beryl spent the day with Cerise in town with her tailor being outfitted for the coming balls and parties. The ball at the end of the week was her introduction to Orlean society, and she had to be perfectly outfitted. She also needed masks since many of the coming parties were masquerades where everyone went in costume, wearing cloth or leather masks to pretend to be someone else for the night.

"I'm afraid no matter the mask you will be spotted with your bond mates." Cerise pointed out, "Some go to great lengths to hide their identity at the masquerades, wigs, padding to change their weight, shoes to change their height, and they refuse to respond to their correct names by acting out some character instead. The prince hired actors to roam about last year, making it even harder to figure out who was who. He even had an actor playing himself so he could roam the room."

"Would I offend anyone if I went in a suit?"

"A suit, like a man?" Cerise asked, blinking, "Well, it would be an inspired costume for the party. I doubt anyone among the upper class would do it. What are you thinking?"

"At home I often wore trousers while riding about town or working in my rooms. I was a student acting as a runner, so no one thought anything of it as long as I wore dresses to anything formal. I was hoping to order a few similar outfits if it wouldn't be too outside of propriety."

"The traditionalists will be up in arms, but the prince himself has little care for their opinions so no one will chastise you for it. The king might frown on it, but he's rarely in attendance with his health lately. He is supposed to attend your ball, however, so for that you will need a gown."

"I wasn't thinking for the balls, just while I'm riding or outside. The rest of the time I would wear gowns or court dress."

"If you confine it to an activity, then I see no harm in it. Most will pass it off as you being eccentric, something attributed to most mages, anyway." Cerise hummed, glancing her up and down, "Terrance, I have a challenge for you. I need five costumes for my friend, two full suits a man would wear to a ball and three casual outfits that a man would ride in the hunt in. The two formal wear should be finer, and perhaps a military look would do?"

"A military uniform perhaps?" The tailor asked, glancing over the young woman with a frown as he sketched out a uniform with tall boots, fitted jacket, and double rows of buttons running down the front, "Would you be wearing a binder to flatten the chest as well?"

"Yes, I wear one to ride, anyway." Beryl agreed with relief, "I would purchase another if you would like the measurements with one on."

"Hair hidden in a half cloak or under a hat, tall boots and the full regalia of a Calvary soldier. A challenge Madame; No one would think to look for a young woman in a uniform for an adolescent man at the masquerade. It will be the talk of the ball." He hummed, snatching up several bolts of cloth and gesturing for Beryl to follow, "Come to the back, young Miss and I will find something simple for you to change into that we can use as a pattern."

An hour later her outfits were ordered and by the end of the week she would have enough dresses to wear through the season along with a massive ball gown to wear at the ball she'd paid extra to have ready in time. She'd have to order more once they arrived at the Summer Palace, but that was still over two months away. She wasn't even sure if she'd still be at the palace in two months with how little progress she seemed to make.

"Well, you will be the talk of the party next week." Cerise said, linking their arms and leading Beryl down the boardwalk towards a cafe set off the main street, "You will certainly turn heads during your stay. I hope you will come to my ball at the end of the month."

"I'm certain to enjoy it much more than the ball this week." Beryl said with a laugh, "I hate being put on display like some jeweled ornament only meant to be observed from a distance. I'm much more content reading and experimenting or being out riding. I've never been one for social events."

"You are doing well for one unused to it. Polite yet aloof, you will have all the men running after you at the ball. Add in the allure of a foreign woman all alone without an escort and they will besiege you."

"I'm not looking for romance, Cerise," Beryl said with a sigh, "I have no time for it."

"You are too young to be so busy, dear." Cerise said smiling at the doorman who opened the tea house door for them and asking the hostess inside for a quiet back table, "You are in a rare position to dally with as many men as you wish. If women are more to your taste, you must be more discrete, but I can point you to some of the more intellectual bent if you wish."

"Perhaps once we reach the Summer Palace. Will you be following the court when they leave?"

"No, I'm too old to be chasing the nobility about the country. I hope you will continue to write to me once you leave however, I've enjoyed our time together and our discussions. It's rare to find someone of such open intellect among the nobility. Do not let them cage you, my dear. You are far too fierce a woman to bear such a thing easily."

"My bond mates would never allow it." Beryl said glancing out the window where Argent sat waiting for them to return, Rune was wandering the alley ways near where they'd left the carriage. "I have a feeling we won't be staying, I've traveled too much to be enjoy staying in one place too long without the road under my feet."

"Enjoy it while you can, my dear. I'm afraid travel is for the young, my bones disapprove of too long spent in carriages the more I age. I'll enjoy a quiet summer and perhaps I'll see you in the spring when the court returns."

They spent the rest of their light meal discussing various places she could visit as the court traveled, or if she wished to leave the court and head out on her own. In Orlean she would expect to travel with a household she couldn't afford if she wanted to continue the appearance of being among the nobility. She'd need to hire a butler or house manager at the least to deal with lodgings and to escort her to any events she wished to attend.

Chapter 11

Meeting with Count Malouel and a Ball

"Thank you for coming, Mage." The Count said gesturing her to a seat while a male servant poured them drinks before disappearing from view in a dark corner of the room.

"I'm glad we managed meet, Count Malouel." She said glancing over at the older man, "The way plans keep changing, I wasn't sure I'd be able to come."

"How is your stay at the palace going?"

"It's very nice, the staff is most attentive." She murmured with a slight glance at the watching servant.

"James, would you mind getting our guest's bond mates some water?" He said with a raised eyebrow.

"Count." James said with a bow, moving to the door and closing it firmly behind him.

"James is a loyal servant, but I can understand your reluctance. Do you have news?"

"It's more the lack of news. I'm not seeing the unrest or magical disturbances that they asked me to look for. As far as I can tell, the only deceptions going on are the jockeying for position that always happens at court. The position of Court Mage is being vied for along with the favor of the Prince and his daughter. I haven't seen the attacks against magic users or the open disdain of spells being used that is everywhere in Arden now."

"The unrest is there, I can assure you." Count Malouel said with a sigh, "The lower castes are unhappy with how the distribution of power depends heavily on the King's favor, few can better their circumstances without heavy bribes that they cannot afford. In Arden all magic comes from the King and is distributed about the country, but in Orlean any magic user who is not noble must pay heavy taxes to the crown. That makes magic and its cures out of reach of all but the elite."

"Can one become noble if that's required to work here? I may need more of an income if I'm expected to stay at court." Beryl sighed, everything with the nobility of any country seemed to come back to money.

"You can be appointed by the crown, which takes many bribes or exceptional favor from the nobility, or a noble can sponsor you. I was to be your sponsor here in Orlean, however you might do better by continuing to curry favor from the prince and his peers."

"They sent me to help unravel the unrest and rumors that Orlean would attack Arden. I'm not seeing anything to suggest either." Beryl said with a huff, "What am I meant to do if my principal mission doesn't apply?"

"For now, keep looking. I've lived here most of my life and there are pressures shifting that I've not noticed before. There is a third party only mentioned in whispers, someone who both the nobility and the lower classes are turning towards. I've yet to be approached, but someone new like you may ask the more... unsubtle questions I'm denied by my rank and position."

"Who should I be approaching? No one I've met has even hinted at an open dislike of the current political situation."

"They will soon, give it time. They are still trying to feel you out and see where your allegiances lie." The count said with a sigh, "You are a mage exiled from your home, they are waiting to see how far you will go to fight against the home that cast you away. For now, keep doing as you are, court the nobility and the Prince, curry favor where you can."

"Very well." She said with a frown. The servant came back in after knocking and the count giving his permission. "It was suggested I hire a staff. Can you give me a few references I can trust? For now, I will continue using the palace staff, but if things drag on, I will need to gather a household and staff."

"I know a few, some of whom work for our mutual friends. I'll send you the list in the next few days. Have you decided on a profession should you stay?"

"The position of court mage is open. If that doesn't work, I can open a shop or take commissions for enchanted objects."

The butler set the water out and the discussion settled into more general topics as James returned to his corner. Beryl had no patience for the polite conversation, but she forced back her frustrations and gave the Count the polite smile he expected from a woman of her station. She stewed the entire ride back to the palace. She needed to be moving, not stuck waiting on something to happen.

* * *

The next morning she woke up in a gloomy mood, storming through her bath and dismissing the servants in a huff when they tried to help her dry off. She dressed for a ride in men's breeches, shirt, and coat before striding off through the gardens towards the stables. If she couldn't move in polite society, she could at least move and take out her anger harmlessly. The stable hands scattered as she approached the barn manager.

"I'm hoping to borrow a horse for a few hours. Do you have any needing to be schooled?" She asked, trying not to fidget at the man looked her over with a frown.

"Take the bay," he said, gesturing to a gelding mouthing at the door latch, "He's a bundle of energy and needs to work some off. Stay in the fields, he's got a mean streak if you keep him in too tight and has dumped quite a few of the boys."

"Is he neck reined or trained to seat?"

"Neither, we've tried neck reining, but he's too sensitive and bolts at even the lighter touches. He's still a colt, even with his size. I can get you a milder mount if you'd like?"

"No, I'll try the bay. Do you have his tack?"

"Start brushing him down, I'll gather everything." He said waving her on and watching as she unlatched the door and shoved an elbow in to the chest of the young horse when he tried to push his way out of the stall.

She brushed him down, tweaking the curious horse when he played with her hair, the hem of her coat, and did his best to get in the way. Beryl let him mouth at things, but the first sign of teeth got a light thump to his ribs or a harsh sound of warning. Once she got him clean, she led him out on a halter and set him up in the crossties so she could pick his feet and get him tacked up with the barn manager watching to one side.

The ride was challenging and Argent and Rune stayed at the wall, watching her force the gelding to behave with amusement bubbling across the bond. Beryl kept her focus on the horse and the patterns they were going through. The horse was young but quick-witted and took the smallest opening to act out. After about an hour, she brought the gelding to a last walk and let him cool down as they did lazy loops about the pasture.

"You've a light hand." The stable master said approvingly as she got the gelding in to the crossties and started to untack and brush him down.

"I've ridden most of my life." Beryl said with a shrug trying to not remember most of the bad tempered nags her uncle had used for transport, her Flox had been the best horse she'd ever sat, "He's got a nice gait but needs a firmer seat then I can give him, a man might handle him better."

"Well, I've always got a few horses that need to be exercised. You're welcome to come down any morning you want the work." He said giving her a knowing look as she stretched her arms.

"Thank you, do you have any that are used to working with dogs? I'd like to take one out later this week with Argent if I can." She said nodding to where the dog waited.

"Only the ones used in the hunts are hound trained. I must ask a few of the Lords if they have any in need of exercise." The man mused, "If not, you may use one of the Prince's mounts."

"If I stay long enough, I may just buy a horse. If you hear of one that might work, can you keep me in mind?"

"I'll keep an ear out, Lady."

"It's just Mage and thank you." She said giving him a nod, "Have a good evening."

"Mistress Mage," He said, tipping his cap and getting back to work without a backward glance.

"*Well, we found one servant who's not afraid of a mage.*" She muttered across the bond absently to her bond mates as they started the trek back to the palace.

"*He was good to the horses.*" Rune agreed, "*Where now?*"

"*A long bath for me and some lunch, maybe more work in the library.*" Beryl said with a sigh, "*I can't understand why we have seen no one using magic. At Cardu it was common to see magic practiced at the palace and around the capital.*"

"*They are afraid of magic, is it forbidden?*"

"*Forbidden to do magic? When would they be allowed to cast? At the pleasure of the King? I haven't seen warded buildings off the palace grounds so far. Would the King keep all the magic to his estate but not use it?*"

"There were several deliveries, Madame Mage." Bertrand said with a bow as he opened the door to her rooms for her, "I had the maids place them in your bedroom. The day's mail is on your desk."

"Thank you, Bertrand." Beryl said with a polite smile. The man was an excellent butler, but it was clear he disapproved of her more eccentric attire and refused to meet her eyes when they talked.

Most of the maids and staff seemed to dislike the changes she made to their suggestions, but none spoke out. They questioned even her refusal to wear perfume, every time they dressed her the scents were offered and returned to their box with disappointed looks. She had no intention of changing everything about herself just to fit into court life. The servants would just have to learn to deal with it if she stayed here.

Boxes covered her bed and after a few quick spells to rule out traps, she opened one to find her new wardrobe. Tugging out a simpler dress than she'd been wearing recently with a grin, she headed to the bath. At least the day was looking up. The ball was tomorrow, and she needed to lay everything out anyway once she'd cleaned up and changed, hanging up each gown and its accompanying objects.

The maids would coo over the new clothes, but Beryl was happier over the trousers and simple dresses she'd bought for everyday wear. She'd need to craft things to sell soon. Most of her money had gone to the tailor. It tempted Beryl to try crafting a gown with magic. It wouldn't hurt to add wards to her new clothes. She'd need to try with something simpler, maybe a toy or doll first, she mused, hunting through her trunk for a shirt she could donate to the project.

"The servants are talking about us." Argent rumbled, settling next to the fire with a loud grumbling moan.

"Are they? Agreeable things?" She asked, watching as Rune trailed into the room a moment later, pausing at the water dish to quench his thirst.

"Sad mage who keeps animals for pets, too alone, too distant." Argent said with another grumble that turned into a deep content sigh as Beryl sat on the rug next to him and started rubbing his ears.

"We need to talk to others more, be seen more if they think we are

distant." Beryl said along the bond with a sigh, *"Have they said anything else?"*

"The Princess asks about us, likes me. The King asks for updates on where we go, the servants think it's his old age and humor him with insignificant things, us at dinner, playing on the lawn." Rune said, trotting over and curling in her lap.

"The King will have more eyes on us than just the servants, if he wanted information he has it." Beryl pointed out, ducking to place a kiss on his small head as she rummaged for her sewing kit.

"Do we find out whom?"

"No, let them track us." Beryl said with a sigh, *"We want them to watch."*

"Prance and hide and let them walk us into the trap?"

"If we have to, we need to see what they are hiding. So if we have to hide behind a smile and dance with those we can't trust, then we will."

"To keep home safe?"

"To keep our friends safe, even if we can't be there anymore." Beryl said standing and going back to her sewing, *"We might not be going back to them, but we can keep them safe."*

Beryl went riding and wandered the palace gardens for a few hours each day, happy to lose herself in the greenery with just her bond mates, even if it wasn't the complete solitude they all craved. It calmed her mind after every evening being full of parties and dinners with arrogant socialites, hoping to use the newest sensation at the palace to worm their way closer to the royal family. So far, most were looking to improve their family's name and fortunes. They weren't connected to the rogue mages she was tracking.

She returned to her rooms an hour or two past lunch on the day of the ball to horrified maids who'd arrived early to get her ready. She sighed and pulled off her boots at the door while they shrieked about her muddied hems. If anything, Argent was worse than her hems.

"I can bathe on my own," Beryl huffed grabbing Argent by the scruff and steering him as much as his bulk would allow towards the bath, "you too, you are mud to your eyeballs and I don't want more work for the staff because you fell asleep and muddy the rugs."

"You want us to wash him, Mistress?" Adela asked with a quavering voice, eyeing the giant dog with fear.

"No, I'll wash him and myself. Just layout my white dress and everything that goes with it. You can help curl my hair once we're out of the bath." Beryl said fighting back a laugh. She never understood how some people could be afraid of Argent when he acted like a lazy puppy to put them at ease. A hard scrub for both of them lasted just long enough to drive her maids into a frenzy when they emerged.

"Why are you afraid of Argent? He's a gentle dog, he'd never hurt you." Beryl asked once they dressed her in her underthings and the two women were brushing her drying hair, readying it to be curled.

"My last master before I came to the palace had dogs," Adele mumbled, "he liked to set them on servants who displeased him. They would growl at anyone that came near them. I was never bitten, but I knew several who were. It wasn't a nice household, but it earned me a reference I could use to move up."

"I'm sorry," Beryl frowned, "dogs treated like that aren't happy creatures either, they are nervous of their masters as much as they are of all humans after they've been treated so badly for so long. Their master must have been a cruel man."

"My first master was like that." Margot agreed, picking up the curling irons from the small blazer, "Many servants have cruel masters but it is the way of things. I'm just glad to have found a stable place to work. After my second master passed, it was almost a year before I could find a position beyond laundry work."

"Laundry work is always hard, especially if you don't have enough hands." Beryl agreed, chuckling at the look Adele shot her, "I wasn't always a Mage, my parents died when I was young and I went to live with my Uncle Jared. He was a cruel man, and I had to work hard to earn enough money to eat most weeks. It was only after he caught me setting a fire ward for a baker he found a use for me."

"But you are a Lady, Mistress." Margot stammered, "You are a guest of the Prince himself!"

"I am now," Beryl snorted, "I started out as a street urchin picking pockets and casting illusions on street corners for coppers. Not everyone starts from a titled position. Some earn it. I served the King of Arden and was granted the title of Mage, but I worked hard to get there."

"What are you wanting done with your hair for the ball, Mistress?" Adele asked, changing the subject, but her hands were gentler as she separated Beryl's hair into sections.

"Whatever you both would like, I'm in your hands tonight." Beryl said, giving them a slight smile and sending a rush of love to her bond mates as she watched Rune cleaning Argent's ears by the fire.

The women cooed over the beading on the dress that caught the firelight and scattered small rainbows about the room. The lace shawl was also beaded, fringed with rock crystals complementing the lace gloves that went to her elbow. No one, not a mage, would see the layers of protection charms warded and sealed into as many stones as she could anchor them. She disliked the heeled shoes that pinched her toes, but she'd discard them if she had to run. There was no way to walk without turning an ankle beyond the slow gliding stride she'd practiced for so many hours under Madame Duve.

Bertrand escorted her from her rooms to the ballroom before handing her off to a line of waiting pages. She wasn't sure if the man even enjoyed his duties, but he was more than competent, making sure he swept away most small and large annoyances before she had the time to realize they'd even been there. She knew they considered it the mark of an excellent butler to have an unshakable ease with any situation, but it left her uneasy with how he hid every emotion behind a mask of indifference.

The young page took her arm and guided her to the waiting line of guests being announced. Argent walked with them while Rune had streaked away to watch from the edges of the room. The Grand

Marshal didn't even try to use her name this time, instead announcing her as Mistress Mage of Arden.

The room was massive, and the stairs gave her a perfect view of King Laron seated on a raised dais to the back. The meandering groups seemed to part as they deposited her at the bottom and made her way down the line to make her first official greeting with the King of Orlean. She hated being this exposed, she thought, gritting her teeth in a polite smile as she curtsied in response to a man, the Count of something, bowing as she passed.

"Pleasure to see you again, Mistress Mage." Prince Zyon said with a brief bow as she dropped into a low curtsey. "I hope you are enjoying your stay at the palace?"

"Thank you, your royal highness. The palace is lovely, I hope to see more of the grounds."

"They are lovely this time of year." He agreed with a slight smile, "I hope you enjoy the ball, Mistress Mage. I may have to steal a dance."

"I shall endeavor to avoid your toes if you do, your royal highness." Beryl murmured, dipping another curtsey and moving down the line to his father, King Laron.

"Ah, the young Mage who was exiled from her country." King Laron said from his chair, waving for her to rise with a dismissive hand, "I hope you are more productive than most of the local mages. Few seem to understand the value of hard work."

"I've never been one for idleness, your majesty." Beryl said, keeping her eyes low, noting the way several people shifted in unease as he insulted mages.

"We shall see." He sniffed, waving her off.

She gave a final curtsy before moving away to stand near the middle of the hall. A few people tendered her polite smiles or a quick welcome as they passed, but no one stayed to talk. A group of musicians played in a hidden alcove, and the prince danced the first dance with a dark-haired beauty before returning to his father's side. So far they had left her alone to watch as couple after couple paired off and groups wandered past. She was trying to decide if she could get away with slipping off the painful shoes when Cerise hurried over to her side.

"Come, you must let me introduce you to the few jewels in this parade of lackeys. I've been trapped next to the Lord Marshall and a local Baron for the last hour. I've never been so glad to see a friendly face. How are your bond mates? Did the cat stay in tonight?"

"Rune is hiding," Beryl said with a laugh, "he doesn't like crowds like this anymore than I do."

"Well, I hope you like dancing. You are guaranteed to get at least a few offers as the newest face in the crowd." Cerise said, fanning herself with a feathered fan, "What did you say to the Prince? I thought I saw his mask crack for a moment. I don't think I've ever seen him so much as crack a smile in the last ten years."

"Prince Zyon must have had a miserable childhood if he had everyone around him bowing and scrapping for that long. He's not too much older than me, is he?"

"Prince Zyon is turning thirty-two this winter. There will be another grand ball if you're still with us. Last year it was full of acrobats and performers contorting themselves into knots." Cerise hummed, beaming and giving a curtsy as someone passed before the smile fell away, "You are what, twenty?"

"Nineteen this coming fall."

"A babe," She said sighing dramatically, "Come, Let us find you a strapping youth to dance the evening away with. Or at least someone who will keep off your toes."

"Thank you for chaperoning me tonight, I'm sure I would have been glued to the wall for the duration without your encouragement."

"Well, with such a guardian at your side," She said, gesturing at Argent and giving a wicked grin, "I'm sure your virtue is safe. No one would dare lay a finger on you with such a threat near their, hmm, jewels."

"Cerise," Beryl laughed, pressing a hand to her mouth, "you are too much. Find me someone to dance with if you must, but I'm not one to let my virtue be sullied even without Argent to keep them in line."

"As you command, my dear." Cerise said with a wicked smile, tucking Beryl's arm in hers as they wandered the hall.

Four dances later and two aching toes she was trying to reject her next offer when the surrounding area fell silent. She watched in growing horror as the Prince approached and her current suitor disappeared after a single glance from the prince.

"May I have this dance, Mistress Mage?" Prince Zyon asked, giving her a deep bow and holding out a hand.

"Your royal highness." She said, sending Argent to the wall with a thought and curtsying as she took his hand, "I'm afraid I am not the best dancer. I am still learning the dances popular here."

"After the last few who accompanied you, I felt the need to show that not all Orlean men are with no grace on the dance floor." He murmured with a tiny smirk that disappeared as quickly as it appeared.

"Then I shall endeavor to not abuse your toes in return." She said straightening with a smile and letting him lead her to the floor as the musicians quickly shuffled sheet music before beginning a waltz, a dance she'd learned in Arden in case she had to attend a ball or dance with her former Master, Darius.

"I must steal you away for more dances if it means having such a witty partner. Most are too afraid to offend to enjoy a conversation."

"How dull, I'm afraid I learned to dance while reciting treatises on magic or history. I feel more nervous when my partner's refuse to talk." She said with a quick laugh.

"Then I shall endeavor to dance with you when the occasion arises." The prince said with a flash of a grin, "How are you enjoying your first ball on Orlean soil?"

"It is looking more inviting." She said with a laugh, "I never expected to attend so many parties and events during my stay. I thought I would study and showing others magic, not dancing with handsome nobility and running away to go ride to the scandal of my maids."

"I must plan an entertaining hunt for you to ride in then. The grounds at the summer palace are more challenging, but there are a few nice jumps here you may enjoy."

"That sounds wonderful, I must see about finding a reliable horse." She agreed happily, making him blink at the honest answer.

"You enjoy riding then?"

"Yes, I love riding and being outside. I learned to ride and drive a cart while living with my uncle and became a messenger in Cardu while they apprenticed me. I rode the town every few days and whenever I could get the time off. It became harder once I gained Argent as my bond mate, but we still rode."

"Will he ride a hunt with you? I'd imagine the field would be too fast."

"Yes, we did slower hunts, but I still rode with the pack occasionally. I enjoy having a magnificent mount and the wind on my face. There are few better things to do."

"You are a most puzzling woman, Mistress Mage."

"I will take that as a compliment, your highness." She said drawing away as the dance ended and giving him a deep curtsy. "I've never been one to fit a mold, Prince Zyon."

"As I said, most puzzling." He said giving her a bow and quick smile before escorting her back to where Argent was waiting by the wall with a smirking Lady Bonheur.

"You are moving up, my dear." Cerise said with an evil grin mostly hidden by her fan, "How was your dance?"

"The prince is a wonderful dancer and conversationalist." Beryl said signaling to a passing server for a glass of punch and trying to discretely fan her cheeks, "I may purchase a fan myself if all the balls are like this."

"This is one of the polite society dances, dear, I must make sure you get the full experience when you attend mine at the end of the month. Things are much less ridged and the dancing can go on until dawn."

"I will make sure to have the appropriate footwear." Beryl said with a grin, sipping her drink and pressing a hand to one cheek. Her feet were screaming, but she kept her head up and started planning the rest of the week for short walks in comfortable shoes.

Chapter 12

Magic & Illusions

Beryl glanced up from the thesis she was reading as a group of robed men passed by. The dark flowing robes marked them as local mages however they ignored her filing into a room off the library. They marked the grey charcoal or black robes with colorful trim to announce the mastery each wearer held. She wasn't sure she would want to announce her abilities so openly, at least for now she could ignore the custom.

A handful of young men and women followed the Masters a moment later before a booming voice shattered the silence of the library, muffled only slightly by the heavy door separating the rooms. It sounded like a lecture on casting illusions, however there was a massive section of the library on the same subject so it might just be a favored use of magic in the region. Arden's mages had focused on wards and runic protection based spells, but Orlean seemed geared towards enhancing appearance and hiding flaws. She took notes but most of it seemed useless, bending light and holding illusions to change eye and hair color, crafting elaborate scenes and entertainments for parties, floating ribbons and controlling small objects.

So much of the society she was seeing in Orlean was all about standing out while still fitting in. Show off your skills and hide your flaws and secrets. Don't look past the surface because the surface is all there is, the only thing that matters.

"They are so shallow, they see nothing but the positions they are pressing for." she told Rune and Argent with a sigh, watching the young apprentices file out of the lecture, each glamoured and spelled to catch the eye.

"Do you intend to hide in this corner all day?" One of the young men asked her with a flirtatious grin, giving her a courtly bow. "A beauty such as you should never be unaccompanied."

"Even beautiful things have to educate themselves." Beryl said with an amused smile. The roguish young man had enchanted a scarf to twist along his neck and arms like a silken viper flashing a delicate tongue or fangs.

"Finally found someone immune to your charms, Alex?" Another asked giving her a short bow as he shifted a stack of books handing two over to her admirer, standing out mostly by his lack of ornamentation while the rest of the students glittered or fluttered with random illusions or animated objects.

"It's true that everyone must learn, Madame." Alexandre said giving the other a brief glare, "However, I didn't see you in Master Rogen's lecture. Are you a visiting apprentice?"

"A visiting mage," she said, giving them both a smile, "I wasn't sure the lectures were open to the public."

"An accomplished mage to have graduated so young," Alexander said, giving her another practiced smile.

"Only the apprentices of the resident Masters attend however I've yet to see anyone turned away. I can check with my Master if you wish, Madame?" the other offered with a shy smile.

"That would be wonderful; may I ask what your names are, Sirs?" She asked, fighting to suppress a laugh at how nonplussed the handsome one was with his friend's interruptions, petting at Argent for a moment to give herself time to smooth her expression.

"Oh," he said with a flush, making Alexandre grin at his embarrassment as he offered a stiff bow, "your pardon, Madame. I'm Eric de Merton of Lebon and my friend here is Alexandre, Chevalier de Giles."

"It is a pleasure to meet you both. I'm Beryl Marcian, but most call me Mage."

"Mage? You're the exiled mage from Arden?" Eric asked in shock before blushing at his gaff, his friend laughing.

"It's a pleasure to meet you, Madame Mage." Alexandre said, taking her hand and bowing over it like they were meeting in court, "Once my friend removes his foot from his mouth perhaps we can retire to the sun rooms? We can introduce you to some local mages or students if you have time to spare?"

"That would be delightful." She said standing and gathering up her notes while Eric snatched up the books she'd been reading and re-shelved them used to the library and its layout, "Can you give me a moment to take my bond mate outside?"

"The rain has eased so a short walk outside wouldn't be amiss." Alexandre said with a grin, offering his arm.

She took it with a hidden sigh; she was already tired of the young man's grandstanding at the expense of his quieter friend. Argent and Rune stretched before separating, Argent following Beryl while Rune stayed hidden under the chair until they left so he could explore. A light mist of rain continued to fall, so it was a quick stroll outside before they showed them into the glass covered solarium.

Several of the other students were practicing to one side, casting small illusions, each trying to outdo the other. Alexandre introduced her before taking the next attempt. The other took his interruption in stride, so it must be a common occurrence. The conjured castle with prison like walls and cloud drenched battlements was lovely, yet Beryl couldn't help but note the blurred edges and missing details. It was a lovely illusion, but it would fool no one for something real.

"So are you Alex's latest ingenue, or did he pick you up on a whim?" Adelaide asked while Diane gasped at her blatant cheek.

"Neither," Beryl said with a small tight smile, "I'm using him to expand my collection. It's so hard to find intelligent conversation."

"Would you care for a turn?" Diane asked, clearly hoping to change the subject.

"I'm afraid I've never studied illusion magic." Beryl said with a shrug, "I was hoping someone might explain a few of the concepts to me. The books seem to leave out a lot of the practical applications."

"It would honor me to assist you, Madame Mage." Eric offered with a shy grin, "I wanted to ask about your bond mate, it's not a common ability here."

She noted the angry look Alexandre hid as he watched them walk away to a more secluded bench. Adelaide went to Alexandre; hanging off his arm as the young women converged, cajoling him into showing them more illusions. Eric seemed oblivious to the tension in the group showing her to a seat and chattering about the latest theories they'd been lectured on.

"You're a runic caster, correct?" He asked, conjuring a small illusion with a gesture, letting the small light pulse in one cupped palm.

"Yes, I learned to use runes almost exclusively." She said not wanting to even hint at her dabbles with wind magics and musical conjurations. She needed a few tricks up her sleeve, just in case.

"We only use runes for wards on buildings or objects where the spell is meant to be permanent. The rest of the time we use verbal commands and gestures."

"I'd heard rumors of chants and singing." She trailed off at his wince. The boy couldn't hide any of the reactions flying across his face.

"Well, yes, however, those are rather frowned upon. It's seen as below many of the more advanced casters to use such things." He said with a frown, "The mark of a skilled mage is casting without grand gestures or even silently. Few can master such control, however. Even the most gifted mages often can only cast a few simple spells without the usual props."

"Props?"

"Many use jewelry or rings to channel the spells, making the casting easier, I imagine it's much like how your jewels work." He said gesturing to the wrist cuffs and collar that never left her skin. "It's rare to see someone wear such powerful pieces openly."

"They are family heirlooms," Beryl said with a soft laugh, "I'm afraid I don't have the heart to change the settings."

"Many mages might see it as boasting." Eric said with a blush, "Not that I mean it as an insult, they will give you some leeway as you're a foreign mage."

"Like having a bond mate does?" She asked watching the latest creation, a maze of rose bushes, collapse into a soft spray of sparks, "There was some mistrust of animal bond mates in Arden but not the level of disgust I've encountered here."

"We see it as lowering oneself to a baser state to join yourself with an animal, it opens the mage to his baser instincts the Masters claim."

"Funny, the most common thing I've shared with my Argent is happiness. To share a constant presence with someone who loves you with all their bodies, to feel his steadfast loyalty and eagerness to see his Mage happy. What is wrong with that?"

"They make you happy?"

"Always, every experience is shared. To know that you'll never be alone no matter what happens? That's a constant comfort." She murmured, stroking one hand down Argent's broad head and sending both her bond mates a burst of love and affection across the bond before adding, "They also can boost your magic or to focus unruly elements of a spell."

"Eric, dear? You must take a turn!" Adelaide called across the room, gesturing him over impatiently.

"I'm sorry," he said with a blush, "perhaps we can talk again later?"

"Of course," Beryl said, giving him a smile, "show me something to cheer everyone up on such a gloomy day."

Beryl settled back, noting the number of rings and small gems hidden on cuffs and sashes. Most glowed with slight sparks of stored magic. Eric stepped into the center of the room and small blackbirds were soon filling the room and swirling between people, only the lack of sound marking them as illusions. She spun a small illusion of light against the table and frowned as she manipulated it. Why couldn't they have a sound or smell to go along with the dazzle of light?

"Would it be too forward of me to ask if I can escort you back to your rooms? Dinner won't be too long off and most of us are heading home." Eric asked as the apprentices gathered their things, the soft chime of a clock's bells marking the sixth hour.

"Thank you for the lesson, I didn't realize it was getting so late." Beryl said taking his arm, "Will you be studying any more in the coming days?"

"Not until next week," Eric said, giving his farewells to the room as he showed her out, "are you enjoying your stay in the palace?"

"Oh, yes; I've tried to leave time to study where I can, but there always seems to be something happening, a ball or a dinner. Tomorrow is the hunt the Prince is riding in. Do you ride?"

"No, I'm afraid I'm more of an academic bent." He offered with a slight blush. She noted one side of his face didn't flush outing an illusion he was holding to hide something.

"Pity, perhaps I'll catch you next week then. I'd like to try a few of the tips you gave me before we meet again."

"Are you riding in the hunt?"

"Yes, Argent misses hunting, and the field is supposed to be moving slowly enough for him to come."

"Your dog misses the hunt?" He repeated, baffled.

"He does," Beryl agreed, not elaborating, "thank you for the escort and the lesson this evening. It was much better than anything I had planned for the afternoon."

"I hope you can join us again. It would be interesting to learn some novel forms to cast even if they aren't illusions."

Chapter 13

The Hunt and a delicate matter

Argent surveyed the gathering hunting dogs and horses eagerly. They'd decided that he or Rune would always be with Beryl, however, never at the same time outside of their rooms. Many knew that the visiting mage had two bond mates, but it was something easily forgotten as her curse forced any bystanders to forget her in moments or to think she was some random mage visiting court. The prince seemed to be one of the few exceptions to her curse's influence. He'd insisted on her participation in the hunt today. He could just be courting a rogue mage to use her talents in what was soon to be his court, however it felt like more.

Her audience with the King had been brief. They had shown her to a stuffy sitting room sweltering from the two roaring fires warming the room. The monarch sat next to one further ensconced in furs and blankets.

"So, you are the mage so many of my courtiers are talking about." He said eying her sharply before smothering a cough with a black silk handkerchief.

"I am called Mage, your majesty, however I cannot say if the rumors about court are about me or some other visiting mage. I've yet to meet any of the mages in your service." Beryl said with a curtsy.

"Yes, rumors can be dangerous things; much like rogue mages." He said looking her and her bond mates over with a frown before reaching for a steaming cup of some herbal drink. "Have you been enjoying your stay in Orlean?"

"Yes, your majesty, the grounds here are very fine and I've wanted for nothing in my time at the palace."

"I'm pleased to hear so," He said with a grimace once he'd drained the cup and handed it off to a waiting servant, "I was hoping we might persuade you to stay and assist us in a few magical endeavors."

"It would honor me, your majesty." Beryl said with another deep curtsy.

"Good, my steward will send you the papers." He says waiving a hand at the man standing to one side, who nods and makes a note in his waiting book.

"Yes, your Majesty." Beryl said with a nod before asking, "May I ask, is this an urgent matter?"

"I would have your opinion on the matter by the end of the week."

"Yes, your majesty;" She said dropping another curtsy as he waved her out, which gave her four more days.

They had announced the hunt a few days ago at dinner, and her invitation was waiting in her rooms by the time she arrived. It thrilled the maids to help her decide on an outfit for the outing until they realized that she intended to ride in the hunt. Beryl had sent them away after their aghast cries over the riding breaches and great coat she intended to wear. She'd never used the side saddles in fashion in Orlean. Most of the women would ride in small phaetons and carts, anyway. Noble women saw themselves as far too delicate to ride in a hunt, it seemed.

She arrived early at the stables to find only the lower class staff and dog whippers were out and readying mounts and animals for the hunt. One of the stable hands showed her to the lovely grey mare she was to be riding, and she groomed her while Argent and Rune got acquainted with the horse. Thankfully, the mare seemed used to dogs and stood steady while they roamed around her feet. They were tacked and idling in boredom while the rest of the field arrived, most collecting their horses tacked and waiting from a harried stable hand.

"Surely you don't mean to ride with the hounds, Madame?" A gentleman asked as he was hoisted into the saddle nearby.

"What is the point of having a hunting hound, if you don't hunt?" Beryl said, waving away the assistance of his groom as she mounted.

"And riding astride?!"

"Riding side saddle hasn't made its way to Arden, I'm afraid." She said with a bright smile as she caught Rune and set him on one shoulder, nudging her horse forward and away from the sputtering man and his smirking valet who was fighting laughter behind a white gloved fist.

"*So much for keeping a low profile.*" She murmured to her bond mates, keeping her head up as they moved through the growing crowd.

"*Let them talk; we want them to court us. Let then try to keep up.*" Argent said with a soft bark.

"*They see us now and we will show them how well we hunt.*" Rune agreed. "*We have to be seen to find the people we need to watch, don't we?*"

"*We might.*" Beryl agreed with a sigh, making sure Argent was keeping up as they wound through the scattered groups of carts with velvet clad women and jacketed men on horseback.

She kept her head up and a polite smile on her lips even as the wave of gossip at her attire and riding style quickly spread. She pulled her horse up to one side away from the carriages and tried to ignore how space opened between her and the other riders. Eventually someone would break the line. She was a foreign woman and mage, and someone would either try to educate her on the error of her ways or join her in being rebellious. She didn't have long to wait.

"You're causing quite the scandal among the court this morning,

Madame Mage." The prince said mildly as he reined his mount next to hers.

"Good morning, Prince Zyon; How are you enjoying the hunt so far?" she asked, giving him a quick glance before returning to watching the milling crowd.

"I have high hopes for the morning's hunt." He said giving her a gallant grin, "Will you be keeping pace with the hounds or staying with the carriages?"

"It depends on the speed of the hunt." Beryl said with a slight grin, "Argent isn't built to race so we may stay with the hounds or I may hunt and let him catch up as he can."

"It should be a fast hunt, you may wish to hang back." One of the other courtiers said giving her and her horse a dismissive look.

Beryl knew she was bristling at the man's tone but couldn't stop the swell of anger at his presumption, "Are you suggesting a woman wouldn't be able to keep up, Sir?"

"Few women will push themselves hard enough to keep pace with a fast hunt. We will ride all day, Miss."

"Then perhaps I shall have to rise to the challenge," Beryl said, giving the man a sharp smile that was all teeth, "Prince Zyon, are we hunting live or riding a dragged course?"

"The course has been dragged, but if we flush a true prey, we will pursue." The prince said looking amused, "The Count Renee has been hoping to flush a boar by the end of the season."

"By bow or spear?"

"Spear." The Count said tightly, "An arrow would do little to stop a full sized boar from the King's forests."

"Are the weapons different here in Orlean? A grown man knowledgeable with a long bow can take down a boar in Arden. A bear might be a different matter. I've hunted small game, myself. What should we hope to see on the hunt?"

"The King's Woods are well stocked with deer and boar, however it's been many years since we tracked a bear." Another man replied watching the exchange with interest, "The field is assembled, my Prince."

"Diplomatic as ever, James." The Prince said, reining his horse around, "Let us get started."

I will stay and watch from the back. Argent said with a huff, *"Rune stays with you."*

"Always," Beryl agreed, disliking leaving her bond mate behind, but there was no way he'd keep up to a fast hunt, *"Our next hunt will be your chance to shine. Be safe."*

Thankfully, the hunt started out slow, letting the horses warm up and going several miles at an easy pace until they loosed the dogs. They waited in an extensive field while the hounds hunted for a scent, setting off again as the dogs howled and took off. The Prince's group peeled off to take a side trail lined by massive hardwoods, and Beryl followed.

Rune disliked riding this fast, but he refused to abandon his bond mate, digging his claws into the leather of the coat she was wearing. The lane was crisscrossed with brush jumps that the other horses took at speed, some riders whooping and calling out insults to each other as they raced. Beryl stuck to the low points in the middle of the jumps, not knowing her horse enough to trust her to make the more difficult heights.

The other riders were skilled and pushed their horses, jockeying for the best spots and fouling each other as they thundered down the lane. Beryl stayed back and to one side to keep her mount out of the competition. She wanted to keep up, not lame her horse or get thrown. At the end of the lane they took an easy canter back to the rest of the hunt, dropping to a walk as the next field came into view.

The next lane of jumps were earthen mounds, giving them something to scramble up and a leap over a small creek that several horses balked at. Beryl's horse trotted through the stream like it was a common obstacle, while the more high-strung jumpers vaulted it like they would melt if the tiniest drop reached them. She ignored the men watching as she cantered on, keeping to the middle of the pack as they finished out the ride.

The forest they headed into was too well spaced and groomed to be a genuine forest, but it made for an entertaining canter as the men dodged back and forth between the evenly spaced hardwoods, ignoring the pounding hooves of the guard following behind them. The rest of the riders were moving at a trot to the last field where the hunt would end, Argent trailing along with the rest of the dogs unhappily.

"How are you enjoying your first Orlean hunt, Mistress Mage?" The prince asked as they reined to a walk to cool the horses down.

"Mage!" One of the other blurted before turning red at the nonplussed look the prince gave him.

"I look forward to the summer palace if the rides are as challenging as you mentioned. However, this was a lovely ride considering I have an unfamiliar horse."

"This is the first time you've ridden this mare?"

"Yes, she held up wonderfully. A lovely canter, I may ask to ride her again if there's time."

"Few women can keep up with the Prince on the hunt, you did well." The Count said, giving her a nod.

"I doubt I would have been able to keep up if I rode sidesaddle, as most of your women do. Do any of the women jump while riding on the side?"

"Yes, a few buts most consider it unseemly."

"Then it is an agreeable thing I never learned." Beryl said with a laugh gathering her reins, "Shall we give the field the illusion we galloped the entire way?"

"After you, Mage?" One man offered with a leer.

"Royalty should always lead, dear sir." Beryl said, arching an eyebrow before cueing her horse for a gallop with a shout.

The string of curses behind her was worth it as the men whipped their mounts to catch up. She let the mare have her head but didn't push her, letting the others pass as they would. They thundered down the lane and into the field in a cloud of dust to the applause of the waiting crowd.

She nodded to the prince and his companions and walked her horse over to where Argent was waiting. The men were accepting drinks, and the ride became more of a mobile party as the day wore on. Beryl waved away the offered wine and found a groom to help her untack and wipe down her horse. While the others rode, she walked, watching her horse's gait. Rune moved to ride on Argent's back, keeping a few feet away as they walked through the tall grass.

"Did she pick up a stone?" a rider in the brown coat of a minor noble asked, leaning forward on his own mount to watch the stride of her mare.

"It's probably nothing, but I thought there was a catch in her stride on the final gallop. I'd rather walk, then make it worse."

"The voice of a true rider," He grinned, "I despair of the horses that some of our peers will ruin in the coming months. They will be sold off if they aren't shot as soon as they get the poor thing home."

"Drink and horses is never a pleasant combination." Beryl agreed with a sigh as the man dismounted.

"John Toussaint, a pleasure to make your acquaintance." He said with a grin, offering his hand.

"Beryl Marcian, but everyone calls me Mage." She said taking his hand and liking the firm grip. Most nobles seemed too concerned with treating the women around them like delicate sculptures to actually deal with them as people.

"Mage? I wasn't aware that any of the palace mages bothered to ride."

"That may be, I'm not a palace mage, so I can't say. I'm a visiting from Arden. I take it you are a local noble?"

"Yes, my family own Glenlight estates. It's near the northern border of Orlean." He said with a light blush, "I apologize if I spoke too lightly of your status as a mage, I'm afraid I know little of magic or its practitioners."

"Then we are even, I know little of how Orlean's magical practitioners comport themselves either. I only know that I love to ride and will continue to do so." She shrugged, glancing over the rest of the field.

"I meant no offense." He stammered, raising his hands as if to ward off her anger.

"And I've taken none," Beryl sighed, turning and whistling for Argent, "do you ride often when you are home?"

"Yes, we breed and sell horses for hunting and general use. I grew up helping around the stables and working with them, it's why I attend the hunt season every year." He said eyes flickering over Argent as he trotted up but gave them a bit of space in case the man's horse wasn't used to dogs.

"You must make many sales during the hunt, is this one of yours?" She asked nodding to the handsome horse he was riding, "He's got a look, leggy but a wonderful broad chest."

"He's still young, but he's got an amazing spring to his gait." John said with a nod, "I've seen your mount in the hunts before, did you choose her?"

"No, I've been helping school horses for the Stable Master here and he arranged for me to ride something stable since I haven't found a horse yet. It's hard to find a horse willing to work around large dogs." She nodded to Argent as they walked, "I've asked around but no one will sell to a known mage."

"Are you planning to stay with the court for now?"

"Yes, I'm traveling to the summer place when the Prince leaves. I'm trying to hire a few servants and at least attempt to have a small household while I travel."

"If you are heading north, maybe you can visit Glenlight, or I could bring a horse or two down that might work. What are you looking for?"

"A bit of everything, I need a horse that can pull a small trap if needed that I can also ride or use in a light hunt used to large dogs and won't kick or react around them."

"Do you care if the horse is older?" He asked, glancing over her with a frown, "That much training and exposure will mean the horse is at least eight if not older. You'll have a dependable mount for years to come, but they might not have the speed or agility of a younger mount."

"I'm more interested in endurance then speed. I travel a lot and I want something that can keep up with me."

"They trained your last horse the same, wasn't he?" He asked, watching her from the corner of one eye.

"Yes, Flox was a messenger horse. Not fast or young or even pretty, but he trucked through mud and crossed streams without complaint, went for miles and traveled rough as needed. He wasn't trained to a cart or trap, but I never needed one in Arden. Here it's much more common."

"You don't like the social restraints that Orlean has for women, I take it?" He asked with a chuckle, "I must introduce you to my sister, Samantha. She is part of a group advocating for social reforms. Allowing women to move about the country without an escort, riding astride, owning their own businesses."

"You don't allow women to own businesses?!" she sputtered, coming to a stop.

"They frown it upon and the few I know of, thanks to my sister, are from the husband leaving the woman the business. Even then they have to have a man stand for them in any court or guild, generally it's a relative."

"Do you agree with what she's advocating for?" She asked, starting walking and accepting the water skin that was passed their way by a servant.

"Yes, things need to change, but I just don't see it happening as quickly as she thinks they will. It may take generations to get all the laws changed so things are more equal." He said with taking the skin and drinking before passing it back to the servant.

"You may be right, Arden still has some that believe that women are beneath them, but they also believe most people are beneath them."

"Rather like most of the aristocracy here." John laughed, "That's most of the reason I dread coming to court each year. My family are considered 'Newly Noble' even two generations in. That they granted us a title for hard work seems to make it some kind of insult to most of the nobility."

"So they will buy your horses but they still treat you as beneath them no matter what your actual rank is."

"Exactly." John laughed, "I take it from your tone, mages aren't so different?"

"There are people hoping to gain status and power in every profession. It is worse for female mages since we are they see us as a way to gain status by adding magic to the bloodlines. Most of us get constant marriage offers throughout school from local aristocrats hoping to stuff us in a back room while they parade their new magical children through the town."

"And yet you are unwed and unchaperoned at a Royal Hunt?" He asked teasingly, "Breaking the mold and proving that a woman can keep up with even the Prince at this own hunt."

"I'm a foreign mage, your country's restrictions don't apply to me." She said with a smile, "Will you be joining the crowds at dinner? I was told it would be more informal than it has been."

"Yes, tonight at least I'm invited." He said with a snort, "Pardon my foul mood. My father may be a Baron, but they rarely treat the rest of us like we exist to the royal court. I don't mind, but the constant snubs get old as the months drag on. I'm ready to get away from the courts for a while."

"Will you go home while the Prince is at the summer palace?"

"Yes, I'll still be at the palace through the hunt season, but I'll get to go home for a few days if they cancel a hunt because of weather or a ball. By the winter I'll be home helping with the pregnant mares and cleaning stalls. Not a glamorous life, but I ache for it when I'm gone this long." He gave her a rueful smile, "Thank you for listening to my rambling, I'm homesick amongst all this pomp and glitter."

"Do you have a favorite horse at home?"

"Yes, we have an old retired stallion called Devon. He's a dark grey going white with age. We still use him for breeding occasionally, but he is used to teaching the younger cousins how to ride and handle a stallion. He's still strong as ever, but has mellowed in his age. He runs with our bachelor band right now, but eventually he will be moved to a pasture of his own, he's getting too old to keep up with the younger stallions."

They chatted as they walked, John was a tall lanky man with reddish brown hair and hazel eyes that seemed prone to laughter. He seemed an untroubled man who enjoyed riding and being outdoors while helping to run the family estate. Her conversation with Cerise circled through her head as they talked. She might dally with this handsome man if he proved trustworthy.

* * *

"Thank you," Beryl murmured as the page bowed and backed out of the room, leaving her with the packet of papers for the King's project. She was still sore from the hunt the day before but had enjoyed the dinner with John, the horse trader. It was nice to find someone so calm and unaffected by the swirling politics of the court. Bertrand returned from an errand with bowls of water and meat for her bond mates, leaving the bowls in their normal place.

"*Smells strange.*" Rune said, backing away from the bowl after a cursory sniff.

"Wait a moment, Bertrand. Where did the meat come from?" She called out, picking up the smaller dish, careful not to touch the meat.

"The kitchens, they make the bowls in the morning while preparing the meat for the day." The man said, watching with a frown as she smelled the meat.

"So anyone working in the kitchens or just passing through could have had access to them?" She asked casting a brief spell over the meat that made it glow a soft red, "Poison, it's not strong but it would be enough to kill Rune."

"The meat looked fine, Mistress, do you want me to alert the guards?" He asked, snatching up the other bowl, so it wasn't near the animals.

"No, ask the Prince's staff for a meeting tomorrow. I'll be testing everything that comes through this door, even the mail. Don't let anyone handle anything without gloves, I'll enchant them to glow if an item is spelled or tampered with in the morning. We may need to reduce the number of staff that services the rooms."

"Very well," Bertrand said, glancing over the room with a troubled gaze, "what do you wish to do with the tainted meat?"

"Take the large bowl but leave the small, don't put it anywhere someone might touch or eat it. Bury it if you have to."

"Yes, Mistress." He says neutrally, gathering up the untouched water dishes and leaving without another word.

"We didn't touch it. We are fine." Rune reminded her even as she dropped to the floor and gathered the animals as close to her as she could.

"Someone tried to harm you, which is never fine."

"We will never leave you, we are with you until the last." Argent rumbled, leaning against his mage.

"I don't know if I can survive losing anyone else."

"Then you will not, Argent will wear his armor and you will as well. We will go into battle ready for the fight." Rune insisted, purring as he cuddled against her.

"No more hiding then." Beryl hummed in agreement, *"Good, I'm tired of hiding and playing the weak women. We'll show them how to fear us."*

* * *

It was the next morning before Beryl got back to the papers from the King. She had an appointment that evening with the Prince to discuss the poisoning and another with the staff to train them in how to use the gloves she'd enchanted. She kept to her rooms, buying time where someone might think the poisoning had worked.

The papers were records of attempted assassinations on the royal family. The letter that accompanied everything was blunt. She was to design something to protect the family and prove her loyalty to Orlean. She would need to see what they already use if she hoped to improve on it, but considering the list of known attempts, their protections must be formidable. Multiple attempts at poisoning, drugging a horse before a ride, spelled hair combs and jewelry that were both gifts and favorite items, kidnapping attempts whenever the princess traveled, and that was just the princess. The attempts on the Prince were more ruthless, open attacks on the road, while riding a hunt, poison and spells much the same as the princess, however there were also forced duels and outright attacks by both lovers and friends brought on by bribery.

She wasn't sure what she could do to shield the young princess from kidnapping, but she could make it harder for anyone to poison either of the royal family with some enchanted objects. She needed to see what they were using first. They should test every plate before they served it, but she'd seen nothing like that at any of the meals she'd attended.

By the time a page arrived to lead her to the Prince's study, she'd come up with twelve possible runic protection wards. But there was no guarantee that he would accept or use any of them. Anything she came up with would be analyzed by dozens of other mages before the family ever used it, anyway. This was a test. If Arden wanted the royal family dead, then she'd be honor bound to leave gaps and holes in the protections to allow them a way in.

"Please follow me, Madame." The page stuttered, taking in her black cloak and the aggressive stance Argent took at her side.

They didn't follow meekly. They stalked the page, forcing him to lengthen his stride until he was almost jogging to the Prince's wing of the palace. She might show her hand too soon, but she felt certain the poison hadn't come from the royal family. Someone was trying to remove her from a position of power. She might as well push back and see who reacted.

"Mistress Mage to see you, your royal highness." The page at the door announced opening the door and gesturing them through a beat later at some sign from inside.

"I didn't take you for the mage to terrorize my staff." Prince Zyon admonished, watching as she closed the distance between them, stopping a few feet from his desk.

"Someone on you staff tried to poison my bond mates. I don't take threats lightly." She snapped back, raising a hand when he opened his mouth to respond, "I know the idea and the poison didn't come from your staff or even your family. They paid someone to poison the meat and disappear. I don't doubt they will turn up dead in a gambling house or brothel."

"You seem to have a grasp of the situation. There are several factions vying for power since the last Court Mage retired. Between that and how we've kept you to us it was bound to happen," he said with a nod, "how can I assist you in ensuring it doesn't happen again?"

"I'd like to hire my staff and either live outside the palace or just outside the general guest rooms if I have to stay to continue my work for the king."

"There are a few scattered cottages at the summer estate sometimes used for long-term guests," He said with a frown, "I can't allow your staff the run of the grounds but they could keep the cottage functioning as you'd need."

"Am I allowed to place wards where I need them?"

"As long as the wards aren't lethal. I know you're working on protections the king requested, you'll be warding this wing before we leave and the family rooms at the Summer Palace as well." He hummed, glancing her over before continuing, "Was your other bond mate injured? Do you need a healer sent to your rooms?"

"No, neither of them ate the poisoned meat." Beryl said with a sigh, reaching to pull Rune from where he was hiding in her hood into her arms, "It also protects them from most simple spells and hexes. I wanted to continue the illusion that one of them might have been harmed until I could speak with you."

"I'm glad to hear that neither were harmed."

"The palace wouldn't have remained standing if it had harmed them." She said flatly, meeting his eyes.

"I didn't realize mages were so protective of their pets." He said tone mild even as his he jotted out instructions for his staff.

"I destroyed an army of northern barbarians being amassed by Rowle of the Red Hand after my bond mate died while I was scouting the area. Any threat to them will be met with deadly consequences. I protect what is mine."

"I will keep that in mind." The Prince said, voice dry as he glanced over the animals. "Was there anything else you wished to discuss?"

"I have the plans for several wards that can be placed on jewelry or simple objects if you'd like the additional protection outside of the palace wards." She said offering the handful of sheets she'd brought. The prince took them without comment and paged through them almost absently. "You aren't trained in magic, your royal highness?"

"No, I know enough to tell if a spell is being cast near me, but nothing beyond that." He said handing the papers back, "I'll arrange a meeting with the king and his advisors to review everything. Perhaps you can summarize what you hope to attempt?"

Beryl checked Rune's collar as she talked, making the onyx stone pulse against her hand, but it didn't draw the prince's gaze. He couldn't see magic, only the gestures or words used to stabilize the spells. She shuffled the papers she'd been reading from before returning them to the small leather case she'd brought.

"It is simple wards you already use, warnings for spelled objects, poison; A pendent or bracelets that warms when a tainted object is near. It rather surprised me you don't have a royal taster for your meals given the number of attempts at poisoning." She summarized.

"They taste the dishes before we bring them into the room. We use only a handful of trusted servants to serve the royal family." He said absently as he absorbed what she'd said, "We don't use enchanted objects, they are expensive and the wards have to be updated at least once a year or the spell fails."

"That's not how runic magic works, your royal highness." Beryl stuttered in shock, "Your mages don't enchant objects at all?"

"I take it this is common in Arden?"

"Very, all mage apprentices also apprentice to someone in a craft that their magic compliments and the items they enchant are sold to cover the costs of their lessons. I worked in the armory under a local blacksmith forging arrowheads and armor."

"A blacksmith?! No mage here would ever consent to dirty their hands with such a task. They would see it as beneath them." He said with a snort, "They give their students projects, but they make no money from the efforts. I can't imagine a female mage accepting such a task, none of the nobility would."

"As riding astride and enjoying a hunt is seen beneath the local female aristocrats?" She asked, keeping her tone indifferent.

"You've already proven a proficient rider," He said with a slight grin, "I will wait to see you do to astonish us next before commenting."

"My strength is in stone and metals, I learned to craft jewelry as well. If you wish, I can make the pieces for your family from scratch if I have access to the tools and a small forge."

"I will have a small workshop outfitted in the cottage. For now, we want the plans for the wards going into the royal wing. Will you be able to provide them in two days?"

"Yes, your royal highness," She said, giving a small curtsy, "I also need to know if you want the runes hidden along the foundation or in the open."

"What would hiding the runes entail?"

"Digging out the edge of the foundation around the building so I can add the runes or setting them internally if you have a basement or lower levels. If it's in the open, I can add them in where ever I can fit them with supportive jewels that will seem like decoration but will help store magic to support the ward."

"Would both work? Having hidden runes are certain points along with the decorative placement to draw the attention?"

"Yes, it will take more planning and the hidden runes will need to be larger, but it can be done."

"Draw up the plans for having both, and I'll have my father's advisers review it." He said with a firm nod that morphed into a grimace as he continued, "You may have to explain some wards and he'll wish to call in Master Mage Deacon to review them as well."

"I haven't met Master Deacon yet, I take it you're not fond of the man?"

"He fancies himself invulnerable to politics because he's a Master Mage and has amassed a sizable fortune guiding other mages in their studies. Most of his proteges are powerful in their own right, and they will owe him for the rest of their lives for his guiding influence."

"Who is his current protege?"

"The heir to the Chevalier de Giles. His father is older and should pass on the title in the next year or two."

"Are there any mages or adversaries in particular that I should watch out for? I'd hate to redo all my work because someone sabotaged it out of jealousy." She asked with a mild smile, hoping the prince would ignore the light dig for information.

"We'll clear the halls while you work. How long should it take?" He asked, ignoring her other question.

"Warding a small town took a day," She said, fighting back a smile at the shock that froze his expression for a moment, "I'll be using more specific wards with more intricate reactions, but the effects will be the same. It should take only four days once I get the supplies I need since I won't be able to work during the day. What stones do you want used?"

"It can be anything?"

"I work best with natural stones and low grade gems, but I've worked with everything from garnets to diamonds. Do you have a preference in color?"

"How many would you need and what sizes?"

"It depends on how solid you want the wards. Setting a large stone at the cornerstone of each building would anchor the spells and power them for several years. If I interwove garnets and small gems into the visible designs on the doorways and in the halls, then it could last for up to ten years and could be recharged as needed."

"You continue to surprise me," He said, writing out a quick list of items, "I look forward to seeing your designs."

"I will send them as soon as they are ready, your royal highness" She said with a curtsey taking the dismissal and starting the trek back to their rooms, they had a long day ahead of them to keep a step ahead of whoever was trying to target them.

Chapter 14

Lady Bonheur's Party

Beryl arrived at Lady Bonheur's party later than she'd wanted, thanks to her maids fussing. She couldn't fault them on the job they'd done on her hair and makeup, however. Today her hair fell in soft waves down her back, red ribbons woven into a crown of braids holding a few sections away from her face. The red and black lace dress draped about her in delicate folds of material, hiding and seeming to reveal small bits of skin hidden by dark lace. It was a daring dress, but she thought Cerise would approve.

The grounds had been opened and small tents with seating filled the lawn while couples and groups mingled on the paths. Several groups of musicians played softly at different points, while several guests joined in song or recited poetry to those near them. Oil lamps and paper lanterns lit the night, filling the garden with a warm glow, moths chasing the flames where they could reach them.

She joined a small group near the drinks, accepting a cup of spiced wine and pausing in her wandering to listen to a young man expounding on the gods and how their gifts were representations of humanity's hopes and dreams. There was a much more open-minded crowd then in the palace at least, she thought with a smile.

"Miss Mage, wonderful! I was hoping you would come." Cerise said, hurrying over and giving Beryl a hug.

"I wouldn't have missed it, Cerise. This looks lovely, you've outdone yourself."

"Let me introduce you to a few people, are your bond mates hiding?" she asked, linking arms with Beryl and leading her along the path towards another open area where people gathered about a small fire pit.

"They are wandering the garden. I didn't realize your property was so extensive."

"The garden makes for a lovely end of season party, don't you think? The cool air is perfect for a few dances and discussion under the stars."

"Madame Bonheur, I don't believe we've had the pleasure of meeting your latest project? Weren't you mentoring a young dancer last fall?" a tall man asked while his wife looked on with sharp eyes.

"Madeline has joined a traveling troupe visiting the southern islands. I've heard she is doing well." Cerise said dismissively, "This, is Madame Mage, an accomplished mage from Arden who is staying at the palace. She has the lovely pets I told you about at my last luncheon, Richard. Mage, may I introduce the Earl of Eastfall and his wife, Lauren."

"It's a pleasure to meet you." Beryl said with a quick curtsy before turning back to Cerise, "Do you take on many projects, Cerise?"

"One must have something to do in their old age, dear. I enjoy mentoring the newcomers to society and assisting them in their endeavors. If one has money it should be used to promote the young and their arts, do you not think?"

"If that is what you like to call it," Richard snorts, "it never hurts to have varied interests."

"Remind me to dis-invite you to my next soiree." Cerise said with a sniff sweeping along without a backward glance, "Come along, Mage, let's find someone with more tact to converse with."

"You needn't apologize for the truth, Cerise. You have helped me in many ways since I arrived at the Palace." Beryl murmured once they'd collected fresh drinks on the other side of the garden.

"I didn't take you on because I needed a project to keep me entertained, dear. They can't see past their greedy natures. If I can help someone who needs it, what does it matter what they do with that help in the end? I'm not asking for recompense beyond friendship and knowing my friend is enjoying their life." She hissed angrily as they wandered the more deserted paths, calming down, "You were so sad when I met you that first time in the palace gardens, so close to tears. I couldn't stand to see you thrown to the whims of the likes of them, with no one to support you at all. All I could see was myself after I'd lost my first daughter, crying in the garden to escape the knowing looks from the other nobility. To not be able to have children is seen as a fault by many since there is no one to pass your name and titles on to."

"No one can even remember mine, so it wouldn't matter if I married or not." Beryl joked softly with a weak smile, "You have mothered all the broken and young that crossed your path for years, haven't you? What more could anyone ask of a mother?"

"Grandmother is more likely," Cerise sniffed, dabbing at her eyes.

"It would honor me to consider you mine," Beryl offered gently taking the woman's hand and leading her to a bench nearby, "my grandparents died when I was very young. I never knew them that I can remember. I have a few cousins left in Arden, but I think I will make a new family here in Orlean. I'd be honored if you would be part of it."

"If you don't mind an old woman visiting for tea?"

"Never," Beryl said fiercely, pulling Cerise into a quick hug while Argent crowded closer to rest his head in her lap, "no one else remembers to get Rune a cup of tea after all."

"Thank you, dear." She said with a chuckle, wiping her eyes so to not smear her makeup, "Let us return to the party. I won't ask you to perform, but if you think of something suitably extravagant to make those imbeciles wilt, I won't stop you."

"I'll keep it in mind." Beryl said wryly, standing and linking her arm jauntily with Cerise, "Lead the way, my dear hostess."

Chapter 15

Shopping

Beryl wandered the shops, trying to ignore the small snubs and comments from the shopkeepers. At the palace she could go about her day without an escort to act as her intermediary between her male counterparts, but here she was drawing horrified glanced from the other female shoppers and their male companions for wandering alone.

"Your pardon, Madame." The shopkeeper said with a grimace, "Is your companion nearby? Would you like to wait in the sitting area for their return?"

"No sir," she said, giving him a polite if stiff smile, "I wish to conclude my business and leave. I have no companion beyond my dog. Are you unwilling to make the sale?"

"Madame, we generally only deal with a lady's male escort. It is unseemly for a woman to deal with such trivialities."

"Sadly, I am traveling alone, sir. I do not have a male relative to shield me from such weighty matters." Beryl bit out fighting to stay polite, "Will you make the sale or should I take my needs elsewhere?"

"This is most unusual, Madame." He said taking the offered

money with a frown but gesturing for the waiting boy to wrap up her purchases.

"I find mages are unusual, sir, even female ones." She offered with a brittle smile, ignoring how the surrounding people recoiled when she said mage.

"Have a pleasant day, Madame." He said giving her a tiny bow before turning his attentions to the next shopper waiting with her frowning escort.

Beryl collected her purchase and led Argent out of the shop without a backwards glance. She'd expected some issues when she refused the offered palace escort. Her maids were horrified that she was planning to go shopping alone and had rushed to find a male to accompany her.

The constant rebuffs and refusals were shocking after living on her own for so much of her life. Traveling without an escort wasn't uncommon in Arden, but here for anyone outside of the poor side of town they considered it insanity. Women around her traveled in small packs with at least one male, often an older relative or husband of one woman. No woman walked alone.

The district was for higher end shopping than she was used to, but she hadn't expected even the middle class shops to refuse her business. They gave her all kinds of reasons, from not having an appointment when others were walking in off the street, to the item she was holding being a display model only and not for sale even when there were more of the goods sitting to one side. Adding today to the latest in a string of horrible teas and small parties she'd attended recently, and she was ready to stab the next person who looked at her wrong.

She'd accepted offers hoping to hear more about the various factions in court and instead had been relegated to a mute doll being handed from person to person. They'd only invited her to dangle her in front of their guests like some cheap prize they'd purchased for their entertainment. The last one, a pompous Baron, had asked her to delight the room with magic to accompany the music before offering her a purse if she came for the next party he was hosting at the end of the evening like she was the hired help.

They made their way to one of the open markets that the middle class used, but instead she stood out more. Few women shopped at all, a handful worked the stalls under the eye of their husbands, but no young women were unescorted in the crowds. She'd hoped to meet someone her contacts with the thieves' guild had recommended, but with every eye following her progress that would be impossible. She'd have to send him a coded message and hope it wasn't intercepted.

At the docks the lower class had shopped and traveled as they would, but they apparently expected those with status to be supervised at all times. She couldn't see a reason for it. The shopkeepers' comments about not sullying herself with menial tasks rankled. There were also no children in sight, not even beggars or pickpockets outside of the port area.

Women with influence or money were seen as fragile and needing male support and guidance at all times. That explained the constant horror her maids expressed at her riding in the hunts, practicing as a mage, or stopping in the halls to speak with various men who she was becoming acquainted with. Arden had much less restricted views on what was acceptable behavior for a woman. They accepted females in the army, as mages, allowed them to work as they pleased as long as they could do the work.

At the palace she was a foreign exiled mage, they expected her to be eccentric and unusual. Outside, she was drawing attention no matter how calmly she tried to go about her business. She'd have to conduct her business through others if she wanted to make the connections she needed. With that in mind she hailed a carriage and directed it to Lady Bonheur's estate, she'd need to discuss things with the woman if she would set things into motion.

"I'm very sorry for coming without notice," Beryl said once they were announced, and they showed her to the sitting room.

"Nonsense, is something the matter? You seem vexed?" Cerise

asked, gesturing for Beryl to take a seat as the maid poured a fresh cup of tea, "Is it the Baron? I warned you about him. I don't know why you keep accepting these invitations. They are the worst of society and are only looking to flaunt you about like the latest trinket."

"I wanted to see both sides of the board." Beryl said with a huff, giving Argent a scone and Rune a celery stick to gnaw at. "I'm done with it, however, I wanted to ask a favor if I may?"

"Anything, my friend. Sucking up to those backstabbers would have gained you nothing but pain. How about a coming out party at my country estate? The court will move to the summer palace soon and you will be able to meet some inland intellectuals at least. I will send out a few notes so you have invitations waiting when you arrive."

"That would be lovely, Cerise. I was hoping to borrow a carriage or trap for a few days. I'd like to visit the coast before the court moves on."

"I have a small property on the coast if you are also seeking lodgings. My driver can accompany you and take you to the court when you are ready."

"The Prince has invited me to Alexandria estate before he retires to the summer palace. They are due to leave for the estate in a week."

"You won't have much time for a rest then," Cerise sighed, "my house on the coast is small, more of a cottage then a grand estate, but it sits on the cliffs and the views are marvelous. When are you wanting to leave?"

"Is tomorrow too soon?"

"It will mean the house won't be ready, I must send a messenger to open the house and bring in some supplies for the kitchens. Only the caretaker is there now. The winds off the cliffs are too much for my bones any more. I haven't been to Cliff Side Estate in several years now, but the caretaker is wonderful and everything will get done."

"I just need a bed and a roof over my head, Cerise, I'm sure however it is will be fine."

"I keep forgetting your eclectic youth, my dear." Cerise chuckled,

"I think you will enjoy it. There is plenty of room for your bond mates to exercise themselves on the property, not a neighbor for miles, so you'll get all the quiet you need."

"I have a small gift for you if you'll indulge me." Beryl said pulling out one of the dolls she'd crafted and a small wrapped package.

"Of you needn't have gone to the trouble." She murmured, taking the box.

"You've been like a mother to me since I arrived and I wanted to leave you with something, even if it's just a token." Beryl said with a smile as Cerise opened the package revealing the small bracelet inside, "I know it's not quite your normal colors but I thought you could wear it under a sleeve if you needed to."

"I gather that it's more than just a lovely bracelet, then?" Cerise asked, waving her maid over to do the clasp for her.

"It's charmed to warn you against spelled objects and foods. Press the bracelet near whatever you are about to touch, and it will warm if they have tampered with it."

"I doubt anyone will try to poison an old woman like me, but thank you for the thought." She said with a frown before turning to the small velvet bear with a smirk, "Have you made me a pet even I can't kill?"

"In a way," Beryl laughed, "touch the jewel on its collar and ask it to do something."

"Anything?"

"Anything a small black bear could do." Beryl chuckled, reaching out and taping the jewel firmly, "Dance."

The bear shivered before slowly lumbering in a circle on soft paws. It reared onto its back feet tipping over on its rear and letting out a silent roar before going back to its original position. Cerise clapped in delight and laughed, commanding a few other minor acts from the doll before cuddling it in her lap.

"It has one other function that's only for emergencies." Beryl cautioned, "If you ever need me, tap the jewel and read the name on the other side of the ribbon. I'll hear you and come to wherever you are."

"You are too paranoid, darling. I doubt I will ever need the precautions you've given me, but thank you for trying to protect an old woman." She sighed, picking up her teacup, "I'm close to retiring from the court. I don't like how the old ways are changing with this latest bunch of flops. They have no soul, no spirit."

"I've learned its better to have the precautions, even if they aren't needed. I hope you don't mind a young mage's meddling."

"Of course not. I know you mean well, child." Cerise said patting Beryl's arm, "Now, tell me. Whatever made you enchant a stuffed bear?"

"I will need some kind of trade, eventually. I thought I might be able to sell small commissions, small enchanted objects I can make in the evenings."

"You can expect to receive orders in the next few weeks, then. I'll show the bear off at my next tea and I should be the latest craze in a matter of days." Cerise said with a grin.

* * *

The coach they took was plain without the plumes and gilt of the royal coaches, and Beryl was glad for it. They were ignored at the inn they stopped at for lunch and to rest the horses. Her driver, Peter, was a middle-aged man who talked in an inaudible voice to the horses as they were unharnessed and led to the stable, chiding them for slacking off in an affectionate tone. The meal was simple but filling, and Beryl was happy to watch Argent playing with a puppy that ambled over to him. The stress of the last few weeks was easing, and she was glad she'd finally decided.

Once they were back on the road, they made excellent time reaching the house just after dark. Beryl grinned to watch the large facade loom over her as they made the way to the door. What Cerise had insisted was a small cottage could have roomed most of the people they'd seen at the Inn. She could hear the pounding of the waves against the cliffs on the breeze and almost feel it through her feet. She longed to bolt straight to the cliffs, but she forced herself to wait, smiling at the woman who opened the door for them.

"Please come in, Miss. Lady Bonheur sent word, and everything is ready for your stay." The housekeeper said, ushering her in.

"Thank you," Beryl said with a polite smile, "I hope it wasn't an inconvenience."

"Oh, no, Miss. Let me show you to your room." The woman said with a smile, showing them down a hallway and up a stairway to a room that faced the sea. "I'll bring up a tray for dinner if you like, I'm afraid the rest of us have already eaten."

"That would be wonderful, thank you. Do you have some chopped meat or stew I can give my pets?"

"Yes, the Lady was very specific that we treat your pets well. We have diced chicken tonight and they will have beef or rabbit along with the rest of us depending on what we serve each night." She said with a fond look at where Beryl cradled Rune against her chest, "I'll leave you to get settled, please let me know if you need anything at all."

"Thank you, we're just hoping to rest for a few days. We shouldn't be in your hair, Ma'am."

"Nonsense, whatever would you get into? Let me get your tray, my boy should bring your bags up once they finish with the horses."

Beryl smirked, remembering some things they'd gotten into while she was studying in Cardu. Even bonded animals sometimes forgot themselves when their instincts kicked in, and having a sea hawk chase a mouse across the library had sent students screaming as they ducked under tables or behind shelves. Kuro had torn into the mouse with relish once she returned to Beryl's fist, making one poor students faint.

"She was a fierce hunter," Argent rumbled, leaning on his bonded with a sigh, and *"She would have enjoyed our hunt in the woods."*

"She would have hated the dancing and parties as much as I do." Beryl thought with a sniffle.

"Kuro would have shrieked at the mages who thought us less, but she would have loved the hunt and the gardens full of loud birds." Rune agreed, purring softly.

"Peacocks, " Beryl corrected with a hiccuping laugh, *"She would have tried to catch and eat one just to prove she could."*

The meal that's brought up was left untouched, and they spend the night curled against each other in the too large bed. The next morning Beryl picked at the porridge and fruit they served her, but her bond mates cleaned their plates. At least the servants have nothing to say about her wearing men's pants and a too large sweater to go wandering the cliffs.

She sat on a stone at the edge of the cliff bottom while her two bond mates played in the waves, trying to cheer her up with their silly antics. Beryl smiled as best she could and sent them her love across the bond even as she couldn't stop the tears tracking down her face, Kuro would have loved the sea. She missed the bird like a limb that no one could see was missing, a part that someone had carved out of her soul and hidden away from her.

Wiping her cheeks, she called them back as the sun set. The cook fussed at the missed meals, but Beryl merely fussed over her bond mates in silence, slipping them bites of bread or meat from her own plate. Tomorrow would be hard, and she wanted just a few more hours to hold the ache close to her heart. Her fingers constantly sought the round jade stone that hung from a leather thong around her neck.

The next morning she went down early, wandering the top of the cliff until the tide moved out enough for them to reach the beach. While her bond mates wandered, she chalked out a sending diagram and set her letter in the middle weighted down by a wave worn stone. The note wasn't one she wanted to send, but it needed to be done. Mage sent the note with a hard shove of magic. The backlash would break his warded table and preventing him from replying. The stone underneath the chalked circle shattered with a snap.

Darius,

I'm sorry, but I can't keep going as I am now.

I'm not meant for this role.

When you receive this, inform the King that he needs to disavow me publicly. I'm done being subtle, I lack the patience for politics. I'm no longer your apprentice, mage, or even a citizen of Arden. I love my country, but I can't bear its chains any longer.

--Mage

Chapter 16

Warding the Palace

The morning after they arrived from the coast, she began warding the palace. She'd expected to argue with the King's advisers, but the Prince had stood up for her work and backed the suggestions she'd made along with opening the royal vaults to her use for the gems and metals needed. The palace was emptying for the summer, and they cleared the halls while she worked.

The continuous casting was exhausting. She worked at night to keep the changes a secret, but a wide-eyed trio of guards and one of the king's advisers followed her about as she made the steady lines of carved runes and decorative scrollwork that would disguise the spell work. I filled each carving with metal and gems to anchor the spells and collect ambient magic to help recharge the spell and strengthen its protections passively. During the day when she wasn't asleep she was working on charms, pendants, and jewelry that the Prince and Princess could wear while still being protected.

"When do you expect to finish?" Prince Zyon asked once she stepped back from a section of wall.

"One moment," Beryl muttered, mind still trapped in the spell as she started on the arched doorway next to them, inlaying the gold, quartz, garnets, and amethysts as far as she could reach without a ladder.

"Go fetch a ladder for the mage." He ordered one guard, waving off his stuttered protest, "How else is she supposed to reach the top of the arch?"

"She's been magicking the stones there, sir."

"Magicking them?" He repeated with a hint of a smile, "I will have to see that to believe it."

Beryl grinned and started the soft chant to lift the stones from one hand to the vaulted arch above them. Soft golden lines of magic caged each gem and slowly raised them to the stone, fitting them into the waiting slots. Only when the last gem was anchored and linked to the growing layers of spell work did she turn to the prince.

"Something I can help you with, your royal highness?" She asked, biting back a smile and raising an eyebrow at the man's stunned expression.

"Would a ladder have been easier?" He asked, smoothing his expression as he examined the archway.

"Yes, but one wasn't offered, so I worked with what I had available." She sighed with a shrug, turning to look down the next stretch of hallway.

"When do you expect to finish?"

"By the end of the week, once I finish the halls tomorrow night, I'll ward the inner rooms and connect them to the base wards circling the foundation."

"Those are already laid?"

"Yes, I did the foundation first since I needed light to get everything aligned." She said with a slight smirk, "I doubt the King would have wanted me wandering the grounds at night with several torch bearers or mage lights hovering about me."

"It would rather have destroyed the illusion of secrecy we have going." He said with a snort, "Half the court knows you're working on a project for the royal family and the other half know something is being done to the wing since their servants have been refused entry."

"Why keep it secret at all if it's a futile exercise?" She asked, moving on and kneeling to start the next section near the floor, "Why not say you're using the spell work to test various mages for the open court position? It would give you a reason to have people working in the halls while also examining their work for future projects."

"You are wasted as a mage." The Prince huffed with a laugh, seeming to surprise himself, "Why did you leave Arden, you're too powerful a mage to have just been thrown away no matter what the rumors are."

"Why do you think?" She asked, stalling as she eyed the guards even as her hands shaped the gestures needed to engrave the next several feet.

"Give us a bit of room, please." The prince intoned, giving the guards a hard stare until they'd shuffled more than just a few steps away, moving to the end of the hallway. "Do I need to ask again?"

"I couldn't stay after my bond mate died. They offered me the chance to work as a spy for Arden, but that's not to my temperament. I'm not a subtle person who wears masks and deceives with words. I prefer to be in the thick of the action." She sighed standing and moving down the wall starting the next segment of engraving with one hand while the other fitted stone in the waiting holes, "I don't think your country is looking to endanger Arden but there is something brewing here that I may assist with."

"My father said you were a poor spy if that was what they had sent you as. You stand out like a bonfire on a moonless night. No one could look at you and think you a powerless girl."

"Too many have," Beryl said with a cynical chuckle, "most simply seek to use my power for their own purposes, at least at your court I'm being paid for my work."

"You weren't paid in Arden?"

"Magic there is at the order of the King. He controls where a mage works, who they are apprenticed to, where you can sell your wares. The laws are rarely enforced outside of wartime, but they are still there. All magic flows from the King at his discretion."

"That's not how Orlean uses its mages." He said with a frown, watching her work in silence for a time, "You weren't paid for your work?"

"As an apprentice to a court mage, all my wages went to my Master. They gave me a stipend to live off of, but I made no money until they placed me as a mage by the King. Once I was given my placement, all new spells had to be approved by the Mage's Counsel before they could be used or sold. The Counsel approved every object before I could sell it and often they kept the best pieces for themselves, paying a pittance of the actual value."

"No one argued with this?"

"Some apprentices thought it unfair, but there was little we could do about it." She shrugged, "Plus the nobler your blood, the better your placement and favors you received when you graduated. I was from a minor family with no title and little money, most outside of my father were merchants and fishers. My father didn't believe in the rules imposed by the Counsel and was reprimanded several times for warding villages or houses for no pay simply because they needed the work."

"Your father was a mage, I take it?"

"Yes, not a well-known or powerful one, but a mage all the same. It ran in his family, but he was all but disowned after marrying my mother." They had reached the next archway, and she fell silent as she placed the next handful of stones and started the spell to carve the decoration into the archway.

"I didn't realize you disliked your home country so."

"I don't," Beryl sighed, "I love my home. I just chafe at the restrictions. I chafe at the restrictions your country places on women. Arden fares better their at least."

"How so?"

"A woman may own and run a shop or business if she has the coin and the determination. They may travel alone if they wish and shop by themselves without censure." She said dropping her hands from the wall and turning to face the prince, "When I went into town alone they refused me purchases because I lacked an escort, they refused me tables and seats at the inns and cafes. They catcalled me on the streets near the docks because the only thing a woman alone can might be is a whore. Why do you deny half the population of your own country a voice and a chance at a prosperous life?"

"Surely you were offered an escort when you left the grounds?"

"I was, that isn't my point." She sighed, turning back to the next section of wards. "I shouldn't need one. Does a man need an escort when he goes to town to make a purchase or to eat at a local inn? Does a man require for his every action to be done by a relative or husband? How many women here have married simply because they can't have a productive life without some man to stand for them?"

"Arden doesn't protect its women?"

"You consider being confined protection?"

"I wouldn't call it confinement."

"It's a restriction you place on all women in your society. I consider that a confinement as ridged as a prison. If I can't live a life on my own, how can I ever want to share it with someone else without resenting their freedom?" She asked, retrieving her bag and gathering the gems she needed for the arch while the prince looked on.

Beryl continued on her work, finishing the hall and starting the next before the Prince gave her a curt bow and continued on his way without another word. She watched him stride away, trying to decide if the force of his gait was fueled by frustration or anger. It didn't matter; she pushed on, finishing the last hallway at dawn before retiring to her rooms.

The next afternoon she started work on the Princess Noemi's rooms. The girl sat at a table nearby, watching from the corner of her eye as the mage worked while presumably looking over the selection of jewelry that Beryl had crafted. Her lady-in-waiting hovered nearby, wide eyed and flittering about the rooms while two guards moved the furniture away from the walls to allow her room to work.

"There you are," Prince Zyon said, coming in and waving away the guard who announced visitors, "are you trying to convert my daughter to your outlandish ways as well?"

"Mage has been showing me the jewelry she designed and warding my rooms." Noemi huffed, "What is she supposed to be converting me to? Magical studies?"

"Our line doesn't have an ounce of magic, it would be a waste of time." He said waving off the very idea.

"My father's family were non-magical, I wouldn't write it off unless they have tested her for talent." Beryl hissed as she stood, twisting to stretch her back, "Some children show no signs of magic at all until the mandatory testing at age ten."

"I'll bet you're testing was off the charts." He huffed glare intensifying when she refused to rise to the prodding.

"They never tested me, I didn't receive formal training until I was fifteen." She said absently gathering her bag and moving it further down the wall she was working on.

"What?"

"It was common knowledge in Arden," She said glancing between the father and daughter as she dug out the next packet of gemstones, "my parents died when I was young and I was given to an uncle to raise, he never had me tested."

"Then how did you become a mage?"

"My uncle had me warding homes and small villages for money," She sighed, stuffing the handful of gems into a pocket, "word started getting around of a hedge mage who was placing wardings that even experienced mages couldn't crack. Eventually the King sent several troops to either detain me or being me in to be fined for using magic without the King's approval. Instead, I was brought to the palace for healing and placed with a Master Mage in Cardu to study."

"But you can't be over twenty," The prince sputtered, glancing between her and his daughter.

"I'll be nineteen in the fall." She said primly before turning back to the princess, "Do you like any of the designs, Princess?"

"Yes, all of them are lovely and would work with my outfits for traveling or the ball when we reach the Summer Palace." She said happily, picking up one cuff bracelet to hand to her father, "Who does your dresses? I don't thing I've ever seen that style."

"This?" Beryl flushed, her cheeks burning. She smoothed the grey linen, "I have ordered several dresses and outfits through Lady Bonheur's tailor, but I made this one myself."

"You keep dipping your hands into the skirts, are there pockets? I can't see any bulges or wrinkles."

"There are slits in the overskirt letting me reach pockets I added to the lining." She said reaching into one and pulling out a pair of gloves she'd shoved there out of habit more than need.

"How wonderful! I might have to commission something from you. Are you making them for others or only yourself?"

"I hadn't considered selling the clothes I was making," Beryl said blinking, "I have some jewelry and a few enchanted items I was hoping to market but not clothes. Most of the tailors in Arden belong to guilds. I wasn't sure if I'd have to apply to a guild here to make the sales or have someone offering the items for me considering you don't allow women to own their own shops."

"That was what I was talking about," The prince snapped, "don't pollute my daughter's head with such nonsense."

"How is it nonsense to think a woman should be on equal standing as a man?" Beryl asked absently, unbraiding her hair and redoing it into a tighter braid. She hated when it frizzed into her face while she was working.

"Is this about me being tested for magic?" Noemi asked, glancing between the two of them uncertainly.

"No," Beryl said, resisting the urge to roll her eyes even as the Prince snarled, "yes."

"Changing the subject," Beryl sighed, "the jewelry is already warded, pick which ones you like and return the rest to me later. If you want a dress, I'll need your measurements and a dress form made in your size."

"Noemi, if you wish to be tested for magic I'll arrange it with one of the mages," the prince said after a long silence his tone stern, "however if you test as having ability you'll have additional lessons added to your day."

"I would like that, father." She said voice soft as she glanced between the two of them, "If I show potential will you be teaching me, Mage?"

"Oh, no." Beryl sputtered, ignoring the relieved look that flashed over the prince's face for an instant, "I don't teach, I'm afraid, and much of Orlean's magic leans towards illusions which I've yet to master. You'd do better starting with a local mage who can tutor you in the basics first."

"I'll send the payment for the jewelry to your rooms once she's chosen." He said stiffly, "I didn't think you'd be able to complete them before the move to the palace."

"I called in a few favors to get a small workbench together. It's not as intricate as I can do, but it's an excellent base design to work from if you want anything changed." Beryl said turning back to the waiting work, "I'll get back to work on the wards, I should have the princess' rooms done tonight and be finished by the end of next week."

"Wonderful, I'll inform the King of your progress." He said giving her a quick bow before turning back to his daughter, "Don't stay up too late or bother Mistress Mage. I expect you to be at your best tomorrow during lessons."

"Yes, father." Noemi said returning the bow he gave her with a deep curtsy as he left the room.

"Will it distract you if we talk?" She asked once the door closed behind the prince.

"No, but I might need to ask for silence when I'm linking wards or if I need to chant." Beryl said with a soft laugh, pulling out the gems and placing them into the pattern, "What do you want to talk about?"

"You said you enchanted objects, what did you make?"

"It may seem silly but I needed something to test patterns and stitches in the fabrics I was using before I tried to make a full dress so I made toys, simple dolls and animals that are enchanted to do minor tasks."

"What kind of animals?"

"I made a black velvet bear for Lady Bonheur. She's been showing it off at several small teas and parties, and I have orders for five more to be made once I'm set back up at the summer palace. I've also made several small cats, dogs, and a horse. I can bring them tomorrow if you like?"

"Oh, yes. I would like to see them. What did you enchant them to do?"

"Just minor things, walking in circles, dancing a few steps, acting like a dog or cat, wagging a tail, things like that."

"*I can bring one.* " Argent rumbled, getting to his feet and wandering to the door.

"*Be careful,* " She sent back with a rush of affection across the bond. The animals were not liking her change in hours any more than she did, but they gamely came with her each night.

"Do you mind letting him out?" Beryl asked the guard by the door, "He will fetch one toy for the princess to see."

"If I have magic, do you think I could have a pet like yours?" Noemi asked moving to sit on the couch near where Rune was curled on the arm, "Would he let me pet him?"

"His name is Rune and you can pet him as long as he tolerates it, he's rather grumpy with the hours we've been keeping." Beryl said smiling as Rune allowed a few small pets before stretching with a grunt and giving the child a head-butt before jumping down to find a quieter place to nap. "You might not want a bond mate. The mages I've met here so far dislike the idea, some in Arden did."

"Why?"

"It's not just having a pet." Beryl said, leaning back and watching as they let Argent back in with two dolls in his mouth, "It binds them to you, mind, body, and magic. You are never apart. It's seen as a weakness by many."

"Do you think it's weakness?"

"No, they're my strength, my love, my honor. They are the reason I get through each day and sleep at night. Without them, I would be nothing." Beryl said hugging Argent to her and rubbing his ears when he dropped the dolls next to her side and rested his head on her shoulder, "They are the missing halves of my soul I never knew I was missing. It is considered weakness because we share the good and the bad. Pain, fear, injury, and death, all of it is shared."

"Pain, fear, and death." Beryl repeated straightening and picking up the slim cloth doll in a dress similar to her own, activating the charm and watching the doll twirl and dip for a moment, "This is Bridget, I spelled her to dance."

"And the other?" Noemi asked sliding to the floor and sprawling on her stomach, hands holding her chin while she watched the doll curtsy and start a new dance ignoring the soft rebuke from her lady-in-waiting like the child she actually was for once.

"This one is a wolf or dog, I haven't named it. It walks, howls, and pounces." Beryl said activating the wolf, "Walk to her."

"It listened to you!" Noemi crowed, snatching up the doll into her lap as it reached her, frowning when it went still, "How do you make it work?"

"Touch the gem on its collar and give it a simple command. It will stop when the command is finished or when it's picked up." Beryl said standing and moving back to the wall to finish the wards while the princess played enraptured with the two dolls.

It wasn't much longer before they led the Princess yawning to bed. That room had been warded first and as heavily layered with spells and wards as Beryl could manage. Only the Prince's rooms were left to be worked on in the next few days. King Lyon would stay here through the summer and his were the only rooms Beryl wouldn't touch, he'd flat out refused the designs she'd offered.

* * *

The king gestured her forward, already going back to his correspondence, "Mage, come in. We already have the model set up and ready for your additions. Master Mage Rogen will review your work once you complete it."

"Pleasure to meet you, Master Rogen." She said with a brief bow, noting the sneer of disgust at the cat riding her shoulder.

"Is this necessary, my liege? There are other master mages more than willing to take on this project at your command."

"I am sure Mistress Mage is more than up to the task."

"Do you have any restrictions to what I do to the models?" She asked as she paced around the model town, eyeing the angles and height of the buildings.

"Surely you would rather know the requirements?" Master Rogen asked, raising an eyebrow.

"Both are equally important." Mage said with a distracted smile at the older mage.

"Play nice, Rogen." The king huffed, ringing for a page, "The wards should protect from damage. What you wish to ward against and how it is done is up to you, Mage."

"I'm allowed to move and change things as I see fit?"

"As long as it does not remove the structures."

"Have this model moved to the Mage's rooms." He instructed the page as they trotted in.

"Was there anything else you require, my liege?" Rogen asked, giving the king his full attention.

"No; thank you, Rogen."

"Have a good evening, my liege." He said, ignoring Beryl as he swept past and out of the room.

"Master Rogen is the top of his field, Mistress Mage. He has served as my magical advisor for decades. I hope to see a similar dedication to your craft if you wish to stay at court."

"I will not disappoint you, sire."

"See that you don't. You won't find much sympathy from any other mages should you fail. Loyalty is prized above all here in Orlean."

"In Arden, loyalty is earned."

"On that we can agree. Prove yourself, Mage, or find another master to serve."

* * *

"I take it the model is complete?" The king asked, wandering around the small tabletop of miniature buildings, "Are you satisfied, Rogen?"

"I will be satisfied once the tests are complete, my liege."

"The model is yours to test, Master Rogen. I'm sure it will exceed your expectations." Mage said, giving the other mage a slight bow.

"You seem to have conserved your strength in the ward's contraction." Master Rogen intoned, examining the weakly glowing lines of power.

"Subtlety is often an overlooked skill when it comes to casting, I find."

"We shall see what wards did you use?"

"The king has the full list. It wouldn't be a genuine test of my abilities if I told you how to counter the enchantments."

"She has a point, Rogen." The king said giving the older mage a sharp look when he looked like he would object, "we will test her work, the same as any other court mage."

"As you say, my liege. Allow me to have the model moved so we won't disturb you with our casting."

"Will others be testing the model?" Mage asked, keeping her face neutral. The more mages that tried to cancel the wards, the stronger they would become.

"We will give every mage at court the chance to verify your construction, Mistress Mage. Many are eager to pit themselves against foreign magics to prove Orlean's supremacy."

"I am happy to provide the challenge, Sire. I hope to learn as much about Orlean's magic during me stay as the other court mages do from my efforts."

"You may find that Orlean is not as willing to share." Master Rogen sniffed, "Some lessons must be experienced, simple book learning won't get you far in our brand of magics."

Chapter 17

Discussions

"Why do you dislike our society?" Prince Zyon asked from his sprawl to one side of the room, eyes sharp as he surveyed her work.

"I don't dislike your society, I dislike the burdens it places on the women who live in it." Beryl said, biting back the sharp retort she wanted to make. She was exhausted, and the Prince had been watching her all evening while she worked, prodding her with questions and demanding explanations for each step of the warding.

"And you believe Arden is some virtuous paradise for women compared to Orlean?" he asked, sipping from a never empty goblet thanks to his personal servant who wandered through once an hour.

"I never said Arden was a paradise. Living in poverty or dangerous situations is less than ideal no matter where you live." She sighed, keeping her eyes on her hands, "Arden has its own issues, I've yet to live anywhere that didn't have some social rule designed to bring one sex or class down just to make another feel better about themselves."

"How did Arden bring the female sex down?" He asked, refilling his goblet. She was certain he was drunk at this point.

"It was less than here. It allows women to own businesses, join guilds, and do the same work as men in any industry. However, there was pressure to marry, especially for mages."

"Especially for mages? How?"

"Families want magic in their bloodline." Mage said flatly, turning away and starting the next section of warding, she'd have to wait until tomorrow to do the final casting to link the hallways and rooms together.

"So they encouraged minor mages to marry to pass on their magic into a family."

"It wasn't just minor mages, I received constant offers while I was at the palace. Thankfully, those offers had to come through my Master and he refused them on my behalf. If you received a bad Master Mage, they had the power to betroth you to the highest bidder. It was an antiquated practice, but it was still done. And it's possible here, a woman's chaperon is often her cousin or brother. They can arrange a marriage should the need arise."

"So neither country is better."

"Exactly what I've been saying." She sighed, starting the chant to move the gems to the top of the doorway she was warding.

"So what would be a suitable solution? It's tradition at this point for the older males of the family to run the household. Would you have me force that to change?"

"No, I just wish they had options." Beryl huffed once the spell was complete, turning to look at the Prince, "Do you have women who run away, disappear or turn up married to strangers?"

"Yes, it happens occasionally. Sometimes the family doesn't condone the marriage, sometimes the woman is willful and refusing to marry the man the family wishes."

"And some of those women are running to the only solution they have, a marriage to a stranger that gets them away from their family and out on their own. They are running for sanctuary." She gave a low chuckle, "Do you have religious orders who take in girls, refusing to allow them to marry?"

"Are you saying they're running to religion to escape an arranged marriage?"

"Not all of them, but there will always be a few who would rather devote their lives to some cause then to be forced to devote it to a man they didn't choose. I was considering joining the healers in Arden who function much the same at one time."

"You almost became a healer? Why, when you are so amazing at magic?"

"My Uncle was a cruel man, he would have sold me off into marriage if he'd known he could make a profit off it. I warded every room and bed I slept in to keep myself safe, wore spells like armor to keep away unwanted advances in the Inns we stayed at. I did everything I could to be unappealing and dangerous to the surrounding men, and they still tried."

"Surely they were punished..."

"I was a poor hedge mage who was still considered a child living in the poorest parts of towns or traveling from Inn to Inn warding towns. There will always be drunk men willing to try for what they might not take during the day. If my uncle had forced me I'd have been sold to as many of them as he could arrange each night to turn a profit, only my magic saved me from that. I was lucky that way."

"Why would your uncle do such a thing? Was he ever punished? A man like that caught harming children here would be put to the death."

"He eventually found me again in Cardu and tried to kidnap me. I never learned what his plans were for me, and I never cared to. They sent him to the mines to do hard labor. He's probably already dead."

"Good, I'd hate to send an envoy to Arden simply to ensure his death." He huffed, collapsing back into his chair.

"So you'd fight for me but not for the other desperate girls and women here in Orlean?" She asked in disgust, "Would you let me prove it?"

"Prove what? There are no women in Orlean who would be

subjected to such things." He muttered, taking a drink from his goblet.

"Do you ever go out in disguise?"

"Rarely, why?" He asked, glancing up in confusion.

"Go out with me tomorrow, be my escort for the day. No royal carriages or gold jewelry, just a middle class woman and her escort out for a day of shopping and a light meal." She offered fiddling with a gem.

"It won't change anything."

"Then you enjoy a day outside of the palace and its royal pressures in my company. Consider it a holiday if you must." She said waving off his reply and turning back to her work.

"I'll go if you agree to never discuss this matter with me or my daughter again."

"Fine." Beryl huffed, biting back the comments she wanted to heap on him as Argent growled lowly behind her, "I'll see you before lunch. Enjoy the rest of your night."

"Aren't you going to finish warding the room?"

"I ward the room, I just need to link it to the underlying spells. I can do that tomorrow night." She said giving him a short curtsy, "Pleasant dreams, your royal highness."

Chapter 18

Out on the Town

"Mistress Mage and her companion, Argent." The guard at the door announced as Beryl made her way into the Prince's rooms the next morning.

"It is much too early for this foolishness." The prince huffed, tugging at the cuffs of his suit.

"At least you dressed for the part, I was afraid I'd have to borrow clothes from the staff for you." Beryl said taking in the tailored if understated clothes the prince was wearing.

"Are we taking the mutt as well? Surely that would defeat the purpose of going in disguise."

"We're not hiding who I am, we're hiding you. No one will be honest while speaking to a man that can order them killed with a snap of his fingers." Beryl sighed, fighting the urge to rub her temples, "I've arranged for a coach to bring us to the markets near the docks."

"I'm not a despot." He snarled.

"I never said you were, but very few people will be anything but polite to their royal family. I want you to see how people act when they don't have to bow and scrap the second you walk in a room."

"No one bows or scrapes!"

"Really?" She asked as the guards saluted their passing even with the disguise and the doorman gave a deep bow murmuring, "Your royal highness,"

"You are infuriating." The prince snarled.

"Good, it will do you good to have someone to bark at occasionally." She said gesturing for Argent to proceed her into the carriage.

"I have plenty of people to bark at," He snapped, straightening his vest and cuffs, "I wasn't aware that both of the animals were going. Are you certain we'll all fit?"

"We'll fit fine," Mage said, turning as she climbed in, "you may have people to argue with you but do they always give you their honest opinion?"

"No one always gives an honest opinion."

"I try to baring being polite, some opinions would do nothing but hurt the other party so those I keep but the rest are there for anyone who bothers to ask. It's amazing how few people actually want to know what a person thinks."

"I don't care to know everyone's opinion, I hear enough opinions from my generals and advisers." He sniffed.

"But they are jockeying for position or power and working for the benefit of Orlean." Beryl said gathering Rune to her as Argent stuffed himself into one corner of the bench half over her legs, "I don't care for position or power, I wish to live as I can with my bond mates. If that means I live poor then that is what I'll do."

"You would abandon your titles and duties?"

"I have no position or titles. I'm an exiled Mage living here under the protection of the crown. For that protection I'll assist you with what magics I have at my disposal but not if it means causing others pain. I'm cursed so that no one can even remember my name much less a title anyway, I have no power outside of your court but I'm willing to leave and search for a different home if it means keeping myself and my bond mates safe."

"I don't understand you at all."

"Nor I you, Prince Zyon." Beryl said with a weary laugh, "What should I call you while we are out today?"

"My middle name is Tobias, I went by Tobi as a child. You may call me that." He said heaving a breath and glaring at where Argent was panting against her shin, "What should I call you?"

"You can call me whatever you like," Beryl said, turning to look out the window as they left the palace grounds and their thick forests giving way to fields of crops.

"Surely you have a name?" He sputtered, "Oh, you were serious about being cursed that first day? Everyone thought it was a quirk or you wishing to abandon your name along with your country."

"If it's merely a quirk, then what was the name I told you that night?"

"I can't remember, it was several months ago." He said waving it off with a frown.

"How about what the reports from Orlean called me?"

"They called you Mage, we were never sure why."

"I was attacked and cursed as a child. The healing sealed the curse so it couldn't be removed. No one can remember my name and no one can remember me speaking of the attack or who attacked me."

"They never caught the person who hurt you?" He asked with a frown sitting up from his slouch.

"No, he was a minor noble in Arden, he was the one who attacked the castle in Cardu a year ago."

"And no one believed it because of your curse?"

"Well, it was thought that he had no magic. I've since learned he's using the attacks to steal magic from children."

"But you still have your magic."

"The spell didn't work on me, so he scarred and cursed me instead." Beryl said pulling off a glove and showing the Prince one scarred palm, "I kept my magic but lost my name. When I was young, the spell was so strong I'd be forgotten if anyone lost sight of me. It has weakened a little, as I've aged at least."

"They assumed the gloves and sleeves were a part of Arden fashion." He murmured.

"It makes people uncomfortable, so I hide what I can." She said with a shrug.

"I can't imagine having to fight to be remembered," He murmured, "how old were you when you were attacked?"

"Five. It took almost a year for me to be considered healed. They sent me to live with my uncle when I was eight. At least by then I was already learning minor magics and knew the basic runes for small protection wards."

"What are you hoping to show me at the docks? I'm aware of the perils of poverty and squalor." He huffed, shifting in his seat.

"Perhaps you are, but do you know why your laws make it twice as hard for a woman to live on her own?"

"I'm sure you will explain it even if I don't."

"I went shopping without an escort because I've never needed one before." Beryl said reaching down to rub Argent's ears, "In Arden I lived with my Master once they apprenticed me, but I took care of myself. I traveled alone, I went shopping alone, and I dealt with traders for the materials my Master needed alone. Before when I lived with my Uncle I was still alone. If I wanted food or a room to sleep in then I had to buy it myself. He did nothing for me except to arrange for have me ward different small towns so he could cheat them out of as much coin as possible. I never saw a coin of money from that work. I worked in laundries, ran errands, and did whatever else I could to make enough money to keep myself off the streets from the age of eight on. I have never needed a companion or guardian to do those things for me, and yet your shopkeepers won't let me buy even a single biscuit without a man handing over the money I worked for."

"You had no one help you in Arden?"

"I worked for what I have, Tobias." She said keeping her eyes on the passing countryside, "That doesn't mean I never had help. Some towns had kind people who gave me meals when I didn't have the coin or a few pennies more for the work I did but I also had people refuse to give me even a copper at the end of a day's hard work because I refused to let them use me as they would. No one is purely good or bad in their actions, everyone has a motive even if it's just to save themselves."

She fell silent, and the Prince didn't comment, settling back into the cushions as they swayed down the road to town. He watched her in silence and she tried to ignore his gaze. It was only as they came to a stop and he gestured her to step down first that he finally spoke.

"I'll call you Meg." He said, watching with a wince as Argent lumbered out of the carriage.

"Any reason?"

"I knew a Meg once, she was one of the most annoying suitors I had as a young man."

"Fair enough," She laughed, "your arm, good sir. We need to at least look like we're together."

"If you insist, my lady." He said giving her a short courtly bow before taking her arm and leading her at a stroll into the crowded market.

"What did you dislike so much about her?" she asked, smiling at a vendor selling bags of roasted nuts and handing Zyon a coin, "Buy me a bag, Cousin? The ride has left me famished."

"As you wish, Cousin Meg." Zyon said with a put-upon sigh buying two small sacks and handing her one along with her change as they moved away, "She was very into appearances, nothing could clash or distract from the picture she was trying to present."

"Such as?" she murmured, eating a nut and blowing on a second to cool it enough for Argent.

"We had to wear matching clothes, agree on anything discussed while with anyone else. There could be no deviation. It drove me mad."

"You don't like being controlled, few people do." She murmured before turning to a ribbon seller and starting a debate on price and lengths. The merchant clucked at her before turning to Zyon with an expectant look.

"I'm making the purchase, sir." Beryl said, keeping her voice and face mild as the merchant ignored her.

"She'd quite decisive, sir." The man said with a chuckle, "What will you be buying today?"

"Whatever the Lady wishes." Zyon said with a frown, "She is the one making the purchase."

"Oh, I wouldn't take the poor woman with such tasks. Perhaps the blue velvet?"

"I'm interesting in the ivory." Beryl said, watching as the prince's temper rose.

"What about you, sir, the green is very feting on a woman of her coloration?" the merchant wheedled.

"She wishes to see the ivory." Zyon said stiffly, glancing at her with a frown.

"Sir." The merchant said with a frown, offering him a length of ribbon to examine without a glance at her.

"I believe we'll take our business elsewhere," Zyon muttered, pulling Beryl away from the booth and hurrying them down the lane.

"Don't rush so, we are just two young cousins on a shopping trip." She murmured, tugging her arm from his bruising grip.

"That man was an idiot."

"He's the worst I've encountered so far, but none will take money from a woman or allow them to choose what to purchase. This way." She said catching his elbow and pulling him down a small lane and into a small square where a woman sat with a begging bowl at her feet.

"A copper for the name of somewhere nearby with excellent food?" Beryl offered, stepping away from Zyon to kneel near the woman.

"The Copper Pot down the lane, the rooms are overpriced, but the food is fresh and the dishes clean." The woman said not looking up as Beryl dropped two copper pennies in the bowl, "Thank you, Lady."

"I have a second offer, one that you are welcome to turn down." Beryl said, placing a silver coin in the bowl.

"I don't whore and I won't let any man strike me no matter the coin." The woman said fiercely, meeting Beryl's eyes.

"I wouldn't ask either of you," Beryl said, drawing out another silver, "I'm not from Orlean, I've never seen women treated so badly without some reason. It happens even where I'm from, but not to every woman. Some can make their way out of poverty without a man's help. They own businesses, work for their coin with their hands and not lying on a bed."

"What are you asking?"

"Come to the inn and have a meal with us. Answer some questions for my friend so he understands what I mean. No tricks, we share a meal and part ways, and you gain another silver."

"And leave me with the prince of the meal? I'm not feebleminded." The woman spat, wrapping her arms around her ribs.

"No, we'll be paying for the meal and room to eat it in first. We won't leave you hanging with the bill."

"And if I say no?"

"I leave you with your silver and walk away to make my offer to someone else." Beryl said, mentally sending Argent to stay near Zyon.

"Why did you choose me? You passed three others begging the way you came."

"Two were faking injuries and would have tried to lure us to a handy alley to take whatever else we carried, and the third was a young man in a dress trying to con the travelers who pass through the docks. You asked for nothing when you need it more."

"Why would I need it more?"

"Because you are a woman without a man in a country that refuses to allow women to do business. You can't even buy day old bread on your own, half of what you earn goes to someone else to make the purchase for you."

"A meal and nothing else?" the woman finally asked when the silence had dragged on.

"Just a meal and some talk," Beryl said, helping the woman stand, "go secure a room for us, Cousin Tobias."

"He's your cousin?" She asked as he hurried away, Argent at his heels like an obedient dog, tucking her coins in a small pouch, "Posh toffs like him don't mingle about the docks much."

"A distant cousin, his family is from here." Beryl said with a grin, "I'm determined to rub some of his polish off before I leave."

"You dress well but you spotted those shames easily, what's your story?"

"I grew up part of a merchant family but my parent's died, I went to live with my Uncle who didn't bother with much so I worked for every bed and bite of bread for years until I found my trade. Now I sell my wares to the like of his class." She said with a nod at where Zyon was waiting for them down the lane, "I hate how he's blind to the people below his station, he needs to see a bit without getting his pockets fleeced."

"So you're letting him dangle his toes to the sharks, but keeping an eye out in case the idiot falls in?"

"Exactly," Beryl laughed, giving Zyon a smile as he got the door, "thank you good, sir."

The staff must have been warned because no one said a word as she led the older woman to the back of the tavern and into the private room though the few loitering drunks watched with anticipation of the potential brawl and sagged disappointed when Zyon stalked past them. Zyon was still fuming as he fussed with things on the table, so the owners or drunks must have been rather crude while he made arrangements.

"You were correct that they overprice the rooms." He said stiffly, pulling out a chair for each of them to one side of the table before taking a seat on the opposite side.

"And they made some insulting connotation given your attitude."

Beryl chuckled, picking up a knife and slicing the heavy bread deftly while the prince watched.

"They informed me that there was to be no fornication in the dining room, we'd have to purchase a room for that."

"How blunt of them," Beryl said with a put-upon sigh as she doled out slices of bread, continuing in a sickening sweet chirp as the first slice set near the other woman disappeared into a pocket, "It's such a pity there will be no fornication or even mild drunken fondling as we have no alcohol."

"I wouldn't recommend the wine, from what I saw on the tables."

"You need to gain a sense of humor." Beryl sighed, falling silent as the door opened and their meal was laid out, a thin soup, boiled vegetables, and a greasy slab of roast steaming on the platter.

"You can carve, dear Cousin." He said eying the knife with a smirk as he took a portion of vegetables.

"What can we call you, Miss? I'm Meg and this is my cousin, Tobias." Beryl asked, taking up the knife with a shrug and cutting them each a portion before setting her plate on the ground where Argent could eat. She would be fine with just soup.

"You can call me Mary, the street boys call me Sister Mary since I give them pennies when I can."

"Kind of you," Zyon murmured, and Beryl bit back another sigh, taking up her spoon to sip at the thin soup.

"What did you do before you lived on the streets?" She asked, thinking of her own times on the street growing up.

"I was engaged to marry a baker. He was a quiet man, but the shop was pleasant and I enjoyed helping with the baking in my father's inn. It could have been a pleasant life." Mary said firmly.

"Did he turn you away?"

"Yes, after my father died, the money for my dowry went to the funeral expenses and to pay off his debts." She said stopping to eat for a moment, Beryl let the silence hang until she continued, "The Inn went to some cousin I'd never met, they sold it out from under me without even a letter or ever having seen the place. Ret demanded his ring back since I had no dowry and married someone else within the month. I left that town as soon as I could, I ended up here begging for whatever I can once the little I'd saved from the creditors was gone."

"You can't find work?" Beryl pressed, hating that she was forcing the woman to spill out the details of her troubled life to prove a point.

"No one will take a woman without a man to vouch for her. I've found a few minor jobs doing laundry or sewing, but no inn or house wants a woman with no references as a cook."

"What is your best recipe?" She asked since Zyon seemed determined to ignore the both of them while picking at his meal.

"Have you had rolled cakes yet? It's a local tradition in the winter." Mary said, eyes lighting up, "Oh, they can be lovely, light with lemon and berries or heavy with cream and chocolate. You must try one before you leave, Miss."

"It sounds wonderful," Beryl nodded, "did you run a house as well, or was it mostly cooking and baking?"

"I ran my father's house and tended to his books and the Inn as he got older. He'd had a nasty fall and wasn't able to help often, but he always tried to do what he could. He finally gave in to a cold during a dreadful winter. The Inn wasn't taking in much, and I was doing what I could to keep things in line, but even the hired help often refuse to listen to a woman's orders."

"I'd say you are more than qualified to work." Beryl said, glancing at Zyon before turning back to Mary when he continued to ignore them and adding a second piece of meat to her plate, "Tell me more about your cooking. The roll cake sounds wonderful."

Beryl left the woman with as much silver as she could spare, making sure she was safe and off the street before they left her. Zyon continued his silence as they made their way back to the docks and their waiting carriage. Beryl left it to him while listening to how Rune had spent the day watching the people on the docks and chasing a few mice. At least someone had a pleasant day, she thought, hoping that Mary could put the money to use and not have it cause more trouble.

* * *

"Thank you for coming, Mage. I have a task for you." King Laron requested, gesturing her to the chair next to his, "This must be done discreetly. Too much is as stake should things become public."

"What do you wish of me?" She asked, trying to keep the weariness out of her voice as she took a seat. The prince seemed more likely to acknowledge the rising danger now that they were in the North, but the King seemed just as determined to keep things quiet.

"You have shown your loyalty in diligently protecting my family." He said taking a sip of some herbal concoction that was scenting the surrounding air, "I would have you protect one more. He is the second in line to the throne and has received anonymous threats, much like the Prince and Princess. I will return to the coast soon and wish to see him protected before I leave."

"Do you wish more wards designed, you majesty?" Beryl asked hesitantly.

"Not unless you wish to outfit him with additional protections. I wish you to take him on as your apprentice. He has shown minor skill in magics, and I believe further training would improve the boy's potential."

"I am not seeking an apprentice, your majesty."

"I am aware. However, no one will look for a foreign mage in exile from her home country to train a royal bastard. He will be safer with you than any protection I can offer. To do so would expose his heritage and force his enemies and mine to act." He said giving into a coughing fit, one hand covering his mouth.

"Apprenticeships in Arden differ greatly from how mages are trained in Orlean." She said with a frown, watching an aid hurry in to give the man a handkerchief and exchange his tea for a fresh cup.

"You may train him as you wish, you will have full guardianship of him until his twenty-fifth birthday or when you declare him a full master mage." He said straightening up and waving away the servant.

"Is he aware of this arrangement?"

"He knows they have offered him an apprenticeship to a royal mage on scholarship. I will pay you handsomely to cover any costs he might accrue."

"I've yet to master Orlean's style of magic. I would teach him runic magic. Surely you would want him taught by a local mage?"

"I want him safe, even if it means his education will be broader than most would consider ideal. Will you accept this task?"

"Will the boy be able to refuse or to choose another master if we aren't an ideal match?"

"If in one year he is still unhappy, I will find a new Master to train him." The King huffed, "Will you accept him as your apprentice?"

"Yes, your majesty, if he accepts me as his master I will train and protect him."

"I will take my leave, he will join you in a moment." He said standing and leaning on one of his personal guard as he left the room.

"Your majesty," Beryl murmured, dropping into a deep curtsy until the door closed.

Chapter 19

Traveling to the Summer Palace

They were finally off for Alexandrea for a few days before heading to the Summer Palace inland in the much cooler northern plains. Already the heat in the coach was oppressive, even with the windows lowered. There wasn't a hint of breeze. Beryl was wearing a simple traveling dress, but even that was quickly soaked through as the journey seemed to go on and on.

The Prince had avoided her in the last few days she'd used to finish the wards and jewelry the Princess had requested. The King's advisors had tested the wards, trying to sneak poisoned items into the royal wing or sending tainted mail to be carried there by a servant. She felt sorry for the servants since the wards escalated each rebuff if it happened within the same day. No one deserved to have a package they were delivering burst into flames without warning.

She was traveling alone, but most of the carriages had four to five occupants wilting in the heat. They stumbled out onto the cobbles drunkenly when they finally stopped for a late lunch at someone's estate. Considering Argent took up the entire bench opposite her, it was for the best, she thought with a snort, imagining the horror of some ladies at the animal hair and dog slobber that would have liberally coated their skirts by the end of the ride. Striding quickly to the wood that edged the drive, she waited while her bond mates relieved themselves before heading inside. She accepted an iced drink and paper fan from the waiting servant and made her way behind the line of others to the ballroom for lunch.

"Eric," She said with a grin, offering her hand to the young man when he gave her a grin from where he was waiting to one side, "I'm glad to see a familiar face in this crowd. How are your studies going?"

"Mistress Mage, a delight to see you as always." He said with a laugh bowing over her hand, "My studies are progressing slowly but surely."

"Always the best kind of progress, I dread when I get blocked and become stuck on a problem for weeks. It can be maddening." She said with a smile, rubbing under Rune's chin.

"How are your bond mates doing? I see they are still at your side."

"Always, they never leave it if I can help it." She offered glancing away as the crowd moved around them, "Are you planning to continue your studies at the Summer Palace or will you be going with the group to Alexandria? I'm told the gardens are lovely this time of year."

"No, my Master has me working on a project and the libraries at the Summer Palace are extensive. I take it you are heading to Alexandria for a few days?"

"Yes, I'm looking at a few horses while I'm in the area and will stay there."

"I haven't heard if the libraries there are worth a visit, you must enlighten me when you return."

"I hope I have time to review them, most of my days will be riding and testing the paces of several horses being brought down." Beryl said with a sigh, mentally adding her search for trustworthy staff for her stay at the Summer Palace.

"You seem to keep busy, we haven't seen you in the salon." He said softly with a hint of rebuke.

"The King has decided to audition my services, I've been making enchanted objects for him to test."

"Are you considering the Court Mage position?"

"I'm not against it but I doubt they will want a foreign mage to hold it, better someone from Orlean who knows the local magics. Right now, I'm just trying to see what I can do to support myself."

"Support yourself?" Eric asked, blinking at her in shock, "Surely you have a patron?"

"Not yet. The royal family is willing to give me asylum, but I need to find a market for my skills on my own. Do the Mages here have their own guild?"

"Guild? No, nothing so formal. Most of the time a mage has a patron, a wealthy business owner who funds their projects and guides the mage to others who might be interested in their wares."

"So you don't market enchanted items in shops or pay for your lessons?"

"An apprenticeship must be purchased, but you stay with your Master until he deems you worthy of taking apprentices of your own. I doubt there'd be much business for enchanted items, they're seen more than novelties then anything worth a considerable amount. Most of the time we're hired out as entertainers or artisans. Those who can paint or sculpt are highly sought after."

"Artisans? What would your specialty be when you go out on your own?"

"I've still several years of work before I'll be granted leave, but I am strongest in enchanting instruments. My father was a violin maker, and they apprenticed me under him before I started showing signs of magic."

"Why have I never seen you with an instrument or playing?"

"The King refuses to have magical instruments on the grounds, he thinks they can sway emotions and ensnare those that listen. It bans even a mage playing a regular instrument." He said with a shrug, "I practice in the evenings at home."

"I have heard that magic can be cast while playing or singing, anyone power hungry enough could try to twist that magic to their own uses."

"No one would do such a thing." He huffed, offering her an arm as everyone lined up to head into the table.

"There are those willing to abuse others around them to gain power in every place I've visited, Orlean is no different. Even I'm being pushed back and forth to join a side. People see my magic as something that could bring them prestige and money. Even your friend Alex seems to jockey for a more noble title." She hummed in his ear, nodding at where the man was escorting a dark-haired beauty twice his age to the table.

"Alex is never satisfied with his position, he only wants to better his family name. He wouldn't harm anyone in the attempt."

"Perhaps not, but harm can happen even if he doesn't push for it. The blindly ambitious rarely consider the cost to those below them."

"You are too pessimistic, he's young and willing to play the field as they say." Eric huffed, "His family encourages it since he might marry well."

"And the hearts he breaks in the meantime?" She asked, directing his gaze to a mage they'd studied with before who had broken from her escort and was leaving the room at speed, "She won't see it as a simple dalliance."

"I'll try to get him to smooth things over," He sighed, "I think Alex only keeps me around to smooth the feathers he's ruffled. Not that any of them would ever look twice at me."

"Nonsense, you've had plenty of admiring glances today that I've seen."

"But you have cast none of them yourself. What would it take to catch your eye?"

"I'm not looking for romance, marriage, or even a dalliance." Beryl sighed, giving him a slight smile as they took seats next to each other towards the end of the table, "The timing is bad for me, ask me again if you are still wanting in a year. I need to find my feet here in Orlean before I consider taking anyone on as more than a friend, Eric."

"Not even the huntsman you met at the last hunt? The gossips have been working overtime on how you two talked for several hours." He said with a serious expression even as Beryl fought to stifle a bark of laughter.

"Mister Toussaint is a horse breeder, Eric. He's bringing several horses to the Summer Palace for me to try. I'm looking for something of an unusual mount since it has to be well trained and used to large dogs."

"Will you have more free time once you arrive? I was hoping to introduce you to a few of the Masters once they start lectures." He asked as the servers started making their way down the table with each dish.

"Yes, I'll still be working on a few things, but I will have time most evenings if you'd like to visit. I'm hoping to have more time for my studies, I'm still fighting with illusion spells for some reason." She said accepting a plate of salad with a murmur of thanks, "I wanted to ask you, is there a way to detect illusions?"

"Why would you want to detect illusions? They aren't permanent spells like your wards." He said waving the salad away and taking a plate of chicken when it passed by.

"Yes, but say I wanted to illusion over a stain on my sleeve. Would someone be able to see it was an illusion or see the stain beneath?" she asked, glad that she'd made sure to have a snack for the carriage for her bond mates. Even with that, they were drooling over the scents of the meal going on around them.

"Well, for a loose illusion you could see the wavering edges of the spell where the light bends. You've surely seen it while you practiced. How the edges look almost like steam rising?"

"Yes, but is there a way to remove that?"

"Not that I'm aware of, would you like me to look into it?" he asked, fiddling with his fork as he thought.

"No, it's just something I was wondering. I want to make spells permanent like wards are, I was trying to think of a way to anchor an illusion without having to constantly feed it magic." Beryl shrugged, "Call it an intellectual puzzle I was pondering."

"You could anchor an illusion to feed from a gemstone, but it would need to be massive and have to be refilled often to keep up the illusion. Even then you would still have the edges of the illusion showing, which would ruin the effect if you were going for something seamless." He offered with a sigh, "It would be complicated to set up and a waste of magic given the need to constantly replenish the gems. If they did, it would be tiny in scale."

"I might dabble with the idea anyway, it's an interesting puzzle." She hummed, "What does your master have you researching if I'm allowed to ask?"

"There are rumors of a crystal that nullifies magic. My master is determined to prove the rumor false."

"I heard about something similar in Arden." She murmured slipping Argent a bite of steak and then a second he passed to Rune, "It never came to anything but I'd be interested to know if you find out more."

"So far it's a dead end, everything I've found remarks on how various crystals are used for channeling magic, not removing it." He huffed a laugh, catching her dropping the next piece to one side, "Do you always have such unpleasant table manners?"

"Only when our hosts refuse to provide meals for my bond mates." Beryl said ignoring the soft laughter from around them, "I heard the crystals were dark colored but never saw one myself. I'll try to jog my memory, but that was almost two years ago now."

"I'd appreciate anything you can share, my master is rather determined and taking my lack of progress as a personal failing."

"Nonsense, he can't berate you if the information isn't there."

"I know, but he expects results, I knew that when I asked to become his apprentice." Eric said with a smile, "I wanted to be pushed to do my best."

"It's funny, mine just wanted me to experiment. I invented fifteen new spells that he licensed to the Counsel by the time I left. I'd made over thirty, but they didn't accept most of them."

"You invented new spells?" He sputtered, blinking at her in shock.

"All the time, I've even created customized runes I use in my wardings. Some are just enhanced variations of existing spells, but a few are mine alone."

"There hasn't been a spell crafter in Orlean in decades."

"You don't experiment? I wasn't aware it's forbidden."

"It's not forbidden, it's just rare." He said watching her for a long moment with a look she couldn't decipher, "My master refuses to let me try untested spells until he's reviewed the work, most of the time it's not worth his anger to suggest a change in the spell's formula. He considers such dabbling unnecessary and a waste of resources."

"They gave me things to research and study along with spells to master each week, but most of my free time was my own to use as I wished. I enjoyed experimenting with runes, so that is what I did." She murmured with a frown, "Is spell crafter a title?"

"A master mage can claim the title of spell crafter if they publish a volume on their work and they accept it into general use, but the King has given the title to a few mages."

"That may have to wait awhile then," She said with a grimace, "I've been told often enough that my writing needs improvement and my essays are worthless."

"That can't be true." He said with a laugh, wiping his mouth and setting down his utensils, a servant swept in to replace his plate with a bowl of frozen custard.

"When did you first have to write essays or explanations on magic?"

"I think around my tenth birthday, they tested me, and they hired a tutor? I can't be sure." He said with a shrug, "I take it you were different?"

"I learned to read and write, but I had little need to practice as a child. Once my parents died, I continued to read what I could, but I rarely wrote anything. I didn't start magical lessons until I was fifteen.

I taught myself magic and warding before that from books or just learning as I went."

"Fifteen? That can't be right." He sputtered, coughing as he snatched up his drink.

"I started casting runic magic at seven. I'd cast minor spells with my father before then but I was learning alone after that until I was fifteen and placed with my Master." Mage said sipping at her glass.

"Then you have no grounding in the basics, the classical forms, the ancient texts!"

"Master Darius insisted I cover as much as possible to catch up but there was too much to review, instead if I could prove that I could cast the required spell without issue and could explain my reasoning for deviating from the suggested runes or spell work then I could move on to the next lesson. I covered five years of work in a single year. It's amazing I even had time to breathe that year."

"That's impossible. You know the forms, I've seen you use some of them."

"If they helped me in what I was researching, they taught me them, if not I studied the basics and moved on." Beryl said with a shrug, "My life has never been stable enough for traditional lessons. I just learned to adapt."

"It still sounds impossible, but it worked since you're a Master Mage." Eric huffed, "Are you hoping to go back to what you missed?"

"That's some of what I'm studying, but I doubt I'll even catch up at this point. I'm just working on things I enjoy."

"Isn't that what all apprentices hope to do once they become a master?"

"They gave me my mastery for my inventions even though I was tested like the other students, I can't say I ever stopped doing what I love."

"Then you were luckier than most." He sighed, "There's no market for magical instruments at the moment so I'll be selling illusions as entertainment part time along with working with my father again."

"So you've kept up violin making?"

"Yes, I go back to my father's shop on vacations and try to keep my skills. I'd have to work full time to ever match my father's ability."

"Work doesn't have to be grand, you just have to be satisfied with what you do." Beryl mused, glancing at her bond mates, "I enjoy warding, I enjoy knowing I make people safe with that I do. I'd do it for whatever anyone paid me, I don't need a room at the palace or friends in the correct bloodlines to make me happy."

"Then what do you hope for? A simple cottage, a grand estate?" he asked, looking genuinely intrigued.

"A simple cottage, a few friends, and enough work to keep me busy. I've never ached to do more. Traveling and adventures are fun, but it's not how I want to spend all of my life."

"Would you ever go home?"

"You mean Arden? No, I don't think I will return. I'm uncertain I'll stay in Orlean yet, but I've grown fond of the area I've seen so far. Have you been to the North much?"

"My family live on the coast, but I've traveled some in the mountains and plains. You will like the forests, think. They are old and full of life, there are many herbs and plants that grow nowhere else I've been told. The wood my father uses comes from a high region of the mountains, I must find you a piece. It's black and red, it looks like marble when polished."

"That sounds lovely." Beryl hummed taking a bite of the custard and then setting her spoon aside, she couldn't get used to how sweet the desserts were here, "I've worked in wood but I'm better with stone. Have you ever tried to do elemental workings? I studied it a bit while I was under Master Darius. It's an excellent technique to train yourself to focus."

"Elemental, do you mean focusing on an element?"

"I mean focusing on the natural magic of a stone or piece of glass, focusing until you can feel the heat of its initial creation, the water as time molded it. It's calming sometimes to let the feel of something pull you to stillness."

"That's not something they have taught me, is it common in Arden?"

"Working with the elements is common, focusing on an element is used to help a novice see what elements they are drawn to. One of my friends was a fire affinity. She had spells constantly backfiring and exploding until she could learn control. She worked with glass and forged metals."

"And water affinity would work with what? Plants and wood?"

"Exactly, I can do a little with wood as well since my affinity is with stone or earth, but I've never stayed someplace long enough to try working with plants. One of my mentors had a sizable garden. Maybe I can try to grow a few things when I finally settle down." She murmured wistfully.

"I'd say start small, I'm afraid I have something of a black thumb." Eric said with a soft laugh, "My sister likes to give people plants as gifts and I've killed more of them then I can list. Perhaps you can talk to one of the gardeners at the Palace, they could give you a few tips."

"Perhaps, it's just a pleasant idea right now." Beryl said with a smile as they took away their dishes, "Are you going to stay or are you heading out again?"

"I'm staying, I take it you're heading out soon?"

"After a polite thank you to our hosts."

"A fair warning, the Lord Taavetti is not an admirer of magic or mages. I'd make it brief." He said with a grimace, standing and pulling her chair out for her.

"That I guessed by the table." Beryl said with a soft laugh, they'd been sat amongst the lowest ranking guests as far away from the hosts as they could go, "I hope to see you at the Summer Palace, Eric."

"As do I, Mistress Mage. Stay safe in your travels." He said giving her a brief bow and pressing a kiss to her knuckles.

Beryl gave her thanks to her hosts and made her way back to the waiting carriages. She was one of the few leaving and she ignored the feeling that she was being rushed out. She wanted to be away from the sneering nobility as much as they wanted her gone.

She wasn't sure what to do with Eric's proposal. She wasn't looking for romance, and in her mind she still ranked him as somehow younger than she was, even given his correct age as a few years her senior. He had a naïveté she was hesitant to tarnish, but she knew he wouldn't understand what she'd gone through in the years before they met.

Chapter 20

Alexandria

Beryl had to admit the gardens at Alexandria were wonderful, full of hidden sculptures and exotic flowers in full bloom. Even the kitchen herbs and garden were laid out in pleasing grids, drawing the eye here and there. The stable was smaller than at the palace but the rides were in her opinion nicer, in wide open fields or the old-growth forests that edged the estate to one side.

She spent her mornings setting up her household, had lunch with the royal family and then spent her afternoon riding or in the library on the few days the weather didn't cooperate. They had sent letters out to Count Malouel to ask for appointments with any staff he might refer her, and she'd also sent a sort note requesting the same to the local version of the thieves' guild. She wasn't expecting a flood of people to arrive, but each day a few arrived requesting an interview.

A letter of introduction had gotten her in contact with one, James Lark who passed on her requests and given her some basic information and expectations from the local guild. They thought her mad to order a bit of every poison available but the guild was more of a merchant organization with a side of black market trading then anything and they will offer goods for gold if she had the coin. She was certain they thought she would poison the royal family, but she needed the herbs, powers, and infusions to make sure none of it would get past her wards.

One person she'd hired without the appointment. Mary would man the kitchen at the Summer Palace cottage. She'd arranged for her to have one of the seven rooms at the "cottage" they had given her on the grounds, along with a bonus to spend on new clothes and free rein to order what she wanted for the kitchens. She should arrive in the North at the same time as Beryl if things went as planned, the rest of the staff would arrive soon after.

"Madame, there is a man here to see you. A Mister Jeremy Cannon, he says he is applying for a position in your household." The butler said stiffly as she finished the correspondence she was working on.

"Send him in, Grant." Beryl sighed, wishing she could dismiss the staff from her rooms at Alexandria. None were comfortable around her or her bond mates, and most disapproved of her methods and relaxed manners. It was another applicant from the guild, she'd sent the last four away the second they walked through the door. Only one had tried to protest, she'd broken his arm and flat out told him to warn the guild that if they sent another spy or rat into her house, she'd kill the next one.

"Thank you for seeing me, Ma'am." The man said giving her a short polite bow. His clothes were worn and wrinkled but clean with his overlong hair pulled back into a low neat tail.

"You're seeking a position in my household? What are your references and abilities?" she asked, keeping her tone mild. This wasn't a rat, this was a soldier who'd been hurt badly none too recently from the still healing marks on his face and hands.

"I have no letters of reference, Ma'am. I worked last as a stable hand for Lady de Campt before they dismissed me for drunkenness. Before that I was part of Count Russo's personal guard, I served for one year until his death." He said eyes on the ground. A thick scar twisted down one side of his face, making him seem to scowl.

"And before that?" She asked, gesturing him to a chair he ignored, keeping his ridged stance even as his bad leg trembled.

"I was a member of the Orlean Calvary until they forced me to retire because of an injury."

"What position are you seeking?" She asked, nudging her bond mates to come to the room. She wanted to see how he reacted to them.

"I can work as a personal guard or with your animals, I have experience with horses and I've heard you are looking to buy at least two for your household."

"I've already purchased one, which has been moved to the Summer Palace and will ride four more this week before we head north." Beryl agreed with a hum, glancing over at the man, "I have one question and I want an honest answer."

"Of course, Ma'am." He said with a quick nod, shifting his trembling hands behind his back. He was fresh off liquor and trying to force his way through the weakness.

"Do you still drink?"

"I try not to, Ma'am but sometimes a man can be driven to it." He said stiffly, eyes on the floor.

"If you work for me, I won't tolerate you being drunk. If you show up drunk, I will send you away for the day until you are fit for work and you lose that day's wages. I won't dismiss you for an issue I was aware of when I hired you, but I won't have you drunk and working near me. You have your demons and I have mine, sir." She said watching as he finally met her eyes, "My Uncle was a miserable drunk and a worse man. For seven years I endured his neglect and abuse because of his habits. I won't have it in my household."

"I understand, Ma'am." He said with a nod before turning to leave.

"I didn't say I wasn't willing to hire you." She snapped, jotting out a note and casting a spell to dry the ink. Opening a drawer, she pulled out a small pouch of coins, "Give this to the man outside, he will arrange passage for you to the Summer Palace. I am asking you to prove yourself, but I'm willing to give you a chance. The purse is your first week's wages should you need to settle any debts before we depart."

"Thank you, Ma'am." He said shakily, taking the items and clutching them hard in his fist.

"I'm sure they warned you I'm a mage." Beryl said giving him a slight smile, "The cottage we'll be staying in will be warded to prevent any alcohol from entering the building. If you want to drink, do it on your own time away from my home."

"Yes, Ma'am." He said with a firm nod, "When will you arrive at the Summer Palace?"

"I travel there at the end of the week. You have two weeks to deal with any business you need to complete. If I don't see you by then, I'll assume you've refused the position."

"I'll be there, Ma'am."

"Good," Beryl said, watching as the door was opened and Argent came trotting in with Rune riding on his shoulder, "Grant, Mister Cannon here will join my staff. Please arrange transport for him when he's ready to join me at the Palace."

"Madame." Grant said with a badly concealed wince, but her attention was on Cannon who watch the two animals with a slight smile pulling at one side of his mouth.

"I hope you're not afraid of dogs, Mister Cannon."

"No, Ma'am. What are their names?" He asked as Rune leapt to the desk and gave her a quick buss to the chin before jumping down.

"The cat is Rune, and this is Argent." She said fondly, rubbing one of his ears as he passed by before sliding to a sprawl on the floor with a happy groan.

"Fine looking animals, Ma'am. I'll see you in two weeks. Thank you, Ma'am." He said with a slight smile, giving her a quick bow and turning to follow Grant through the door.

"What do you think?" She asked, reaching to trail a few pets along Rune's back, making him start a soft purr.

"They hurt him, it twists him with pain." Rune murmured.

"A fighter, he shifted to protect you as the mean one came in." Argent rumbled, grumbling as he shifted on the hard floor.

"You think I need a guard at the palace?"

"It never hurts to have a large pack when danger nears."

Beryl hummed agreement, starting another letter to have his room ready. She didn't doubt he'd make it, even if he had to walk the entire way. She made a few notes to herself. His room would need wards against nightmares, herbs under the mattress to help with sleep. She might as well do something similar for the rest of the guest rooms while she was at it.

The next evening she was back out after lunch trying a bay gelding with John Toussaint extolling its virtues. She was wondering what his true motive was since the horse was too green for what she needed, shying at a worker trimming a hedge and blowing and sidestepping whenever Argent was near.

"A lovely ride but much too green." She said dismounting and pulling off her glove so she could scratch at the horse's withers and along its jaw, "Perhaps you'll have something more seasoned when I visit your estates? Will your sister be there, she sounds like an interesting individual?"

"Yes, she's eager to meet you. I've mentioned you several times in my letters and she's intrigued about the foreign mage who rides so well." He said with a faint blush as she loosened the girth and starting putting up the stirrups quickly getting the other side for her, "I'd enjoy showing you my home along with some of the horses, the grounds are fine and there are some nice trails. The northern forests are much older than the ones you'd have seen on the coast. They were said to be a home for the gods and were left untouched through the centuries."

"It sounds lovely." She agreed as they walked back to the barn, "Will you be staying for dinner tonight? I was hoping we could continue our discussion from earlier, I have a book I think you would enjoy. I could give it to you then if you like, or perhaps when we see each other next?"

"I'm afraid I have some matters I need to attend to after this and won't be able to attend dinner. Tomorrow? I have an older grey that you might enjoy. Care to say the same time as today?"

"That sounds good, I'll see you then." Beryl agreed, giving him a sunny smile as the groom took the horse, pushing back the annoyance that they wouldn't let her untack or care for any of the horses she was riding here.

"*When are you going to mate?*" Rune asked, making her choke on air once they were back in their rooms.

"*Why would we mate? He doesn't even want to hold my hand.*" She huffed, dragging off her sweat-soaked clothes and waving the maid out so she could bath in peace.

"*He wants to mate, he watches you like a male scenting a female in heat.*" Argent agreed as Beryl lowered herself into the water with a sigh.

"*He's a wonderful man, but he's just selling me horses. He has to be polite until the sale is final.*"

"*The one you rode today didn't suit you. Why did he offer it if he knew you wouldn't want to buy it?*" Rune asked, peeking over the edge of the tub to sniff at the oils that had been added.

"*There are customs for how to offer to court a lady, he hasn't done them.*"

"*Perhaps he doesn't know the customs, he is a young male.*" Argent offered, walking in and sitting on the rug to one side.

"*He's older than me.*" Beryl pointed out, "*I'll be nineteen in a few months and he's in his late twenties at least, maybe even thirty.*"

"*Then he knows his customs, perhaps you do not. His scent says he wishes to mate with you, even if his actions do not.*"

"*He's supposed to make a formal offer to court me, he has said nothing.*" Beryl sighed scrubbing herself down, "*I won't throw myself at someone who is unwilling, he has to say something.*"

"*It's a rut. Why do humans make things so complicated?*"

"*You'll have found the secret of the ages if you can answer that.*" She laughed, finishing her bath and getting ready for bed.

* * *

The rest of the week went quickly. She didn't find a second horse that caught her eye, but she rode every day. Most of the time it was with John Toussaint testing the paces of his horses, but sometimes the Princess took her pony out and they walked the garden trails chatting with Argent, easily keeping pace. For such a young intelligent girl, the princess seemed to have few friends her age. Beryl was packing her things the day before they were to leave when Noemi raced in, bouncing with excitement, the stuffed wolf clutched under one arm.

"The test worked, I can learn magic!" She crowed, spinning in place, making Rune jump for the safety of the bed as Argent barked and danced around with her.

"That is wonderful news, Princess Noemi." Beryl laughed, catching her hands, "When will you be starting lessons?"

"Father will arrange it once we're settled at the palace, but I get to learn. I can't wait! Will you teach me something?"

"Something small," Beryl chuckled, giving the girl's hands a squeeze before she moved to her bags and dug out a small clear crystal, "have you ever seen crystal lights?"

"Yes, they have them in the libraries." Noemi said expression serious even as she continued to bounce in place.

"This is small, you activate it by concentrating on the light." The small crystal glowed softly, "You can use the rune for light as well, but just focusing on what the light should look like will work for a small crystal like this. Try it."

The girl took the crystal gingerly, frowning at it with increasing intensity, "It won't light."

"It takes practice." Beryl said starting back packing her things, "Don't try too much and if you get a headache stop for the rest of the day, you don't want to burn out your power before you've even started lessons."

"Burn out?"

"Doing too much magic too quickly can make you sick. It gives you a high fever and you can collapse if you aren't careful."

"I'll be careful." Noemi said with a firm nod, "Thank you."

"See that you do," Beryl said with a smile as Rune wandered to the edge of the bed and meowed until the girl gave him a few pats with her free hand, most of her attention still on the gem in her other palm.

Chapter 21

The Summer Palace

Beryl wandered the party, trying not to frown. She wanted to be at her cottage organizing her household and working on projects. Instead, as soon as they arrived, the Prince ordered a party to be thrown the very next night, sending everyone into a frenzy of preparation. It seemed like she'd be busy with several balls, parties, and the Prince's birthday mascaraed at the end of the month. She glanced over the royal table and caught the Princess yawning, she'd been surprised that the girl had stayed up as late as she had given the lengthy carriage ride the day before. They hadn't arrived until late the night before and Beryl had barely wandered through the cottage they had shown her to before warding her room and collapsed into sleep curled against her bond mates.

She joined a small group of minor nobility near the edge of the dance floor. She had not wanted to dance herself, but a woman a few years older was more than happy to explain the various dances and point out a few of the nobles to watch out for. Lady Viand was a shy woman and kept back from the rest of the chattering women, making eyes at several of the dancers. Beryl rather liked her small, witty comments that went unnoticed by the rest of the group. They watched in surprise as the Prince accepted a dance with an older woman gliding across the floor, making the other couples seem clumsy.

"I wasn't aware the Prince enjoyed dancing. He seemed to dislike the one dance I shared on arriving to Orlean." Beryl said to her, keeping her voice low as they chatted.

"That is Lady Camille, she taught him as a young man. Whenever the royal family is in the North, she insists on a dance to prove he hasn't forgotten her lessons." Viand said, gesturing to another woman watching the dance with her fan, "Madame Claudette Derain, her current apprentice. She will teach the Princess while she is here at the palace."

"He is very good, I'm afraid I don't know the correct patterns for most of the dances here. He must have dreaded for his toes to dance with me after all the fumbles I had that night."

"You haven't danced tonight, did you wish too?"

"Not unless someone asks." Beryl said with a sigh, "I don't enjoy it myself, but watching is always a pleasure, seeing how the others enjoy it. Do you dance?"

"I rarely get to dance, I play piano and often get pressed to play at any gathering I go to. I like the balls at the palace since I get to participate and talk a bit."

"You must be very good," Beryl said with a smile, "the small parties I've been to are much the same for me. Everyone seems to assume a mage wants to show off their skills to the crowd."

"Are you on adequate terms with the prince?" Viand asked, changing the subject, "He's looked over here several times during his last dance."

"I'm assisting his family on a few projects. It surprised me the princess stayed this late, but she seems to love dressing up for balls." Beryl said, noting that the girl's chair was finally empty, so they had sent her to bed.

"The traveling may have worn her out." Viand said softly, "They keep her schedule full with classes during the summer since the hunts and they put parties off for the fall."

"So things will quiet a bit with the heat? I'd hoped they would." Beryl said sipping at her iced drink, "It amazed me no one fainted at the last ball on the coast. I barely made it myself even with cooling runes."

"You enchanted your clothes to keep you cool?" Viand blurted, blinking in surprise.

"Yes, and they can be warmed as well, which works better than my cooling charms." Beryl shrugged, sipping at her drink. She did what she had to, learned what she needed to get things done. She'd never tried to hide that about herself, no matter how it seemed to unnerve people when she wouldn't fit into a convenient category.

"Are you a tailor as well?" Viand asked, glancing over the other woman's dress. It was an unusual cut, but kept with the current fashions.

"No, I make some of my clothes and enchant whatever I buy. The princess is trying to get me to make a dress for her, but I don't think I have the skill yet."

"Are you the mage making dolls? I've seen the wolf you made for Noemi, it is lovely."

"Yes, I started the dolls to practice my sewing. I've sold a few to the ladies of the court for presents if you are interested in commissioning one." Beryl said before going still as she realized the Prince had finished his dance and was approaching them.

"May I have this dance, Mistress Mage?" He announced, watching as the few people around them backed away to give them room, Viand gave him a deep curtsy before hurrying away.

"I'm afraid I only know a few of the local dances." Beryl whispered, watching the surrounding couples already starting an intricate pattern, a few missing steps as they tried to monitor the prince.

"Then we will wait for the next song. A waltz, perhaps?" He said gesturing for a page and sending them off with instructions for the musicians.

"May I ask why you wish to dance with me? There are any number of women who would be delighted to take a turn with the royal prince. Miss Viand seemed interested." Beryl said glancing to where the woman had retreated near the wall, watching them with a pained look she was trying to hide in her fan.

"Perhaps it is because you are one of the few who seem to ignore the title." He said taking her hand and leading her along the hall to one balcony. "Few look at me as if I'm simply a man, it is refreshing to feel I'm being judged on my own actions instead of a few centuries of tradition."

"And Miss Viand? She was an amiable woman who would have loved a dance with you."

"You are too observant, Madame." The Prince said under his breath, giving her a sharp look, "They originally meant Miss Viand to be my first wife before my father changed his mind. We grew up together and have kept in touch as the years past. Noemi is fond of her and treats her like an Aunt."

"She still loves you, you can see it in her eyes when she watches you." Beryl added to the silence that stretched between them, ignoring the flinch from the prince, "You shouldn't cast her away, it's rare to find someone willing to love anyone that deeply."

"We will have dinner later in the week, I can't be seen to openly favor her at the moment. It would be dangerous for her." He said hissing a sigh between his teeth.

"And yet you danced with me at several balls and most of the court is gossiping that we are having an affair behind the King's back." She said offering him a tight smile to his hard glare.

"You can protect yourself, she isn't." He snapped, turning away with a huff, "Every time we talk you make me regret it. Are you normally this frustrating?"

"I'm generally this honest, I can't help it if you take the comments badly."

"Few people speak openly with me." He said with a sigh, leaning on the railing, "No one wants to offend a member of the royal family, but you don't seem to care. Why is that?"

"You are a person, the same as the lowest worker or servant here. I treat you the same as I treat them, I'm honest until a person gives me a reason to not be. You haven't done so yet." Beryl sighed, reaching across the bond to check on her bond mates.

"You are a strange woman." He chuckled, offering his arm, "Are you ready for our dance?"

"Whenever you are, your royal highness." She said with a smile, letting him lead them out of the balcony and to the dance floor. She'd need to speak with Miss Viand again. She was connected to things somehow.

* * *

The next morning she started organizing her cottage in earnest. Mary arrived and immediately took over the kitchens, spending the evenings pouring over cookbooks from the small library the cottage boasted and questioning Beryl on her favorite foods and what she ate when stressed or happy. She even questioned what Beryl's bond mates liked or disliked and how much or often they ate each day so she could have separate plates ready with each meal.

She still needed to hire a maid and house manager to run things while she was traveling, but mostly she needed an escort. The main issue she was running into was that she needed a chaperon to attend several meetings, and she didn't want to force one of her recent acquaintances into a harmful situation while she hunted for the followers of Aegis. She needed someone with enough standing to be an acceptable chaperon, but not one of the upper nobility whose reputation wouldn't allow them to travel the places she needed to go. It was proving to be an impossible search. No noble would sell their time to attend meetings or to work as a servant to a foreign mage.

She'd put out word of what she was looking for to her limited contacts, but little had come of it so far. She interviewed the two very minor nobles that arrived. One was desperate for money to shore up his household after his mother bankrupt the family after his father's death, the other was escaping a controlling family trying to force him into an unwanted marriage. Both would last a month before they sold her secrets to the highest bidder. She sent them both away with the name of another contact who might be willing to at least see them in action before dismissing them outright.

The man shown to her office a few days later was someone who could fade into a crowd, at a ball he was overlooked and forgotten much like she was once the event was over. His features were average if pleasant enough, making him look like a serious but well-meaning man at first glance. He dressed in well-tailored if plain clothes meant for ease of movement and comfort more than style, and the various shades of brown and tan brought out the highlights in his olive skin.

"A Mr. Benjamin Bryant to see you, Madame." Mary said dipping a quick curtsy once the door was open.

"Thank you, Mary. Can you bring some tea in a moment?"

"Yes, Madame." Mary murmured leaving, Beryl needed to find a maid quickly, it was wearing on Mary to have to serve in such a role.

"How may I assist you, Mr. Bryant?" She asked, setting the dress pattern she'd been working on to the side. The wards had warned her there was someone at the door, but she saw no point in hiding what amounted to a hobby. "Please have a seat."

"Thank you, Madame." He said removing his jacket and taking the offered chair. It wasn't very comfortable, so she didn't blame him for shifting in the creaking leather, "I was hoping to apply for the position of house manager if it is still available?"

"It is available. May I ask why a man of your standing needs such a position?" she asked, letting her eyes linger on the family crest displayed on his ring and cufflinks.

"May I be blunt, Madame?" he asked, suppressing a sigh.

"Of course," Beryl said mildly, "I find it refreshing after the constant diversion and innuendo of the courts."

"I don't need to work, I have a small estate west of here, but I worked for years on the family estates as the bookkeeper and house manager. With the marriage of my older brother, he has taken over the duties I had taken over from my father. They didn't need me muddying affairs at the estate while my brother finds his feet. My father is still there to give guidance if it's needed, and the recent bride expressed her dislike of me lingering about the house."

"If you don't need work, why are you here?"

"I dislike being idle, a friend recommended I look for a small position to keep my mind occupied. I could have spent time at my estate, but again I would be mostly idle. Managing an estate as small as yours would be a few hours' work a day, Madame. No offense meant, but it would be work."

"No offense taken, however, my affairs will soon branch out in complexity. I intend to purchase property here in the North next year and to sell wares to various customers. I may purchase a shop in the capital or hiring merchants to get my wares into shops about the country. I may be a mage but I come from a family of fishers and merchants, I grew up on stories of bad seas and deals gone badly. I know just how much work it takes to make a merchant house rise, and I hope to start trade between my contacts in Arden and Orlean."

"That is no small undertaking, Madame." He said leaning back into the chair as his eyes flickered with the speed of his thoughts, "My family has connections with several trading interests, I'm familiar with dealing with such endeavors."

"It is still years out and only if things go the way I hope they will in the next few years. For now you are correct, I have few affairs for you to deal with. What do you plan to do with the rest of your time?"

"I have some correspondence I need to keep up to help with the family estate and my house but it's the work of a few minutes a day. I entertained perhaps writing a book but I take it you have another task for me if I join your household?"

"Only if you accept the addition," Beryl said watching him, he had a small spark of magic but it was untrained and just meant his family lived to a rather healthy old age, "I have contacts and meetings

I need to keep where I need an escort, a chaperon. Some of these meetings could damage a person's reputation if they came to light, and I don't wish to damage a person's standing unwillingly."

"I can understand a need for discretion and have acted as a chaperon before for several cousins. I take it I'm to ignore anything discussed during these meetings?"

"Only if you wish it, I also would need you to sign a magical contract for the terms of your service. Have you ever done so before?"

"I have not, I take it they are more binding than regular contracts?"

"In this case, yes." She said pulling out a sheet and handing it over, "It will prevent you from speaking, writing, or sharing the information you learn while under my service to anyone not already granted permission to know it."

"Who would have permission?" he asked quickly reading over the contract.

"Myself and the other members of our household unless I indicate someone else at a later date."

"Will what we are keeping secret be dangerous?"

"It is possible, which is why I need the magical contract. I can't have this information getting out. I can swear that it will not harm the royal family or Orlean. It is to save lives and to keep those around me safe."

"But it could be harmful, that's why you are warning me." He said watching her with sharp eyes she approved of. Her old master at the thieves' guild would have approved of him, she thought.

"I understand if you wish to decline the position."

"Would I be allowed to distance myself from my family to protect them as well?"

"As long as it doesn't cause you issues in the future, I don't want to cause issues with your family because of working for my house."

"Frankly, Madame, my brother and I disagree on how a house should be run." He said skimming over the contract with sharp eyes, "It's the foremost reason I had for leaving the family estate, his new bride wishes to keep up with the best of society with little regard for the state of the rest of the family coffers. A little distance would not hurt my standing or estate."

"I often have to make similar purchases to keep in fashion with the King's Court."

"You have a position in the Court, Madame, she does not and is using my family's money to seek alliances above her station. Once she realizes that I have gained your employment, she may seek to use that to her advantage." He said shifting uncomfortably.

"She will find that pressuring a mage differs greatly from attempting to dazzle a lady of the courts." She said waving away the issue, "I take it you will sign?"

"I have been looking for work to keep me occupied, Madame, and working for you looks to do so. I doubt it will bore me if you are working on as many things as this rooms shows." He said waving at the various tables, "You have dress designs next to daggers and leather work, letters and merchant tally books next to magical tombs. I think I might even learn something from such an eclectic environment."

"Wonderful," she said, taking back the contract and clearing off a table for it to lie on, "are you used to magic being cast around you?"

"No, none in my family have more than a very minor talent. My great grandmother grew magical herbs and flowers that were sought after in her time, but no one in this generation shows the skill."

"You have a hint of magic at your core, so you may see things more clearly than most. Did you notice the wards on the property?"

"I noticed something coming in but couldn't place it and didn't want to be rude and linger, a blue line that I couldn't seem to find on a second glance."

"You first few days may simply be attuning you to the wards placed about the house, I can set them to alert you if there is a disturbance or if the person at the door means the occupants harm." She said casting and smiling at his soft gasp, "You can sign at the bottom but I also need a drop of blood or a bloody thumbprint, the blood anchors the spells to you."

"Will the household be protected from spells as well?" he asked, accepting the pen and quickly signing his name with a flourish after she did the same.

"To the best of my ability, each of the staff is being given a protective piece of jewelry and I'm offering to ward weaponry or clothes that you wear often. The jewelry will heat if something you are reaching towards is spelled to harm or poisoned." Beryl said watching him prick his thumb with a folding knife, sealing the contract with a slight flash of magic as the blood hit the parchment. "I've also warded the property against magical attacks and some physical attacks. Later, I'll show you the runes to activate the full wards that would prevent anyone not attached from entering. It locks down the house until myself or another mage deactivates or destroys them."

"Does the palace grounds have something similar? It would be invaluable if an attack happened." He asked as she collected the paperwork and put it away.

"Sadly, the royal family doesn't agree with you on that. There are wards and I've added to them, but they refuse to allow for such extreme protections. There is also a spell on the basement that prevents entry and keeping you safe from fire or other magical attacks. If they attack the house, you are to activate what you can and retreat to the basement until I return." She started a quick tour of the house, pointing out small wards and where things were as they talked.

"You think there will be an attack, it's not just being protective." He murmured as she showed him the heavily warded staircase down into the basement.

"Why do you say that?" she asked, heading upstairs and pointing out the empty rooms he could choose from.

"The grounds are already patrolled, and since it is a royal property, it has to be heavily warded, I expect. You've warded the house like you expect those protections to fail."

"I hope I am wrong." Beryl whispered, "Come to the study, the tea should be ready."

The tea service was waiting when they arrived back in the study. A small fire had been lit and a tray of small sandwiches and treats left waiting on a low table. She gestured him to a chair by the fire and poured them both cups, mixing a third cup with extra milk for Rune, who for whatever reason had decided he liked the taste. Argent was in the kitchen with Mary while Rune watched from a pillow hidden in one corner.

"Why are you preparing for war? Do you have proof that one is coming?"

"Who said anything about war?" she asked, setting Rune's cup on the edge of the hearth while Benjamin watched with a frown.

"Are we expecting another person for tea? Do you have a child?"

"No, but I have a bond mate who is very fond of tea scented milk." Beryl said laughing softly as Rune came out of hiding and gave the man a haughty look, curling his tail about his feet before lapping daintily at the cup.

"What is a bond mate?" he asked hesitantly as she sat down.

"An animal that bonds to a mage for life. I have two, Rune," she said, indicating the cat, "and Argent a hunting hound."

"We've gotten off topic," He muttered, "why are you preparing for an assault on the palace?"

"Because I've seen it happen," Beryl said taking a sip of her tea with a sigh, "it is rare but some mages see visions of the past, present, or future, things they have no logical way of knowing without some magical or divine intervention. I've seen war and death my entire life. I've learned how to direct the visions so I can gather more information, but I have no control over what I see. A war is coming and I've done everything in my power to limit the damage to those around me."

"When?"

"I've been preparing for it for most of my life, I know it will happen soon, but I can't say if it will be this year or the next."

"How do you know?"

"I see my two bond mates and I see some people I know from

Orlean, they are close to the age they are now as much as I can tell. I thought for a while I'd pushed the path far enough along to change things when I bonded to a sea hawk, I never saw her in my visions. I lost her last year. Once I met the Prince, I knew it would happen here."

"Is that why you travel with the court?"

"Yes, I can only hope that I've given everyone enough protections to keep them from harm. If not, then I will be here waiting to run to their aid."

"What would you have me do? I'm not a fighter. I limited my stint in the army to managing the troop lists and rations." He said with a grimace, "I won't be much aid to you in a battle."

"You've seen enough to know how to prepare, I want you here to help get people to safety. You will be the only one I'll let move through the house wards, if you drag someone with you it will lock them inside the wards and safe. Are you regretting agreeing to work for me?"

"No, I wasn't looking for an adventure, but it definitely won't be dull." He said with a slight smile as Rune leapt into her lap, "Is there anything else you need from me tonight? If not, I'd like to return to my estate for the night to get things settled. I'll return in the morning to start work, I have a lot of things to consider."

"Have a good night." She said standing and cradling Rune in one arm while she showed the man out. It didn't take long for Mary to bustle in to collect the trays once she settled back into her chair.

"I hope you didn't scare him away, Miss. He seemed a reliable enough chap." She tutted, collecting the used cups but topping off Beryl's and nudging the sandwich plate closer, "Your hound has been begging in the kitchen all day."

"Would you like me to get him to stop?" Beryl asked, taking a sandwich and offering Rune a tiny sliver of meat before taking a small bite to stop the other woman's frown.

"Oh no, he's careful to stay out of the way and he barked to let me know the afternoon delivery was at the door. I spoke with the cooks in the palace and they've agreed to add our supplies to their order each week for the price you offered."

"Good, you're welcome to order what you need from the markets or go into town as you like." Beryl hummed taking another bite, "I'll also have a box of material arriving soon for the next few dresses I want to work on. I need to get started before everyone gets busy for the Prince's birthday celebration."

"The palace is already buzzing, they say the Prince has ordered twice the normal number of entertainers and if the weather holds they will hold it in the gardens."

"That should be interesting," Beryl murmured, trying not to wince.

She'd already scared two gardeners half to death who'd used the masked tunnel entrance to store tools. They thought it was a simple folly built to look like a small temple that time had turned into a ruin. There was no telling how many people would trip the wards that night if they were running about masked in the gardens. She would inform the Prince at their next appointment.

"Jeremy should arrive tomorrow, have you aired the guest rooms?"

"Yes, they are ready and waiting. I added the fresh herbs under all the mattresses. Are you certain they help with sleep? The smell was rather strong."

"It's only because I placed them today, the smell should be gone by tomorrow night. Tell me in the morning if it's bothering you, I can try a minor spell instead."

"Are you certain it's needed?"

"Tensions will run high with everyone starting new jobs and staying in an unknown place. I'd like to have everyone fresh instead of snappish and mean because of lack of sleep the first few weeks, myself included. All it does is help you sleep deeply so you don't dream as easily, it doesn't prevent you from waking if you need to." Beryl reassured her, "Let me know in the morning if they bother you and I'll help redo the laundry."

"Nonsense, the palace staff would never let me live it down if they knew the Head of House was doing laundry. You do enough as it is." Mary huffed, "Go take your hound on a walk, get him out from under my feet while I cook dinner."

"As you wish," Beryl said with a chuckle gathering up her coat, "I found some cress on the creek's edge, I'll bring some back."

Chapter 22

Princess

She wondered if the prince even knew that she was forging weapons and armor on his grounds. The spacious garden shed attached to the cottage had been perfect to rework in to a small forge with the materials the royal family had provided. They may have asked for jewelry, but this large a forge was large enough to suit her other needs. Jeremy watched in shock as she'd started the fires before disappearing to change, returning in rough work pants and donning the leather apron she'd set aside earlier.

The carters who'd delivered the blacksmithing supplies had lingered, watching as she'd unpacked and sorted things to her liking. They'd scatted finally when she started warding the assembled forge and tools. Beryl ignored them, casting to allow the forge to get much hotter than normal and to keep some of the heat instead of bleeding it out into the air. Her tools were also warded to keep them from heating or sticking to any metal she was working.

"Are you going to work through dinner?" Jeremy asked gruffly rubbing at Argent's ears when he leaned against the man for a long moment.

"I'm almost done." Beryl huffed, tugging out the red hot dagger she was attaching to a crosspiece from the fire. "What weapons do you favor besides the short sword?"

"I can use a bow but have had no call to practice. They only allow personal guards to carry a short sword and dagger while traveling in Orlean. Once you have your own land, you can outfit me as you wish." He said, watching as she checked the placement before casting on the cooling metal.

"I want you outfitted as best I can. I'm not in a safe position yet, and I've already had several paltry attempts made to poison myself and my bond mates. Whatever you deem as necessary can be purchased and I will enchant it to ensure your safety."

"Enchanting it how?" He asked hesitantly, "What are you adding to that?"

"I'm casting runes into the dagger to ensure it remains sharp, to strengthen the metal, to reduce the chance it breaks, and to bind it to myself and my House. No one else will wield this blade without harming themselves." Beryl said finishing up and quenching the dagger with a quick ladle of water before setting on the anvil to cool, "If you wear armor I would work it to turn aside blades and block spells that might be cast against you. I can spell your boots to muffle your steps and your bracers to protect you from poison."

"You expect that much trouble?"

"I'm an exiled mage taken in by the Orlean royal family. I have few patrons and many enemies." Beryl said stripping off her gloves and the apron ignoring the way the man eyed her scars, "I expect danger but I have no way of knowing what direction it will come from right now. I would rather be over prepared then under."

"You could kill with a word with your magic. Why bother with weapons?"

"Have you ever heard of a mage killing in anything other than self defense outside of the old stories?" she asked, arching an eyebrow, "It doesn't happen. They stripe them of their magic and are left in prison to die if caught."

"Surely it can't," He trailed off as Rune trots out of the gloom, bounding up to his normal place on her shoulders.

"A mage who kills is a dead mage. Our magic comes from the earth and air, to use it to kill someone outside of self-defense is taking that magic for granted, it goes against the oaths we swear when we leave our masters. They bound the oath to our very core and will burn out that mage's magic if they use it to harm another intentionally. Only rogue mages aren't bound by oaths." She murmured eyes on her work as she cleaned up.

"You expect me to guard you from magic?"

"No, I expect you to guard me from the non-magical threats while I protect everyone else." Beryl snapped tossing down the rag she'd been using to clean her tools, "An open attack on me is something I can counter, what's to stop them from attacking anyone else around me? What's to stop an attacker from killing innocent bystanders?"

"You said only rogue mages kill without killing themselves."

"Who said the attack will be from a mage?" She snarled casting a spell to put the forge to glowing embers ignoring how the man flinched at the flash of fire and light it caused, "It could just as easily come from a random noble who is offended that a foreign mage is gaining power in the court. They have all the time and money I don't. They can send mercenaries or hire poisoners, they can bribe my staff, they can send poisoned or spelled gifts meant to harm those around me out of spite. They can attack anyone around me and I won't let them be injured because of me."

"You expect an attack, you're not just preparing for the off chance."

"I was warned of things brewing here while I was in Arden. I know there are groups who would love to corrupt me and use my power for their own purposes."

"Then why stay here? You could run and get somewhere safe and easier to defend. You've surrounded yourself with snakes coiled for the strike."

"Yes, I have." She said giving him a grim smile, "I've set myself in the middle of a war and made myself the third party. I'm the target of both sides because they don't know where I stand."

"You made yourself a target, why would you do that?"

"Because if I don't thousands would die." She sighed, pushing the wide doors closed and letting him hold them together while she fixed the latch, "You have your nightmares and demons that haunt your rest. This is mine. Since I was a child I've dreamed of a raging battle, death taking everyone I fought to protect, leaving me alone and broken on a battlefield while fire consumed the world."

"Nightmares are just that, they can't happen just because you dream it will."

"My dreams have a tendency to come true. I found you after all, Sargent Cannon." She said giving him a tired smile as she turned to go in.

"You dreamed of me?" He asked, grabbing her sleeve and pulling her to a stop.

"You and Mary, the Prince and his daughter," She sighed, "I've dreamed of death and flames for my entire life. Crystals that shatter and weapons that burn an army to ash as I watch. I only hope that I can prepare everyone as much as possible to give them a chance of changing their fates."

"So you don't see the future, it can change."

"The future isn't set in stone, it can change just like anything else. Everything is twisting and turning with every action we take. I'm just trying to force things on to a better path."

"And if you can't?" He asked letting go, "If you can't protect those you wish?"

"I've done it before, I've seen a castle shattered and burned to ruins in my dreams. It still stands, I just have to hope I've done enough to keep the battle small enough that we might prevail." She said opening the door, "Good night, Jeremy."

"Good night, Ma'am." He said frowning as he turned away from the light, wandering into the shadows of the garden to think.

* * *

"Watch carefully," Beryl told the princess, twisting the bracelet so a curved blade slid out, "this isn't for hurting anyone, it's to help you escape. If anyone ever ties your hands, you can twist the bracelet and run away. It activates the jewels when you press this sequence, once pressed people will ignore you unless you draw their attention. It's a turning spell, it diverts attention from whatever I place it on."

"Did you need something like this when you were my age?"

"Yes, most children wouldn't need or understand the need for something like this, but I used magic to keep myself safe and I think you need the same protections. Since you can't cast the spells yet, this is the other option." Beryl said closing the bracelet and slipping it into the girl's thin wrist, "I hope you never have to use it, but if you do, it's there. Wear it at all times if you can, even in the bath. Get used to the feel on your wrist, only you can remove it."

"This will keep me safe?"

"No, the guard and your father will do everything they can to keep you and everyone else in the palace safe. This is just in case something happens, anyway." Beryl sighs, "Your father won't give me permission to teach you the other methods I learned at your age."

"What methods?"

"Are there any female guards?" Beryl asked, changing the subject.

"No, the guard doesn't accept females." Noemi said, frowning at the change of subject.

"Do any of the ladies at court do archery or work with swords?"

"Not the nobles, but some of the ladies-in-waiting are trained in weapons so they can protect their Ladies if they kill the guards. I'm not supposed to know that, but Sabine has a cousin who was taught to use daggers and she told me."

"Is there someone at the palace you can ask to teach you?"

"You think I should learn to use daggers?"

"No, I think you need to learn to break a hold if someone grabs you." Beryl huffed, "Ask Sabine's cousin if she or someone she recommends can teach you how to get away from someone, where to kick or hit, and how to fight back if someone picks you up. Your father won't let me teach you, but if you are quiet about it, you can still learn what you need."

"All right," Noemi said, settling the bracelet against her skin, "will you tell me what you're wearing to the mascaraed? I'm going as a cloud dancer, the dress is lovely, and my teacher helped me charm ribbons to flutter about as I move."

"That sounds like fun." Beryl agreed with a grin, "I'm going as a soldier, I want to see who will recognize me so don't spoil the secret."

"I won't tell, promise." The princess agreed, fingering the bracelet, "Is the bracelet a secret too?"

"Yes, you can tell your father if he asks, but not anyone else."

"All right," She said with a frown, "do you keep many secrets?"

"Few," Beryl said, changing the subject, "how are you lessons going? Are you still having issues with casting wards?"

The princess explained her progress and jotted down a few books that Beryl recommended. They chatted about her lessons and the goings on at the palace for a while before she was called to bed by her maid. Beryl wandered the corridors of the royal wing, checking the wards and adding minor spells to strengthen them where she found issues.

"Please ask the Prince if he has a moment." Beryl said to the guard outside of his rooms trying to steel herself for the upcoming conversation. The prince had dismissed her offers to further ward the royal wing or to ward jewelry or weapons for his own use.

"Please go in, the Prince is waiting in his study." The guard said, returning and holding the door open for her.

"Thank you." Beryl murmured with a slight smile, making her way to the second door and knocking. A page let her in with a brief bow, ignoring Argent as he padded past.

"Thank you for seeing me, your royal highness." She said giving a deep curtsy to the man as he glanced up from his work.

"That will be all, Andrew." He said waving out the page with a glare, "Are you here to persuade me to sequester my daughter away in a temple or force the entire family to wear armor under our shirts?"

"Something is draining the wards on the edges of the property and the ones near the entrances in a few areas. I've strengthened them, but something is pulled the magic away without tampering with the ward."

"Can you work around it?"

"I don't like the fact that someone is taking magic from the wards protecting the Palace. The wards on the foundation are hundreds of years old and even those are being drained."

"Where are the weak points?" He sighed, tossing down his pen.

"The entrance to the royal wing, the servant's entrances, and the wards that border the western forest trails."

"What would you have me do? Search the servants?"

"They have to be carrying something in that is weakening the wards."

"Contrary to rumor, we rarely search our servant's quarters or force them to hand over their personal property."

"Even if they were trying to poison the royal family?"

"By that count, I could have you thrown in the stocks for owning herbs that could harm others. Many people in the court use herbs for various reasons, I can't order a mass search without proof."

"Then I'll find proof." Beryl huffed, digging out a sheet of parchment and handing it over.

"What is this?" The prince sighed, holding the rough map to the light.

"A drawing of the wards, their weak spots, and the unwarded tunnels under the palace."

"There are no tunnels under the palace, I would have been told of them." He said tracing the path of a tunnel to the edges of the property.

"You can check with the King or have the old maps pulled, but I found an entrance to one in the main garden already."

"Where does it lead?"

"Out into the forest, I warded the entrance to alert me if they use it but we need to find the others."

"You are certain there are more?"

"The stone here is excellent for building, and the grounds have been shifted and remodeled many times over the years. That could have been tunnels for escape or servants could be used against you if you aren't aware."

"I am not a complete idiot," He snapped, tossing the paper to the side, "I'll have the royal archives searched. There should be some record of these tunnels in there."

"I know you think I'm being paranoid," she started only for him to break into a bark of laughter.

"Paranoid is warding the grounds, paranoid is offering to ward the royal wing, paranoid is covering my daughter in so many wards she outright glows to mage sight according to my advisers. There is nothing I would not do to protect her, so I'm willing to ignore it, but you are battening down the palace like a war is coming. A war that I have no indication exists!"

"They warned me of unrest when I sailed from Arden."

"And yet there is none that I am aware of. Whatever unrest your former companions warned you of doesn't exist."

"Have you ever heard the name Delorean?"

"I have not."

"What about Aegis?"

"Never, is there something I should be aware of?"

"A cult was growing to power in Arden when I left. They traced the skirmishes on the northern border back to a group of rogue mages who claimed to worship the god, Aegis. Delorean was a top-ranking member."

"I have never heard of such a cult here in Orlean. Unless you have proof of their existence or proof of them plotting to overtake the country, there is little I can do."

"An apprentice mage in the Palace mentioned that his master is searching for magic stealing crystals. The followers of Aegis use them to subdue those who aren't followers. They could be what is draining the wards."

"Have they found a crystal?"

"No, but they were found in Arden. I collected them myself for the King."

"Have you found any evidence of them here?"

"No, however,"

"No, bring me proof and I can increase the guard or search the grounds. Without proof my hands are tied, Mage."

"Can you increase patrols near the forest and in the gardens?"

"Not without evidence." The prince snapped, slamming a hand down, "No further changes will be made without evidence of a danger to the royal family or its retainers. Dismissed."

"Goodnight, your royal highness." She said giving a short curtsy and heading to the door.

"What happened to the woman beggar?" He asked heaving a sigh as she paused by the door, "I sent a purse to be given to her but she was no longer at the Inn."

"She works as a cook in my household, your royal highness. You are welcome to come by if you wish to speak with her."

"I thought we agreed you could call me Tobias."

"Not where others might hear, your royal highness."

"The room is empty save us."

"And yet someone is listening behind that painting." Beryl said gesturing to the large painting of the King to one side, "Good night, your royal highness."

She left the room, ignoring the roar of the Prince for his guards. He had asked for proof, even if it was just his servant Andrew spying for the King. She needed to bring the danger into the light soon if the Prince continues to refuse to increase the protections. The wards would fail within a week without her reinforcements.

Chapter 23

John

"How long are you going to string that poor wretch along? He's been all but groveling for your hand all week." Jeremy asked, stepping out from his spot against a tree when she passed.

"Groveling? John hasn't been groveling. And what about my hand? We are talking horses!"

"And he's wearing his God blessed colors and wearing the emblems of his house Gods. That's probably his best tunic."

"Well, yes, he's been overdressed for riding, but I thought he was trying to impress me. What do you mean House Gods?"

"You've seen how some people wear certain colors most of the time, they're showing their affiliation with one god and asking for their blessing."

"And you do this by wearing a certain color?"

"Well, and by praying at the house shrine or leaving offerings."

"I haven't seen any temples in Orlean, where are the shrines if everyone is praying to their own gods?"

"There are no public temples, every house has a shrine used to worship your god. Even the palace has one somewhere for the royal family. Every wing of the estate has one for any visiting guests."

"My rooms didn't have a shrine."

"Maybe some visiting dignitary had a fit, and we removed them." He shrugged, "Even your cottage has a small one off the main entrance."

"The boot room where someone keeps placing flowers in the niche. Oh, I'm so stupid. How did I miss this?"

"I take it your people don't worship the same?"

"No, we don't have personal shrines. We go to the town temple to make offerings and pray. There are many gods, but we don't wear their colors to ask for a favor. Some will wear a pendant with their patron god, but most don't. The temples also serve as places for healing, and any money given goes to the healers to treat patients who can't afford the treatment."

"Prayer is considered private here, you don't share it with others outside of the family. You can proclaim your House God by wearing his sign or colors. Your man was wearing a pendant to the god of the hunt and a green tunic marked with gold, showing that Brennan was his patron god."

"So he was asking me to court him by wearing his house god's colors?"

"While courting we wear our colors to show that we have a good House God and the person we are courting does the same. If we see the gods to be compatible, we pray for a blessing."

"Compatible?"

"A god of destruction and one of plenty aren't going to get along, are they? Some more nontraditional families ignore such things if the match is good. The woman might take on the House God of the man's family while keeping her own God as a personal devotion." He recited before scrubbing a hand over his face, "I can't believe I'm explaining this. You should talk to someone who follows the gods. My family were never that devote except to Chiron, the god of plenty."

"Do you wear his mark?"

"Yes," He said tugging out a chain which held a small silver coin showing her the relief on one side, "the god of money and increasing fortunes, not that it ever did much good for my pockets."

"I'm not sure if Ruth even has colors, Bain is black to represent his darkness." Beryl muttered, frowning, "Are their books about this?"

"There are books on everything, but it might make you look like an idiot to ask for them. They are for teaching small children."

"Mary wears blue in the kitchen, what god is that?"

"How can you not know the gods when you're god touched?" He asked in exasperation, spinning to a stop.

"You mean the dreams."

"Yeah, to see such things you have to have a god guiding you. Have you felt drawn to Ruth or what's his name?"

"Bain? No, they saw Ruth as a skilled mage that walked the land healing all that came before her. On her death, she became a goddess after the old gods raised her to the heavens. She was the goddess of fertility, new growth, and healing. Bain is the male opposite of Ruth. He is darkness, destruction, the unbinder and the bringer of change, he gathers the souls of those who die and lays them to rest. I never felt drawn to them, I attended the events each season, but I never felt their touch or attention. Not even the minor gods seemed to draw me."

"Minor gods?"

"Everyone else below Bain and Ruth like the god of thieves or patron of bakers."

"We don't rank the gods like that, every god has his own abilities and strengths and one isn't above the others, though some families would disagree."

"How will I know when someone is wearing their god's colors or if they're just wearing a color they like if not everyone follows the old traditions?"

"The colors of House Gods are worn on important dates or events even if the family doesn't wear them daily, plus the decoration on the cuffs or hem will depict something favored by that god if not his emblem."

* * *

Beryl watched the stable-hands eyes widen as she galloped up. She dismounted and handed over the reins, storming past without a word. John watched her approach with a stunned expression. She knew he'd never seen her so disheveled, her hair tangled and windblown while she only wore a men's shirt and breeches with her greatcoat.

"Is something the matter?" John asked, stepping forward to meet her headlong rush with concern.

"I need to say something and I hope you won't take offense."

"Whatever you need." John agreed, waving the riders back to their work and leading her to a small bench set to one side.

"I think you've been offering to court me. It's not the way we do courting in Arden and I will remove myself if I'm wrong, but I enjoy your company and our time spent together and would like to continue spending time with you." She ran her hands through her hair in frustration as he watched her dumbstruck before pulling him down for a firm kiss, "If you want to court me I'm willing, if not I'm sorry for the presumption."

Spinning she marched back to her horse, mounting she pushed it to a trot, waiting to see if he would call her back. He didn't. She'd known it was a gamble offering herself like that, but it wasn't like she had any reputation or title to worry about at this point. She walked the horse in loops until it was cooled down before heading back. Waving away the stable hand, she took her time untacking and currying the mare before handing her over to be put away.

She was calm by the time she finished and refused to be ashamed of voicing her affection to someone she was coming to consider a friend, if not more. The walk back to the cottage was short, and Argent watched her mournfully from his spot at Mary's feet as she kneaded dough. Rune came down the stairs to join her as she dropped into a chair at the long table. Neither bond mate had enjoyed being left behind for this task.

"Help me with this," Mary said, dropping a bowl and spoon in front of her, "those two have been worrying about you all day. Is there something I should worry about?"

"It's a personal matter." Beryl sighed, standing to shed her coat and twist her hair back out of the way before washing her hands.

"So the horse trader has done something. Do I need to send Jeremy to knock some sense into the man?" She asked as they both got to work.

"No," Beryl huffed, shoving the mixing bowl across the table, mixed and ready, "I offered him a courtship. He has yet to reply."

"Then there is nothing we can do for it today." She said crisply, "What would you like for dinner?"

"Whatever you like." Beryl shrugged, fiddling with a spoon left to one side.

"What did you mother feed you when you were sick?"

"Nothing we could get here." Beryl laughed, standing and stretching, "She was a merchant's daughter in a family of fishers. Milk fish stew or fish bone broth with honey bread."

"This far north I doubt we could get much beyond lake trout." Mary said doubtfully, "How about a beef stew with brown bread and honey?"

"That would be good. I will get cleaned up."

"Go take a long bath and brush out that rat's nest. I'll wrap your hair so you have curls for the dinner party tomorrow."

"I doubt even curls will win over the local mages." Beryl said with a snort.

"It never hurts to put your best foot forward." Mary announced, waving her up the stairs with a spoon covered in cookie batter.

She was wrapped in a thick dressing gown on a stool before the fire, feet covered by Argent's bulk when Mary came in. "There is a letter for you, Madame." She murmured, handing over the letter before she started brushing out the other woman's long hair, sectioning it so that thin strands could be twisted up for the night.

Dear Mage,

I am ashamed to say your offer this afternoon struck me speechless. I have been hoping to court you but was waiting on introducing you to my father before making an official request. I did not mean for you to doubt my advances, I only wish for your happiness and you seemed happy during our time together.

I wished to know you more the moment I set eyes on you riding in the Prince's hunt. Once we spoke, that wish only deepened. I offered my family's horses because of this need, we wouldn't make a sale to a random guest of the court.

It would honor me to court you if you will still have me.

Yours in friendship or however you will have me,

John Toussaint

Beryl mulled over the letter while Mary twisted her hair into tight knobs. She tried not to wince as her scalp tightened along with the hair. Why wasn't there was a magical way to curl your hair without hot irons and twisting until your scalp screamed?

"Is it good news then?" Mary asked once she was over halfway done.

"He wishes to court me and would like me to travel to meet his family so I can be formally introduced to his father."

"That is marvelous news, isn't it?"

"Yes, but he said he didn't ask me sooner because I had no family to ask." Beryl said fiddling with a ribbon, "Do you think that will be a problem with his family? I'm not even sure he's told anyone beyond his sister about me at all."

"You are a woman with your own household, soon to own property and looking to open your own shop in the coming year. You have your own money and the favor of the royal family. You don't have a title yet, but I doubt it won't be soon to come given how much you have done for the King. Any man would be lucky to have you. Surely you've been courted before?" Mary asked, pausing her work to glance down at her with a quirked eyebrow.

"Yes, but in Arden I was courted because I would bring magic into the bloodlines." Beryl sighed, accepting the pat on her shoulder as Mary went back to fussing with her hair, "They eyed me as a broodmare for future children and not as a person. John is the first person who as wanted to court me as myself and nothing more."

"That is a rare thing in the courts. Few marry for love unless both families have other siblings to place into better matches. Even among commoners, most have their eye out for someone to improve the family household."

"He is the firstborn of his family and will inherit the estates. Most families would push for a political match to bring strength or money into the household. My family discussed contracts with other mage bloodlines, even when I was as young as three. They decided nothing before they died."

"He does not seem to care about your magical ability. You have both political strength and power if not the funds to offer. His family may overlook your lack of family name if the man is insistent, but they may insist on a long engagement."

"If we make it to discussions of marriage, I may insist on a long engagement. I feel like I am barely getting my feet under me after being exiled, and yet things keep arriving to throw me off course."

"That's how life works." Mary said with a snort, tying a cloth around Beryl's hair to make it easier to sleep on. "Has he seen you work magic?"

"No, we're riding or walking about the grounds. I've had no reason to cast while we've been together. Do you think I should find a reason?"

"Perhaps just to gage how comfortable he is with it. You cast constantly in the house and if he isn't comfortable with magic being cast around him, it would make for an uneasy relationship."

"He accepts Rune and Argent and doesn't treat them as pets.

That is more than most of the people of Orlean will do." She pointed out.

"They are not all you are, you may share a love of horses and animals, but if he doesn't accept your magic, can you say you will be happy?"

"No," she sighed, nudging her bond mates over their link to climb into bed, "he doesn't understand the bond either. Most mages would refuse to share their mind and soul with one bond mate much less three. I've already lost one bond mate, I won't lose another no matter who asks it of me."

"I take it you are skipping dinner?" Mary asked with a sigh, gathering up her supplies, "What will you be wearing tomorrow to the dinner?"

"The green silk and I need a ribbon for Rune, something ridiculous." Beryl grimaced, climbing into bed and gathering up Rune for a cuddle, "They think bond mates are animals, we might as well use that to our advantage."

"Ruffles and curls, you will have them thinking you are hunting for an arrangement." Mary chuckled.

"That is their dilemma, I just want to be acknowledged as an equal mage so I can work without half the mages in the country badmouthing me behind my back."

* * *

Beryl made her way to the ball with careful steps along the garden paths. She should have taken a carriage even for the short distance, but she wanted to get as much air as she could before being stuffed into the overheated ballroom for the evening.

She felt like she was drowning in pleats, ruffles, and lace. It was better than the utter disgust Rue was feeling at having the big silver ribbon at his neck. Argent padded jauntily along, wearing his red ribbon with pride, making the cat hiss at him as he passed.

"Both of you behave. We need to be on our best behavior tonight.

We hope to be underestimated, but these are the magical advisors and researchers for the crown. If we are lucky, they have allowed the apprentices to attend and you two can wander listening to gossip." She murmured, settling Rune along her arm. She embroidered the ribbons and her dress with protection spells and Beryl wore her cuffs and collar openly. Hopefully, they would be immune to an open attack at the palace, but the ball was a perfect place to make a rival mage look incompetent with a well cast spell.

"Why they wanted to hold a ball to introduce me to magical society is beyond me. We could have simply held an informal meeting or lunch to discuss what branches of magic I might be able to learn or teach in Orlean."

Heading inside she swept through hidden corridors, the servants she passed stared in shock at the Lady hurrying through their domain with two animals in tow but did nothing to stop them. She slowed once they reached the public hallway leading to the ballroom, taking a deep breath. She wasn't early, but it wouldn't do to arrive looking like she'd walked either.

"Your name, my lady?" The page at the door asked checking his list as the couple before her entered, "Are you waiting on your escort?"

"Mage Beryl Marcian, called Mage. Unaccompanied." Beryl murmured with a tight smile as the page checked her name off the list of invitations.

Gods, she hated how many stupid rules society made to box people into their predetermined places. Arriving without an escort was already a mark against her but she refused to hang off the arm of a stranger for the entire night, she'd considered asking Benjamin but he'd have been stiff as a board amongst a room full of mages.

The page handed off a slip of paper to a boy who ran ahead of them to the next door, waiting impatiently until the last announcement was finished and the couple headed down the staircase. The herald took the paper and managed to announce her name and title before she glided past him down the wide staircase. Perhaps it would be a good night after all.

Small groups of people mingled about the grand ball room while servants flitted about with trays of hor d'oeuvre and glasses of wine. She was glad they had abandoned trying to hide her bondmates; she wanted them at her side and safe where she could see them in this crowd of magic users. It was a pity she didn't know more mages here in Orlean. She could use a friend to help curtail the more venomous glares she was earning.

"Well met, Lady Mage." Rogen said as she approached the corner the Prince and the King's advisor were occupying.

"Prince Zyon, Maser Mage Rogen," She greeted them with a smile and a deep curtsy, Argent coming to sit at her feet.

"I see you declined to leave the animals at home," Rogen said with a sniff, "How are you enjoying your garden cottage?"

"The cottage is delightful," She said turning to the Prince with a smile and tapping Argent lightly on one ear to forestall the building growl, "It is the perfect location, your highness, thank you for allowing me to opportunity to stay there."

"You are most welcome," Prince Zyon said, accepting a glass and allowing Rogen to cast a quick detection spell across it before taking a sip.

"Are you wary of poison or magic in such a large gathering?" She asked raising an eyebrow, "I would think few would stoop to attaching the Crown Prince at such a function with so many skilled practitioners on hand to retaliate."

"Few would, but that doesn't mean one can't be careful," Rogen snapped, "perhaps you should circulate instead of monopolizing the Prince's attention."

"Enough, Rogen;" Prince Zyon said with a suppressed sigh, "This is after all meant to be her introduction to Orlean Magical Society. Who would be the best to escort Mistress Mage about the room?"

"Surely so powerful a mage needs no escort, my prince."

"Astonishingly, I agree. If I may have your leave, Prince Zyon, I will circulate as I may until the entertainments begin."

"As you wish," He said, looking concerned as she gave him a deep curtsy and turned to make her way to the next group to his left. Rogen watched with sharp eyes as she curtsied to the group.

"Lovely evening, gentlemen;" She said, glancing over their number and trying to place names to the faces and crests they wore. Each wore a Master's belt with several colored cords representing their disciplines. Almost everyone in the room had the silver cord for illusions, while these groups seemed to contain those more comfortable with weather casting.

"Good evening, Lady Mage;" One said with a curt bow, "Is it simply Mage or is that an Ardenian title?"

"I am Beryl Marcian however, I often go by Mage." She said simply not wanting to hash out the details of her curse yet again for someone who didn't actually care and would soon forget anyway, "And you are?"

"I am Master Mage Hogan, this is Master Mage Trent and Volaire." He said gesturing to each man who gave her stiff nods, "It is surprising to find the Prince so enamored with a foreign magic user. You must have promised much to be allowed to stay here with the King's blessing."

"Surely you have had visiting mages from other countries?" Beryl asked mildly stroking a hand along Rune's back, "Arden is well known for accepting any mage that wishes to stay and use its libraries."

"Do many of your Arden mages have familiars?" Master Volaire asked with a frown, "It is not a common ability here and often see as polluting your soul and magic with the animal's baser nature."

"About half of the mages I knew had a familiar at one time, it is fairly common to gain one while a child is first learning magic. They serve to ground the child's magic as it grows and matures leading to a stronger mage."

"You are not long out of your apprenticeship yourself, I have never heard of so young a master." Master Trent said with a sniff of disdain, as if she excelled at such a young age simply to annoy him.

"I was tested and found competent in my first year of apprenticeship. I stayed one year to complete the required training my master wished of me however I was crafting my own spells by fifteen and they saw no reason to limit my studies by preventing my Mastery."

"So they contested the decision?"

"Such things are always contested, sirs." She said handing off her glass to a passing servant, "It was a pleasure speaking with you, sirs. Allow me to take my leave and continue to meet the rest of my peers."

"As you would, Mage." Mage Hogan said with a frown waving her on in clear dismissal.

The rest of the night didn't improve. The only women mages present were married to a mage or widowed. None had arrived unaccompanied, and it was a scandalous rumor circulating the room that she had done so to show the Prince she was available for marriage in hopes of stealing his heart. Beryl fought not to laugh hysterically as the rumors of her voracious appetites for men and power filtered behind her.

The Orlean mages as a whole saw her as a naïve child who sought a powerful marriage or someone who sought power through alliances with the royal family and their retainers. She kept up a polite mask but felt that the evening had been a colossal waste. No one here was willing to discuss magical theory beyond trying to prove how unintelligent she was by not knowing every vessel of the crown and spell crafter in Orlean magic. She noted the names and families of those she met, but most of them she could only hope she would never have to deal with often while she was in Orlean.

Rune and Argent were either treated as disgusting relics of old-fashioned magic better left behind or a sign of Arden's waning magical power. None were willing to accept her as anything more than a gold digger or prostitute, even the women seemed baffled that she wished to discuss magical theory and refused every offer to allow a nearby single man to accompany her for the evening.

Several illusionists who built castles and filled the room with mist and the rushing sound of waterfalls provided the entertainments. Everyone clapped politely, but Beryl wished she could see something more elaborate. Surely the Prince would expect something spectacular instead of the illusions that while more detailed than what she had seen of the apprentices work was still hardly something that would ever be thought real. The colors and pulsing lights seemed garish in the crowded room. Couldn't something be done to make the illusions more interactive with the guests?

The Prince waved her to the front when the last illusion was dismissed.

"Mage, may I present your mastery cords for the disciplines that Arden acknowledges. I hope to see you gain more cords in the coming years." He said handing over the three cords, red for fire elemental magic, bronze for warding, and black for a spell crafter. The crowd murmured as she accepted with a curtsy, stepping so the side so they could see the colors. There had not been an acknowledged spell crafter in Orlean in decades.

The next few hours were tedious, and she finally begged release, pleading a headache. It was nearly midnight, and even the prince looked relieved to be able to head to his rooms. Walking back along the garden paths, she bit back the impulse to scream her frustration to the stars above her. Why could no one see her own power and worth without trying to tie it to the surrounding men?

Chapter 24

Gaining Momentum

Beryl exchanged a sigh with Argent as she straightened and moved to a chair, giving Rune a chin scratch as he settled in her lap, Argent leaning against her legs. They had been waiting on her new apprentice for over three hours, no student would do this to their soon to be new master unless there was some massive travel accident. Did his carriage flip?

Maybe the boy would be skilled enough to assist her in some small way. She could only hope, she mused, trying to figure out where she would fit lessons into her already busy days. She had too much to do to take on yet more. She could only hope he was competent enough to carry some of the load.

"William of Westedge," the page announced, striding in and holding the door for the tall young man behind him. Beryl restrained herself, but she wanted to curse. The boy she'd been expecting was over twenty. He shared the inky hair and sharp chin of the King, but the Prince had the same.

"You are the Master Mage wishing to take my apprenticeship? This must be a joke." He sputtered, glancing around like he was waiting for someone to leap to his rescue.

"They offered you a paid apprenticeship to a Master Mage. I'm the only royal mage without an apprentice. If in one year you wish to change masters they will arrange it." Beryl said, setting Rune on the arm of the chair and standing.

"I haven't agreed to the apprenticeship!"

"Then why bother to come if you don't want the opportunity?" She asked, making her way to the fire and readying a spell as the bastard prince snarled and paced to one side.

"A noble doesn't have to explain his situation to a no name mage who is too young to be a veritable master of the craft!"

"Shall I explain it for you then?" She asked waving the fire into a roaring blaze in a shower of golden sparks, "You have been living off a trust for your entire life. Your clothes are last year's designs yet you wore them to the palace so they are the best you have. You've misused funds or something withheld them from you to curtail your expenses. You came here because an apprenticeship means a small stipend and free food and housing until you are declared a Master Mage or are dismissed."

"If they apprentice you to me, you will receive a small allowance dependent on your work and compliance with any rules I set. You will have practical and palace worthy attire provided since you will accompany me on various errands. If you embarrass yourself or anyone else in your company at an event, I will prevent you from attending another until I've decided your work has improved."

"This is insulting. I refuse." He spat, storming across the room.

"Very well," she magically rang the bell for a servant and called for her cloak, "the offer will be available until the end of second day."

The young man seethed as she collected her things and left without a backward glance. She wanted to snarl and scream herself. How in the world was she supposed to teach and protect a young man who saw her as a child? She had no rank in his eyes, so he would offer her no respect. Her bond mates were silent as they made their way back to the cottage. How did you teach someone who did not want to be taught or even to work?

"That was a short meeting, Mistress." Mary said, taking her cloak before Beryl could toss it on a chair and following along as she climbed the stairs to her rooms.

"I need the guest room made ready for a long-term resident." Beryl grimaced, "Once he arrives you are to touch nothing but his laundry and linens, he will care for everything else if he agrees to stay."

"Not the new maid I take it?" she asked, her voice dry but eyes twinkling.

"No, Jeremy gave a reference for a young woman he knows that needs a better situation. Olivia will arrive next week." Beryl sighed, arriving at her bedroom and changing, "The new resident will be my apprentice if he agrees to the contract. We will need to monitor him the first few weeks. He's used to being given whatever he strikes a fancy to, don't let him take advantage of you or anyone else on the staff. I'll have Rune or Argent staying with you if I'm not available."

"Surely he won't be that awful?" Mary asked, taking the dress Beryl handed her and hanging it up.

"I'm taking no chances." Beryl huffed, pulling on a pair of pants and an oversized sweater, "He's much too old for a traditional apprentice. I started at fifteen and they considered even me too old. He's in his twenties and afraid of magic."

"Is he some nobleman's son, then?"

"Yes, what do you know of Westedge? He wasn't announced with a title, but he acts like he has one."

"Westedge is a small duchy near my hometown to the East. The Duke doesn't travel, so he's never at court or any of the local events. I wasn't aware he had a son, his wife died some years ago."

"Perhaps he indulged the boy after his wife's death." Beryl mused, pulling on her boots, "Whatever the cause we might be stuck dealing with the aftereffects. I have a feeling that little will happen without a struggle for William of Westedge."

* * *

Beryl tried not to groan as she watched the drunk young man stumble from his carriage. She was glad Jeremy was out running an errand so he didn't have to deal with this. The carriage porter helped him to his feet before he could hit the ground, only to earn a slurred curse.

"William of Westedge, how delightful to see you. I take it you are agreeable to the apprenticeship?" she asked pleasantly, masking her annoyance as best she could.

"I am, Madame." He mumbled giving her a shaky bow turning green as he straightened.

"Very good. May I have your hand to add you to the wards?" she asked, holding out one hand.

"You've added personal wards to the palace?" He blinked, frowning at the cottage before him as if just noticing it.

"The Prince granted me permission along with use of the cottage."

"Why in the world would you stay out here when you could be in the palace?" He asked, swaying in place as he offered his hand.

"I prefer my privacy." She said taking his limp hand and pressing a charged spell stone into it even as she added his magical signature to the wards. She watched his eyes go wide at the surge of magic.

"Oh, gods." He choked, ripping his hand out of her grasp and stumbling to his knees to vomit into the shrubs.

"Are you ill? I've never seen that kind of reaction to such a simple spell." She asked gesturing for the porters to finish with the bags, she would slip the driver a few coins for the workers.

"I apologize, Madame. I'm afraid the drive has done me in for the day." He gasped, staggering back to his feet.

"Let me show you in." She said ushering him to the door, "Mary, please show William to his room. Perhaps a pot of peppermint tea to sooth his stomach?"

"Right away, Madame. This way, please." Mary said, taking his arm and leading him inside.

"Do you wish us to help clean up, Madame?" the driver asked, accepting the coins with thanks.

"No, he will see to it himself in the morning. Can I ask you a favor before you leave?"

"Madame. How can we help you?"

"I need his things searched for alcohol before they go in the house. One of my servants has issues with it, and we don't allow it inside at all."

"Leave it to us, Madame. We'll bring the trunks in once it's sorted. I'll watch the boys to make sure they don't get any ideas."

"Thank you, gentlemen." She said wandering over to the puddle of sick and spelling it away with a grimace. She doubted the young man would be up to doing much for the rest of the day.

"Do I want to know what you spelled the young man with?" Benjamin asked with a resigned look.

"I'll be his legal guardian once the contract is signed, he has already given verbal agreement so I can legally cast whatever I feel necessary to ensure his health and safety."

"And his recent illness?"

"A healing charm that helps to purge the body of alcohol. People don't react well if they are already blind drunk."

"That wasn't the only spell you cast. I saw three lines of runes."

"I'm regretting teaching you that technique." Beryl sighed, "The second spell was to cause an adverse reaction to alcohol if he drinks over three glasses a day. The third linked him to the wards of the cottage."

"He won't be happy when he learns you've spelled him against his will."

"I doubt he will ever bother to ask."

"Madame," he sighed in exasperation, glaring at her with a resigned sigh when she didn't respond.

"I will inform him once we sign the contract and we finalize his protections as my ward." She said after the silence had stretched on too long.

"Thank you, Madame." He huffed, "While I doubted it will

improve things. In the long run, I've found it best to be open about such things."

"I refuse to have a drunkard for an apprentice, much less one staying under my roof. If he can prove his restraint I will remove the spell."

* * *

Beryl woke early the next morning. The air was cool and a low mist hugged the grounds around the cottage. She stretched and started her dagger practice and wind forms before heading outside to work on sword and staff forms until breakfast. William had yet to appear, and she sent Mary to fetch him for breakfast. He wouldn't be eating in his rooms if she had any say in the matter.

He'd slept the day away after his arrival, not bothering to come down for dinner. Everyone could hear a shouted exchange followed by a slamming door. Beryl waved Jeremy back to his chair when he stood looking ready to tear into the boy. The wards had indicated no injuries.

"That boy needs to learn manners." Mary huffed, moving to finish setting the table, everyone helping once she pointed to what needed to be moved.

"Do I need to speak with him?" she asked, finishing her tea and placing the cup and saucer by the sink.

"No, I said that breakfast was ready and his presence requested downstairs. He asked for a tray and a bath drawn. I explained the magical tabs and repeated that he was to eat downstairs."

"And the shouting?"

"He called me a dimwitted whore unworthy to lick his boots before slamming the door." Mary said stiffly, "They have called me worse."

"You shouldn't have been called anything," Jeremy growled unhappily.

"I'll inform him of the house rules on such behavior after break-fast. I can assure you it won't happen more than once." Beryl said grabbing a hot cake and a bowl of fruit to take to with her, "Enjoy your meal. If he emerges send him to my study."

"Shall I bring some tea up, Madame?"

"Thank you, Mary. That would be lovely. Olivia should arrive later today. Please make her welcome and show her to her room. I'll meet with her after lunch to complete her contract."

Beryl could hear them muttering to each other as she left, but she didn't have time to calm the room if she would make the alterations needed before William emerged. She was just finishing the last touches on a thick sliver chain bracelet when he was announced.

"Are you a jeweler as well?" He drawled, dropping into the chair behind her without waiting for her to acknowledge him.

"Yes, I specialize in magically crafted pieces that hold protection wards against harm or poisoning. This one will be yours once I'm finished."

"It's hideous." He sniffed, eyes flitting about the room like he was pricing the various objects, if he was thinking of stealing he'd was a bigger fool then she'd thought.

"It can be glamoured into any illusion you have the power to cast or to blend into your skin." She said finishing her casting and turning to take in his untidy sprawl, "Are you still agreeable to an appren-ticeship?"

"I would not be in this hovel if I wasn't." He sneered, watching as she laid out the contract and gestured him forward.

"The contract is ready, I suggest you peruse the terms. You have all day to make your ultimate decision."

"I am decided. When do we start my classes?" He asked, snatching up a quill and signing at the bottom.

"We start lessons tomorrow. I expect you up and dressed in clothes less likely to be ruined while working outside." She said handing him the bracelet as she signed, duplicated the contract, and filed the original away. "Are you certain you don't want to review the contract?"

"No, I am here to learn. Give me my first assignment, Master." He drawled picking at his nails while surveying the room.

"First, there are a few rules of the household you need to be aware of." She offered, pouring a cup of tea and handing it to him before fixing her own. She returned to the desk turning the chair to face him as he returned to his chair abandoning his copy of the contract on the floor next to him.

"Is this necessary?"

"You've already broken two of the rules since you arrived. Given you were unaware of the rules at the time, I will withhold punishment for any offenses given until we start lessons tomorrow morning."

"Punishment?! You must be joking. I am here to take lessons and learn magic, not to be threatened like an unruly child!"

"You are not a student, you are an apprentice. As such, your Master has complete control. We expect you to bid by your Master's decisions in all matters."

"I did not agree to those terms!"

"You signed a magically binding contract for a minimum of one year of service, I'm afraid I cannot revoke it until that year has passed."

"I have things I must see to, duties I have to perform. I can't be stuck here!"

"We can schedule any required duties with my house manager and myself. I wasn't aware the Duke of Westedge had passed on the management of the estate to you."

"He hasn't," William seethed, snatching up the contract.

"I see, and what duties would you need your schedule rearranged for?"

"I am courting a woman of the court, not that it is any of your business! I wish to annul the contract."

"Per the contract you will have one day free to do as you wish each week. As for annulment, you may review the contract at your leisure and seek counsel, but it is a magically binding contract for the next year. Neither of us can easily cancel it."

"I need a carriage, I would like my father to review this." He snapped, waving the crumpled parchment.

"Very well, I will send for a coach, but I expect you to return by lunch tomorrow to discuss your training." She agreed easily sending a note to Jeremy with a small surge of magic that William tracked with wide eyes, the parchment folding into a swan shape and soaring past them and out the door, "The coach should be along in a moment if you would like to wait in the courtyard."

She stayed in her study and watched the young man pacing manically back and forth before throwing himself in the carriage the moment it stopped. Making a cup of tea, she settled into wait as the rest of the staff gathered. Mary passed out cups and offered muffins that only Argent was willing to wolf down happily.

"Are we done with the brat?" Jeremy asked, setting his cup down with a clatter when no one seemed inclined to start.

"No, he signed a magical contract without bothering to read it." Beryl sighed, waving away their retorts, "He's bound as my apprentice for the next year whether or not he likes it."

"Kores damn him, does he have no sense at all?" Jeremy sputtered, dabbing at the tea he'd spilled down his front.

"You haven't been around royalty much. They are either so pampered they wouldn't know how to wipe their own nose without instructions, or it has forced them to grow up and realize that their decisions have consequences. Most of the nobility at least are still people under it all. He's been sheltered and never had to face or even decide about his life. It will be a rough transition if he's been as isolated as I think he's been."

"Isolated?" Benjamin asked, fingers twirling his ring.

"He claims to be the heir of Westedge, yet Mary's from that area and has never heard of him. He may have never left the estates until he came to court."

"So he's a country lord fallen to the vices of palace life?" Benjamin surmised, earning a snort from Jeremy.

"Not exactly," Beryl sighed, debating how much to reveal, "if I tell you anymore it must fall under your oaths of secrecy. Not even to the boy himself."

"He's that important?"

"The apprenticeship is valid, but they instructed me to protect him at all costs should things go badly." Beryl sighed, setting her own cup aside.

"If I am to protect the brat I'd like to know why." Jeremy said glancing over the others.

"We are already keeping your secrets, Madame. One more is hardly a burden." Mary pointed out with a frown.

"You say that now," Beryl muttered, standing with a huff and going to each person and reinforcing their protection charms before she continued, "William is a royal bastard. I suspect they raised him as royalty and may even know his parentage. I don't know who fathered him, but he is next in line should the King and Prince die."

"A brat like that on the throne, Metros preserve us." Jeremy groaned, cursing the gods.

"The contract gives us one year to get his head on straight. Even if the unthinkable happens, I will still be his master until the contract ends."

"Does he know of the threats on his life?"

"No, I would inform him today, but then he had a tantrum over the contract." Beryl tugged at her hair violently as she unbraided it, needing something to do with her hands, "He is at least wearing a bracelet with every protection charm I could manage since yesterday."

"What do you need from us, Madame?" Benjamin asked.

"I need you to treat him as an apprentice. His blood has nothing to do with him while he is here. I expect him to treat you as I would and I want any attacks, verbal or physical, to be called out immediately. I won't tolerate anyone abusing those around me no matter what their rank."

"He will not take to lessons or guidance easily if he's used to being catered to." Benjamin pointed out with a slight grimace.

"That will be my task and I've dealt with enough bullies and brats, we just need to find what pushes him in the right direction."

Chapter 25

Working with William

Beryl was just finishing lunch when the wards announced the arrival of William's coach the next day. She waved the others back to their meal and quickly made a pot of tea to take back to her study. She doubted the boy was going to be any less prickly today simply because they had informed him of his mistakes.

She watched from the window as William gathered himself before knocking on the door to the cottage. This wasn't going to be a pleasant conversation. At least he appeared to be sober this time, if still looking exhausted and ill. They would have to work on that. The boy needed someone to direct him to healthier outlets.

"William of Westedge is here to see you, Madame." Olivia said softly showing the young man in, Beryl noted the leer he threw the maid's way and added that to the list of things to discuss.

"Thank you, Olivia." Beryl murmured, gesturing William to a chair, "Would you care for tea?"

"No, thank you." William said stiffly, taking a seat, "I've reviewed the contract and been advised to complete the contracted apprenticeship. I am at your disposal, Madame."

"Very well, do you wish to discuss any of the points of the

contract or should we start with what you will be learning and the rules of the house?"

"You mentioned rules of conduct previously." He bit out with distaste, "I take it your ideals differ from those of Orlean society?"

"In many ways." Beryl said with a sigh, stroking Argent's head and taking a bracing breath before she began, "First of all, all staff in this house is to be treated with the same respect you give myself. If I find out you have abused or maligned any of the staff in any form, I will punish you as I deem necessary."

"What would these punishments comprise?"

"Physical work or labor. You will be assigned chores about the property, given tasks that suit your current level of training, or assigned physical exercises such as running laps or extra weapons practice."

"You expect me to run about like a commoner?"

"I expect you to do as instructed, you will only be forced to such menial tasks if you ignore those instructions. No one outside of the cottage will be aware of your punishments and unless you do something egregious, you will not be punished off its grounds."

"What of my lessons?"

"I practice two crafts along my magical endeavors. I expect you to assist me in at least one. You may choose to learn blacksmithing or crafting magical items such as the jewelry I make. I personally think you will be more suited for blacksmithing."

"Are you joking?"

"Every apprentice works to craft objects to be enchanted. Unless you wish to learn from an outside source, these are the options open to you."

"When would I learn magic if I'm working at becoming a blacksmith?"

"Every morning you will rise before breakfast and have weapon's practice. After breakfast we will have lessons in magic and its applications. There will be a break for lunch and in the afternoon you will learn to craft objects or watch me work on larger projects to expand your knowledge of the magical craft."

"I will have no time to myself?"

"You will have every seventh day for yourself as well as the days I assign you a project to work upon. Once the project is completed and presented to myself, you will have the rest of the day off to do as you wish."

"Very well," he gritted out, clearly fighting with his temper, "what will I be tasked with today?"

"Today we will test your magical aptitude." Beryl said standing and gesturing him into her workroom, "Show me your best skill, Apprentice William."

"As you wish, Madame." He huffed, taking off his coat and shaking back his frilled cuffs.

The next half hour was painful as she watched illusions waiver and collapse into showers of sparks as William became more and more frustrated at her lack of reaction. He didn't attempt any warding magic at all, sticking to visual and auditory illusions that verged on mocking, echos of tittering laughter or taunting shouts rang in the room from various corners while towering castles and mountains flicked like candle light floating midair. Finally his hands dropped, fists clenched as he fought to slow his breathing, sweat coating his face.

"Do you know any magic other than illusions?"

"It is the principal focus of study for Orlean mages. I impressed my previous tutors with my detailed images."

"They are quite detailed," she agreed, rolling back her sleeves and gesturing him to a place near the wall as she gathered some supplies, "let me demonstrate a few things that I will be able to teach you."

"Very well," he huffed dropping into a chair in one corner and gesturing for her to proceed with a small smirk that faded as she chalked a complex runic circle into the floor, "what exactly are you hoping to cast with that?"

"Just protecting the floor, I doubt the housekeeper would want to deal with charred floors every time I summon an element."

"Summon an element? I've never heard of such a thing." He scoffed, shifting deeper in his chair as the wards activated pulsing sickly red.

"It's not exactly a well-known branch of magic, but we task every apprentice in Arden with communing with an element until they discover their strengths and weaknesses. Some show affinity with fire and stone, others to water and earth. Those with a strong elemental sense can use a simple fire run to control fire in ways another would need extensive chanting and assisting warding to control. It can be a dangerous art to practice." She said gesturing and causing a small flame to burst to life in the center of the circle, "The wards keep the heat contained and channel it outside to the forge where it can dissipate safely without causing damage to the house."

The fire suddenly roared to the ceiling, filling the circle and lighting the room with dancing shadows. There should have been impossible heat as the fire roared brighter turning white blue before it subsided but the room remained comfortable. She twisted the flames into several shapes, birds, a running hound, a tree before she let it collapse into itself and go out with a soft puff of smoke. William was pale as she carefully broke the runic circle and stared to explain simple runic spells and their meanings, casting small wards and charms as she went. It took nearly an hour of demonstrations before she finally started cleaning up the mess she'd made of her workroom.

"Do you have any questions?"

"I've never seen anything like that." He breathed, "You can truly teach me to do such things?"

"Yes, however, you need to understand that in Arden mages are bound from causing harm with their magic. Only the King can order a mage to turn their magic on another. To cast even a simple tripping jinx on another with intent to harm is to lose your magic."

"But Arden uses their magic in war, everyone knows it."

"We did centuries past, but now mages don't take part in wars beyond protecting the troops, healing, and enchanting weapons or armor. We scry for the enemy camps if asked, but just as often they have ordered me to scout on foot. Magic isn't meant to be used to injure, it's a gift from the gods and the earth. Using magic to kill drains the magic from an area killing the soil and wildlife making it unlivable for generations to come."

"So you couldn't cause an enemy to burst into flame?"

"No, generally I spelled them to sleep when fighting."

"You've been to war? That's impossible, you're too young." He scoffed, his arrogance returning.

"I went to war at sixteen." Beryl said with a chuckle, "The soldiers thought me a useless girl as well at first. Let's go to dinner, you need to meet the rest of the staff. Tomorrow morning during practice you'll see just how useless I am on the battlefield."

"No one would send a sixteen-year-old girl to war."

"Why not? They send boys that age."

"That's different."

"I will have to show you the difference. I hope you like roast with sage, Apprentice. Mary has been cooking all day, so we should have a good meal waiting."

"Was that Mary who showed me in?" He asked with a calculating glance.

"No, that was Olivia. She is my new maid and is not here for your attentions."

"Excuse me?!"

"Abusing the staff includes pressuring them to obey you. They have the same authority I do when it comes to your behavior. If they order you to leave them alone, you are to do so. If I find you have been tormenting my staff, there will be weeks of running in your future, Apprentice."

"My name is William." He snapped.

"You haven't offered to allow me to call you that." She said keeping her tone mild, "Would you prefer it?"

"Anything is better than Apprentice."

"You will still be Apprentice Westedge should we be in public, but in private it will be William." She agreed, gesturing him to a chair as they arrived in the dining room. The rest of the staff quickly stood as they entered, taking their seats as Mary served.

"Everyone, may I introduce William of Westedge, my new apprentice." She announced thanking Mary as she passed her a plate, "He will be staying with us for the next year."

"Wonderful to meet you, William." Mary said with a tight smile, passing him his plate and continuing down the table.

"To your left, William, is Benjamin, our House Manager, across the table is Jeremy, who will assist in your weapons training and Olivia, who you met previously."

"Pleasure to meet you all." He drawled with a frown fiddling with his goblet, "Is there anything stronger to drink?"

"No, alcohol isn't allowed in the cottage. If you wish to drink, you will have to do so in your free time." Beryl said flatly.

"Surely you are joking. My father has a marvelous vineyard. I can arrange for a shipment to be sent for."

"May I be blunt?" Beryl asked, waiting for his uncertain nod before continuing, "My Uncle was a miserable drunk who treated everyone around him like trash. I won't have alcohol in my household. Not now, not ever, and no offer of fine vintages will change my mind. If you wish anything stronger than cider, then you must find it on your own. The property is warded and you won't be allowed to pass the threshold with any type of alcohol. I suggest you don't test the warding."

"Very well," he said, setting his goblet to one side, "I apologize if I've misspoke."

"It is nothing," Beryl said waiving the matter away, turning to the rest of the table, "Benjamin, how has your day gone?"

* * *

The conversation was stilted, and Beryl retreated to her rooms as soon as she was able to do so politely. She'd need to push William tomorrow morning, but for now she'd had all the interaction she could take for the day. She couldn't deal with both of their issues right then, a night apart would give them both some distance.

She wrote a brief letter to John and left it sealed on her desk to send the next day. They'd been writing each other steadily with John pressing for her to join him at Glenlight estate in the coming weeks, but she'd been putting the decision off too afraid that something would go wrong while she was away. The prince seemed determined to ignore her warnings and continued to hold events and hunts on the grounds while attending parties at various nearby venues. She was at her wits' end trying to keep a step ahead. At this rate, half the region would be warded and covered with protections from the coast to the mountains.

The next morning she ignored the grumbles from William as he staggered along behind them. They trailed single file down the path into the woods behind the cottage to a handy clearing they had been using for weapons training and archery practice. William was still overdressed, but he'd learn today exactly what they would be putting him through. Argent and Rune wandered the edges of the meadow, keeping out of the way.

"What weapons have you learned so far?" she asked, tossing her bags to one side and stretching while Jeremy set up the archery targets to one side.

"I took lessons in sword fighting from Sword Master John Assant, he was the regional champion for eight years running."

"Very impressive, what kind of sword did you use?" Beryl asked mildly, dropping into a split and ignoring the way the two men both looked hastily away with a mental groan.

"A rapier, my father wished me to be the best at whatever I attempted."

"You learned formal dueling?" She questioned him absently, already nodding along with his response as she twisted and stretched.

"Is there anything else?"

"Many things as you will soon see." Beryl sighed, standing and gesturing for him to join Jeremy where he was laying out weapons, "Jeremy will coach you in sword work, I use a short sword, daggers, and sling myself. I don't have the length of limb needed for a rapier. Warm and up and show us your stance, if you please."

"Your servant is going to be teaching?"

"Jeremy Cannon served in the Army, he is well versed in sword work. Don't underestimate him."

"He wouldn't last five minutes in a duel! He's crippled!"

"Then it's a good thing we aren't dueling, isn't it," Jeremy spat, "would you care to give the boy a demonstration, Mistress?"

"Not yet. I'd rather he learned this lesson himself." Beryl said gathering up her daggers and moving to the first target, "To the first blood if you please, I need my apprentice fit for work this afternoon."

"As you wish, Mistress Mage." He said, tendering her a mocking bow.

"You expect us to duel?" William asked, exasperated, as Jeremy advanced and gestured the younger man forward.

"I expect you to fight, whether or not it is a duel is up to you." Beryl huffed, gesturing for them to start with an absent wave of one hand.

"What was it you said, five minutes? Step forward, Billie my boy."

"My name is William, servant. Respect your betters."

"I've yet to see you lift your blade, Billie boy. Come at me, or are you too pampered to know the edge of a blade against your skin?"

"You felonious upstart! I will see you hanged!" They met with a crash of blades, William trying to win by brute strength in his fit of rage. Seconds later he was sent flying by a harsh kick from Jeremy.

"The first lesson a soldier learns is to never attack in anger, it dulls your blade. Up, again!"

"You know nothing of dueling!" William snarled, thrashing to his feet and taking a fencing stance.

"I never said this was a duel, boy. You fight to kill or survive, there won't be any of that polite tapping of blades here. Show me what you know, Billie. Come!"

They clashed and parted, William trying to dart in for a killing strike only to be bludgeoned back with sweeping blows that sent him dancing backwards. He didn't know how to fight back with Jeremy pressing into his space and soon went sprawling from another blow to his side.

"You are dead if you lose your feet in battle, up!"

"Give me a moment," William snarled, chest heaving as he staggered to his feet.

"You won't be allowed time to catch your breath on the battlefield, move or die, Billie."

"This isn't a battlefield!" he gasped, lunging for another strike only to have his sword knocked from his hand.

"Then why are you losing?" Jeremy asked, not bothering to stop pressing the young man backwards until his back hit a tree.

"Stop, I yield!" He shouted, gasping as the sword tip pressed against his neck.

"First blood, Mistress Mage." Jeremy announced, stepping back and sheathing his sword.

"Noted, Jeremy. How is your trainee?" Beryl asked, retrieving her knives and wandering to join them.

"I protest this barbaric treatment," William spat gingerly, feeling at his neck for nicks.

"Also noted," Beryl sighed, "I learned from a soldier when I was fifteen, William. I worked on sword patterns with a staff and short sword however you are tall enough to use a full sword. Jeremy will be your trainer in its use. Every morning you will train with him for one hour before joining me to learn daggers or staves. You can take a break while Jeremy works with me on my form."

"This isn't proper dueling."

"No, and it's not meant to be. This is fighting to stay alive and to protect those weaker than yourself. You won't learn moves that can be used in a polite duel while under my tutelage. I'm teaching you to survive to fight another day."

"Why would I ever need to know such things?"

"If you are going to be around me, you need to be able to protect yourself. I have many enemies and I won't have your blood on my hands because you are too stubborn to learn."

"You are a mage, who would want to harm you?"

"I've already had three attempts to poison myself and my staff. Jeremy has been offered bribes to reveal the details of my routines and the household staff's during meetings in the palace and elsewhere. You haven't joined a safe household and if you don't want to be injured, you need to be ready for a potential attack. I expect you to be armed and if possible wearing light armor whenever you leave the cottage or palace grounds."

"That is absurd. Why would they be attacking your staff?"

"The nobility dislike having outsiders in their midst, and I don't fit what many consider a proper magic user. I don't have the same political views considering I was raised as a poor commoner from a fishing village. I treat commoners and nobility alike, and it has led to many enemies in my life. I am currently employed to protect the royal family, and eventually whoever is hunting them will come for me as well. I don't want those close to me dragged into the bloodshed if I can help it, which is why you are going to receive training and protections as much as I'm able to provide them."

"Enough chatter," Joseph called out, scooping up William's discarded sword and tossing it to him, "clean your blade while you rest. Come, girl, let's get going and show this boy a proper bout."

"Whenever you are ready, Captain." She grinned, taking a ready stance and saluting him with a dagger.

"Imp." He scoffed, waiting for her to close the distance between them.

"Cur." She offered back with a laugh as they feinted and blocked, dancing on light feet about the clearing. Neither gained much ground with the other, both dodging feet, elbows and headlong rushes. Beryl ducked a slash and tossed a handful of soil into Jeremy's face making him stagger back cursing as she knocked his sword aside and mule kicked him with both feet, tumbling away before he could bring his own dagger into play. Scrambling, she lunged forward, straddling his chest and placing a dagger against his throat.

"I yield." He conceded, tossing his dagger away and allowing her to back away carefully.

"Why is he allowed to yield when I wasn't?" William demanded from his collapsed sprawl to one side.

"Because she never took her eyes away from me or sheathed her weapons until I was beyond striking distance." Jeremy huffed, standing and gathering up practice weapons and a skin of water he tossed to William, "Get some water into you and then we'll start going over the basic stances for the sword and staff. You could do with a brush up on your stances as well, Mage."

"Of course," Beryl agree easily finishing wiping down her daggers and taking the skin for a drink herself, "never drink too much when you're already winded, get up and walk. Your previous instructor should have taught you that at least."

"We rarely did over three passes before a break and not at the speed you two fight." He grumbled, sipping from the skin she tossed him.

"True fights to the death are rarely about endurance, either you are dead in three blows or you are fast enough to kill you opponent or run away. In battle there is no time to stop until they call a retreat, I'm hoping you never have to see such fighting but it never hurts to train for an extended fight." Jeremy huffed, catching the water skin and taking a drink before tossing it next to their gear, tossing William a practice sword, "Try this on for length, if you seem adept we might try a broadsword later."

"If he's trained to a rapier, I'd lean toward a lighter weapon that leaves him room to move."

"If you're wanting him light on his feet, he must train with you more than me." Jeremy huffed, rubbing at his bad leg, "Most of what I know if for foot soldiers or calvary, fighting with a short sword, shield, or a spear from the ground and mounted. You can't go carrying about a shield and spear so we are going to focus on short sword and dagger work while I try to find a heavier rapier you can practice with."

"You can't wear weapons openly on palace grounds."

"I can and I've asked for dispensations for my House, I'll make sure the guards are aware that your allowed." Beryl said waving away the concern, "Let's get started, the morning is wasting."

"Come get in line, face me." Jeremy said gesturing them forward, "First stance."

They went through their standard practice with practice swords for an hour before dismissing William and having a brief bout with practice swords. They walked back to the cottage afterwards and Beryl smirked at the young man's groans. He had no idea what awaited him after breakfast. They separated to clean up, and she wasn't surprised when it took another hour for William to join her in the workroom.

"What will I be learning today?" He asked, glancing about the room like she might have another bird of flames hiding in a corner. At least he was showing some enthusiasm.

"Today will be spent testing your aptitude for the various elements," Beryl said gathering up the needed supplies and scattering them across the warded table she'd set up early that morning, "you will concentrate on each item before you and attempt to force some change with your magic, the orb in the center will respond if you have any affinity with the elements that make up the items."

"What spell should I be attempting to cast?" He asked, taking a seat with a frown.

"Nothing, the goal is to get your magic to rise to the surface and interact with the items." She murmured, reaching out and lighting the lone candle with a gesture, "Your assignment for tonight before bed will be to pick an element and meditate on its properties. You need to understand how your magic reacts before you can truly achieve a powerful ward or spell."

"This is all I'm learning today?"

"Once we know what elements you favor, we can tailor your learning toward spells that favor those elements. I favor stones and fire so my wards are extremely strong, but I'm not adept at spells based on plants or healing. I can cast basic spells, but the more advanced spells take massive effort. You will be the same, we need to know your elements before we proceed, if you want more you can start learning how to read and write the standard runes used in runic crafts." She said setting two books to one side of the table, "You have one hour to work on this, concentrate."

"How will I know if the element is reacting?"

"You will feel some part of the element in your mind. Fire generally makes me hear a roaring fire with warmth in my chest." She said reaching out and cupping her hand behind the flame for a moment causing the orb to pulse with a deep red light, "The orb will react differently depending on the strength of your magical connection to the element but that can be deepened with practice."

"How long until I can cast a runic spell?"

"Complete this assignment and I will show you a simple spell to practice in your strongest element." Beryl allowed amusement flowing between her and her bond mates at his sudden eagerness but it was tempered with weariness, she'd seen too many power hungry students burn themselves out attempting magic beyond their means to trust this sudden thirst to learn.

"Have your previous tutors explained magical burnout?"

"Yes, however, they assured me I didn't have to worry about it." He huffed intent on the candle and frowning in concentration.

"Leave the candle a moment," She snapped, moving it from his reach with a gesture, "they said you never had to worry about burnout? Any mage can burnout, your power levels don't matter. I've suffered from burnout."

"They said illusionists don't suffer from burn out since it's a milder magical endeavor."

"That is ridiculous. Any spell can be draining if you over reach or do it too many times in a day. Did they teach you the signs of burnout, exhaustion, irritability, burning in the joints and muscles, fever?"

"No, they said it wouldn't be an issue."

"You weren't studying warding, it could be an issue now. You need to be careful, if you start to feel weak or dizzy, we need to stop practice for at least a day to allow your magical reserves to recover."

"It's that serious?" William asked, blinking as she set the candle back before him.

"Healers are watched extremely carefully because they can easily become overextended. Warding is just as draining, and if you aren't watching, it can hit you hard when you overextend yourself. I was sick for weeks with fever and weakness right before I left Arden, thanks to spell backlash. I'm not saying it will affect you, but I want you prepared in case it does."

"I'll be careful."

"Very well, try not to stare at the candle too long." Beryl murmured with a small chuckle, "I'm going to be working on warding some new jewelry for the Princess' ladies-in-waiting, if you need a break you are welcome to observe."

"Ah ha." He hummed absently, mind already fixated on the flame in front of him.

* * *

The next few days fell into a pattern of training and lessons. She tried to keep things varied, to keep the young man interested, but so far he was doing rather well. He was slow to easily pick up runes, but he'd tested strong for earth and water so he would have a mild affinity with fire and air as well. He seemed to resent the fact that fire wasn't his chief strength and rejected her wind scrying outright. She wasn't sure he'd do any better today if his mood continued to worsen.

"I've written my father asking for my training rapiers to be sent. I'm not sure why I would need something sooner." He huffed as she showed him the correct way to start the forge fire and which runes on the pipes to activate in what sequence.

"You will learn at least one trade while working as my apprentice, I can teach you blacksmithing or jewelry making. What you pick is up to you, but this afternoon we will be smithing and warding a simple dagger. I already have the basic parts ready to be attached so it should not take us long to start adding the runes."

"What will I be doing?"

"Today is observation. Tomorrow you will work on stoking the forge to the correct temperature and making and warding nails."

"Nails." He repeated flatly watching as she assembled the blade, tang, and

"Once you can prove to me you are capable of warding a nail with at least three separate runes, I will teach you how to craft a dagger of your own."

The lessons dragged on with William reluctantly doing the work and Beryl correcting him at every turn. She'd managed to get him to enchant small objects, but he declared it useless and the lessons became endurance tests to see which would lose their temper first. Beryl had never thought of herself as mild tempered, but the boy seemed to have a knack for testing her patience. When he turned in a slap shod warded snuff box the night before his day off she was close to confining him to the house but finally let him go so she could have to time to arrange some of the more unsavory meetings she'd been putting off.

Jeremy was easy enough to pass off as a bruiser she'd hired to rough up the competition, but Benjamin was a thief's perfect target on market day, distracted and too well mannered to raise a fuss if he lost his purse. The trip into town had been a last-minute decision, but she'd heard of a local thief who was acting as the intermediary for the region's guild master, and she wanted to arrange a meeting. Jeremy was at least being entertained by the range of aghast expressions Benjamin had managed since they arrived, Beryl thought with amusement. Having the meeting in a brothel had been a nice touch.

"How may we assist you this morning, good sirs?" The hostess asked with a blooming smile as Benjamin all but squeaked while he turned scarlet as her dress, "I might have to steal you away for the night, good sir. It's rare to get such an honest man in a place like this."

"We are here to meet Madame Lacene." Beryl offered with a small smile, "Would you care to wait in the lounge, Cousin? Perhaps a glass of water would help cool you down. You are rather flushed."

"Of course, yes, that would be lovely." Benjamin sputtered, taking a waiting woman's arm and letting her lead him to the lounge area.

"This way please," The hostess murmured, showing them upstairs to a private office, "Lacene will be right with you."

"Thank you," Beryl murmured absently, checking on Rune, who was waiting outside while Argent paced unhappily to one side of the room. The women had cooed over him as they entered, then laughed delightedly as he climbed the stairs.

"Not clumsy," he grumbled, sitting finally by the window.

"You are the strongest dog I know, nothing is clumsy about you. Dog just aren't meant to be graceful on stairs."

"Cats are always graceful," Rune purred with a shaft of amusement across the bond.

"Sadly, humans and dogs don't live up to the pretensions of cats." Beryl murmured moving to stand next to Argent, *"Your ungraceful moments have won us many friends in our travels, it's not a fault to struggle with something you are unsuited to."*

"I love you both no matter your grace." She murmured for his ears alone as the owner of the brothel finally joined them, "Thank you for meeting with us, Madame Lacene."

"It is rare that we receive female callers, Lady Mage." She purred, gesturing them to the seating area to one side, "Are you hoping to find something more... pleasant to while away the hours? I have a young man you may find interesting?"

"As tempting as that sounds, I'm afraid I've come on business instead of pleasure."

"How may I assist you this evening? Your request was rather vague."

"I have heard that you are quite well connected in Orlean and its major cities, I'm looking to start a small business and would like to test the waters before I attempt to purchase any property. I've heard certain members of the nobility are inconsiderate of females doing business."

"Orlean isn't the most hospitable country for a female business woman, that is true." Lacene agreed, pouring them each a cup of tea and raising an eyebrow at Jeremy when he refused and moved to the door so he was out of the conversation, "I inherited this business from my previous husband, may his soul rest."

"I am sorry for your loss, but you have done well for yourself. Your name is known throughout the region and you have establishments up and down the coast. You've clearly learned to advance even in a country that doesn't enjoy elevating its women to the same status as their men."

"Few would speak so openly of Orlean's faults. You out yourself as a foreigner by doing so, Lady Mage."

"My pardon if I speak too bluntly, Madame. I've little patience for working in the shadows, and yet I find myself placed there since I've arrived in Orlean." Beryl said keeping her tone pleasant as she took a tiny sip of the tea, "The more comfortable I make myself, the more attempts against my life I uncover. I'm fairly certain I would have been safer to stay living as an exile within Arden then I've found myself currently."

"So you truly are the exiled Mage? I doubted the request when it arrived. Why would a powerful mage need my assistance?"

"While I am a mage, I am also a woman and under the same restrictions you found yourself fighting before your marriage. May I be blunt, Madame Lacene?"

"If it means coming to the point of this meeting, please do."

"I find myself in the need of information that the men about me are keeping out of my hands in order to keep me, in their minds, safe.

Previously, I worked with a merchant's guild to ward various buildings for small bits of information or favors. Many of these buildings were gambling parlors or brothels were men relaxing from their day might say things they wouldn't say to their own wives. I wish to offer a similar trade with your establishments if you are willing."

"I fail to see how such a trade would benefit my business, Lady Mage."

"Protections to lock violent customers outside of the property or doors so they can't damage anything in a drunken rage. Wards that will alert you to such issues while in your office. Protections against fire and self repairing window glass should any be broken."

"I've never heard of such protections."

"I was one of the few mages in Arden to perfect their crafting. I've warded villages across Arden, and the wards have lasted over five years now. The mages who surveyed my work said they could last as long as ten, more if they were repaired every five years."

"And you are offering these protections to me for information?"

"As well as assistance in meeting various contacts that you may have."

"I also design jewelry," Beryl offered trying not to sigh as she removed the extra bracelet and necklace she was wearing and laid them on the table, "these are charmed to warm when the food offered is tainted or poisoned, like with the mild sedative you placed in the tea. They can also be warded to glow slightly when a connected item is activated, I've seen it used for scouts in the army to warn outriders of attack, you could easily use it to warn the girls to close up shop."

"You're offering weapons of war to a brothel?"

"I offered them to the brothels in Arden, why not here if it means you know your girls and boys are safe while they ply their wares?"

"Why did you drink the tea if you knew we dosed it with something?"

"The bracelet told me it wasn't deadly, and I doubted you would try to kill me simply for making an appointment. The tiny amount I drank would have little effect on a mage anyway, our bodies protect themselves from most minor diseases and sedatives."

"Perhaps we can come to a small arrangement," Lacene murmured, picking up one of the pieces gingerly, "who crafted these?"

"I did." Beryl said simply keeping her body language relaxed nevertheless, hands in lap, chest up, shoulders back.

"You do very detailed work for something meant to have such a simple function."

"I've crafted simple silver or gold chains as well. I prefer using gemstones, the wards and enchantments last longer. The royal family hasn't complained of my designs yet, the Princess herself has requested another full set in green emeralds. It should complement her well."

"Green would be a lovely color on her fair skin." Lacene agreed faintly, holding one stone to the light before carefully setting it back down gently, "These are rubies."

"I intend to sell some of my work once I find the right shop but for now I am only doing custom work which means I use more high end gem stones."

"Did you design the net of jewels the princess wore at the last ball?"

"Yes, it took me a fortnight to craft and set the jewels, but it was stunning against her black hair." Beryl agreed easily. She might not want the protections, but for a chance at the most popular items on the market, she might be willing to deal.

"Everyone in Orlean is clamoring for the jewelers name. You could make a fortune on reputation alone, why bother selling in a shop?" she pressed, making Beryl sigh. Money controlled too many people.

"Because the money means little to me, I want a quiet, simple life that I doubt I will ever have." Beryl said with a bitter laugh, "I intend to sell various wares and services but keep the supply of the truly intricate pieces to private buyers. Perhaps if a woman openly owns a shop visited by the royal family, it will make things easier for other women."

"As one business woman to another, the trick is to make yourself indispensable to them." Lacene said returning the jewelry to Beryl and rising to start a fresh pot of tea, hopefully undrugged this time, "They have to bend the rules if they wish to keep you, do they not?"

"True," Beryl agreed with a wry smile at the woman before her, she'd clearly clawed her way to her current station and would be a formidable partner if they could manage to not irritate each other.

"Craft something small but elegant for two of my girls, I'll have them on the arms of the most eligible bachelors in town by the end of the week. By the end of the month with the Prince's birthday party, we'll have the entire town talking. You have something over the top planned for the party, I hope?"

"Not for myself, but the Princess will drip with onyx so plan for something dark like purple amethysts or something similar. I've heard the Prince will wear white for the masquerade, but no one dares breathe a word of what his actual costume is."

"And you? As the crafter, they must see you showing off your best."

"I'd intended to go incognito, better to judge the reactions to my latests works."

"Few are going to miss the Mage accompanied by such a large dog everywhere she goes. You haven't garnered the usual gossip, but word has gotten out." She offered with a small smirk, "The rogue mage who has had multiple meetings with the King and Prince, is often seen talking easily with the Princess. The mage who hires those most would consider unredeemable and yet has inspired staunch loyalty to anyone who asks about you, they refuse to reveal anything beyond singing your praises. You're a puzzle that half the kingdom is hoping to solve."

"I'm just a woman trying to make her way in the world whatever way I can."

"Yet, you say you don't care for money. Surely you wish to turn a profit?"

"Not beyond the expenses I have. I've never dreamed of being rich, I just wish a small cottage by the sea and enough work to keep me busy."

"You don't enjoy the court life."

"Not that I dislike it, I just have no stamina for the constant gossip and drama." Beryl said with a shrug, accepting a fresh cup of tea, "If you like I'll make a handful of simple bracelets for the girls. They will warn against drugged items and have a small healing boost if activated."

"Activated how?"

"A drop of blood to the stone."

"Blood magic? That isn't considered barbaric by your country."

"I wasn't aware it was frowned upon here. It takes a touch of magic to activate a ward and everyone has a touch of magic in their blood, even the non-magical."

"I would not be comfortable with such a system, I doubt the girls would use it."

"I'll see if there is another way," Beryl frowned, "For now I can layer some basic protection wards for them to try out."

"I'll tell them they are from a guest, not everyone has the best view of magic at times." She offered with a tight smile.

"That I am aware of," Beryl chuckled softly, "it seems to be a common factor of life no matter where I travel. Just because something isn't understood, everyone is immediately suspicious and calling it dangerous."

"People rarely jump to embrace the new unless it benefits them. Perhaps you need to bring magic to the people?"

"I'm not sure we could. Even if every apprentice was mass producing trinkets or light globes, they would never be able to get enough made for every home. We could make enough for the rich and lower nobility, but unless someone finds a way to make crafting less draining on the mage, it would be grueling work."

"Says the woman who works a forge by herself." Jeremy snorted from by the door.

"I hope to eventually hire help. I have to purchase a house first. There is no use training someone local if we're just going to move."

"Where are you hoping to buy? I have a client who works with families looking to consolidate their estates. He may be able to assist you. Let me grab his card from my office."

"Thank you."

"Don't thank me yet, Darling. I have comprehensive plans for our partnership. If your jewelry takes off as I hope, I plan to own at least ten percent of the business, if not more. Perhaps in a few years we'll both be able to retire to the seaside." She said with a wicked grin as she stood and strode to the door, "Stand aside, soldier. I'll just be a moment."

"I doubt I'd ever be able to tear you away from the city, Lacene. You're too wicked for the country." Beryl called back with a smile as the woman winked on her way out.

"That woman is going to be trouble," Jeremy grumbled as the door shut behind him.

"That was a given whether or not she agreed to an exchange." Beryl laughed softly, "There isn't a gain without a little risk, Mister Cannon. We just have to keep the losses, even with the gains. I hope you are ready for our next meeting, she's the least of your worries."

"And I thought guarding a small household would be a comfortable retirement." He muttered with a snort, "The entire house is nothing but nutters."

* * *

"Thank you for coming," Prince Zyon said, waving her to a chair as he worked on various papers scattered about his desk.

"I am at your disposal, your highness." Beryl said with a curtsy before taking a seat.

"Your wards have caught three poisoners in the last few weeks. We are interrogating the servants now to find who pressed them to it."

"Why wasn't I notified sooner?" she demanded, straightening in surprise.

"We wished to give you time to adjust to your new apprentice. He is not the sort of young man I would have pictured you taking on."

"The apprenticeship is a favor for his family. Thankfully for both of us, the contract is only for one year." She replied mildly, keeping her tone light. He wasn't aware who the apprentice actually was then.

"How are lessons going?"

"Apprenticeships are done differently in Arden, your royal highness." She huffed, tired of explaining, "He will be learning a trade along with lessons on magic and its uses. He has refused to learn the crafting of jewels or jewelry so he will learn blacksmithing."

"You are teaching a noble to blacksmith?" He sputtered, dropping the paper he was sorting through.

"Yes, your highness; I learned at fifteen. I see no reason a boy of twenty cannot do the same."

"I keep forgetting how young Arden trains its mages, eleven wasn't it?" He huffed, going back to his paperwork.

"Yes, most learn at least two professions alongside magic and the same lessons that might be given to other young nobility."

"Blacksmithing and jeweler?"

"And what Orlean would consider spell-crafting. Most of the spells I use are unique to myself and not what is generally taught in an apprenticeship."

"That is a rare title here, will you be publishing your accomplishments?"

"Once I'm more settled, perhaps." She demurred, "What do you need me to do? I can strengthen the wards, but I was planning to go on a brief trip. Should I postpone?"

"No, no, go on your trip. Now that they have caught the poisoners, things should quiet down for a time." He said waiting away her protests as he rang for a page, "Adjust the wards as you would but do not cancel your travel for some misplaced sense of duty. You have protected every inch of the grounds and given us the means to protect ourselves. You have done enough. Focus on your new apprentice for now."

"As you wish, your highness." She murmured, frowning as she stood as his dismissal and made her way to where she'd left William in the corridor.

"We will rework the wards on the palace tomorrow." She told William as he fell into step as she swept past.

"Yes, Mistress;" He muttered, eyes flickering about the hallway as they passed sections of warding.

"Master," she corrected absently, "a mage is a master of their craft no matter the gender."

"Yes, Master Mage;" He intoned with a grimace.

"Call me Mage if you like. I only expect the title amongst the nobility, anyway."

"What will I be doing tomorrow while you correct the wards?"

"You will observe, take notes, and once we are finished your project will be to ward a small object in some similar fashion. If you show skill, you will assist me in adjusting the wards the next time we need it."

"And the rest of this afternoon?"

"Your choices are weapons practice or survival lessons in the woods."

"Is there another option?" he asked with a sigh.

"If you don't choose, I will choose for you."

"Weapons practice," He groaned.

"For choosing, I will let your spar with myself instead of with Jeremy." She offered with a wide smile at his defeated expression.

* * *

"Why are we practicing at night? We won't be able to see." William whined, glaring as the other two armed themselves without complaint.

"That is the point, learning to fight in low light." Beryl said cheerfully.

"Only thieves fight in the dark." William sneered.

"Or soldiers," Jeremy said with a snort, "buck up, after this you get to play sneak with Mage."

"Sneak, in the dark?" William squeaked.

"You never played after dark as a child? You track her, she tracks you. One person hides while the other hunts." Jeremy asked, watching the boy with a frown.

"This is ridiculous."

"My trainer called it Hide or Death." Mage said with a grin, "It can be a lot of fun."

"You have a dog, I'd never get within ten feet!" William snapped.

"Argent and Rune won't be playing tonight." Beryl said lighting the next torch, "You are competing against me. Sometimes it is necessary to hide and not lead a trail or track someone at night. It takes practice, and yes it helps to have a trained dog to track the scent but that can be hampered by using game trails, dropping urine or herbal extracts to confuse the dogs, or doubling back and using streams to break the scent trails."

"When am I ever going to use this?"

"Probably never, but I believe being prepared for every eventuality. I'd have died four times over if I hadn't learned to hunt and track. Magic can only go so far, you are a strong earth mage, try to feel the ground around you for things that shouldn't be there."

"Is this necessary for the boy?" Jeremy asked once they had sent William out to hide, "He thinks you are mad and the King might agree if he saw the training regimens you have him keeping."

"I keep dreaming of hunting in the dark, franticly searching for something. I'd rather keep him safe if the visions bare out then have him lost in the dark defenseless." She sighed, shouldering the long staff she'd been working with, "I'm hoping this is a vision that doesn't come to pass."

"You will need something he can show off publicly as well."

"I know, I've already requested a room at the palace to use as his apprenticeship project. I'm waiting on the King's agreement before I give him that assignment."

"Asks for a garden, the boy is skilled with plants if nothing else." Jeremy grunted.

"Something I need to remind him of," she said with a sigh, heading down the path to collect the young man from his spot behind a tree, "He should use the trees to hide, not to announce his position."

Chapter 26

A Party

"Why are your pets dressed that way?" William asked frowning as Rune wandered by sporting an enormous pink bow at the back of his neck while Argent wore his armor polished to a mirror shine, the shark skin and mail making him look rather deadly with his heavy hunting collar.

"We are going make a statement no matter what we do. We might as well be well dressed." Beryl said, handing him a book and pencil as she accepting her cloak from Mary.

"It looks lethal." He muttered, flipping through the tomb.

"We mean him to; Argent is a hunting hound, after all. He tracks and harries boar or bear until the huntsmen can arrive." Beryl said with a sigh, watching as William halfheartedly paged through the book.

"This book is blank." He pouted, hefting the small volume, "What am I meant to do with this at a party?"

"You are meant to write in blank books." She sighed, tweaking his arm as she passed, "Note which topics are discussed that you wish to learn more on. Try to be discrete about it, no one likes to know they are being observed."

"I can be discrete." He snapped, shoving the thin book in a pocket, "I don't need a book to remember names, I've been attending events since I was five and father expected me to recite everyone I meet of importance to him the next morning."

"Don't sulk." She said fighting to keep her tone even, "Be grateful that I allow you to attend. Any more attitude and you'll be staying in working on essays for the night."

"Yes, Mistress." He bit out, fighting to not appear ungrateful. He wasn't used to being held accountable for his work, much less his attitude.

"I am under extra scrutiny because of my position at court, because of this you will be under constant observation and judged accordingly. Your rank will mean nothing, you are here as my apprentice and as such your behavior will reflect on my status as well."

"I won't embarrass you."

"That is one thing I am not worried about," she said, "I am a political nightmare given my status in my home country. I am trying to make sure that view does not impact your own standing at court. Prove to me you can handle yourself tonight and I won't subject you to unnecessary lessons."

"Very well."

* * *

The carriage ride to the front of the castle is silent, all of them are making sure their masks are in place before they reach the crowd. William watches the gentle softness and humor he'd only just started to notice disappear behind a stony mask of disinterest. He tries to mirror the same, but he is nervous. What will they expect of him?

Before he's always been the party's darling, wined and dined and had his every whim catered to. The last few weeks have left him feeling abandoned and exhausted. The Mage expects him to act like a prince and excel at his craft while still being polite to everyone around him, servants included. Servants have been little more than furniture in his life once he was taken from the nursery and given his own room.

He's sent several letters to his friends only to receive short chilly replies now that he is no longer supporting their adventures and time in the taverns. He thought they would be more supportive of his outrage at being forced into an apprenticeship, but few showed a lick of sympathy. None had been willing to help fund or engineer his escape.

The constant snubs and looks of disdain were not something he was used to dealing with. Everyone they met seemed to think both of them were worse than some random poor degenerate who was headed to an early grave via prison. The only ones that were polite were the more eccentric families who had no interest in social climbing or hobnobbing with the royal family. It was infuriating.

William fought to keep the disgruntled sneer off his face. Attending this ball was meant to be his introduction into society at his Master's side and he was being treated like the son of a penniless noble struck with wasting disease. Evelyn, the woman he'd been courting for the last year, refused to look at him and was on the arm of a wealthy landowner who'd recently become widowed. He was left sulking at his Master's elbow or hidden in the edges of the crowd. Neither was a position he enjoyed.

Watching his new master twist the surrounding conversations was interesting, at least. Considering her age and gender, he'd assumed she'd be overwhelmed at courtly discourse. Instead, she easily avoided the utter power hungry or bores and danced enough even if it was clear she was unused to the steps of some turns. She was well versed in politics, hunting horses, and even discussed various makeup and scent trends with one Baron's wife to her delight and his mortification.

Her cat was nowhere in sight while the hound waited at his side for his master to finish the dance. He resisted the urge to kick it. If they were linked, the mage would know. Wiliam wouldn't put it past the dog to bite him, no matter how lazy it appeared. He had no experience with animals belong horseback riding and he'd been told bluntly he was no natural.

Not a single woman had asked him to dance, and most of his friends didn't have the standing to attend something like this unless as someone else's guest. Mage had given him a disapproving look at leaving her side but had left him to his solitude until the conversation ended and she was asked to dance.

"If you glare any harder, the gentleman's wig will combust, Apprentice. Is there something I should know?" She asked, coming to his side like it was a fortunate place to stand and not her actual destination. Her social competence irked him.

"My promised fiancé is on his arm." William ground out, forcing his face to remain a mask of irritation and not the rage burning in his gut.

"I see, my apologies." Beryl said with a soft hum shifting further into the corner next to him, "She took the news of the apprenticeship badly then."

"I wouldn't know, she isn't returning my letters."

"Then she doesn't have the maturity needed for a suitable match. Did you discuss your prospects beforehand?"

"Why would we?" He snapped, frustrated with the conversation. Why couldn't she just leave him be?

"You were about to propose and never discussed your future life together?" She asked, arching an eyebrow.

"She wished to live in a titled family and bring that reputation to her family name. How we would live together didn't matter."

"I see."

"You don't agree with the match?"

"Even a match done as a business deal should consider the couple's personalities and plans for the future. If you knew she was against magic, would you have taken the apprenticeship?"

"Possibly, it promised to be a chance to improve my standing." He snapped, raising an eyebrow in return.

"You may yet; if you manage a decent showing tonight, you may accompany me on the evening ride with the royal family in two days."

"A decent showing?" he asked warily.

"No lurking in the shadows glaring," she said with a sigh, "Find Master Ranel for me, I wish to ask him about an alternative sword form being developed."

"Sword Master Ranel is here?" he sputtered, scanning the room.

"A fact you would know if you'd bothered to listen to the surrounding conversations." She said taking his arm, "Discussing dressmaking may bore you stiff, but that doesn't mean you can allow your intelligence to rot from neglect."

"What did you learn from her? She's a gossiping housewife."

"The Baron is the head of a major trading company. He travels most of the year and his wife entertains in his absence nearly nightly. She is known for holding large mixed company dances on the last day of the week and small intimate dinners with up-and-coming business owners and minor nobility as her schedule suits. Her husband may be the head of the family, but she controls the major trade decisions. Any major change in regional trade or supply comes to her ears weeks before the King's advisors will ever hear of it."

"And this helps with magic how?"

"Knowing where to apply it." She murmured, taking a cup from a passing server and smiling to an older gentleman on the arm of his bored looking granddaughter, "Are the crops not producing as expected? That will affect prices, drive up costs for basic supplies. Does the king send a mage to assist with the harvest or let the markets play out? If a plague breaks out, where are the healers sent? If there is a war, do the mages ward the borders or the front? Do the mages stay home and only supply weapons and charms? There are a thousand possibilities and as an advisor to the royal family I must be ready to answer questions on any possible threat to the country and its people."

"I've never heard of magic being used to prevent disasters or assist wars. Battle magics were banned centuries ago."

"Magic cast to hurt and destroy turns on the user. Most battle mages died from their own spell work long before they banned the practice. Magic used to heal and build on what is already natural builds on itself and spreads to strengthen whatever is around it. A spell cast on a farmer's field will spread and strengthen the surrounding fields far past the energy the mage placed into the earth."

"Will I learn to do such things?" he asked when it was clear she wouldn't continue.

"If you show promise. It takes years of study and depends on what elements you show talent in."

"You've said you can cast with elements that aren't your strengths, surely I would be able to do the same."

"With years of training, it all depends on what direction your training goes in."

"Direction?"

"A smith is rarely taught to garden as well. We will align your training with your abilities. A fire inclined mage would go into smithing or glass making, water into pottery as a craft, but they may work on the coast or travel with the fleets to ensure pleasant weather or to guide ships around reefs. You won't be working a forge your entire life if you do not wish to."

"Good," he grunted, wincing as she elbowed his side hard.

"Pay attention this time, I expect details tomorrow before your lessons." She breathed as they approached the sword master.

"Yes, Master Mage."

* * *

The party was finally winding down, leaving William exhausted, nauseous from the one glass of wine he'd snatched, and frustrated with the world in general. He'd never had the head for the political manipulations that his father thrived on. Wandering around the party being treated like a leper wasn't him having a grand time.

His master was on the balcony talking with a few of the current masters of their disciplines. He'd been sent to wander and enjoy himself, but everywhere he looked all he could see was the tittering laughter of the elite socialites mocking his downfall. A month ago he'd been the darling of his hometown and set to marry the most eligible young noble woman his age. Now he was apprenticed to a foreign mage, too stuck up to even use her own name, with dirty animals hanging off her even during a party at the royal palace.

What was he supposed to gain from such a situation? He'd lost all his money, social standing, and his father's favor in a matter of days. He'd signed the agreement to apprentice to a royal mage hoping to use the proximity to find a better situation and instead he was shackled to a woman barely older than he was who was supposed to be teaching him magic, not swordplay and smithing.

"Apprentice Westedge, wonderful to see you out and about again." Master Mage Rogen said with a smile, gesturing for the apprentice to come to his side.

"Master Rogen," William said with a bow, waving away the wine a passing server offered as he straightened.

"Your master has been keeping you busy as of late. It is good to see you back in our social graces. How are you enjoying the evening?" He asked with a tight smile, turning to look back at the dwindling party.

"I have been learning much," William said hesitantly. It was obvious the man had no love for his master and was hoping the apprentice would drop something he could use during the conversation. He might not like the woman, but he wouldn't be selling any secrets without a modest incentive.

"So I have heard, blacksmithing and enchanting objects." Rogen hummed with a moue of distaste, "I will be looking for an apprentice in the coming year if you decide to return to the Orlean branch of magical study."

"I am contracted for the next ten months, but I will keep your offer in mind." William demurred politely trying to keep his face a serene mask, the man certainly was willing to off just enough to make him want to press him for more.

"Make sure that you do, your father has been supportive of the arrangement, I take it?" He asked, taking a sip of his goblet.

"He wishes I would study a profession more suited to our bloodline, but I enjoy magical studies." William said, trying not to wince. His father would be delighted if he managed to break the contract, but he doubted this mage would do so without striping him of everything he could get.

"Being a mage for the court is one of the highest positions available, barring the royal family themselves, of course. Let me guess, he wishes you to study law?"

"Studying law is the more traditional choice, yes." William agreed mildly wishing he'd grabbed a drink simply to have something to do with his hands.

"And yet every court member has a background in law. Studying something outside of the normal scope does broaden your options and make one more of an asset to the courts. My own apprentice sadly shows no aptitude for the rigors of legal studies."

"A year studying foreign magics is something few at court can boast of," William pointed out with a wry smile, "I expect to have a number of offers by next season."

"A year is more than enough time to form opinions of foreign magics and their cultural impact. I doubt the mage herself will be a permanent feature in the courts. You may well be the expert in Arden's magic in a few years' time." Rogen teased back with a twisted smile of his own.

"You don't believe she will stay?"

"Female mages rarely stay in society, she is a passing distraction for the royal family." Rogen said waving off the matter entirely, "In time they will pass her over for more familiar couriers who have earned their favor."

"Surely she would retain favor for the work she has done."

"Favor wanes for work that has already been bought and paid for. Don't you agree?" Rogen asked, arching a brow as he gestured for a fresh glass of wine.

"Perhaps," William murmured, accepting a cup of his own with a tight smile. There was no way he was drinking while the master mage courted his attention.

"Enough talk of politics, come meet my good friend Count Reginald." Rogen said, guiding them to the other side of the room in full view of his own master.

"It would honor me, Master Rogen." William murmured, giving the group they were approaching a polite smile that was received with bright flashes of teeth like tigers scenting a bleeding doe.

"Gentlemen, Master Mages, may I introduce William Westedge, apprentice to the foreign Mage from Orlean." Rogen said giving him a glittering smile full of false pride.

"How goes your studies, Apprentice Westedge? Has the rogue Mage been filling your head with Ardenian policies and merging minds with animal filth?"

"Not that I have seen, sir." William murmured with a tight smile, "I'm afraid I did not catch you name, Master?"

"Dalmas, I teach illusion magic here at the palace." The mage said stiffly, "Has your master started illusions yet? I heard that she was pestering the apprentices here in their practice sessions for tips, not even able to cast her own illusions."

"It seems they prefer more concrete uses of their magic," William deflected with another smile turning to the next gentleman, "What are your views on the matter, sir? Would you wish to pursue illusion magic extensively or branch out?"

"I have little use for illusions, Thomas Wentworth," the portly man huffed, waving for a fresh glass of wine, "I run the wine merchant guild for this region. I've heard rumors your master is driving the mercantile guilds batty trying to sell her own good and magical items without a chaperon. What is the world coming to?

Unmarried women seeking to snatch the coins from our purse, is Arden so ridiculous?"

"I couldn't say, I know Mage is a proponent for fair wages and protections for those under her employment." William offered, swallowing a mouthful of wine and praying his words didn't get back to her ears. There were just too many ways an innocent conversation could be twisted by men like this.

"Yes, a drunken soldier, two disgraced wretches pulled from the gutters, and the minor head of a merchant family. She seems to collect the worst of the trash the rest of the country has tossed aside," the last man said with a sneer, "discounting yourself of course, Westedge."

"Of course, I would never dream of taking insult." William said with a bitter smile, wonderful, she was dragging him down along with her, "I didn't catch your name, sir?"

"Kent, Master Kent." The man sniffed, "My primary worry is for Orlean, what can we hope for when the King is employing such riffraff?"

"Exactly my concern," Rogen agreed with a smarmy smile, "these Ardenian mages have little to offer and in tempting our own apprentices to dabble with these animal bonds they could pollute an entire generation."

"And having such close contact with the royal family, surely Prince Zyon hasn't been swayed by these foreign magics? Are we certain she isn't enchanting the royalty?" Wentworth asked, looking disturbed.

"That is one thing I am certain of, she hasn't attempted to do more than use her meager warding abilities. The royal family is grateful for her assistance, nothing more. This popularity will pass once the court moves next season. Mark my words, gentlemen." Rogen said soothingly.

"It is a pity she isn't more appealing. Few are going to offer a marriage to such a plain mage." Master Dalmas said with a sniff, "What would a mage need with selling trinkets?"

"Selling such insignificant things couldn't possibly affect other merchants." William inserted with a mild expression, "How else would a woman mage earn her funds?"

"Marriage like any other wretch without a penny to her name, not that she even has that. How does one even manage to be cursed nameless?" Dalmas asked, gesturing for a fresh drink.

"Sadly, that was done in childhood. She has little control over what a random madman did to her, Dalmas." Rogen chided gently, "She is a passing fashion, gentlemen, we must plan on how the country will strengthen itself while we wait for these foreign mages to lose interest and leave."

"How does her presence make any difference to the country?" William asked only half jokingly, how did a single mage matter in the grand scheme of things?

"A mage with the ear of the royal family has immense power if they choose to use it." Rogen said with a smirk, "Swaying the prince into acknowledging her uncommon beliefs draws those beliefs into the preferred views of those about the royal family. A commoner should never have the ear of those in power, it dilutes the power of everyone above them."

"Shouldn't royalty be aware of the needs of those below?" William asked, mostly to see how Rogen would control the conversation. Was he after more power or seeking to undermine Mage out of spite?

"I only wish to see Orlean prosper, wether that is under this king or the next." Rogen said dismissing the question, "Power and prestige are nothing without the proper guidance. Your master appears to be looking for you, Apprentice Westedge, do give her our regards."

"Of course, Master Mage Rogen." Williams said, giving a quick bow to the group at large, "Thank you for the stimulating conversation, gentlemen, you have given me much to consider."

William joined where his master was waiting to one side without comment beyond a single long glance. Did the other nobility and mages truly think she had that much influence and power? Most dismissed her openly but considering they worried over her impact on the royal family bringing about new policies that were more Ardenian leaning, she had more power than they liked.

He brooded the rest of the night, watching his new master skillfully chatter with those willing to gather into her circuit. She made no move to approach those who openly disliked her beyond a polite greeting as they passed by. She wasn't trying to openly cultivate relationships with anyone that his father would have pressed for. What game was she playing? Was Ardenian politics so different?

Chapter 27

Relatives

William scowled at the parchment in front of him before tossing it to the side with a groan and grabbed his coat. Mage had requested an essay of what he had learned from his previous lessons. After seeing her spells cast so casually, it had blown his old teachers out of the water.

Over and over he realized that his tutors at home had bordered on incompetent. He'd learned the basics of all the important subjects a member of the nobility was expected to know, but so much of it was proving useless with his new apprenticeship.

Mage didn't care for the pomp or rigor of status, and her servants openly expressed their opinions of him and his behavior with no fear of reprimand. The only one who treated him normally was the maid, Olivia, and she was a timid thing, terrified of everything. The rest of the staff at the cottage were antagonistic or disproving.

The cook, Mary, seemed determined to mother him in some twisted way, pressing cake and tea on him when he wandered in, unable to sleep no matter how exhausted he was from armed training. Working the forge was torture, nothing he did was good enough, and he ruined most of the steel he was trying to hammer or cast on. The nails or arrows warped and shattered before the runes could set wasting the day's work and efforts in an instant.

Sword training with Jeremy was the only area he could say he was slowly improving. The man's constant goading left his temper frayed, and he payed for it in bruises and extra assignments from his master. Normally this kind of stress would have driven him to drink, but with none available at the cottage he wasn't willing to risk his tentative footing to go out in search of a bar or inn to drown his anger. It would have to wait for his next day off so he could go off the palace grounds.

His life was in ruins, and no one around him seemed to care. He snarled, kicking at a loose stone. His father expected him to magically attain some prominent position, while most of his friends seemed content to live off their family wealth without even learning the smallest trade. None but Andrew had even responded to his letters. His Master seemed determined to find an area for him to excel at, but everything he touched fell to rust and ruin.

Dismissed from the forge after mangling two daggers, he'd been tasked to sharpen and ward and too worked up for the essay they had assigned him. He stormed through the gardens and paths that covered the palace grounds. Turning a corner, he barely missed flattening an older woman, catching her basket to the gut and sending it flying.

"I apologize, Madame." He huffed with a cough, catching her elbow to make sure she was steady on her feet before he snatched up the offending basket and shoved it back in her arms.

"It's been years since a young man swept me from my feet," She said with a snort gathering her scattered belongings, he moved to help her after a beat praying nothing was broken, his first allowance as an apprentice was still weeks away, "I refuse to count you among their number."

"I'm sorry, I should have been watching where I was going." He muttered, handing back the last package and opening his mouth to ask about the strange-looking items when she spoke over him.

"What were you running from in such a huff? I'm afraid my driver dropped me at the wrong entrance. I've been walking for miles, it seems."

"I was just walking. If you need directions to the palace, I can accompany you?" He said offering his hand as she stood. Maybe he'd be able to beg a bottle of something from the kitchen staff there.

"No, I am looking for the Mage's cottage. Are you familiar with it?"

"Yes, Madame;" He said biting back a sigh and giving her a brief bow, "I am her apprentice, William of Westedge."

"Wonderful!" The woman said, smoothing her shawl, "Do you mind guiding me?"

"Of course not, Madame." He said offering his arm and pulling on the mask he'd used at countless dinner parties.

"How are you finding working with your master?" She asked as they started walking back to the cottage.

"I've only been apprenticed a short time, Madame. I couldn't hazard a response just yet."

"A very polite response," she said with a grin, "Someone has taken care in your lessons of discourse at least."

"My father insisted on the best tutors available." He murmured, biting back the bitter taste the words caused, "They educated me as befitted my station."

"He did. You are the spitting image of your great grandfather. I was but a child myself when he passed, but you share a remarkable likeness."

"Really? My mother lamented that I didn't share her darker skin."

"Sometimes it skips a generation or two. Skin, eyes, even the family nose." She said with a chuckle, "I am happy to have caught you, young master William."

"Do you know my master well?"

"We have exchanged letters however, she seems a knowledgeable woman of the world. Are you learning much from your time with her?"

"It isn't what I expected from previous tutors," William said, "Her abilities are nothing like what they use in Orlean."

"From what I have heard, her abilities are unique to herself more than her country of origin." The woman said with a cackle, "Do not look so glum, things will pick up."

"Why do you say that?"

"Because wether you want it or not, it does come true. Time moves on." She said giving him a long look, "There it is, I can see the roof from here. I won't keep you any longer. Thank you for walking with an old woman."

"It's no trouble,"

"Nonsense, go, enjoy your day, Apprentice. It is too nice a day to be cooped up indoors bending to social niceties." She said giving him a curtsy.

"Very well, have a pleasant day, Madame."

"You as well, young man."

* * *

"Thank you for allowing me to meet my nephew. The king would have never allowed a visit with him staying on the grounds."

"I know what it's like holding a secret no one else will ever believe. He is struggling to adjust to the apprenticeship, but he shows promise if he can learn a little patience."

"Most young men in my experience suffer from such a deficit." She snorted, taking a sip of her tea, "A lovely blend, a custom mix?"

"Yes, my maid Olivia shows a deft hand at choosing the best blends. I hope to expand the gardens to allow her more space to dabble."

"I would be more than willing to accept any experiments you deem successful if this is the first result." she hummed, "What can I do to assist William? I doubt he wants for much, but I would like to do something."

"Perhaps a few letters of encouragement or a few books?" Beryl offered, "He seems to have received more mothering from the staff than the people he lived with. A non relative treated as an aunt is not too far-fetched."

"I'll think on it, I don't want to stir trouble for him just as he's getting settled here."

"I'm sorry the tea with him didn't happen. He needs support even if he doesn't realize it." Beryl sighed.

"It turned out well. This was before I was just an old woman he met and not some social obligation." She sighed, "He seems an angry young man."

"He has had his routine removed and him normal day to day rewritten. It will take some time to accept the changes."

"And if he doesn't?"

"Then hopefully by this time next year I'll have a better option to offer him."

Chapter 28

Lessons in Magic

William paced along the trail, wishing he could fill his hands with flames and destroy everything around him. Nothing was going right. His father had written demanding a letter on his progress. He'd sent off a terse note with lists of essays and books he was studying, but knew he couldn't put off the man forever. He was furious that the pending engagement had fallen through and was scrambling to find a new master for William, but none would touch him considering he was already contracted for the next year.

There was a good chance he'd show up unannounced and demand the contract be revoked, magically binding or not, if William couldn't get him to calm down. William had sent a book full of the consequences of voiding or ignoring a binding, but doubted it did much good. The man was an expert at ignoring facts that didn't fit his plans.

A series of sharp barks and cries brought him to a halt. A pair of fox kits just gaining their red coats were tumbling about, oblivious to him as they razzed and chased each other up and down a rolling bank. He leaned against a tree and watched until they disappeared over the top and didn't return.

His father was determined to push his son into a wealthy marriage and exalted position of state. He had groomed him his entire life for a life of politics and state functions, but William had never excelled at his studies; he wasn't drawn to the law or state craft that his father seemed to deal with so easily.

He was a fair hand on horseback and his sword work was steadily improving under Jeremy's demented training, but there wasn't anything he could say he honestly wanted to do with his life. He'd been told his place his entire life, to suddenly have options was terrifying. He would be disowned if he stepped out of line to his father's plans, but he couldn't give up on his life before it began. The problem was that he wasn't sure what direction to go in. Magic was becoming much harder than he'd ever envisioned.

Olivia was singing softly as she weeded the vegetable garden, and he went the long way around to leave her to it. She only ever seemed happy when he caught her alone, working at some task with all her attention. As soon as she noticed a man nearby, she locked herself away and would only reply to direct questions or commands. It was painful to see the spark in her eyes die.

* * *

"Come, knead this dough. I need an extra hand for dinner tonight if you have the time." Mary said, gesturing him to the sink to wash up as he came in the back door.

"What are you making?" He asked, breathing in the sharp herbal scent and failing to identify whatever she was chopping.

"Mage has requested a rolled roast as we have company coming for dinner." Mary huffed, going back to her cutting board, "And before you ask I don't know who, just that you are both eating in the formal dining room for once."

"And all the fruit?" He asked as the other half of the table was buried in baskets of berries and several kinds of plums.

"Sugared fruit tarts." She huffed, tossing the squash in a bowl and laying out more herbs to chop next, "There will be leftovers for breakfast the next few days."

"Right," William sighed as he started kneading the dough. He would have heard if his father was on this was for dinner.

"Alright, what has you twisted up in knots?" Mary chided taking the dough from the wood in front of him, "Here work on these nuts before you knead the dough out of existence."

"My father is unhappy with my apprenticeship and seeking a way to end the contract."

"Do you wish him to?"

He opened his mouth to reply but found himself at a loss. He wasn't learning much magic yet, but he was learning other things. How to manage an estate, how to calculate supplies for a journey, how to fight in an actual battle and not the polite bouts he'd learned under his father's sword master. Mage was teaching him history, dagger work, and how to heal with bandages and herbs. He'd proved a failure at the forge but instead of getting angry or stopping lessons she was trying different tactics, unique methods, hoping to discover what his block was with her brand of magic.

She never complemented his work unless he'd done his best. Beryl expected him to learn and wasn't satisfied with a sloppy attempt like his other tutors would have accepted. She pushed him to challenge himself and he was enjoying it, even wearing patched dirty clothes and constant bruises and burns from the forge.

He'd been annoyed at first when she refused to heal his bruises, but as he improved he understood the enjoyment of hard worked muscles and the hard sleep of the exhausted. He'd earned the calluses on his palms with hours of sword practice, far beyond what his old master would have allowed.

He realized he'd been standing there thinking like a village idiot and flushed, but Mary simply handed him the nutcracker and went back to work. None of them pointed out his gaffes or moments of embarrassment, not even Mage. At home, he would have been mocked by his father or babied by the staff.

This was the first place they had allowed him to simply be William, no title or surname necessary. When they went to the palace, his apprenticeship superseded his rank and title. The other apprentices were open in the disdain of his position, but many still tried to gain his attention to use him as a stepping stone to the royal family or his master's attention. They may mock Mage behind her back, but they still respected the power she held so casually.

The royal family was another surprise. The princess was a solemn girl in court or at events, but became a regular child out of the public's eye. Prince Zyon himself seemed to have a running argument with his Master over women's rights of all things, but otherwise was a courteous courtier and a doting father. They were a normal family outside of their duties, a much more functional one than even his own.

He finished the nuts and handed off the bowl. Mary waved him out of the kitchen, but not before giving him a handful of the dark ginger cookies he loved. Today was his day off and at home he would have gone out to gamble and drink in town, but now he went to his room to bathe and study yet another runic manual in hopes of inspiration.

Runic magic seemed to be formulaic at the onset, but much of the power in a spell depended on the mage's personal inclination to original materials and elements. Mage was inclined to stone and fire, while his own inclination seemed to be more earth and water based. There should have been enough overlap to allow him to learn her specialties, but so far the only progress he'd managed were wards on small wooden boxes. Spells cast on metal exploded or fizzled out with no warning of a miscast.

He heard a carriage pull up, but his room faced the back of the house. Finishing his toilet, he headed back downstairs. The woman who was shown into the dining room wasn't what he was expecting.

She could have been his grandmother for all her finery and refined air.

"William, may I introduce Lady Cerise Bonheur. Cerise, William of Westedge, my apprentice," Mage said, gesturing to each of them as William gave a quick bow.

"Lovely to meet you, Apprentice Westedge." She smiled, giving his hand a firm shake as he guided her to her seat, "How are you finding the apprenticeship?"

"I am learning a great deal, Lady Bonheur."

"Cerise, please," She said waiving away his attempt to pull out her chair for her, "I am an old young man, not dead, and I have had enough pomp and posturing during my days as a lady-in-waiting."

"I apologize," he mumbled as he moved to his own seat, glancing at Mage, but she seemed absorbed in watching the other woman.

"Thank you for coming, Cerise. I hope the drive wasn't too miserable?" Mage asked, gesturing for Mary to serve drinks.

"Long, but the countryside was as lovely as I remembered." She said taking a glass of tea with a murmur of appreciation, "I've brought the paperwork on the houses you wished to view. Are you certain you don't wish to look more inland? The coast isn't the healthiest of places during the winter. That's why the court moves as it does. There was a horrible outbreak of disease when I was a child that killed many at court."

"I can winter in the mountains if I must, but I promised someone dear to me we would live on the coast and I would like to keep that promise."

"Well, all three houses come with a sizable property, two have out buildings that could be converted to accommodate your workshop or a small private dwelling or two. They are of varying acreage and would need maintenance to a one I'm afraid."

"I don't mind a little work, Cerise. Do they have stables?"

"Nothing of notable size but enough for a riding pair and something to pull a trap or cart as you indicated."

"Ah, Mary, you have outdone yourself." Mage grinned as they

brought the large roast in. The main course was served and talk moved on to Mage's current projects and the work William was doing with the apprenticeship. The Lady Cerise was deft at making sure they included him in the conversation, no matter the topics that came up.

"How are your projects coming along, Mage? Are you still planning to open a shop?" Cerise asked before humming around a bite of tart.

"Yes, eventually; I've had to put that on hold for now with the cost of the house, but I hope to sell small items in the coming year. Several merchants have expressed interest in protection amulets and the stuffed animals."

"Stuffed animals?" William asked, blinking.

"You haven't shown your apprentice your wares yet?" Cerise teased with a small grin like it was a subject Mage wasn't eager to discuss.

"It is a silly thing, I made stuffed animals and enchanted them to move. I had several commissions for them from the ladies of the court. The princess is quite taken with a wolf I made for her." Mage said dismissively.

"You stuffed animals?" William questioned, trying to picture the princess playing with a stuffed dead thing.

"No, I made dolls from cloth. Did you not have a cloth bear as a child?" Mage asked with a frown, "I had a small bear from my parents, I think."

"No, my father wasn't fond of such things. I received practical gifts, tools for my education." Willam said dismissively, trying not to wince at yet another thing they had denied him as a child. He would have to look for children's toys next time he was at the market.

"What has Mage been teaching you, William? She was still leaning toward illusions when we first met." Cerise informed him with a wicked smile, "How are your studies progressing?"

"My studies are progressing slowly," William said trying not to fiddle with his glass, "I'm still learning many of the runes used and Mage has been teaching me other skills to fill out my days."

"He is being too polite," Mage said, giving him a look he couldn't decipher, "Our magical leanings aren't compatible. I lean to stone and fire, he to earth and water. Most of what I excel at will be a struggle, and I struggle to teach what he should know."

"Then he is as much a teacher as you are." Cerise said with a nod, "A hard mentorship on both sides, but you both improve and learn. A worthwhile endeavor, it seems."

"True, William has helped me greatly with my illusion work." Mage said with a smile, conjuring up a tiny sparrow and sending it hopping along the length of the table. It looked real, even casting a tiny shadow that seemed to flicker in the candlelight.

"You've already surpassed me. How did you suppress the glow?" He asked, watching as the illusion hopped onto a goblet and appeared to drink.

"I know increasing the depth isn't a wonderful answer, but I tried to anchor the runes to the center of the image and not the edges."

"I wasn't aware that was possible." William said, frowning as he tried to plan mentally how it would work.

"I've already believed in working around the rules." Mage said with a light blush, "Not everything you read or are taught is the truth or the best way for you to do something. You need to experiment and find your own rhythm and method for a casting."

"As with all things in life, the accepted method isn't the only way." Cerise agreed with a hum, "You must compliment your cook. This is the best bread and meal I've had in years. I believe I will have another slice."

"She will be happy to hear it. Shall I ring for dessert?"

"I may never fit into this dress again, but ring away." Cerise said with a peal of laughter, "Have you crafted anything new for the shops, Mage? The bear you gifted me is delightful, and I've pointed a few families your way for jewelry commissions."

They devoted the rest of the meal to comfortable conversation, and William realized it was one of the first more formal dinners that he could remember enjoying. None of his family or his father's acquaintances would have gone out of their way to keep him in the conversation or to include his interests. The few friends he went drinking with were just there for the entertainment, few if any would have bothered to ask how he was doing in his studies or pushing him to explain his thoughts on anything.

* * *

"We need to speak of your work ethic, Apprentice Westedge." Beryl said as he joined her in the forge.

"I've done everything you've demanded."

"You've done as little as possible of everything demanded. The only one who says you are showing improvement is Mister Cannon." She sighed, setting the snuff box to one side, "What I asked of you when you warded this snuff box?"

"To make it fire poof and resistant to damage." William recited only to yelp as she drove an iron spike through the box and tossed it into the roaring forge next to them.

"You are to try again, take another box from the workroom. I expect you to test your work before you turn it in this time."

"Yes, Mistress." He bit out, watching as the box was consumed in the fire.

"Can I ask you a frank question, William?"

"You are my Master, you can ask or demand what you wish of me." He said sagging back against the worktable behind him.

"Do you wish to learn magic?"

"What?"

"At first you seemed willing enough to learn magic, but you've stalled out in your progress. Do you still wish to learn magic or has the sword play become more to your liking?"

"I enjoy the swordplay and the discussions I've had with Mister

Cannon about history and various battles," William said haltingly, "however I am contracted to you to learn magic."

"No, William, it contracts you to me as an apprentice. The contract says nothing about what you must learn while under my governance. If you wish to focus on Mister Cannon's teachings, we can change your schedule to do so. You have a talent for magic, but the memorization of runes and their casting isn't a strength of yours. I would like to teach you the more varied forms of magic, you already know the basic runes for control so we can dabble in various arts that you might be more suited to."

"Would we continue as we have, half the day in the yard, half in the study of magic?"

"That depends on you. Would you like to continue as we have, keeping the training at weapons in the morning."

"Would I still have to work the forge?"

"Not if you dislike it, I've been speaking with Benjamin and we can afford an errand boy to help me in the forge if you wish to pass on that duty."

"Please, I realize you value crafting things with your hands, but I can't seem to keep the metal straight. It almost seems to twist in my hands."

"Twists?"

"When I'm hammering it out." He explained miming hammering at the forge.

"Perhaps it's something else, come with me." She said gesturing him up as she activated the sequence to douse the forge and headed out the door without another word.

"Where are we going?" he huffed, waving to Jeremy and at the open shop as he hurried after Beryl, Rune a few steps behind them.

"Have you ever worked with water?" she asked once they were deep into the woods behind them, "Or earth?"

"Not beyond the focusing exercises you showed me."

"What do you feel when you focus on them?"

"The water is cool and flowing, the earth hums and seems to cling if that makes any sense."

"Have you ever gardened or kept plants?"

"Never." He huffed with a snort.

"Did anyone ever send you flowers?"

"The maids kept flowers in my rooms, why?"

"Did they seem to last a long time?"

"Not that I noticed. How would I know how long flowers last? You think I'm making mistakes at the forge because of flowers?"

"I think working the forge goes against your innate magical strengths." Beryl said leading him into the bank of a tiny creek, "We know your strengths are earth and water from your testing. I thought the forge would suite you because of your connection to the earth. My stone sense comes from my connection to earth and fire so I assumed yours would to, I should have remembered my training. My Master thought glass would suit me for it suited him, I spent weeks wrecking every piece I tried to enchant before he let me move on to metal."

"What am I supposed to do with a creek if my strength is earth and water?"

"First take off your shoes, you need to feel your connection to the elements." She said dropping to the ground and pulling off her own boots and stockings, "I'll demonstrate but I'm very weak in water so it will not be very impressive."

"What are you expecting?" he asked, watching from the bank as she walked into the water.

"There's a vein of copper somewhere that way." She said with a laugh, gesturing up stream, "It's hard to tone back my stone sense enough to hear the other elements sometimes."

Reaching out a hand, she closed her eyes and focused on the water flowing over her feet. She focused on the earth and plants around them, the mud beneath her feet. Slowly the water climbed against all natural forces up her shins. It hung a few inches below her knees for a moment before splashing back as she staggered.

"It takes a lot for me to do that." She huffed, leaning over and waiting for the dizziness to pass, "Your turn, William."

"You think I can move the water?"

"I think you can do a lot more than move it. We're starting small."She reminded him with a grin going to lean against a nearby tree.

William gave her a doubtful look but slowly stepped into the water. The water was icy, but he barely reacted as his feet settled into the silt at the bottom. Reaching out a hand, he closed his eyes, frowning in concentration as he pushed for the connection he'd been studying for the last month. Instead of clinging to him, the water surged, rising about him in a glistening dome.

"William, open your eyes." Beryl called out grinning as the young man let out a yelp as the dome collapsed, dousing him with water, "Water is your element, care to try for earth?"

"I'd rather not be covered in mud."

"Concentrate and will yourself dry, the water should respond." She offered as she scuffed through the leaf litter, looking for something.

"That should not have worked," William huffed, stepping slowly out onto the bank.

"And yet it does, hands." She said offering him something she held cupped between her palms. "Close your eyes and concentrate on the earth beneath your feet and in your hands."

"Yes, Mistress." He sighed, taking the offered handful with a grimace. She doubted they had ever allowed him to play in the mud as a child.

"He is a grower?" Rune asked, watching as a thin green stem popped from between William's cupped hands.

"Earth and water." Beryl agreed, *"No more forge for a while until he gets his powers under control."*

"Good," Rune huffed, allowing Beryl to pick him up. He hated the harsh clang of the hammers.

"Goddess!" William breathed as he opened his eyes, taking in the young pine tree he hadn't been holding before.

"Come along, Apprentice. We will need some supplies if we you want to keep that growing." She said placing Rune on her shoulder and starting back to the cottage at a slow pace.

"I can keep it?" He asked blinking at her in shock as he stumbled trying to pull on his shoes while keeping the plant and its soil in one hand.

"The rooms are yours to do with as you wish. Add all the plants you like as along as you care for them. Mary and Olivia won't be watering them for you unless we are traveling."

"Can I grow more things?"

"That will be your project this week. You will work with Mary in the small garden behind the cottage. Learn the feel of the various plants and how to care for them. Try channeling your magic into them gently. Just a sip at a time. The extreme growth the sapling went through would be very stressful for an older plant."

"What if I kill them?"

"That is why you need to go slowly. Working with growing plants is similar to healing, feel the entire plant and learn what it needs." Beryl said with a grimace of her own, she'd gotten lost in the other person too easily and let her power drain away too quickly in her lessons, eventually she'd been recommended to keep to minor injuries and leave the broken bones to the healers.

"Could I learn to heal as well?"

"Eventually, once your abilities stabilize, we would need to find you a teacher. I have basic skills in healing, but with your affinity with water you could be a powerful healer with training, but that is some time away. For now, focus on your training with plants, once is in hand, we'll broaden out to the harder skills."

"Such as what?"

"If you can sense plants, then you can sense when there is a disturbance in them. You should be able to track animals through the forest, find water, know where the trails are, know what areas are dangerous and what to avoid just by expanding your senses. It takes practice. Keep up your nightly meditations on your elements. It will help deepen your understanding of the element and strengthen your focus as you train."

"Is this how you feel fire?" he asked, examining one dirt covered palm as they walked.

"Like you found a friend or brother you never knew you had?" Beryl offered gently, "Elements are a weaker version of bond mates. They can be a comfort or a raging inferno that powers your spells."

"Bond mates, you mentioned that before. Your pets feel like this?"

"Deeper but similar," Beryl sighed, "once I find an estate to purchase we'll start exposing your to different animals if you like. Not every mage finds their bonded and some refuse to try."

"My last tutor said it was disgusting." William mumbled, glancing between her and Rune.

"Some think it so, when you bond with an animal, you share everything. Your heart, mind, and magic are shared which can increase the reserve you have available for spell craft, but it also means you share their pain. People used to capture bond mates to control their mages."

"Which one did you bond to first?"

"I met Rune in the Palace kitchens in Cardu. He was the tiniest kitten I'd ever seen, but he climbed right up and claimed me. Rune was the runt and the rascal of the litter, always into something. He even fell into a pie once trying to steal scraps." Beryl laughed, scratching the cat under his chin.

"And the dog?"

"Argent was one of the King's hunting hounds. They already considered him an older dog, but the bond eased his aches and pains. He should live to twenty or more now."

"They don't live as long as you do?"

"No, the magic we share extends their lives, but they are still animals and don't have the life span humans do."

"The rumors said you lost an animal. Was it a bond mate?"

"Yes, Kuro. She was a Shiro, a sea hawk. They killed her in the north of Arden during a battle."

"I'm sorry, I didn't realize what they were to you."

"Few do, we make sure they underestimate them. Bond mates are smarter them most animals and once the bond settles, you can share emotions or even mind speech in a powerful bond."

"But they don't always travel with you," He mused, petting at his tree's needles, "are they spying for you?"

"At times, they have tasked me with protecting the royal family, and I need to keep abreast of the latest rumors and gossip. Most of the time they are wandering and enjoying the day."

"What do you think I would bond to?"

"It's different for everyone. Master Darius, my old master, said a bond mate was the god's representation of your soul." She said with a shrug, "I always thought it was the god's way of giving you support and strength. My bond mates have taught me so much in the last few years, I'm not sure I would have made it this far without them."

"But how do you tell?"

"You just know, just as you will instinctively know what they need and what they wish to be called. The magic itself will force you to strengthen the bond until it settles, fighting it just hurts you both."

"They chose their own names?"

"Yes, I offered suggestions, but they picked the one they liked. Argent was already named and wished to keep his name as it was."

"What do you think I'll bond with?" He pressed again, glancing at Rune with a frown.

"Do you like cats or dogs?"

"I don't know, I never could do much with them." He shrugged, "I rode a fair bit growing up because they expected it that I have the skill, it was never for fun."

"Do you have a horse you'd like brought down? If not, I'm sure John could find one suitable. You may need a good mount if we have to do any traveling."

"You rode with the Prince in his last hunt, didn't you?"

"I did, Argent likes to hunt, so we might go on the next with the slower crowd if you wish to join us."

"Your bond mates go with you?"

"Your bond mate is part of you. You don't leave an arm or leg at home when you go out." Beryl said a bit stiffly before softening her tone, "There are tales of bond mates who were forced to give up a lot to stay with their bond mates. One mage bonded to a dolphin and joined a fishing fleet so he could stay nearby. Most of the time a mage bonds to what he or she is familiar with, the one who bonded to a dolphin had sailed and traveled by sea often as a child. I traveled as a child with my uncle, but I often slept in barns or in the kitchens with the cats and dogs."

"You were not raised as a mage? I thought you were from a family of mages?"

"My father was a mage, but they disowned him for marrying a merchant's daughter. The rest of my family are merchants and fishers. I didn't know them well, however, they sent me to my uncle when my parents died while on the road. My uncle was a crook and a gambler who had lost all of his family's money at the tables and only kept me hoping to turn a profit. The Marcian name isn't something to garner respect anymore." Beryl said ruefully. Maybe it was a good thing that no one remembered her name. Let it be forgotten along with the rest of her past.

"My father expects exceptional things from me." William breathed after they had walked in silence for a while, "They have trained me all my life to take an influential position in the nobility. Everyone expected the best from everything I did, but no matter how bad I was, they praised me. I came to hate them because of that."

"What do you want to do?"

"I don't know," William confessed, frowning at his seedling, "not what they expect from me, I think."

"If you wish to continue learning magic and weapons here, you can extend your contract once it ends. If not, I can try to find you a similar situation where your family won't be able to decide for you.

You don't have to decide now, think on it. We've got the rest of the year to figure out something."

"Yes, Mistress." They made their way to a nearby potting shed the grounds keepers used and found a small pot for his seedling before heading back to the cottage, "Mistress, why do you go by Mage?"

"I was attacked as a child and cursed by a rogue mage. Now no one can remember my name."

"Will you tell me?"

"My name is Beryl Marcian." She said facing him squarely and giving him a sad smile, "Good night, William. Water your tree before bed. It will need a bit of care over the next few days to recover from its rapid growth."

"Good night," William said, hesitating like he would say more before turning away for his rooms.

Beryl stayed up and made sure they sent a simple supper to each of their rooms. She would have to dig through her books to find tombs that might help William in learning his elements. She'd need to introduce him to musical magic. She had a feeling the esoteric unstructured magics would be more suited for the young mage. Beryl hoped he found a bond mate in time. It would be a wonderful grounding force, something that he could lean on that would expect nothing from him but simple care and love.

"The scars on your arm, how did that happen?" Beryl asked, examining his latest creation in her office with a sharp eye.

"I don't remember, but my father has always said it was from a dog when I was a child, a hunting hound."

"Ask your father when you see him in the holiday, take this as a gift if you like." She said handing him the intricately warded box, "It is well crafted and could store sensitive documents."

"What is my next project?" He asked uncertainly, taking the box back with a glance at the faded scars on his wrists.

"I'm arranging it with the palace, it should be ready when you return."

"I don't know why he is insisting on my attendance. I have missed more of his yearly balls than I ever attended." William said with a frown, fingers tracing the designs of the box, "His letters say he is searching for a way to transfer my apprenticeship."

"You have more than half a year left, there is time to make your decisions. While I'm away, you will have time to speak with him." Beryl said offering him the seat across from her, "Now, back to your studies, a local healer has agreed to allow you to observe her work in the next week. If you prove adept, she will schedule days for you to assist her."

"Men don't heal."

"Nor do women wield a sword or bow. Stop filtering everything through how you expect them to happen. Not everyone is satisfied to follow society's expectations of them." She snapped.

"I apologize, I mean that the patients may not allow me to treat them." William murmured with a wince. He couldn't do anything right today.

"Healer Diane is a formidable woman, they will allow you observe and test your skills. Those who refuse will be seen by her apprentices. If you prove to lack the skill needed, we will move on to other areas of magic."

"Such as?"

"Working with ice." She said handing over a thin book, "I want you to have a basic understanding of healing before you attempt to cast anything with ice. It is very easy to injure yourself with these spells."

"Surely fire is more dangerous?"

"Fire burns the outside of our skin, but it is very hard to cause internal damage. Our bodies are water based, and it is common to see lost fingers and toes in failed casting. One apprentice I knew lost the use of an arm while training." She said harshly, "This is one art you cannot rush. Read this at least twice, write a summary on the basics of its use and the dangers. You won't cast until I am certain you are ready."

"Yes, Mage;" William said eying the small book with a frown, "Is this something I must learn if it is that dangerous?"

"I won't force you, but given how strong your skill with water is you need to understand all its forms, ice is the next logical step. After ice, we study weather and manipulating enormous bodies of water."

"The sea?"

"Yes, but first clouds, wind, and storms. Then currents, waves, moving objects within or on the water, and using both wind and water at the same time." She said with a smile, "Go pester Mary, dinner should be ready soon."

"You don't think he's going to refuse to allow me to return, do you?"

"He may be your father, William, but he can't refuse to allow you to leave his estates. You are of age and can leave whenever you wish. If you want to return then do so, the cottage will be here waiting or you. If he gives you trouble, send me a message using the stone I gave you. I doubt he will deny me to my face."

"It might surprise you, the man is stubborn when it comes to me."

"Perhaps, but for now don't worry about it. We still have a week until you have to leave."

"Very well," he sighed, "I know he is planning something, I never went home for the holiday during school."

"Whatever it is, as my last master said, we can only plan for the worst and hope we are worried over nothing. You are as protected as I can make you, now it is up to you to survive."

"That isn't funny."

"It wasn't meant to be, negligent parents and people in general have to be endured at times. I can't fix that anymore, then I can stop Argent from being a dog. Occasionally we have to deal with the bad in our life until we are in a better position to cast it out."

"Who did you cast out?"

"My Uncle," she said, gathering up a coat and gesturing him out of the room, "Come, I want to walk for a bit before dinner. Go bother Mary."

"I am not a child." He muttered, hating that he sounded just like one.

"No, you are a young man dealing with an untenable situation to the best of his ability." She called over her shoulder before whistling for the dog as she headed down the stairs.

"Deal with it until you can cast them out of your life. Right." William huffed mussing up his hair, "Why didn't I think of that."

He'd given up trying to deal with his relatives as a child. All of them simply wanted to control him in some shape or form, even if it was the strange distant affection that his mother showed. Forcing himself not to stomp moodily down the hall, he wandered through the kitchen and outside without bothering the housekeeper. He wasn't up to yet another conversation.

How was he supposed to cast his own father away? His mother had removed herself from the situation years ago. William couldn't see his father letting him create any distance. Even here at the palace he sent constant letters and messages probing to see what William was learning and if he'd made headway on breaking the contract.

He wasn't sure what about his scars had disturbed the woman. He could barely remember receiving them, just days of fevered dreams and waking eventually back in his room worn thin. He had suffered nightmares for months afterward and his mother had kept him close for once, watching over him like someone was coming to snatch him away.

Chapter 29

William Goes Home

"William, come meet Master Trenton!" The Baron of Westedge boomed across the ballroom as William made his way to where he'd stationed himself in front of the massive fireplace.

"Good afternoon, Master Trenton, Father," William said giving them both a bow, "This year's ball will be the talk of the town, you have outdone yourself, Father."

"Master Trenton, this is the boy I have been telling you about." The Baron said, waving to the man next to him.

"A pleasure to meet you," Trenton said, giving him a tired nod, "but as I have been explaining to your father, a magical contract cannot be canceled on a whim. I would advise you to wait until the trial period is over."

"I agree," William said, giving the man a bow, "Thank you for taking the time to explain things to my father, Master Trenton. I am sure things will work out for the best once the contract is complete."

"Nonsense, nothing is ever unbreakable." His father rumbled, gesturing at a servant for another glass of wine and pointedly ignoring the quick escape of Master Trenton. He'd been a massive man in his youth and he still kept the powerful-looking shoulders and arms, but his love of wine surmounted it with a large gut hanging over his belt.

"Come, there are a few people I wished to introduce you to. It is time you started meeting the family's business associates. Once your apprenticeship is sorted, I expect you to assist with our holdings."

"Father, I hoped to speak with you after the ball. There are some matters to discuss beyond the apprenticeship."

"We will talk tomorrow." He said emptying his cup and thrusting it as William, "Fetch me a fresh glass and one for yourself, boy."

"Yes, Father;"

"Don't be so sullen, boy. We will find you a proper master who understands that you have other duties that will take precedence. It is high time you started attending court and building relationships with your peers at the palace."

"My current apprenticeship has afforded me several new introductions, Father, the prince and princess among them."

"You will need supporters and friends among the nobility, William. Royal favor comes and goes. They will forget this mage in time. She is nothing but a passing fancy."

"The contract is for at least a year, Father."

"There is no reason you can't start planning for next year now." He huffed, guiding William to one side of the room, "Miss Ravenel was hoping to meet you. Her father as you know has a title and lands that would pass to you in the coming years. It would be an excellent match."

"Surely it is too soon to be courting, Father."

"Nonsense, there is no harm in opening discussions with a proper house."

* * *

His father refused to discuss anything beyond the light gossip and chatter that he'd grown to hate at events like tonight. He let himself be shown around like a prize stud and kept a polite smile on his face, but he longed to let the wine blur out the rest of the hours until he could escape. William had had two glasses, but he waved away the servants offering more. His stomach turned even as they made their way to the dining room for a fashionably late dinner.

He made a mental note to visit the kitchens and ask for the biscuit recipe he'd loved as a child; he mused, nibbling on the bread as they waited for the next course. It was one of the few things he missed living in the cottage with his new Master. The few fond memories of his childhood were loitering in the kitchens or if he was honest, hiding from his tutors in the one place they would never look. Why would the son of a Baron happily spend time in the kitchens?

It was so late it was the next morning when he finally escaped the after drinks and cigars post dinner and went to the one room no servant would think to hunt him down, the library. He'd studied more since joining his new master in his entire life, and it made him curious to see what his father considered worthy of knowing. His father did his reading in his study, a room that they had barred William from since he was a child. They left the library to dust and silence outside of the occasional use as a showroom to impress a visiting aristocrat.

Everything was a show with his father. Every word and gesture, the meal served, the wines selected to show off his personal cellars. William had grown up being tutored in which family or house were the ones he should impress or the ones to avoid because they weren't the same caliber of nobility as they were.

His mother was non-exist when it came to the parties and dinners that his father threw. She spent more and more of her time traveling as William grew until it was rare to see her outside of his even rarer visits to her family estates. She didn't bother to send a letter on his birthday once he was off to school, but he'd envied her independence from the heavy hand of his father growing up. They had married to consolidate trade interests in her family winery and the income it brought to the family, but it wasn't an advantageous match. His parents had no interest in each other, and both were rumored to keep several lovers at a time.

The library was dark and cold, but he conjured a few mage lights to hover about while he started the fire roaring with another quick set of runes with a small smile. This at least he was becoming skilled at, even if his father would dismiss it as petty tricks. He hadn't been expecting a selection of magical tombs, but the collection seemed to lend toward bad classical fiction and old historical novels that his tutors had mocked while teaching him history.

Settling into a velvet chair near the fire, he paged through one travelog he'd loved as a child. The detailed prints of exotic locals had led to a few aborted attempts to runaway from the estates that never amounted to much more than hiding in the woods for a few hours until he got tired or hungry. He was certain even if he tried to leave now, his father would just track him down to complain about his marriage prospects.

William eyed the scars on his wrist with a frown. That summer had been a blur for as long as he could remember. He had caught a nasty fever and spent months sick or delirious. By the time he recovered, the wounds on his wrists were healed and he accepted the story about the dog without comment, even if he couldn't remember being attacked.

The dreams from those fevers filled weeks lingered long after his recovery, leaving him bolting from the bed screaming or sleep walking to the stables with no memory of how he got there. They had sent him to boarding school after that to distance him from the trauma of his illness according to his father. He'd always thought it was so he wouldn't be inconveniencing the household then concern for his health.

It least at school he'd been out from his father's control for the first time in his life and it had been heady freedom. To be allowed to choose his own friends, his own activities after classes were over. The first year had been wonderful, but in the next he'd been outed as the son of a Baron and lost most of his friends because of pressure from their parents or the social jostling as the children of minor nobility tried to earn his favor. Only Andrew had stuck by him through the years, a minor enough noble to be beneath notice from his father.

Finally he could put it off no longer, and he headed to bed with a sigh. He hated the ornate rooms they had given him when he came of age. It was yet another room meant to impress more than be functional. When he returned from school, he'd drank himself to sleep every night to manage even a few hours of sleep. For now, he read a runic journal Mage had given him until he finally fell asleep in the too soft mattress and pillows. Tomorrow he'd try the couch near the fire. This would be a long holiday if it kept on like tonight.

* * *

It was well into the next evening before his father emerged from his wing of the house for a late lunch. William had been up early considering the few hours he'd slept, but the early mornings at the cottage had pushed him up out of habit. The servants looked shocked to see him wander into the kitchens and conversation ground to a tense halt as the door silently shut behind him.

"Carry on," He said with a grimace, "I was just hoping to grab a pastry and talk to the cook."

"Chef Moore is out at the market, sir." One of the serving girls said, hurrying up with a tray of pasties for him to choose from.

"No, I meant Cook Evens. Is she still working at the manor?" He asked, piling a few pastries into the offered napkin.

"No, sir; She retired some time ago. Is there something we could help you with?"

"Not unless you know her recipe for her cinnamon biscuits." He said with a small laugh and a nod to the room, "Thank you,"

"Sir, she still lives in the village if you wanted to visit with her. She's on Copper Lane."

"Thank you, I'm sorry, what is your name?"

"Mandi, sir."

"Thank you, Mandi." William said giving her a brief nod and left the kitchen trying to ignore the rush of conversation as the door shut behind him. He'd never hear the end of it from his father if he thought William was consorting with the staff.

* * *

He wandered back to the library, nibbling his pasty. It was much too early to call on the cook now. She had not shared her recipes with the staff when she left, considering how dry this pastry was. Knowing his father, she was sacked and replaced with a new chef who knew the up-and-coming dishes were in fashion. It had been years since he spent time at the manor, so it was possible he'd missed the change. After all, why would anyone expect him to care that the old cook retired?

They had renovated the house several times since he left for school and he wandered unfamiliar corridors and peeking into redone sitting rooms once he'd finished with breakfast. He glanced at one room with bright purple walls with a sigh at the expensive fabrics and furnishings that would be cast aside in the next year or two as quickly as his father had purchased them. The grounds and stable at least seemed untouched, even if the horses he remembered were long gone.

They had sold the stable of hunting horses off while he was at the palace and all that was left were the carriage and cart horses, two rangy looking horses for messages or errands, and a single black stallion kept for selling breeding rights. He'd never considered the manor home, but now it had been reduced to a shell of its former memories and lacked any comfort he might have found there.

William took a ragged-looking bay out the next day with the stable master, but he could walk if he had to. He'd never been allowed to go to the village as a youth, but had ended up at the local tavern enough to know just how painful a trudge back to the manor it could be while drunk wearing new riding boots.

It was a slow morning waiting on his father to start his day. He studied and worked on a few letters, but he would rather be out in the gardens working on his magics or practicing sword patterns. There was no telling how his plants were doing with him gone for two weeks considering the winter weather setting in. He was certain the staff would go into fits if he tried to work outside during his stay. He'd never felt so useless. There was nothing he could work on or accomplish during his stay that would have any real output. He doubted talking to his father would change anything.

William was about ready to climb the walls when he was finally summoned for dinner, his stomach having long forgotten the small sandwich he'd grabbed for lunch. His father was waiting for him in his fine brocade jacket and velvet vest, making William self conscious in his own tailored suit of simpler cloth.

"Good of you to join us, William. Have a seat."

"Thank you, father." William said, biting back a sigh and taking a place next to his father's right hand. The rest of the long table was empty. The next party wouldn't be until the following night.

"I've asked the chef to make a few of the more up-and-coming dishes, I'm sure you've tasted them at the palace."

"I'm sure it will be wonderful." William hummed, fighting to keep his hands still. He doubted they had served anything like this at the cottage, he thought, eyeing the massive fish and breaded shapes being brought in.

"The wine is from one of your mother's vineyards. They have been having quite a good year, I hear." His father continued as the servants moved around them serving and pouring, "I've arranged for my tailor to come tonight, we need you outfitted for tomorrow evening."

"Of course," William agreed, praying he could talk the tailor into something less extreme than his father's wardrobe leaned.

"How have your studies been progressing?"

"Well, I've been learning how to manipulate fire, grow plants, and have mastered warding boxes. I brought my last project with me as a gift if you would like to examine it later."

"Warding against what?"

"Tampering, theft, damage from water or fire, and the box is nearly indestructible."

"Interesting," The older man said, "what of your other studies? Are you keeping up with your sword work?"

"Yes, one of Mage's retainers has been working with me on sword, shield, and spear. They say I am improving daily."

"Good, good,"

"I had hoped to discuss a few matters with you after dinner if you have time, Father."

"What do you need, boy? More funds? A dalliance causing problems?" He asked with a leer before downing his wine.

"Nothing like that, I was hoping we could talk about some family business and a few things I'm struggling to remember."

"Struggling to remember? Nonsense, if you can't remember then it is better left forgotten."

"Like when the dog attacked me and I was so sick. I don't remember it well, and one servant said that my scars aren't those from a dog bite."

"Nonsense, they do not understand what they are talking about."

"They work with hunting hounds, Father. They know what a dog bite looks like." William pressed, trying not to wince as his father's replies got sharper with every question.

"Then they are an idiot." He snapped, "I won't speak of this further."

"Very well," William sighed, trying to ignore the ingrained need to search for his father's approval. He knew it would never happen, but he couldn't seem to stop himself from trying repeatedly.

The rest of dinner was polite conversation about how the family business was doing and the various investments. William kept trying to point out small irregularities in the stories his father boasted about, but we pushed aside them. Only pleasant news could be discussed.

The missing silver items that had been sold, or the farms and fields lying fallow and disused on the ride in were brushed aside as minor issues that would soon be corrected.

William was sure his father had put the family in serious debt but could find nothing but rumors and his gut instinct to prove it. On the outside the manor was more prosperous than ever, but there were too many minor things that didn't add up. They had cut the staff in half. The wine cellars were mostly empty, and most of the rooms sat unfurnished once you left the ground floor.

He wrote to his mother and several of the more cautious families he was certain wouldn't take his questions straight to his father or his other allies. They might at least be able to give him an outside opinion of what was going on with his family estate.

He also sent a letter to the cottage for Mage with all his findings, asking that she help him look into his family's finances. With the apprenticeship contract in place, it bound her to assist him with matters such as these, even if he was believing she would have done it without the magical binding.

* * *

The actual holiday to celebrate the dead wasn't celebrated at the Westedge household. It meant a massive party for others who didn't wish to traditionally celebrate the holiday and a brief prayer for the dead at dinner the next night. William eyed the shifting crowds in the ballroom with a sense of despair. He didn't know a single face in the crowd.

His family wasn't large, but it looked like none had attended this year's event. He smiled politely and bowed as needed, but kept to the edges of the room. He wasn't sure why anyone had bothered to come except to get away from their own unpleasant family events.

"You look rather miserable, music not to your taste?" A young woman asked as she lingered near the wall, examining the mural that wrapped the room.

"I've found that I dislike events where I know only a few of the guests." He said matching her rudeness more out of shock than any inclination.

"Then perhaps we should be introduced? Miss Patria of Woodover." She said dropping into a precise curtsy.

"A pleasure to meet you," He said, giving her a curt bow, "William of Westedge."

"Pleasure to meet you, William, if I may call you that." She said with a smile, "What brings the house heir to sulking in the shadows at his own party?"

"Excuse me?" He sputtered, glancing at her in shock.

"Your father announced that this event was in your honor, yet you seem to be hiding,"

"Are you normally this blunt?"

"Would you like me to be fashionably polite?" She asked with a sigh, "The party is delightful, however I miss the more traditional celebrations. How about you, sir?"

"I couldn't say."

"It's nice to celebrate the old ways occasionally. What traditions does your family follow?" Miss Patria asked, sipping at the spiced wine being served and giving him a wry smile. It was the only nod to tradition in sight.

"I'm afraid this is tradition for my family," William said with a bitter smile, gesturing out at the milling crowd before them, half dancing, half mingling, "we've never celebrated at the graves or mausoleums. My father has always enjoyed being a host more than small intimate events."

"You don't hold a remembrance at all?" She asked blinking in shock, "I'm sorry, that must have sounded rude. I thought a little sanity would help your mood."

"No, it is fine. My mother did when I was a child a few times, but I can barely remember it now." He said with a shrug, watching Miss Patria as she turned to watch the dancers with a blush.

"Perhaps next year you can come visit our estate for the holiday. It can be very cleansing to grieve for your lost loved ones." She offered unhappily.

"Even if you didn't know them?" He asked waving away a passing servant offering small cups of sugared fruit or tiny minced pies.

"Those in our past still can impact our present," She said earnestly, reaching up to fiddle with a locket, "sometimes it takes listening to the histories and stories of our families to reconnect to the people who matter in our lives."

"Who did you lose, if I may ask?" He asked hesitantly.

"My brother, Simon;" She said opening the locket to show him a tiny portrait, "I always miss him this time of year but we are meant to reflect on the dead, are we not? It is what connects us. I would be home with my father doing the remembrance dinner now if not for your father's insistence on a family member attending."

"I apologize, he should have made an exception."

"We have invested in your family's wineries and shipping. To not attend could have endangered that investment."

"Only to my father, I wish I could say it wouldn't have mattered, but appearances are everything and to be snubbed at a private event would have enraged him."

"Is it true that you will take over the family business in the coming years?"

"I honestly do not know," William huffed, moving so he could lean against the wall, "I'm apprenticed to a royal mage for the next year, after that I'm uncertain which path I'm headed for."

"If I may be blunt, your house and it's dealings could use a more level head."

"While I agree I've never been one for managing money and while I'm attempting to correct that oversight, few would back me as the head of the family."

"It would give you time to reconnect with your family if you wished to, surely not all of them are as bad as your father?"

"And if you don't wish to reconnect? If you wish to remove yourself from a hurtful relative or home? Does retelling stories every year help then?" He asked, forcing himself to watch her reaction and not the figure of his father on the other side of the hall.

"Distance can be a kind of death," She said, looking at him with sympathy, "A person doesn't have to be dead to be lost to a family or person. We can still grieve for the pleasant memories they shared with us and for the person they can no longer be."

"And if it is the home you are leaving?" He asked, glancing at her in surprise. He hadn't expected to have such a conversation tonight.

"Homes are not permanent things." She said with a hum as she considered the dancers on the floor, "We have estates passed down through the generations and locations we cherish, but home is something that changes with time. I plan to marry and my childhood home will no longer be mine when I move to my husband's house. I will have to rebuild a home where I end up."

"I had never considered that, homes changing. I don't think I ever considered the manor here home. Not since I started going away for school."

"Few people realize that life changes and what may work for you in the past can become a burden with time."

"You are a strange woman, Miss Patria."

"So I've been told," She said offering a bitter smile of her own, "Few people will face the truth in their lives. I wasn't given a choice growing up, and it made me strange."

"I wasn't saying it was a bad thing," he huffed offering his arm, "would you care to dance, Miss Patria of Woodover?"

"I'm a family of no consequence, sir. Your father invited us to publicly snub my father when he didn't attend."

"All the more reason to rub it in his face you decided to attend in his stead." William said with a laugh, "I'm offering nothing more than that and a dance with someone who has no plans to use the occasion for anything more than light conversation and a distraction from his own family complications."

"I had intended to leave before the next dance, but I won't turn such a rare offer down." She said with a shy smile, taking his arm, "As long as we both understand each other."

"Frankly, it's a delight to find someone to have an honest conversation with. Few here are approving of my apprenticeship, and it affronts the rest on my behalf. A dance is a minor price to pay for an evening of sane conversation during the holiday. If nothing else, it will appease my father to see me dancing and will grant your family some time in his good graces."

"Very well, lead on sir, and we shall converse for a while longer."

"As you will, my lady." He said with a genuine smile as he lead her onto the dance floor for the next song.

Chapter 30

Visiting Toussaint Estate

"Wonderful to meet you, Madame Mage." John's father, Richard, said standing stiffly and taking her hand once she approached, "John has told us much of the mage he has been seeing so often of late."

"I hope I live up to his expectations then," Beryl said with a smile, glancing back at John as he blushed faintly. "You have a beautiful home, John has promised me a tour of the stables later. They look extensive."

"The life and blood of this house is horses, Mistress Mage. May I introduce you to my daughter, Samantha?" He said gesturing to the red-haired woman at his side.

"A pleasure to meet you," Beryl said with a curtsy, "I've heard we will have much to discuss on the topics of women's rights in Orlean."

"A fellow supporter, how wonderful!" Samantha crowed, giving a firm handclasp when Beryl offered her hand.

"Can we leave the politics until after dinner, my dear? I'm afraid my back is demanding a chair." He said giving them both a stiff bow and moving to the chair by the fire.

"Of course, Father. Let me show Mage to her rooms, John, why don't you make father a brandy and perhaps something for your guest?"

"Tea or water will be fine, thank you." Beryl blurted, offering her arm to Samantha with a wicked smile, "Perhaps you can share some childhood stories of John while we walk?"

"I believe I shall enjoy your visit, Mistress Mage. Has he told you about his adventures with a young colt and the pond?" Samantha declared with a wide grin, linking their arms together and leading her out of the room with their father chuckling behind them.

"What have I done? I never should have introduced you two." John groaned before laughing as Samantha turned back and stuck out her tongue like a naughty schoolgirl.

"Well, what do you expect? I've always wanted a sister, and you refused to conform." She declared, tugging Beryl along the long hallway and to the front staircase.

"Your home is lovely, Mistress Toussaint." Beryl murmured letting go of her arm and gathering Rune up so he didn't have to climb, Argent thumped to a seat at the bottom refusing to bother with the stairs until he had to.

"Please, call me Sam. Everyone does." She said leading the way up, "Well, everyone but Father. He's a bit of a traditionalist when it comes to names."

"I take it my lack of one caused a bit of an issue then?" Beryl asked, hitching her skirt a hair higher as they climbed to the third floor.

"John explained that you go by Mage after a curse took your name away when you were a child. It must be awful to not have a name, I can't even imagine it."

"It's not as bad as you think, at least the curse is wearing thinner." Beryl shrugged, "When I was very young, people forgot about me entirely if their attention wavered at all. I became something of a brat for a time, trying to make sure I wasn't forgotten, I'm sure."

"That would be horrible for a child, however, did you cope?"

"Even as a child, I had my magic. I learned early to cast small protections and wards to alert me if my guardian was leaving without me." She sighed, trying to decide how to explain it, "I've lived with my curse so long it's become my normal, I barely remember living without it now. I'm not sure I could say living with a name was any better than without it. I'm happy enough as I am, I don't think I'd change it even if I could now. Everyone knows me as Mage, my true name no longer matters."

"That's a very optimistic way to look at it." Samantha said showing her to a large glass door opening to a large balcony over-looking the fields behind the house, "This balcony runs the length of the house and we take breakfast here most mornings if the weather is fine. Your room is just down here."

"Do your animals travel everywhere with you?"

"Yes, once we retire for the night, Argent, the hunting hound will join me. I hope that is all right?"

"Yes, John explained, it binds them to you. I'm afraid we haven't had a mage in the family in so time, so you might have to explain things at times."

"I never mind explaining, it's when people don't ask questions I run into issues." Beryl offered with a wry smile, taking in the nicely appointed rooms they had shown her to, "The room is wonderful, especially the view. You must have amazing sunsets here in the mountains."

"And sunrises, most of the bedrooms are on this side of the house, so you won't be woken at the first crack of dawn. I'll leave you to freshen up. The porter should have placed your bags in the dressing room. You'll hear the bell once dinner is to be served if you don't make it down beforehand."

"Thank you, Sam."

"I have a feeling we will like each other, Mistress Mage. I hope my brother keeps you. If he doesn't, I might." She said with an impish grin as she ducked out of the room.

"Here's hoping they still like us by the end of the trip." Beryl hummed with a sigh as she let Rune jump down to explore. Dinner

that night was awkward with an older aunt arriving just as they are sitting down to the meal.

"Aunt Beatrice, is everything all right? I thought you weren't due until the end of the week?" Richard asked, struggling out of his chair even as Sam rushed to his side to help him up.

"I heard you were having visitors and decided I wanted to see this Mage myself." She told her in a tone harsh, "Who knows what John has gotten himself into while at the Palace!"

"Mistress Mage, may I introduce our Aunt, Beatrice Judith Toussaint." Sam said, giving both of them a curtsy and drawing the older woman's attention as Beryl approached.

"What are your designs on my nephew? And what is your correct name, no woman goes by something as silly as Mage."

"My full name is Beryl Marcian. You may call me Beryl if you wish, but I am called Mage. I've gone by Mage for most of my life." Beryl murmured, giving the woman a deep curtsy, "It is a pleasure to meet you, Madame Toussaint."

"I am not sure I can say the same," She sniffed, "John, I wish to speak with you in the parlor."

"Yes, Aunt Beatrice." John said, shooting Beryl an apologetic glance as he showed his Aunt out of the room.

"Well, you've met the disagreeable crone in the family." Samantha said with a groan, "Shall we continue with dinner or retire to the sitting room for drinks?"

"Samantha, do not talk so about your Aunt. She is family." Richard huffed, offering Beryl his arm, "Forgive the disruption, Mistress Mage. If it's agreeable with you, we shall retire to the sitting room and I'll have the servants whip up a few sandwiches while we wait on Beatrice and John."

"That would be fine, Mister Toussaint. I don't wish to cause your family any strife." Beryl agreed, taking his arm and strolling to the front room where a maid was already lighting the lamps.

"Trust me, it would have happened no matter who John brought home." Samantha said with a sigh, waiving the maid away as she stoked the fire and added an extra log, "Aunt Beatrice has always had lofty ideas of what John, as the firstborn, should accomplish. John has side stepped those expectations, but marriage is the one she will demand a word on. That doesn't mean that it changes anything between you and John. She's just an old windbag trying to control those around her that seem to be malleable. She gave up on me after I started my work for women's rights. She rather firmly believes a woman's place is in the home and at her husband's side."

"Thankfully, John seems to have no issues with me owning and running a business." Beryl murmured, "What is it you do with the women's rights movement?"

"Our group holds rallies at various government meetings and pushes the leaders for legislation to expand women's rights and ability to govern themselves without the oversight of a man. It would amaze you how many young women I knew growing up who married to keep the family estates. There is a booming marriage trade run out of the financing bureaus when a family runs low on funds or has a death with no man left to take over."

"I've spoken with some nobility about this, few even realize how bad it is." Beryl agreed, "They pressured me to marry in Arden but thankfully I had a good Master who insisted I wait until after I was through my training to even entertain a marriage, especially one looking to add magic to their bloodlines."

"Exactly, women everywhere are being pressured to marry to improve their situations, and in Orlean it is easy to become destitute without a man's support." Samantha said triumphantly, "The ruling class are men so they are so far outside of it they can't conceive of it being an actual problem."

"Not everyone sees the constant need of male accompaniment as assistance. When I arrived it seemed more like a cage, I was so used to traveling alone and doing as I needed when I ran errands that to find out that not even the shopkeepers will sell to an unaccompanied woman was ridiculous. I've been running my household and business for years and yet I can't buy a single ribbon here without a man to hand over the money for me."

"What business are you intending to start? John mentioned you were looking into shops on the coast?" Richard inserted, changing the subject and earning a huff from his daughter that made Beryl smile.

"I make and enchant jewelry and small objects. I also have made dresses but I'm still learning how to mass produce those kinds of things, I've worked with custom orders or making things as a project to learn a new magical technique. Enchanted objects don't seem very common in Orlean, so most of my sales so far have been from the jewelry and dresses. I brought a few gifts I'd planned to share tomorrow so I might get your opinion on what might sell among your peers."

"You needn't gift anything, I'd be willing to give my opinion on whatever you like." Samantha said with a laugh, "John mentioned something about dancing bears in a letter. Was that something you enchanted?"

"Yes, I made several enchanted stuffed animals that dance or walk about. At the moment they are seen more than a passing amusement but they helped me learn to sew." Beryl sighed, "It's strange but most of my commissions in Arden were wards and protections, blades charmed to be sharp for longer, houses protected from fire. My jewelry never sold, I gave them out as gifts. Here everyone seems to focus on appearance and wealth, I know it was a part of the courts in Arden as well, but the royal family there weren't so invested in the balls and parties that Orlean seems to favor."

"The nobility is all about appearance here, you have to be in the most fashionable outfits and going to all the best parties or you are less than nothing. It is maddening, I've been to some local parties and there isn't a single coherent thought in some of those ladies' heads beyond the next dress or party. They have no interest in improving themselves or learning to discuss more intellectual topics or pursuits."

"Don't paint the entire nobility with that brush, I've had some wonderful conversations with women at those same balls. It's only amongst their peers they flutter and pretend, get them to one side and they often have a ruthless intellect when it comes to business or dealing with people. They don't realize that same strength could be used in other areas."

"Are you planning to stay with the courts as they travel between the palaces, Mistress Mage?" Richard asked as the maid returned with hot mulled wine and cider for them with small finger sandwiches and treats to nibble.

"I'm hoping to purchase a house on the coast as well once the Court travels back next spring, my household is growing and I will need somewhere more permanent for my forge and studio." Beryl said, taking a mug of cider and letting Rune have a sniff before she sipped. It was still much too hot to drink. She shifted the mug in her hands absently wishing she could take off her gloves, she'd become spoiled with going without while they stayed at the cottage.

"Smells nice but it is hot." Rune mused absently curling on the arm of the chair as Argent claimed the foot of the fireplace with a groan.

"Perhaps Mary can make some cold for you next time." Beryl murmured, sipping gingerly.

"Forge? You do all the jewelry by hand then? I thought you were enchanting already crafted pieces?" Richard asked, frowning in confusion.

"I can enchant objects as well, but I prefer to design and craft it myself if I can. The magic seems to settle better into something I've made with my own hands. I was hoping my apprentice would show an inclination for blacksmithing, but he is leaning more towards plant based magic."

"Where is he this holiday? Does he have a family?"

"He is visiting with his own family this week. I didn't wish to offer the estate as a possibility without asking first myself, and he was eager to join his father for the festivities." Beryl said hesitantly.

"He is more than welcome any time you wish to visit." Richard said firmly, "I'm afraid we celebrate little of the rites in this house. We will stay in on the longest night and the day before is the cleaning of the tombs on the estate and a day of prayer, but the day after is used to rest and recover more than celebrate any grand feasts as some families do."

"Arden doesn't have a day to celebrate the dead. We have a small party to celebrate the end of the season, but nothing as elaborate as was being planed at the palace. I'm glad to be away from the pomp and festivities for a while." Beryl said with a wry grin.

"Are you not a fan of the Prince's parties, then?" Samantha asked, "I thought John has said you attended them weekly?"

"I'm more of just a natural homebody," Beryl shrugged with a laugh, "I'm content to work on my estate, complete my magical projects, and spend the evenings with a good friend or two. I don't mind the parties, but the constant parade of events can be very tiring."

"Are you required to attend many?" Richard asked absently as he selected a sandwich from the offered tray with a murmur of thanks, "I did not think John was attending anything but the larger events."

"The princess requested that I attend last week so I could see her in the latest dress I crafted. She was quite proud of helping to design it." Beryl said selecting her own sandwich and two more for her bond mates. She ignored the slight wince from the maid as she dismantled the rounds and gave them the meat.

"You are designing clothes for the royal family?" Richard asked, exchanging a glance with Samantha, "I didn't realize you had such esteemed customers."

"Just for Princess Noemi, but both her and her father have purchased several pieces of warded jewelry from my stock and requested more to be custom designed for the coming balls." Beryl said, "I've been helping the King on several larger projects and might be in the running for Court Mage in the coming year. I haven't decided if I want to accept that title if it's offered or not yet."

"It is rumored that they poisoned the last Court Mage." Samantha said looking concerned, "Aren't you worried that it might be dangerous to accept such a position?"

"I've been told that I'm already acting as the Prince's Court Mage, the King has agreed to allow me citizenship in the coming year so even if I don't take the position I will still be able to live here without fear of being sent back to Arden."

"So the rumors you were exiled from Arden are true?"

"Yes, however, I was given a full pardon from the King. The person who attacked the palace has yet to be caught, but they exonerated me from those charges. I could return if I wished, but I think I'm still needed here for now." Beryl murmured, she'd only found out about that a few days ago in a letter from Count Malouel.

"Will you be attending the Prince's Masquerade? It's supposed to be quite extravagant this year." Samantha asked brightly, changing the subject with a wide-eyed look at her father.

"Yes, I will be in costume, though I hope to sit out most of the dancing and events this time." Beryl agreed, fighting for a tiny polite smile.

"Oh, you must teach me the trick if you escape the attempts of the older mother's matchmaking." Samantha said.

"I'm afraid it's traveling with an intimidatingly large dog and for the Masquerade I'll be hiding in plain sight." Beryl said smiling as the other woman laughed.

"Oh, will you be disguised? What kind of costume are you planning?"

"A rather non-conventional one, I'm afraid." Beryl said with a grin she smothered as the door opened to readmit John and his Aunt Beatrice. Everyone stood to greet them.

"You seem to rather enjoy the unconventional." The older woman snapped as John showed her to a chair and moved to stand next to Beryl, pressing a hand to her shoulder for a moment.

"I couldn't say, Ma'am." Beryl said stiffly, trying to keep her tone polite, "I'm not from this country and am still learning what is considered traditional here in Orlean."

"You seem content to follow the courts about, swanning about looking for handouts." She snapped waiving away the maid offering her a drink, "John here seems convinced that you are a paragon of virtue, Miss Mage."

"I would never claim to be without fault, Ma'am. I don't believe anyone is without some fault they struggle to overcome."

"And yet you continue to attend those hedonistic events the Prince continues to demand while you are courting. You even live on the grounds!"

"I have been engaged by the King to complete several magical projects for the royal family. They have graciously allowed me to stay on the palace grounds while I find a home of my own." Beryl said firmly ignoring the glare the older woman was sending her way, "I have attended several events, I even met John for the first time at a hunt the Prince requested I attend when he found out I was fond of riding."

"Yes, John mentioned your fondness for animals." She said glancing at Argent with a sniff, "Surely your beasts could have been left at the palace?"

"As a mage, I am able to magically bond with animals. It's a permanent bond and distance can be painful, my bond mates go where ever I do."

"Surely not to the palace?" She spat with a look of disgust, "Animals are filthy and have no place in the home."

"That is a pity that you think so." Beryl said, standing and handing her plate and mug off to the maid who appeared at her elbow, "They go everywhere with me, even to the palace. They have attended dances, balls, parties, and even private audiences with the royal family. I have no intention of leaving them behind. If it makes you uncomfortable to have them here, then I will happily leave."

"Now, I'm sure Beatrice did not mean that you are not welcome, Mage." Richard said, struggling to his feet.

"They are a part of me, body and soul. If they are not welcome, then neither am I." Beryl said, turning to John and taking his hand, "I will retire to my room for the night. Goodnight, John. I hope everyone has a good evening."

"Let me walk you, Mage." John said ignoring his Aunt's continued insults as they left the room and he shut the door firmly behind them muffling the words. "Let me apologize for my Aunt. There was a reason she wasn't invited this weekend. I will tear strips out of my cousin for him telling her about this visit."

"It's not your fault, John. Everyone has an evil seed in the family, I'm just happy you never have to meet mine."

"Nothing she says will change how I feel about you, Mage. I intend to court you and if you consent to eventually marry you. No one in the family can change my mind on that, not even my Aunt that is so set in her ways she's more statue than human."

"There are a few things we need to discuss, anyway. Will they talk if you are gone for too long?"

"It doesn't matter, let's go to your sitting room. We can talk there in more privacy." He said taking her hand and leading the way upstairs, frowning as Argent fought his way up alongside them, "Is he always this bad with stairs?"

"I'm afraid so, enormous dogs weren't designed with steep stairs in mind."

"Then your next house will need to avoid them. Perhaps once you return to the coast I can accompany on a few trips to visit estates you are considering. There has to be at least one with a bedroom on the first floor."

"If not, I might be able to afford to make alterations if the sales of my work continue as they have."

"I'm glad you're doing well, I know you were afraid at first that Orlean wouldn't be accepting of magical items."

"Arden is having a rather bad backlash against magic and mages at the moment, I was afraid it was the same here. I'm relieved more than anything." She said thanking the servant that was lighting the fireplace in the small sitting room as they arrived.

"Will you be needing anything else?" he asked, glancing between the two of them.

"No thank you, Raymond. We should be fine for a while but can you bring more water for the animals and perhaps a small dish of meat?" John asked glancing at Mage for confirmation.

"That would be wonderful, thank you." Beryl agreed with a grateful smile.

"As you said, they are part of you, therefore I should treat them the same as I would have treated you." John said with a small blush as she stretched and brushed a kiss to one cheek, "What was it you wanted to discuss?"

"I have one more thing to show you before I can allow you to court me." Beryl whispered, fiddling with her gloves, "I'll understand if you decline to continue the courtship."

"Nothing you could show me would make me discontinue our courtship, Mage. I wish to be with you no matter the danger. I know being near the royal family isn't a safe position, and I am willing to accept that danger if it means we are together."

"That is good," Beryl said, pulling off her gloves and showing him one palm, "but I meant something else."

"Gods, are you in pain?" he asked, taking one hand and lightly tracing the jagged scars, tilting her hand to better see in the firelight.

"Most days, no. Sometimes the scars become irritated or I do too much and split the skin. When I was cursed as a child someone injured me and left to die, I was found and healed but there was too much damage to prevent scarring."

"How extensive," he asked before trailing off.

"Everywhere but my face." She said pulling her hand away and replacing her glove, "I understand if you need time to decide."

"There is no decision, Mage. I wish to court you and eventually marry you. I mourn the fact that someone injured you and you still have pain, but it doesn't put me off my decided course. I am yours any way you wish to have me."

"I don't want to cause issues with you and your family."

"It entitles them to their own opinions and mine will not be swayed by anything they have to say." He said firmly, taking her hands and squeezing them lightly.

"Think it over anyway." She pressed, "Beauty isn't something I can offer you."

"My decision won't change, I want to learn every inch of you that has been hidden away for so long. I want to know the good and the bad and to share with you my own faults and strengths. Our love won't be less for it, I promise you."

"How are you so accepting of everything?" she asked, pressing against his side for a moment.

"I refuse to throw away the chance of our happiness because of a few problems. We will work through whatever comes. You don't abandon a foal because it is having difficulty. You cherish it and hold it close while it grows into the horse you hoped it would be."

"And if it doesn't grow as you wanted?"

"You love what it is." He said firmly, taking her hand in his as he wrapped his arm around her, "You don't throw something away because it has a few chips. A favorite mug is better for the wear. We will be too in the long run. Are you willing to keep trying?"

"Yes, I don't want to lose you, but my life isn't easy or safe. I will always have impossible tasks to accomplish and people I must protect. I can't be the sheltered wife waiting for you to return at the end of the day with dinner ready and waiting. I'll never be a normal wife or mother."

"I wouldn't want you any other way then as you are. If the gods bless us with children, I will happily stay at the estates while you travel as you need. If not, then I will stay and run the estates or we will find a home wherever you are needed. My sister could take over the estate from my father if needed. If not, the estate can be sold and we can find a new home. My home will be where you are, the rest is unimportant."

She glanced up and the kiss that followed was a natural extension of their touch. They kissed, John peppering her mouth and cheeks with soft kisses before pressing a firm kiss to her temple as he gathered her close. His wiry strength held her up and supported her. For once, being held didn't feel like a cage limiting and confining. She pressed a last kiss to the corner of his mouth before drawing reluctantly away.

"They will be asking the servants to break us apart soon. Give your father and sister my best, I didn't mean to cause any strife in your family."

"Trust me, all the blame rests on my Aunt. She's always pressed for me to marry a distant cousin to keep the estate in the family as it were. She would have disapproved no matter who I brought before her. You are perfect to me. She is the one who needs to learn some manners."

"Thank you," She murmured as he gathered her close once more, "go, or we will have Raymond back in here to fetch you."

"Have a good evening, Mistress Mage." He said, drawing away and giving her a deep, courtly bow at the door once he'd straightened his waistcoat.

"You as well, Mister Toussaint." She said with a blush, dipping into a deep curtsy with a soft laugh.

"There is the smile I was seeking." He said with a triumphant grin, "Now I can face my dragon of an aunt with ease knowing my lady smiles."

"Go, you idiot." Beryl laughed, "I will see you in the morning."

"Good night, Mage. Until the morning." He said with a smile, ducking through the door and closing it gently behind him. Beryl laughed softly before heading into the bedroom to get ready for bed. It was early, but she was tired with all the drama of the day.

"*Can we keep him?*" *Argent* asked softly as he padded to the folded blankets on the floor at the foot of the bed and settled with Rune curling against his feet once he was still.

"*He would make an excellent mate,*" *Rune* agreed, "*He fights for you and makes you laugh.*"

"*That is up to him, but I think he wants to stay. We will have to* see."*Beryl* said with a soft chuckle, wandering over to her bags only to find them empty and her garments hung and waiting for her in the closet. Selecting a nightgown, she changed and hung up her dress before going to sit and unpin her hair.

Would John be fine with her going about ungloved or in men's clothes? He seemed fine with her riding in men's trousers and had called her lovely frequently when she was both in formal dresses or planning to work on the forge and in her simplest clothes. John had no issue with her working the forge or making weapons, he'd complemented her work but had no interest in weapons himself. He'd yet to see her practice. Perhaps she'd need to introduce him to Jeremy and have him attend a session?

It still amazed her he was content to see and be with her as she was. Nothing she'd revealed so far had resulted in him wanting her to change. She'd never been with anyone who didn't want her to conform to society. Most had issue with her crafting weapons, using magic, or dressing as a boy. John had seen all of that and shrugged it off without blinking. She wasn't sure anything she did would force him to change her unless it was to keep her safe, even then he might fight, but he would probably let her do what was needed. He might even be at her side in the battle. She couldn't decide how she felt on that.

* * *

Mage dressed carefully the next morning wearing a conservative grey linen dress and lace gloves, her hair pinned up in a soft cascade of curl. She brushed Rune and Argent down before they descended the stairs to relieve their bladders for the morning. Beryl wiped their feet free of mud with a rag before they headed back inside. The dining room however was empty, and the servants directed her back upstairs to the balcony for breakfast. She was glad of the thick shawl she had wrapped around her shoulders when she stepped out on to the white planking. The breeze was constant and chilling.

"Mage, wonderful!" Samantha said directing her to a seat next to her at the small table, "You needn't worry about Aunt Beatrice coming down, she's eating in her rooms this morning."

"I wish to apologize for my sister's actions last night. I can assure you her comments have no influence on the rest of the family. She will leave this morning and won't be attending any more family functions until she can learn to curb her tongue." Richard said formally retaking his seat once they were seated.

"I just don't want to cause any issues with the family because my presence." Beryl said slowly, hating how she seemed to constantly apologizing for things she had no control over.

"You aren't the issue, my dear. My sister has always believed that she has more control of this family then she does. None of us share her beliefs in this matter, and that is the end of it. You are more than welcome to be here, we have no issue with your bond mates, and there is no issue with John courting you. Should things turn serious, then you will be welcomed into the family with open arms." Richard said seriously, "Now, enough of such talk. Let us enjoy this chilly morning and this lovely weather while we have it, I'm afraid it will storm in the next few days if my bones are right. Soon it will be much too cold to eat out here."

"Perhaps John can show you a few trails today." Samantha offered as John opened the door and stepped out to join them, rubbing Argent's ears as he passed, "Are the animals able to keep up with you on horseback? I know you mentioned going on hunts."

"Rune will accompany we if we are going a long distance. If Argent is coming, we have to go at a slower pace, but he can keep up. We used to run messages for the castle in Arden, and they both have been all over the countryside on horseback. We saw more than enough storms and mud on those rides."

"Did you use the messenger horses or a horse of your own?" John asked, accepting a cup of steaming tea as he took the seat next to Richard across from them.

"I had an older messenger horse I purchased on my first trip to

Cardu. He was called Flox, I rode him the entire time I was in training. He wasn't a gorgeous animal, but he was steady and worked hard, good with dogs and children, willing to truck along no matter the weather."

"Aye, those are the ones you miss." John sighed before breaking into a chuckle, "My first horse was like that, a long nose and barrel on a stocky body but he trucked along no matter where we weathered me learning to jump and hunt with resigned grace."

"What was he called?" Mage asked, accepting a bowl of porridge sweetened with honey and full of dried fruit. Food meant to warm you up from the inside out.

"Brownie," John laughed, "I was five when I received him as a birthday gift and the name stuck. He's been retired for years now, and it surprised us he's lasted through last year's winter."

"He's picked up another cough," Samantha said offering around a tray of biscuits and pots of jam, "I've tasked our new groom with his hot mash twice a day and he seems to be doing better staying in the smaller paddock near the barn in the day and in at night. He's turned into a cantankerous old man in his old age, nipping at anyone who comes near his door but begging for treats all the same."

"Not much different from when I was still riding him." John laughed, "Perhaps we can go tour the barn today if you don't mind being out in the cold longer?"

"No, that would be lovely." Beryl agreed, glancing out at the mist covered mountains and fields around them, "Will we be riding?"

"Samantha is planning a small feast for dinner but as long as we keep it short we should manage a gentle ride so your bond mates can keep up." He agreed clearly already planning out their path in his mind as he absently swirled a spoon through his porridge.

"Shall I tell you a secret, Mage?" Samantha offered in a whisper as everyone fell quiet eating.

"I'll do my utmost to keep it." Beryl agreed with a grin, sipping at her tea.

"John hates porridge, but it's the only thing our cook will make for breakfast in the winter. He eats it because he has to, but you can see him steeling himself for every bite."

"It's not that bad," John said with a grimace, "it's just the fact that its porridge."

"Even with the honey and fruit? I don't like it plain but sweet, it's okay."

"I'd just rather have anything else, biscuits are good." He said with a grin, taking a bite of his now that it was slathered with butter and jam.

"That's good to know," Beryl laughed, "I'm rarely picky with what I eat, I rarely eat much for breakfast, but porridge is as good as anything. What are we planning for the holidays tomorrow? I don't want to be in the way if you have any rituals to attend to."

"We don't hold with many of the rituals. Today is for preparations, and tomorrow is for contemplation of the gods and our ancestors. We will clean the tombs in the morning, spend the day in prayer, and stay up that night to hold a vigil for the dead through the night. Our vigil is more a gathering to share time with family and to remember stories from the past. We gather in the house by the fire and stay until first light, remembering our ancestors."

"That sounds nice." Beryl murmured, she'd never had time to honor her parents or ancestors herself.

"Perhaps you can join us and light some incense for your ancestors before we retire to the fireside." Richard offered.

"Yes, I know you're far from the tombs of your ancestors, but that doesn't mean you can't join us in prayer." Samantha agreed, casting a glance to John who agreed, "You are welcome to join us or not, I know Arden doesn't celebrate the end of the year the same."

"I don't mind joining you, I just don't want to be in the way."

"Nonsense, if I have to insist you come to make you comfortable, I will. We want you to be welcome and you may join us or not, but you will be welcome to do either." Samantha said firmly, standing and picking up the teapot to refresh everyone's cups.

"Thank you, I would be glad to join you."

"Good, now that that discussion is over," Richard said with a chuckle, "Samantha tell me how this year's colts are doing again, I'd like to bring them in for the winter along with the older stock but most should be fine wintering in the fields with the shelters. Do any of the shelters need repairs?"

"Yes, Father." Samantha said starting to list out what work they needed for the barn and fields before the first snow of the season hit, John chiming in with which horses he'd like to work with in the spring for the next year's auctions and hunts.

They were still discussing horses and foaling when Beryl excused herself to go change for the day. She was happy to see plates waiting near the door of fresh meat for her bond mates. Setting them inside near the fire, she went into the bedroom to change into something she could ride in. She dug out her heavy woolen greatcoat and a thick scarf and gloves for the ride. Hopefully, it wouldn't be as cold once they were in the woods, the barns at least should be an enjoyable break from the weather. The breakfast outside had been pleasant, but there was a sharp bite to the air outside of the shelter of the house. John had grinned when she joined him in boots and breeches, showing her down the path to the first massive stable.

"I wanted to show you another mare you might like to ride today, I think she will suit you. She's one of our younger mares, but she miscarried badly and won't be able to be used for breeding stock. She's been lazing around the pastures the last year and is ready for a little work. By spring she should be back in condition if you are interested."

"As long as she doesn't have any lasting issues, I don't have a problem with trying her, I'm not sure I will have time to get her back into condition or rehabilitate any injuries."

"Oh, no. She's fit, she's just not been worked more than once a week. If you're looking for something already in working shape now, then I can keep looking, but I think you will both compliment each other."

"I'm more than happy to try her, she sounds lovely."

"Sorry if it seems I'm selling her to you," John laughed, showing her to a stall to one side, "I think you will do well with each other. She's trained to pull a small phaeton or ride side saddle should you need, she's comfortable with cats and dogs, and is trained to hunt. She is suited for what you need."

"Oh, she's lovely." Beryl laughed as the massive golden head hung over the stall to greet them, "I've never seen these outside of farming, I didn't know they could train one to jump."

"She's on the small side for a draft. We bred her mother with a hunter stallion and we hoped that she would be a more versatile hunter, but she doesn't have the stamina for the fast hunts and her jumping is middling. She would make a great traveling mount going between cities, but she'll never be the flashy ride most of our buyers are looking for." He said nudging the horse back so they could go into the stall before offering her a sugar lump while Beryl looked her over.

"She's got solid hooves for sure, no leg issues?" Beryl asked, running her hands down one leg and lifting the massive hoof. The frog was clean and dry and the hoof wall looked healthy with no lines or separations showing.

"No leg issues and an amiable disposition." John agreed, standing in the door with Argent while Beryl checked the mare over with a quick hand while the horse let herself be inspected with a bored.

"She's no ladies' horse, that is for sure, but I like the look of her." Beryl said patting the thick neck and watching as Rune minced about the stall but was ignored by the horse, "What is she called?"

"We call her Sunny but her official name is Brilliant Sunbeam." John said with a laugh giving her another sugar cube, "Would you care to take a ride now or complete our tour?"

"Let's complete the tour, I'd like to see the stallion you've told me so much about if that's okay?"

"After you," He agreed, stepping out of the way so they could exit the stall and grabbing a halter as they headed down the hallway, "he's in a paddock at the end of our second barn. Devon's turned into a well aged old sire, but he can still be a bit of a brat if you don't know his tricks."

"It's the same with people, everyone has their quirks."

"Are your bond mates the same?"

"I think so," Beryl shrugged, "they have their own likes and dislikes, their own personality the same as any animal or person."

"So you can feel when they are happy or upset?"

"Yes, sometimes they don't understand human issues, but they are just as emotional as we are. They tend towards being happy and enjoying life more than we do, I think. I don't think they complicate things as much as humans do."

"How do you mean?"

"They don't understand why we have to have certain clothes for certain times. Why men and women are forced to dress differently. They have a hard time with social issues, things like rank and social standing make sense but they don't understand how someone can be of lofty rank through birth, for animals rank is a facet of personality and strength. They don't understand not having to fight for a leadership role."

"They are much more complex than I would have imagined. Is that because of your bond?"

"They understand things better because I'm able to explain them to them across the bond, but some things don't translate."

"Like what?"

"Like courting," Beryl laughed, "they didn't understand why humans are so silly about mating, going through all these steps and hoops when it's clear that you like the other person and would like to spend time with them."

"I imagine mating is much simpler for animals." John said clearing his throat, changing the subject as they reached the pasture, "Here's Devon."

"He's much smaller than I imagined, I'd built up a magnificent charger from your descriptions." Beryl said taking in the mid-sized grey stallion grazing to one side, John clicked his tongue but was ignored by the older horse.

"He knows it's not time to come in yet." John laughed, "I used to think he was some knight's charger that my father had found and brought in, it wasn't until I grew up that I realized how small he is for a stallion. Even so, he used to jump obstacles that would make every other mount balk. He had no fear on the course during a hunt. Let's go grab, Hinton, and be on our ride. We can swing back for Sunny and tack up there."

"Lead the way."

The ride was nice, Sunny was wider than she was used to riding but had an easy gait that seemed to eat up the trail. She fussed a bit whenever Argent crowded her, but didn't kick out. Beryl hoped she would settle with time once she got to know Argent. She could see the horse working out well, she would need to try her on a small cart but it was looking promising.

That night at before dinner they were relaxing in the sitting room while Samantha examined some of Beryl's work. She'd brought two stuffed animals and a few small pieces of jewelry or clothing for each member of the family. She'd taken care to do varying shades of brown and green for John, since that seemed to be his favored shade.

"These are lovely, Mage." Samantha cooed, playing with the stuffed kitten that was tussling with Rune on the floor until Argent came and scooped him up to take him mewing back to Beryl, "Is he all right?"

"He's fine, he's just complaining about dog spit." Beryl laughed wiping the small cat down with a pocket handkerchief, "I hope you like the gloves, I wasn't sure what everyone would need but we always need gloves in winter."

"They are perfect, thank you, Mage." Richard said gravely, "The older I get the more I appreciate a warm pair of gloves."

"Let me go grab something from my room. My friend in town gave me an unusual crystal that might work for your jewelry." Samantha added standing and hurrying out of the room.

"She's always on some new item or another, at least this time it's not half the books at the local store." Richard huffed, "Crystals are the latest craze I'm told, different ones have unique properties and healing abilities. Some local women even claim to have healed their children with them, but I've yet to see anything that couldn't be explained away as nonsense myself."

"Here we are!" Samantha called out, coming back into the room and setting down a small box that made Beryl stand with a frown where had she felt that sensation before?

"These are the crystals from Sarah?" Richard asked, standing and moving to join Samantha at the table where she was laying out several dark crystals as Beryl and John joined them.

"Yes, like the one I gave you for your room. They are supposed to heal minor illnesses and improve the humors." Samantha said, offering the largest crystal to Beryl.

"Has anyone been sick recently?" Beryl asked, backing away from the black crystal Samantha was holding out.

"Father hasn't been feeling well the last few weeks, and one of my friends has fallen sick with a cold. It's been going through many of the families since the summer." She said with a frown, watching Beryl uncertainly, "Everyone has been sharing the crystals about since they are supposed to help with such things."

"Are their families known for having magic?"

"We are and my friend Marge is slightly gifted, I don't know about the others. Do you mean the crystals have something to do with the illness going through town?"

"Yes, they absorb magic." Beryl said, swallowing thickly. She could feel the pull on her magic even with so small a crystal, "Set it on the table and I'll show you."

"What now?" Samantha asked, setting it to one side and stepping back.

"Watch," Beryl murmured, moving forward and casting the illusion of a small butterfly above the stone. It sucked a thin trail of golden light into the grey crystal, making it pulse with a bleak light. It didn't take long for the image to flicker and fade. With a last burst of light, the image collapsed, dissolving as the sparks of magic were drained away. "That crystal has been draining the magic out of anything that comes near it. Everyone has a small amount of magic naturally within them, losing even a tiny amount can make you sick or lethargic. You need to get rid of the crystals, can I take one to show the Prince?"

"Take them all, if they are making people sick then I want them out of my house." Richard said frowning at the dark stones and Samantha shoved them back in the box and snapped the lid closed, "Samantha, have the maids gather up any other crystals in the house and write a note to Sarah, we need to warn our neighbors before anyone becomes even worse. There have already been several deaths in the community. What if the crystals are making our illnesses worse?"

"I'll see to it," John said, leaving the room to deal with the servants.

"They very well could be, losing your magic makes the body weak and more susceptible to disease. It also makes illnesses harder to fight off." Beryl said rubbing her hands together as she stared at the box, "I've been hunting for crystals like these since I was an apprentice. They were all over Arden. Someone was draining the magic from children and the land. We never could find the leader of the cult, but they said they were the followers of Aedus."

"There is a temple in the mountains to Aedus. One cousin goes sometimes. They were trying to get me to attend a holy day but I don't get along with Regis very well so I declined."

"Do you think I could meet with him? If the temple is giving away crystals, then the King needs to know."

"I can get you a letter of invitation to his next revel but he's the worst kind of man, Mage." Samantha shuddered, "We put up with him because he's family but he's drained the accounts of my Uncle with his gambling and drunken revels. He will treat you like a whore if he meets you unaccompanied, and he knows all of our servants and friends that might escort you."

"I could go." John pointed out, returning from speaking with the servants, "It's not like we can send her alone."

"Regis would never believe you wanted to join the temple, John. It would be like me showing up and asking for a tour." Samantha huffed, "Maybe your apprentice could go with you. He's around your age isn't he?"

"He's a few years older, but he could pass off being a distant cousin escorting me." Beryl sighed, turning to Richard, "There is no worrying about it now, I know a little healing magic if you'd like me to ease your pain a bit."

"Do you think it will help?" Samantha asked, moving to stand by her father while John hovered behind Beryl like he wanted to draw her close but didn't.

"It can't hurt, I can't heal bone damage, but if it's more inflammation and magical drain, then it should ease things for at least a few days. I'd like to offer a touch of healing magic to anyone was near the crystals, just giving them a spark of magic should help restore their own reserves."

"Let me get the upstairs maids. Both have been feeling poorly."

"Only if they are willing," Beryl said, taking Richard's hand with a smile, "I won't force anyone to accept magic they don't trust. Is this all right with you?"

"Go ahead, my dear. I must admit this winter has been hellish on my old joints. Much worse than unusual, but I assumed it was old age catching up with me at last."

"You will out last the lot of us," John said softly, moving to give his father's shoulder a squeeze before moving away to give them room, "do you need anything, Mage?"

"Nothing but a moment to concentrate and perhaps to rest a bit this afternoon. Healing isn't the easiest spell for me."

John murmured something else, but her attention was on

Richard. She could see the pulsing red of his joints and the dark sickness clinging to his lungs as she eased magic into his body. Most healers used pinpoint attacks to heal specific areas, but Beryl lacked that kind of control with healing. She flooded the body with a steady stream of magic instead. This healed a little of everything and forced the body to start healing itself now that it had the magic and energy to do so. She pulled back, noting that the red areas were already starting to dim while the lungs seemed a bit clearer. Blinking, she pulled back and jolted when she ran into John who was right behind her.

"Are you all right? You wouldn't answer us." He said steadying her as Argent moved to lean against her other side.

"Sorry, the spell takes all my concentration. I can't hear anything or react while I'm healing, all I see is the patient."

"The maids are here, can you treat them now or should it wait?" Samantha asked, moving to check over Richard with a frown.

"I can heal them now, I'd rather not let it wait if they are willing."

"Once I explained the crystals, they were more than willing to help me gather the lot and want to be checked over." Samantha said, calling for them to come in.

"Are you certain we need to be cleansed, Madame?" One asked moving forward hesitantly, "I know we haven't been feeling well but something as small as that doesn't call for a mage healing? The last I heard of one was when the Queen fell ill."

"You don't have magical healers at the temples?" Beryl asked surprised, "In Arden anyone can go to a temple for healing. Those that can pay do but you are healed whether or not you can pay. I thought perhaps the tinctures and such were for minor illnesses while they saved healing for those seriously injured or ill."

"The only one's who receive healing are the family of mages or the favorite of the royal family. No one has access to healing without the money to pay for it," Samantha whispered, "which is why we were so grateful for you offering."

"I'd planned to send my apprentice to a different mage for training in his healing gift, but if you don't have access at all that might need to change." Beryl mused before shaking her head and gesturing the first maid to a chair, "That's for later. Would you take a seat? You might feel a warmth going through you but nothing should hurt."

It was quick to review the two maids. Both were low in energy and magic but didn't have any true issues. They sent both to rest in their rooms for the rest of the day once she was done, leaving them alone with a box of dark crystals and no one wanting to touch them.

"Let's have dinner and retire early, I think we all have had enough excitement for the day. I'll place the box in the safe for tonight." Richard said, gathering it up with a grimace and leaving the room.

"I think I'm feeling better." Richard said with a small determined smile as he stood and offered his arm to both women, "Let us retire to the dining room and forget this issue for now. Tomorrow we mourn our departed and we will need our energy for the long day."

"You seem to be moving better, father." Samantha agreed, taking his arm with a sigh, "With everything going on I'd forgotten dinner."

"What feast have you planned for tonight? I might actually have a bit of an appetite." Richard hummed, giving Beryl a wink as he showed her to a seat before pulling out the chair for his daughter.

The dinner was surprisingly lively, with Richard regaling them with different tales from the family history and his travels in his youth. John and Samantha pestered Beryl for stories of her own and she told them a few of the more spectacular magical accidents she'd had while training and a little about her friends she'd left behind in Arden. Samantha was enamored with the stories of her work with Troche and the thieves' guild though she passed it off as a merchant guild in Cardu. John walked her to her room again and lingered while Rune and Argent got themselves settled by the fire.

"I have a feeling I will not be much use to you in your travels."

"What do you mean?"

"You seem to have done so many amazing things all on your own, I can't imagine traveling as you have so far from my home and family. Even when I travel with the courts, I'm never more than a day's ride from some relative or cousin I could call on if I needed to."

"I would have loved to have that kind of support growing up," Beryl sighed stepping into his arms and pressing a kiss to his jaw, "I don't have many clear memories of my parents and my uncle was a bastard who should have never been given the care of a child. I did what I had to because there was no one there to lean on, I think that's why I was so relieved to find my bond mates. I had someone who would never leave me alone every again."

"They are like an extension of your soul, aren't they?"

"Yes, I don't think I would have made it here today without them. They taught me what it was to love, to want for someone to take care of me even when I could do it myself." Beryl sighed, leaning into his chest, "I may never need you to support me, John, but I want it. Would that be enough for you?"

"I will take whatever you can give me, Mage. I just wish I could help you more." He said tucking her close and pressing a kiss to her hair, "I'll never be a fighter like you, I can ride into battle but I've never been one for weapons or fists. I won't be able to protect you from the dangers at court or elsewhere, but I can offer you a safe harbor to return to whenever you need it."

"I doubt I'll ever live a quiet life," Beryl said with a soft laugh, "but I would like to try for a time if you can put up with me going away when my feet start to itch. I've never stayed in one place for very long and I'm uncertain I'd be able to stop traveling, not when my magic is burning my blood and pulling me along in its wake."

"Then whenever you are ready to rest, I'll be waiting. I'll follow where I can, but I'm no mage either, you're traveling to places I can't follow. All I can ask is that you return to me."

"I can promise to try," Beryl said with a hiccuping wet laugh, "I never promise forever, no one gets to keep such a promise."

"I did not mean to see you cry," John sighed, curling against her and stroking her shoulders, "I will promise for both of us then, I will wait for you to return and you will try to arrive, eventually. That's all that any couple can ask of each other. You will have a new sister in mine and a new father if you wish it, I'm certain Sam has already made this your room so I hope you like it."

"She is a menace," Beryl chuckled, drawing away and wiping her eyes, "she would have me living here already if it wouldn't seem so unseemly."

"I think she'd do it to antagonize my aunt if she thought she could get away with it." He offered with a small smirk, "Did you hear the story of when she decided I would be her friend and sister no matter the fact that I was a boy? They forced me into dresses every afternoon for a year. They have informed me I look very well in rose."

"You do," She said stroking his cheek with one hand, "however I adore you in green. It makes your eyes dazzling."

"I shall have to remember that," He murmured, ducking to catch her lips in a gentle kiss, "there, now you are more yourself. Rest tonight, I'm afraid tomorrow will be a long day of stories, history, prayers, and incense."

"Remembering the dead is meant to be painful, I think." Beryl sighed.

"You needn't attend if it will vex you. I'm more than willing to make any excuses you need."

"No, I'd like to attend. I have enough dead in my family, I might as well remember them for the good and the bad." She said leaning in for a last kiss, "I will see you in the morning."

"Good night, Mage."

"Good night, John."

Chapter 31

Visiting the Dead

Beryl dressed somberly in blue wool the next morning, leaving her hair in a simple braid and leaving everything unadorned. She stuffed her kidskin gloves in a pocket for when they were in the tombs, but left her hands bare. Today wasn't a day for hiding her scars. Rune rode her shoulder while Argent kept close to her side. Neither liked where her mind was today.

"Have a seat, Mage. John should be back in a moment from feeding the horses." Richard said gesturing her to a table, "We are having an informal meal today. The servants have today off to tend to their own relatives' graves if they are able, so we will keep to simple fare today."

"That is fine," Beryl said, taking a seat, "I can cook as long as you aren't expecting anything too fancy or help with the horses as needed, I'm not afraid of a little hard work."

"The cook has left us with a smorgasbord of stews and meats to heat at need, and John is well used to the barn work. We shall make do quite well," He said with a chuckle, "but thank you for the offer. You might have to give Samantha a few lessons. Cook has banned her from the kitchen after her last attempt was more charcoal than biscuit."

"I learned from the cooks at the palace in Cardu, so most of my meals are fit for a squadron of soldiers." Beryl chuckled, "It takes a lot of practice for baked goods. Mine were never anything but edible since I was studying more than cooking. When are we heading to the tombs?"

"Directly after the meal," He said with a nod, "it is a bit of a hike to the caves used by the family."

"You don't bury the dead? There were cemeteries while I was on the coast."

"Yes, on the coast they use mausoleums or burial with a headstone, but here in the mountains most towns have a cave or mausoleum built underground. It can be unnerving for some to be under the earth, so I wanted to warn you before we go."

"I was terrified as a child," Samantha said fiddling with her toast as John came in and threw him a mock glare, "my brother stayed up the night before my first real visit filling my head with awful stories of the dead talking or moving about during the night. It was another few years before mother persuaded me to go."

"Something she never lets me forget." John said with a huff, taking a bite of bacon even as he slipped a piece to Argent below the table.

"That hound will be the size of a pony if you keep spoiling him." Samantha scolded with a frown even as Beryl slipped him a biscuit with much less notice but a wink to John.

"He'll run it off soon enough," John said with a laugh, "you should have seen him at the hunt, he's got a burst of speed that surprises you."

"I'm just glad you don't mind them at the table, you would be amazed at how much fuss some people kick up for a small cat and dog." Beryl sighed rubbing her cheek against Rune's, "When we traveled I stayed in many a barn because the innkeeper refused to have a dog in the guest rooms."

"That is ridiculous. He wouldn't bring in any more mud than the regular merchants that went through." John huffed, turning to Richard, "Have they already left the supplies at the caves?"

"Yes, it was seen to yesterday. Everything is ready." Richard said slathering butter on the last bite of bread on his plate with a sigh, "Thank you for the healing yesterday, Mage. I am feeling much improved this morning."

"I'm glad, I hate that those things came into your home at all."

"Is everyone finished?" Samantha asked as she stood, grabbing a tray and starting to gather up used plates as Beryl and John recovered what they could reach, "Leave the food, it should be fine to sit out."

"Let me grab my coat and cane and we will head out. You may want one, dear." He told Beryl as he passed, giving her elbow a squeeze, "There is a nip in the air, we may see an early snow sooner than we'd thought."

"Surely not this early," Samantha scoffed, returning with an armload of coats and scarfs that she distributed.

"You can never tell in the mountains, I've seen it snow in summer a few years." Richard laughed as John helped Beryl into her heavy wool coat with a stolen kiss, "I'm thinking we will have a harsh winter, the leaves are already turned and falling and that doesn't happen until after the holiday."

They fell silent as they headed out across the rolling grass lawn that backed the house. The gravel drive gave way to a dirt path as they skirted the pastures and entered the woods that bordered their land. Beryl tried to concentrate on the landscape, but her thoughts kept returning to their purpose, remembering the dead. She'd been gone from Cardu for over three years now, her friends would have moved on with their lives. Beryl did not understand if they knew about her pardon or if they still assumed she was a rogue mage. It didn't matter, she wouldn't be returning to Arden anytime soon.

She had too many dead in her life to think about. Her parent's had died while they were away traveling, out trying to earn back some money they had lost while she was healing. She knew that both her parents had loved her and she treasured the few memories that stood out, but the last year of her recovery was a blur of pain and worry. She'd had a good childhood before that but those memories were blurred with time now leaving only scraps, singing with her mother as she worked about the house, playing with a toy horse that had been her favorite, sitting with her father while he smoked a pipe and blowing at the lines of fragrant smoke to blur them.

She hadn't been there when Troche breathed his last. She'd arrived too late, clutching at his still form as she tried to wake him from a slumber that wouldn't end. She'd shoved magic into him recklessly with no training or skill, pleading for it to work and knowing in her heart it never would. She'd clutched at her beloved thief until someone came and pried her fingers away. Later she learned it was a healer who knocked her out when she wouldn't be reasoned with and carried both of them to the temple, calling for her master once they identified her.

She'd held soldiers as they screamed and cried through their healing. She'd held beggars, and the drink addicted as they shook themselves apart with withdrawal. Held them as they succumbed and went still in her arms. Some things not even magic could fix. She'd trained in healing every day since she was free at the temple, refusing to lose another friend if she could. Next time she would be ready even if she didn't have an impressive gift for healing, and somehow even then it was never enough.

She'd cried until she had no tears and could only gasp in choked sobs while reaching for the bond mate that was no longer there. Kuro had been her fiercest protector and champion, she'd raged and revealed in her freedom, refusing to bow to anyone. The sea hawk had helped Beryl to express some of the anger and pain she kept deep in her heart for most of her life. She'd finally learned to allow herself to admit that things hurt her, she'd choked it back for so long while she lived with her uncle. Tears and anger did nothing to change her pain, so why bother? Now she stood in anger for those around her, hating to see anyone hurt senselessly for any reason.

She jolted as John wrapped an arm about her waist, pulling her close with a small frown, "All right?"

"Yes, just thinking." She said stopping when it tugged at her arm, "What?"

"You look cold," He murmured, wrapping his scarf about her neck and scooping up Rune from where he was standing to dump him in her arms, "be a furry hand warmer for your mage, she needs the warmth." The cat's sudden outrage at the manhandling made her giggle while Argent bowed playfully and took off in his ungainly gait to bound his way, zigzagging up the path to the others tongue lolling he bounced up on his back legs to swipe a kiss across Samantha's cheek to her horrified shriek making everyone laugh.

"Mage, come control your dog!" Samantha shrieked, "That is disgusting. He was eating things from the road!"

"He was eating nuts," Beryl giggled, cuddling Rune to her chest as they caught up with the others.

"How do you know? It could have been horse manure for all you know."

"He knows better than to do that." She said linking an arm with the woman and throwing John a warm glance in thanks, "I'll keep him off you."

"I like dogs, I just don't enjoy the slobber." Samantha sniffed, "Rune is more my kind. Can I hold him?"

"If he wants," Mage said, loosening her hold so Samantha could catch Rune when he jumped into her arms, making her squeal all over again.

They walked the rest of the way, chatting about Samantha's attempts at various hobbies. She'd yet to find anything that seemed to suit her, and she pestered Beryl for details on her jewelry crafting and dragged a promise from the reluctant mage to at least let her have a small lesson. She wasn't looking forward to having the enthusiastic woman in her forge, but she could do something simple with beads and wire instead.

The entrance of the cave loomed ahead, and they all fell silent as

John fought the heavy door open and Richard lit the waiting lantern. The progress was slow as they headed down a short corridor and along a series of stairs heading deeper into the mountain. John lit other lanterns and torches as they passed, making Beryl wish she'd thought to bring a light orb. The surrounding stone was a pale grey, catching the light in soft sparkles as they moved, their steps echoing to sound like an entire troop of mourners were making their way into the tomb.

Finally, they reached a long room with benches carved along one side. The rest of the vaulted room was in darkness, but she could see niches carved every few feet or stacked several high with carvings marking each hole. John went down the long hallway lighting more waiting lanterns and at the very back a low fire that vented to somewhere above. There had to be over fifty markers trailing along the walls.

Samantha started opening the waiting bags and sacks to one side, pulling out fragrant branches and bundles of herbs, humming to herself as she worked. She portioned out some of each as John took up a long handled broom and started sweeping. Beryl took a seat by the door and tried to see what she might help with. Richard was wandering the hall, stopping at certain graves to press a hand to the carvings and murmur a prayer too low to hear in-between wiping the edges and carvings down with a rag.

"Do you know 'The Winding Way'?" Samantha asked Beryl after a while when John finished his task and started collecting the bundles to take to each grave.

"No, it's a song?"

"Yes, it's an old folk song around here that everyone knows. It's about a pair of lovers who are parted by a war and the man traveling to reach home again." She said humming the refrain again louder while John laid the bundles along the open tombs, "I have the voice of a crow so I won't make you suffer through having me sing it."

"John has the best voice of the family, takes after his mother."

Richard said coming to collect a bundle of herbs and a few candles as John huffed and started to sing along to her humming.

"Mother had a wonderful voice." Samantha agreed once the song ended, "She'd sing all night long if there was someone to sit up with her by the fire. We used to beg to stay up for one more song over and over again until finally father forced us to go to bed."

"She was a wonderful mother, she loved the two of you like you were part of her heart reborn." Richard laying the herbs along a niche and setting a candle in the middle of the entrance. He leaned forward and pressed a kiss to the stone before he lit the wick, "Wait for me, dearest."

"I've never had anyone to sing with. They would sing in the inns sometimes, but nothing I'd care to repeat." Beryl whispered watching them go from grave to grave commenting something about each person like it was an old friend they were visiting, sharing a memory about each.

"I brought your tobacco, Great Uncle Phillip. Hope Great Aunt Mary is letting you have a pipe."

"You would have loved the colts this last year, grandfather, one is a lovely dove grey we are calling shadow."

"Would you care to light some incense at the alter, Mage? We light some for the gods and those who aren't buried here." Richard offered, handing her a few thin sticks and following along to the alter near the front to light a candle to leave next to the trough of sand that held the incense they'd already lit.

She knew you were supposed to offer a prayer for the dead when you lit the sticks, but thing she knew seemed right. She watched the smoke trail into the air and hummed one of the songs they used to sing at the temple of Ruth while the healers worked. Ruth, grant me your fires to burn the sickness from this place. Bain, accept the souls that come your way. Judge them fairly and grant those peace that have earned it.

She watched the incense until John came to collect her, moving them to the benches near the fire. They spent the rest of the night in conversation, everyone telling stories and memories about the people they used to know. It was early in the morning or very late when everyone had been silent for a time that Richard finally asked Beryl to say a few words.

"Mage, would you like to share anything about those you've lost?"

"I think I've lost too many to name right now." Beryl said with a tight smile, "I'd rather not drag their spirits across the sea without a good reason. Let them rest for now."

"As you wish." He hummed, glancing over to the marked candle set to one side, "It's time to go. Help me clean up the bags, John."

"Yes, father." John agreed, fighting back a yawn as he helped gather up the waiting sacks and boxes while Samantha handed out everyone's coats.

"Do you leave the candles?" Beryl asked as they took one lantern while blowing out the others. The wood in the fire had long ago burned down over the coals.

"Yes, we'll come back after the new year and clean up the wax and leave new logs to dry until next year's holiday." Richard agreed, offering her his arm since John's hands were full, "Did you enjoy the remembrance?"

"Yes, I think I did." Beryl hummed watching with a smile as Rune jumped into the box John was lifting and curled up letting him carry him along with the supplies.

"Your animals are rather surprisingly intelligent," Richard hummed, watching Argent amble along with the group, "most animals would have been fussing or playing, but yours were content to sit in silence for the entire night. Did they understand the significance of the rituals?"

"I'm never sure how much the understand of purely human concepts, but they liked the stories and knew they needed to be polite during the rituals." Beryl said with a shrug, "I'm not sure if they understood that the ritual was to honor the dead or if they could do the same. They were content enough just to be with us during it."

"I believe it was more they were content to be with you for the ritual, dear, they all but clung to you or John all night."

"I didn't mean for them to be a bother." Beryl said only for Richard to laugh.

"They were nothing of the sort, I just wish a few of our horses were as well mannered." He snorted, turning back to John, "Do you remember your first dog, the mongrel?"

"He was a terror," Samantha huffed, stroking a hand down Argent's back, "he ate anything that was left sitting still, shoes, gloves, table legs! An utter mess that never got better until he finally ran away."

"He was a perfect dog, he slept at the foot of my bed, protected me from bullies on the walk from school." John huffed, "I bet Rune doesn't keep your feet warm at night."

"No, but he is a perfect ruff when its cold." Beryl chuckled, collecting her bond mate from the box and sharing a cheek rub, "It sounds like he was a perfect dog, everything anyone could want in a puppy."

"Too bad for all that he was dumb as a box of rocks." Richard chuckled, "He ran out the door one day after John went to a party or something and never returned. We went over half the mountain looking but never found a sign of him."

"A pity, he sounds like a wonderful dog." Beryl mused as they headed into the house.

"Would anyone care for a biscuit before bed?" Samantha asked, uncovering the bread and ham.

"Can I request three without seeming a glutton?" Beryl asked tugging offer her gloves and stuffing them into a pocket.

"Oh! Your hands, are you all right?" Samantha gasped, catching her arm before Beryl could pull away.

"Its fine, it's from a long time ago." Beryl said, jerking back and stuffing her hands under her arms, "I'll see everyone for luncheon. Goodnight."

"John, go and see to her." Samantha insisted as John took a seat with a sigh.

"I already know about her scars, rehashing the memories won't comfort her now." He huffed, rubbing Argent's ear and getting up to open the door for him, "Go on up, give a bark if she doesn't let you in."

"Is she all right?"

"She was attacked as a child and it took months to heal. She's scarred, but it hasn't changed her personality or the way she lives. She tries harder because she knows they bother people, she hides her arms and hands because she doesn't want others to judge her on her skin. She isn't her scars."

"I just assumed the gloves and such were a fashion from Arden," Samantha said trailing off, "she's had such an awful life, how is she so kind? She does so much, I don't think she ever stops working on something."

"I'm not sure she knows how to stop." John chuckled making up several biscuits with ham and passing them around the table, "She's had to work hard for her entire life, everyone around her has always tried to use her magic for their own advantages, to use her for their own betterment. I'm not sure she's ever really had friends, she talks a little about people she left in Arden but she's not planning to contact them or go back."

"Then we will have to be her friends, you want to make her part of this family and we will have to make her feel like she is." Samantha said with determination, "I always wanted a sister, maybe this time I'll get one."

"We've only just started courting," John chuckled, sipping at a cup of water.

"Then you will have to make sure you don't mess this one up, I don't think we'll let her go now that we know her." Richard huffed with a wide grin, "She is a wonderful girl. We shall have to teach her what its like to be part of a family, she should fit right in with how unconventional ours is."

Chapter 32

William's Father

"What is he doing?" William groaned in frustration, resisting the urge to beat his head against the desk.

"Something wrong?" Benjamin asked, hesitating as he passed William's room.

"What do you know about running a family estate?" William asked, tossing a stack of paperwork to one side in frustration.

"Quite a lot considering I ran my family's for a number of years. What exactly is the problem?" He asked, stepping into the room.

"My father is bankrupting the estate, but his books and logs don't show it. I've found debts and expenses that aren't being paid, but no one is demanding payment." William said, scrubbing a hand across his eyes.

"Has he given them promissory notes or items to hold to cover the debts?" Benjamin asked, shifting closer to the desk with a frown.

"I don't know. Those holding the debt won't talk to me, but several of our properties have quietly been sold along with antiques and livestock from the main house. They have let servants go until only a skeleton crew remains, barely enough to cook and clean."

"Would he be the type to hide money?"

"If he had the money most of the county would know, lavish parties, renovations, hunts. My father was never a man to save for a rainy day." William huffed, the last windfall he was aware of had been spent on a season of parties and events that were still the talk of the area.

"And yet he has some small item that is keeping him solvent." Benjamin hummed, "Would he deal in blackmail?"

"It is possible, I just don't know. Someone is paying off his debts and keeping the family to their set standards. He made an offhand comment about needing me back to 'even the keel' but I could look too deep into a random phrase."

"Your father wants you back at home?" Benjamin asked, coming further into the room and taking a chair to one side.

"He's been trying to cancel the contract for the apprenticeship but since that isn't possible he's trying to find me a master he approves to take over the apprenticeship instead. I met with three Masters while I was there for the holidays."

"Have you found an independent solicitor from your family's influence?"

"You think it might be necessary?"

"If it involves your family in unscrupulous dealings, then it would be prudent. I can give you the names of a few my family has dealt with."

"I don't have a lot of funds at the moment," William said.

"Ask Mage, if your family is using you in some illegal fashion or trying to force you into an unpleasant situation, then it is her duty as your Master to protect you as she is able. Paying for a solicitor is part of that."

"I do not wish to become even more indebted to her."

"She is your master, guardian, and teacher. She won't see this as a debt." He pointed out, digging out his pipe, "Do you mind?"

"No, can you help me with these ledgers at least? I know he is recording the payments somewhere but I cannot see it." William asked as Benjamin lit his pipe.

"That is something I can do," Benjamin agreed with a grin, moving to join William at the desk, "How many years is this?"

"The year before my birth, the year of, when I turned sixteen, and when I turned twenty. I couldn't risk taking anything recent." William said with a grimace.

"That is a decent enough range, let me see." They spent the next few hours sorting faded notations and account ledgers into a lined chart on a separate piece of paper.

"The money coming from your mother's estates seems to have stopped on your sixteenth birthday, but these payments increased. Here and here, however the amount was halved around your twentieth birthday."

"That was the year I moved out, I stayed with friends. Father and I were always fighting, and it became too much."

"When did you go back to living at home?"

"I didn't, not really. I travelled with friends, only returning for holidays if father insisted or if mother was visiting."

"What years were you home more than gone? Does it match this?" Benjamin asked, showing him the shifting payments from an unknown account.

"Yes, the more I was home, they paid father more. That makes no sense." William muttered, looking over their findings with a frown.

"Leave it for now, your father is struggling to keep the estate solvent. What do you intend to do about it?" Benjamin asked, starting to tidy the desktop.

"Is there anything I can do? Even if I acquired the money, my father would spend it frivolously and there wouldn't be any change." William said, throwing himself out of the chair and pacing in agitation.

"Then you need to either remove yourself from the problem or remove your father."

"Remove my father? You mean take over the estates?"

"If that is what you want to do, if not let him bankrupt the estates and keep your finances separate in accounts he is unable to access."

"What would you do?"

"I would take over the estates but running a household is something I enjoy, it's why I took over the accounts here." Benjamin offered with a shrug.

"I just hate to see him hurt so many people in the process. They sacked my old nanny without warning or a reference when she left. Her family is destitute and barely getting by."

"But you helped them."

"I gave her a written reference and the names of several families to apply to for work."

"And the money from your apprenticeship, I would wager."

"I gave what I could, they needed it more." William said with a grimace, he'd left his entire purse behind when he rode out of their home.

"Which is why Mage will cover the cost of a solicitor, because it is something you need." Benjamin said with a sigh, "Write up your options and we can decide on your next actions in the coming week. For now, you may pay off his solicitors discretely but it will cause trouble if word gets back to your father or the collectors try to pressure you for more funds."

* * *

"How is he coping?" Beryl asked, gesturing Benjamin to the seat across from hers.

"Surprisingly well," Benjamin said with a sigh, moving to pour himself a cup of tea, "he suspects his father is being paid off to keep him at the estate. The man has gambled away most of the family money and lands and looks to lose it all soon if something isn't done. He's yet to make a connection to where the money is coming from, but he suspects others among his father's associates already know of whatever circumstance brought this windfall to his family."

"What do you need from me?" She asked, watching as the man slowly relaxed into his chair with a groan.

"The funds to hire the boy one or more solicitors and an estate manager. With family backing and blunt force, he may save his estates and allow his father a quiet retirement."

"Will his father accept that?"

"From what I have been able to glean from the palace gossips I rather doubt it is possible but one must consider all options available." He offered with a shrug, sipping at his tea, "Do you have anything stronger?"

"I didn't take you for a drinker," she said with a grin, going to fetch a bottle of liquor she kept for guests.

"I don't enjoy the level of inebriation most seem to, but it relaxes the mind after a very trying day. "He huffed, rubbing at his temples before giving her a mild glare, "I dislike lying and not telling William of his suspected heritage is still lying in my eyes."

"I don't disagree with you." Beryl said, adding a small measure to her own glass, "At least the boy is thinking now. Once he asks questions, I can force the issue on the prince and get him to speak with William. It will never be an open secret, but it would bring some closure and support the boy desperately needs."

"That boy left his entire purse at the home of his old nurse after finding out they had sacked her without a reference or severance after a lifetime of service to his family."

"She was the closest thing to a mother he had, his own abandoned the family as soon as she was able." Beryl said with a sigh, "Now his mother doesn't even bother to acknowledge his existence."

"She supported the household until his sixteenth birthday, but I doubt there was much love growing up under two people who married for convince and money."

"It happens more than you think," Beryl murmured, "people are often happy with what their life gives them, but not always."

"William is coming to realize just how dysfunctional his home life was, sadly."

"His adult life won't be any easier, at least as a mage in a royal court they will give him some measure of protection from relatives and outside influences." She said sipping her drink with a sigh, "There isn't much more we can do for him without some higher powers taking notice."

"He'll still have court life and its intrigues. You know how stressful that kind of life can be." Benjamin pointed out with a frown.

"But he will have his supporters." She pointed out, setting her glass down.

"I have no intention of abandoning the young man." Benjamin huffed, accepting an offered refill with a grimace, "Back to the topic at hand, if he does not come to terms with his heritage, we might have to see about hiding a royal bastard from the nobles that want to use him."

"It wouldn't be the first time, not that I have personal experience in it but if he wants to run away to another country and change names, I have the connections to ensure no one here would take a second glance at his travel documents."

"Your skills are both varied and terrifying at times, Mistress Mage."

"Sadly, I don't disagree. I didn't have a normal upbringing and most of my adult life has been one of constant education and trials. I can only hope to spare William the extremes I went through." Beryl said finishing her drink and returning the bottle to the cabinet, "Goodnight, Benjamin."

"Goodnight, Mage." He murmured, watching the fire as she headed to bed, leaving him alone with his thoughts.

* * *

"You asked about my scars before, I tried to talk to the servants and my father and no one will discuss them. They flat out refused to speak on it. The servants that were there at the time have been dismissed or disappeared. Not even my old nurse would speak on it." William said, pacing before the fire in her study.

"Do you truly wish to know?" Mage asked, setting down the tea she was serving with a click of porcelain.

"Yes, I can't get it out of my mind." William grunted, "Why would they hide an injury? If it wasn't a dog attack, then what actually happened?"

"You haven't been exposed to enough violence to understand the history of such marks. They are faint since you were very young when it happened, which is probably a blessing." She said, her face a blank mask.

"What happened? Why don't I remember?"

"I can only guess, William, whatever actually happened would have to come from your family." Mage warned him with a sigh, "The marks on your wrists are from rope or shackles, bindings left too tight and too long on a child who struggled. To have left scars they went untreated for days and you were not healed or your own magic wasn't up to the task. Your magic may have been dealing with starvation or internal injuries and keeping you alive in its own fashion. The small cuts and other marks are from knives, I can only assume you were injured in the kidnapping or in trying to get away."

"You think they kidnapped me?"

"I think you were held and ransomed, after all, you were returned home and survived." She said with a sad smile, "Most kidnapped children are not returned, your parents must have paid quickly to have you returned mostly unharmed."

"Unharmed?" William repeated, eyes on his scarred wrists in the flickering firelight.

"If they refuse the ransom, a determined kidnapper will send a finger or ear as proof that the child is still alive to try to force the random through. If they aren't answered after that, then the child is discarded and the kidnappers move on."

"Discarded how?" He forced out, sucking in a harsh breath.

"The children are abandoned or killed."

"How do you know all this?" He demanded, why would a mage know such things?

"One of my apprenticeships was to the Thieves Guild in Cardu, while my master dealt with trade and merchant deals more than illegal matters, I was told of what would happen if I was ever kidnapped and attempted to use for leverage against my master."

"Kidnapping children, is that common?"

"Kidnapping potentially powerful children can be, stealing an untrained mage and keeping them to train and do as they wish. They always seek power and many would pay dearly to have a mage at their beck and call, no matter how that mage was obtained."

"Is Arden that barbaric?"

"No, there are laws in place, but it does still happen. There will always be those who wish to use those around them to increase their own power and to earn money they have wouldn't have otherwise."

"Why me?"

"Why not? No one ever believes they will be the one injured or hurt. It doesn't happen to those around them, so it can't happen to them." Mage said, pouring the tea and handing him a cup, "You were a magical child from a wealthy family, that would have been enough."

William sputtered on his first sip. The tea was laced heavily with whiskey, "Why wouldn't they tell me?"

"Such things are considered traumatic to a child, perhaps they didn't want to harm you further by forcing you to remember it."

"They aren't telling me something, why would they lie about something that happened when I was a child?"

"I don't know why they would lie, parents lie to their children to spare them pain, perhaps they just don't wish to harm you with the truth."

"Father is already lying about the estate's finances, this is just one more lie."

"Eventually he will have to come clean with you, you are going to take over the estates when he retires."

"He's not going to give me the estates until he dies, he'd never admit that he's unable to run them himself."

"'Then you need a way to show that it benefits him to have you take over the estates. Does he enjoy traveling?"

"He travels during the winters normally, I was surprised he wanted me home this time."

"You might have to offer to fund a trip or send him off to deal with traders while you stay to manage the estates."

"Benjamin suggested something similar, that or acknowledging that my father is a bastard and give the estates up as lost."

"Are you willing to walk away?"

"I don't know,"

"You have time, for as long as the contract is in place and as long as I am able even if it isn't I'll assist you in what ways I can. I have no experience running an estate myself, that is why I hired Benjamin."

"Could I do the same?"

"Only if it was someone too honest or too loyal to be swayed by your father." Mage said with a sigh, "Your situation is more complex, until there is a way to prevent your father from contesting any changes you press forward every step will be a fight. If you decide to step away, I will find lawyers and others to support that decision. The choice is yours."

"Why did you abandon you uncle?"

"He wasn't as kind as your father, you were ignored, they punished me at every step of the way. When I received an apprenticeship in the capital, he tried to kidnap me back so I could continue to make money for him selling wards. The city guards arrested and sent him to the mines as punishment."

"So you made him pay for his crimes."

"Your father will be harder to corner, as the head of your family it allows him to do as he sees fit with the estate's funds." She said with a frown, "We will move your wages to a separate account, one that he has no control over. Benjamin would be the best to ask about that, Orlean's laws may be different from what I know."

"What if he still tries to take it?"

"Then we give it to someone you trust, I can keep it in an account until you are ready and give you funds as you require, Benjamin or a friend could do the same if you wish to have someone more impartial."

"I just don't know,"

"We have plenty of time, go get some sleep and we will talk more tomorrow."

"You aren't going to promise it will be better?"

"I don't promise what might not be possible." She said with a bitter smile, "Dealing with family is always complex, not everything will always have a happy ending. It will get better eventually, and that might take a lot of distance and time."

"Goodnight, Mage." William murmured with a sigh, setting down his empty cup and moving to the door.

"Goodnight, William, try to get some rest. Let it wait until tomorrow, there will always be something else to work on or worry over in the morning."

Chapter 33

Heritage

William presented her with his latest completed project when she returned to the palace at the end of the holidays. She eyed the blossoming plants, seeming to shiver in the icy winds. A winter storm had chased the coach all the way back and black clouds were already building behind them to bring the first snow of the season or at the very least an icy coating to everything.

"You are doing well in your work," She said giving him a tight nod, "however you are ignoring the natural order of things. Just because a plant can bloom out of season doesn't mean it should. Without protection these blooms will be killed tonight in the frost, all the energy you poured into them will be lost and wasted. Perhaps if we had a greenhouse, it could have worked, but I think for the rest of the winter we will have to find smaller projects for your attention."

"I'm sorry, I should have considered the weather."

"This was your first major attempt at using magic in plants, and you pushed an entire garden into a midsummer bloom. In the days I was gone, you forced grapes to grow and dormant branches to bud. It is a major accomplishment, I'm not belittling that fact. You did well, I just didn't want you to be disappointed tomorrow when it's gone."

"Tomorrow?"

"You see the storm brewing? The entire time in the mountains they were worried about an early snow. You can sense water, reach for the storm, feel its strength. At the least we are in for icy rain, at the worst there will be snow tonight."

"I should have realized that making a garden bloom this late was a poor decision." He sighed, kicking at the gravel path as they went in.

"I have a task for you the next few weeks if you are willing, don't say yes before you hear the details." She chuckled, holding up a hand, "I have several visits to make to various estates. I need a chaperon who is known for wild parties and drinking."

"I have had nothing since I arrived." He murmured slowly, fiddling with a ring, "I thought about it over the holidays but I got sick the one time I tried and my father kept having the servants shove wine at me. He wanted me distracted from something and I needed to be clear headed."

"Are you afraid he's mismanaging the estate?" She asked, moving into the kitchen and pouring them both cups of tea as he took a seat at the kitchen table.

"He's getting money from somewhere and keeps sending letters asking for more. I found one copy he'd tossed away." He said fiddling with the cup and she set out fresh dishes of water for her bond mates and wiped down the counter, keeping her back to him as he worked out what to say, "They always said I would be placed in a high-ranking position in the courts but none of my family are high ranking, they enjoy an estate and a rich lifestyle but they have little real power."

"And now someone is paying your family."

"I want to know what they are paying him for. Did they sell me into some kind of contract or marriage I don't know about?"

"As far as I know they haven't done so, but I can make a few discrete inquiries if it worries you."

"Why else would they be receiving money? The only way I can have a higher rank from my family is if I married into another family or they purchased a position from the King, but that wouldn't bring in money like they are receiving."

"If I told you, why would you be able to keep it to yourself?" Beryl asked turning back and raising a hand to stop his interruption, "You could talk about it with anyone on the staff or myself but this secret doesn't leave the cottage. I wasn't ordered never to tell you, but I doubt it is something they would have wanted. This would fall under your contract and would require a binding to keep you from saying anything."

"It's that important?"

"Yes, to other people it is very important, but it is something that will affect you only if you allow it to."

"It's not bad?"

"It is a fact, facts are neither bad nor good. People will try to use you because of it, and they have protected you from that until now. If you wish, it can remain a secret and you can go on living your life as you wish. You only have to act on it if you wish to."

"Could I discuss it with my father? He knows about it already if he's asking for money from whoever caused all this."

"I will add him as an exception," Beryl sighed, taking a seat and offering one hand, "anyone who already knows about this secret and has verbally confirmed it to you is voided from the contract. Will you let me cast the binding?"

"Yes, I need to know what's going on." He said taking her hand with both of his firmly.

"Very well, just remember that no matter what it reveals you will be my apprentice for the next year, which means you won't have to act on this until the end of the contract, which can be extended if you wish." She said starting the runes to place the binding.

"It is terrible news then," William sighed when she finished, "I wish I was better at runes, you can do so much with them."

"You have to go with your strengths once you learn to master water and earth we can return to runes if you like." She sighed, standing and refilling both of their mugs, "When I arrived at the palace, they tasked me with placing protections on the royal family. They were receiving death threats, and the King wished for his family to be protected at all costs."

"You still do that, you've adjusted the wards every few days since I arrived." William pointed out with a frown.

"And they are still having people trying to sneak poisons and enchanted objects charmed to kill onto the grounds." Beryl said sipping at her tea, "My wards have slowed the attempts but not stopped them. The King wished for me to protect someone else who was receiving death threats. That is why you became my apprentice."

"Someone was threatening me? Why wasn't I told?"

"I have no proof, but I suspect your father was using you as leverage to gain more money. If you were safe, he received the money but you are of age now and any day now they could declare you independent. Once you are married, he'd no longer receive whatever stipend they gave him for your care."

"Why would he receive money for keeping me safe? That makes little sense."

"Why would he push you to be the best at everything and yet never expect much from you? You were born into a rank he could never attain, one you didn't need to earn, and one that could never be bought. They gave him you as a child to raise out of the way of the perceived dangers of you place of birth."

"They gave him, you mean I'm not his son."

"No, I don't know for sure who your father is, but I can guess."

"Who?"

"The King himself requested your protection, either you are a son of the Prince at a very early age or the son of the King."

"You're saying I'm a bastard of the King."

"I'm saying it is possible, I have no way of knowing if it's true. They tasked me with protecting you and if doing so means you learn the truth, then it is worth it if it keeps you alive."

"People want to kill me because I'm the King's bastard."

"If Prince Zyon dies, then you are the next rightful heir to the throne. If you accept it, hopefully we never have to deal with such a situation."

"But, why me, I'm just,"

"You are the son of royalty, no matter your flaws or strengths, your blood grants you that. It's up to you to decide what to do with that power."

"What do you mean?"

"You don't have to become royalty, you can continue as you have or strike out on your own. It's your decision what you do from here."

"They refused to acknowledge me. If they'd planned to do so, it would have already happened! They don't want me as anything more than a pawn to be brought forward when and if the Prince dies."

"They also could have decided you seemed content with your life and wished to keep you safe. There is no way to guess why the King has done as he has but he wanted you safe and if that means away from your family then you are as safe as I can make you here." Beryl said watching the emotions play across the young man's face, anger warring with pain, "I can try to arrange a meeting with the King but there is no guarantee that it will go well for anyone."

"Stop talking in riddles, what do you mean it won't go well."

"Anytime an unknown heir appears, it casts doubt on the current heir and their position. Doubts lead to economic instability and violence most of the time when it's in a royal family. Orlean is enjoying the first true peace after decades of war with various factions and countries. Exposing you as a potential heir could undo years of work to distance Orlean from its violent past and put you in the crosshairs of anyone who wishes to control Orlean."

"Some of my father's friends often talked about when I 'reached my potential' like it was some fabulous joke. You think they wanted me as a puppet leader?"

"You were a known drinker and gambler who spent his father's money like water." Beryl said flatly, "They saw you as someone they could control, a few wild nights out, a few debts you couldn't afford to pay back, and you are being pressured to push through legislation that benefits only their interests."

"I only played the tables because my friends enjoyed it, I was there for other distractions." William huffed before realizing what he said.

"So they ply you with women and drink until something scandalous happens and then blackmail you for the same effect." Beryl sighed, "They know your heritage so your father has been talking about you with at least his regular acquaintances."

"Baron Westedge," William snapped, "he's not my father."

"Very well, however, he was the man who raised you." She sighed, "Something I learned a long time ago is that you don't have to love or even like your family, no matter what anyone else says. I hated the uncle that raised me, but my friends became my family. You can't say that Mary isn't a mother to half the people here, can you?"

"She'd mother anyone who stood still long enough." He huffed.

"Or maybe she just sees people who need a little extra care since they've received so little in the rest of their lives." Beryl sighed, "There is little we can do tonight. Tomorrow we'll discuss if you'd like a meeting with the King. He might not grant it until we head back to the coast in the spring. It would look suspicious for me to run back to the coast without an excellent reason."

"It's waited my entire life so far, a few more months won't matter."

* * *

Beryl did her best to ignore her apprentice's attitude in the coming days. He'd had a shock and his entire world had been upended. That was unsettling, no matter how much they prepared you for it. He stormed about, slamming door and leaving the house in exasperated huffs, striding down the forest paths kicking at leaves and pebbles as he tried to vent his building anger. Finally, Jeremy had enough and dragged the boy to the courtyard to practice with staves until he could barely stand.

"Are you going to keep up appearances if we go out, or should I find another escort?" She asked with a sigh, setting a mug of tea next to his elbow while Mary tended to a nasty bruise on his forearm.

"Isn't a royal bastard supposed to storm about in a rage?"

"In stories it's generally melodramatic brooding," Mary informed him with a snort, "you need to find a better way to lose your anger then letting Jeremy beat you to a pulp."

"Let me see your wrist," Beryl sighed as she switched places with Mary, "I can't do much with a cracked bone, but I can ease the strained muscles and bruises a bit."

"It isn't that bad, you shouldn't waste the magic on something so small."

"I don't see any injury as small," Beryl said, taking his arm and pressing a wash of magic into the muscles and bones, "perhaps we should start healing magic next. You won't be able to do much for your own injuries, healing yourself is always the hardest, but we can start with injured animals or plants that are found on the grounds."

"I don't wish to stop training, I feel like I'm finally making progress with the staves."

"I'm not asking you to stop, I'm asking if I need to find someone else to travel with me in the coming week. I'll be going to several rather unsavory locations and parties with known gamblers. If you don't feel up to confronting that, I need to know now, not while we're in the middle of a dance."

"I'll be fine."

"People will not be polite, they will insult your family as they know it, insult your status as a man, and do whatever they can to drag you to their level to make a scene. If you are feeling at all unstable or raw, then I'd rather you stay. I can find someone else to take."

"I have to confront the reality of my situation, Mage." He sighed pulling his arm away and blinking at the change as he chaffed his hands together before the fire, "Would you rather I do so in the midst of a royal birthday party or the next dinner you are invited to? I can't hide here forever, no matter how much I wish to."

"I don't want to rush you, William. You don't have to do this now if it will strain you."

"I would like to go, at least to the first one." William said, "I know it's going to be hard, but I'd like to help you."

"Very well," Beryl said, handing his tea to him, "tomorrow night we are going to a gambling den, dress appropriately."

"How delightful," Mary murmured dryly, "should I bother with dinner or will you be eating on the road?"

"We will eat in town, make what you like for everyone else." Beryl said, resisting the urge to sigh, "How is Olivia settling in? I've barely seen her out and about."

"She's a timid thing, she cleans in the morning while you lot are out and helps me with the baking before retiring to her rooms if we don't need her. She'd eat all her meals there if you didn't insist that we share breakfast. She has a fine hand with the mending if you want an assistant for the sewing." Mary said gathering up a basket of mending that she was working on and moving to the chair by the kitchen fire.

"She needs a mind healer," Beryl sighed, "maybe once I find a house on the coast she'll calm down a bit. It might help her be away from the crowds in the city or the palace."

"What is a mind healer?" Mary asked, looking uncertain.

"Is this something else that Orlean doesn't do? A mind healer is a healer that specializes in healing wounds of the mind. They often send former soldiers fighting night terrors or memories of the war to mind healers to help them adjust to their return to regular life outside of the army. It can also help those that were traumatized in other ways."

"I don't think we have those here unless it's something that only the wealthy can afford." Mary frowned starting to sew, "It sounds like something that might help however, could you do such healing?"

"No, they never trained me. It takes years to learn how to treat such wounds, and I only managed a day or two a week at the healer's temples with my apprenticeship. I must ask the Prince next time we speak."

"I've never heard of such a thing." William said, standing and putting his mug away, "Are we training in the morning?"

"The same as every morning," she agrees with a nod.

"I'd like to try the wind dancing again if you are willing." He said, fiddling with his cuffs as he rolled them back down.

"Whatever you wish as long as you don't mind doing sword practice first." Beryl agreed, "At the end of the week we are going to the docks and you need to brush up on your dagger work if you're going to go wearing weapons."

"What is at the docks?"

"Information," She sighed, standing and rinsing her own mug before putting it away, "it's late, I'm for bed. Good night, everyone;"

Chapter 34

The Greenhouse

William eyed the empty greenhouse and tried to picture it full of life and plants instead of broken pots and garden supplies. They had used it as storage for some time. It would take days to just clear the floor and till the rock hard soil.

"The prince has requested the greenhouse be a gift to his daughter. It is meant to be a surprise so you can't discuss it with her. I know growing an entire garden in winter won't be easy. Given the scope, you may request help of the staff, but this will be your project to accomplish if they are needed elsewhere."

"Yes, Mage," He said unenthusiastically when she raised an eyebrow, waiting on a response.

"Before the presentation, you may incorporate illusions to enhance your work. I'll be examining your work weekly and expect you to ask for assistance should you need it."

"Are other apprentices given such extensive projects?"

"It depends on the master, they expect some to exceed the scale set to other mages. Considering our patron is the royal family, they will expect us to exceed the normal standards."

"I understand."

"Ask for help if you need it, William. This is an enormous project for any mage, much less an apprentice." She said with a sigh, "You have several months, take your time and plan what you want to bloom when. Try to conserve your magic where you can."

"Jeremy won't be able to do the digging."

"I'll be interviewing staff this week. I would like a helper for the forge, and we might as well start planning for the new property next summer."

"What positions are available?"

"Stable hand, gardener, maid, and gamekeeper."

"We need another maid?"

"I may offer to move Olivia to kitchen staff full time, she enjoys it and isn't suited to deal with visitors."

"You will keep her on?"

"I don't abandon someone just because it might not suit them for a position. If it had become clear, you were unsuited as a mage, we would have found you another position in the household until the end of your contract. You don't throw a life away because it doesn't fit in the box you hoped it would."

"My father wouldn't approve of gardening as a project."

"It's not his project, William. It is yours. This is just one facet of your magic, I have an idea for a separate project to keep your family happy."

"What other strengths? I'm hopeless in the forge and he wouldn't approve of Jeremy teaching me sword craft."

"Does your father hunt?"

"He does the polite hunts our neighbors throw. More drink and conversation, then actual hunt." William said with a grimace, "I thought to show him weather working but it would take something extreme to impress him."

"No storm calling just yet, lightening is impossible to control on a good day. We don't need a death to prove your strength." She hummed thinking out loud, "Your illusions are improving.

Perhaps we could devise a small entertainment for one of his parties?"

"You've already surpassed my training. That candle fooled me for several minutes. I would have kept trying to blow it out if you hadn't cancelled the spell." William pointed out dejectedly.

"We just need to combine your abilities. Your water and air manipulation would work if we added a few small illusions. Call it an alternative form of enchantment."

"You enchanted an entire ballroom. Word has gotten out and my father will expect something on that scale."

"He may have to live with being disappointed," Beryl sighed, "I'll think on it."

"Any suggestions for the garden?"

"The princess is fond of coppery colors but loves flowers of any kind. However, she is also eleven, turning twelve. Don't go too extravagant, no matter her station."

"She seemed to enjoy the tea party you attended with Miss Viand. Would a space with private seating be appreciated?"

"Yes, that would be a lovely idea. She dotes on Viand like a beloved Aunt, she might assist you with the purchases for an appropriate tea table and chairs if you ask."

"How are the purchases being handled? The plants alone won't come cheap."

"The royal family has extended a line of credit. Give me a list of what you need and I will see it ordered."

"Very well."

"Don't give up before the project has even started. Come, let's go back to the cottage. Take the afternoon to outline what needs to be done to ready the space. Tomorrow the work can begin, for now it can wait a few hours."

"What was your first major project with your master, Mage?"

"I was something of a spell crafter. I had already designed several new wardings when I started my apprenticeship. Master Darius saw my bond mates as my first project. The largest one I worked on was warding half the town from fire. I was also apprenticed to the local merchant guild and warded businesses they contracted along with the docks. My last project was warding a fort on the northern border."

"So you didn't create entertainments?"

"No, some apprentices performed at small parties for their masters, but we crafted enchanted objects or useful wardings for the city and its people. Arden believes in using magic to improve the country."

"People distrust such items here." William said with a grimace.

"Some did in Arden, no one trusts a thing they can't understand. Fear and anger go hand in hand." She sighed, "When I left Arden, a cult was attacking mages and making distrust grow. Spells were failing, and they blamed mages for many problems, real or not."

"The king gave magic out to the peasants?"

"If something can help everyone, shouldn't everyone have access?" She asked in the mild tone he was learning it meant something important.

"That isn't how things work."

"Not here, not yet;" She agreed, "but not everyone believes that magic should be hidden away, only available to the nobility."

"What would a farmer or merchant do with magic?"

"Protect their storehouses from damp and rats, treat diseases before an entire district dies of plague, heal injuries before it leaves someone permanently disfigured and unable to work." She said easily, "Everyone deserves the chance to have a decent life, William. Food, shelter, a chance to earn a living."

"You make it sound like a business."

"Money earned in a business goes back into the shop to improve it. Why shouldn't money and magic gained by the nobility goes back to the workers who support them?"

"That is treasonous talk. The nobility have earned our place through centuries of warfare and conflict."

"And yet it was the people under the nobility who died in those wars.

The people your ancestors swore to protect for offering them a work-force and army. You have your position because of thousands that lived and died on your lands. They deserve what little support you can offer?"

"My father would say they owed us for our guidance over the centuries."

"No one man knows everything, even the king has his advisors." She said, "Not all nobility start as such, William."

"It isn't the same."

"Would you say your own ancestors were less for having started as a peasant?"

"They gained a title through loyalty and diligence."

"What of me? I am the daughter of a merchant's daughter and the son of a fisher. I have no titles to my name beyond Mage. I am not of noble blood."

"You have magic."

"So does every person on this earth. Every plant, animal, and human has at the very least a tiny spark of magic. The very stones hold it. The only difference is that we are able to draw it forward to use it to some small purpose."

"Having the ability to manipulate magic puts us above the rest."

"The King isn't magical, are we above him?"

"He is the King, he's above such distinctions."

"Is he? My father believed that all humans were equal. A king may have more power, but he doesn't have more worth than the most impoverished fisher when it comes to the right to live."

"What does any of this matter?"

"You will be a powerful mage, William." She said coming to a stop, "With power comes the responsibility of wielding it. You will need to choose how you use that power. Do you spend your life making pretty illusions for the masses or to improve the lives of those around you?"

"Does it matter as long as you make a living?"

"As long as you are satisfied with your life, no. It is your decision."

She said with a sigh, starting to walk again, "I just want you to understand that you have options."

"Options," He repeated in frustration, how did having options change things?

"I never had these things explained to me growing up. I had many people try to use me and my abilities for their own benefit, with no thought to the harm it might cause me. I fought my way free and made my way here, I don't want you to go through the same trials they forced me to endure."

"Surely the royal family," he started only to trail off into silence.

"The royal family will use you for their own benefit as easily as anyone else. You must decide if you will give your time and magic to them and if the benefit outweigh the loss."

"They are your patrons." He pointed out with a frown.

"And yet even then I would not agree to every request blindly. We both have the right to say no."

"And the greenhouse?"

"It is a test of your skill and ability to plan. If you gain your mastery, they will ask more of you. It will be up to you to decide if you stay on as a royal mage or pursue something else." She said gesturing for him to follow her out of the greenhouse.

"My family expects royal favor." He huffed, that would never change.

"But do you want it? You are the one who has to live with the decision, William."

"You are the strongest mage I have ever met, Mage." William muttered, shortening his stride to keep pace with the shorter woman.

"They allow mages be eccentric, it gives us some leeway in society when it comes to rules and restrictions. Few women would be able to live and run a household alone in Orlean. As a mage, I can do so because I hold a position of power. A fisherman's daughter would never be given even the most basic courtesy I receive if she did the same."

"Of course not, it would be unseemly." William snorted, stopping to one side of the royal gardens when she hesitated at the next path.

"Why?" She asked mildly, giving him a smile at his confused look.

"It just would." He said mulishly.

"So I am an exception to the normal rules of society?" She asked, arching an eyebrow.

"Well, yes." He huffed with a nod. She was the strange one here.

"Why?"

"I don't know, you just are!"

"No one should be an exception, William. Think on it." She said with a sad smile, starting down the path back to the cottage.

William blinked after her in shock, but quickly caught up. Why would he need to consider the rights and abilities of people below him? What did it matter if the gardeners weren't treated the same as he was? His options in life wouldn't be the same as theirs, surely?

* * *

William eyed the line of runes he was carving with a frown and sat up, stretching. With a groan, he arched his back and glanced over at the other workers who were assisting in readying the greenhouse for planting. His father would have thrown a fit to see his son grubbing in the dirt, but William was finding the project surprisingly enjoyable.

He marked down a few questions for Mage in his journal before moving to the seed trays laid out to one side on tables. He could have forced them to grow, but they had months to get the plants placed and matured before the greenhouse needed to be presented.

The gardeners were a constant source of information and advice. They were wary of using magic with the plants and argued over whether the magic stressed the plants or affected their future growth. As a compromise, suggested by his master after he'd stormed back one afternoon, they had started a project, one tray of magically forced seedlings and one only tended by the gardeners. So far they couldn't find any differences, but it was interesting to compare the two methods. He thought his next attempt would be to alter the stems to be thicker and more stable to support more blooms.

He wasn't used to working on projects with anyone, much less a bunch of older men and women who were commoners. All of his friends and acquaintances were noble or at least wealthy enough to be considered of the same status, he'd always thought such people were below him but he was quickly seeing how wrong that view was. Jeremy was a commoner, and he could kick his butt sideways every day during training. These gardeners knew more about plants and the area's conditions than any book he'd studied trying to prepare for the work. They also worked long past his own endurance. They worked without complaint and grudgingly were coming to treat the young noble as someone worthy of working with.

"How goes the scribing, Apprentice Westedge?" The head gardener's wife asked, coming over to inspect the trays.

"The warming wards and charms are complete. We need to decide where the control runes will be hidden." He said.

"Most of the lads aren't going to touch a magical control." She said with a sigh rehashing an argument that had been ongoing for weeks, "I agree controlling the temperature of the greenhouse will be useful, I just can't see them touching anything magical willingly."

"What if it didn't look magical?"

"What would it look like then?"

"A button or lever, something for them to adjust as needed."

"It won't have glowing runes or anything?"

"I can hide those behind a cover. It would be like the new steam machines or the water powered weaving looms."

"Those aren't accepted either, but it's easier to explain than a magical button. We can try it, put it near the workmen's entrance so they can adjust it before leaving." She said with a nod, glancing around the space with a frown, "No one ever adjusts to change well, the world is speeding along without us, I think."

"Isn't that kind of the point? You learn to adapt?" William asked with a frown. That was what Mage was constantly telling him.

"It gets harder to adapt as you age. The new inventions and magics are lovely, but I still prefer seeing things mature with time. Magical things like the lights are useful and something small that everyone can afford, but the grand wards like you are placing here are out of budget for most gardeners. Your Mage seems to want to see magic as useful for everyone, but there is only one of her for everyone in the country, magic only goes so far from the palace."

"She wants to open stores in the major towns so that more people can purchase the light orbs and crystals. She also crafted some kind of rock that goes into the fireplace that keeps the heat from the fire even after the wood has gone out."

"That would be useful in the northern mountains, I'm from a tiny village up that way and we would freeze on the nasty winters no matter how much wood we tried to burn."

"That is what she wants, useful magics." William said, still getting used to the idea himself, "I think that's why she learned to sew. She wanted something she could make that people would use."

"She makes clothes?" She asked, blinking in surprise.

"Dresses for the royal family and other things, toys and blankets. She added warming charms to my heavy coat and spells to keep it clean and not tear." He said, showing her the embroidered line of design along the inner lining.

"Does she make ordinary things? Gloves or work aprons?"

"I think so. She could make gardening gloves that don't get wet or let the mud soak in, probably."

"Is this something you are learning?"

"No, but one of the housemaids has a fair hand and is learning the basic charms. I'm not patient enough for the detail it takes, I bled all over my last attempt." He chuckled with a grin, Olivia was turning into a grand seamstress and was either found in the herb garden or by the fire sewing in the afternoons.

"I may ask your mistress if she could charm some work clothes. Keeping the mud outside would endear her to most of the staff here."

"I'm sure she would," he said, hesitating before forcing himself to continue, "Can I ask, why aren't you a head gardener here? You do more than twice the work of most of the other gardeners."

"I was offered the position once, but I wanted to spend time with my children while they were young. Now that they are grown, I work in the gardens more." She offered with a shrug, "Some women want the family more than the work, others find what they need in the work. I wanted both, but had to give the time to the children when I could. Now I am content with what I have. If I was a head gardener, I'd never have time to rest."

"Mage just seems so determined to do everything herself."

"Some women are like that, when they had little help early in life. She has learned to get things she needs done herself because others wouldn't do it for her. That is a hard habit to unlearn."

"She never seems to need help with anything,"

"That doesn't mean she wouldn't like it. Perhaps I will drop by for tea later this week, I heard she is crafting her own blends?"

"That is Olivia, I started a tea garden as a project for Mage and she is harvesting the plants. She has made some amazing teas so far. Olivia is also the one doing the embroidery. She is very talented."

"Mage attracts talented people to her." She said giving him a grin, "My husband was groaning that she got Benjamin Bryant to run her estate. He made his family farms a formidable force in the area. She will never want for funds if he is managing the books."

"I didn't realize he had a reputation for management." William said uncertainly.

"Only in certain circles, when word came that the farms were going to his brother, the collective groan could be heard in the next county. Most of the produce you eat here comes from those farms. His brother has made a frivolous match in marriage and the woman is grasping for a title with everything she has. She will bankrupt the estate in the end, I wager. At least Benjamin found a good station to use his talents."

"He's been helping me with a few matters, but I didn't realize he was that skilled."

"Ask him about where to invest, the boy has a mind like a trap when it comes to where to place your bets. His grandfather was the same way, it's a pity that age has taken that from him. Ruth bless him, he told Greg to sell the cotton and not save it last year and we made three times what we do normally for the farm. My youngest, Tomas, will apprentice with the glassblowers because of that windfall."

"That is wonderful, congratulations."

"He is the artist of the family and would have done well at the farm, but in the city he will use his gifts. Does the Mage work in glass?"

"No, she trained as a blacksmith, actually. I believe her first master worked in glass."

"Truly? I thought that was just palace gossip."

"Yes, she was trying to train me, but I don't have the knack for it."

"Gardening is just as noble a profession." She said with a sniff, making him grin, "Enough gossip, let us get back to work."

"Yes, ma'am;"

Chapter 35

Lessons in Spy-craft

Beryl knew she'd shocked William the first time she snatched his goblet and demanded a toast from the gaming table. Returning the goblet without batting an eye, she waited for him to realize it was empty and pinched him when he went to order another. He gave her a glare as she went back to fawning over his neighbor at the card table.

"Fold," she murmured as she rose, and tipsily bumped into him on the way to gather her dropped scarf.

"It's a winning hand." He hissed, scowling at his cards.

"You're a drunken gambler, disgruntled at losing his money." She huffed, "Lose, it's the King's money, anyway."

"You aren't letting me get drunk." He muttered in annoyance.

"And yet the table thinks you've had six cups. Play it up." She hissed before popping him on the shoulder with her fan and scolding him loudly before turning back to the other player and applauding his winning hand.

"Come dance, Cousin." She whined, tugging at his sleeve, "Prove to me I'm not just a lucky charm for the table."

"This deck is cursed." He cussed, tossing down his cards in disgust and scooping up his remaining chips.

"What are we doing here?" he snarled in her ear once they were on the dance floor, dancing much too close for even distant relatives.

"Looking for someone" She offered with a wry grin, "Once we find him we need to be invited to his next party."

"Who are we stalking?"

"Maximilian of Chambers-down or one of his minions."

"Max? He's the worst of the worst, that is scrapping the bottom of the trough if you are looking for him."

"Exactly, he'll know where every dirty secret is buried and who's holding the shovel."

"You're cultivating a relationship with the scum of the earth?"

"And brothel owners, gamblers, thieves, and every black hearted dealer I can find with a sliver of a soul left." She said leading for a few steps when he stumbled in the dance, "Scum are always out for themselves, you just have to make sure their survival depends on your own."

"Where did you learn to do all of this? You spy, gamble like a street wench, and the lies trip off your tongue like honey."

"Mostly the Inns and brothels that my uncle frequented as we traveled. The women were always willing to trade secrets and gossip for a few calm minutes and a cup of tea. I also spent a year employed to the thieves' guild of Cardu. They had a similar network of merchants and thieves that traded information for magical protections."

"Does the Prince know what they hired?"

"I doubt the Prince knows, however, the King does without a doubt. He was counting on me going places that a regular mage would have been barred from. It's why he chose me. No one else would get their hands dirty."

"William!" someone crowed from across the dance hall, "I didn't know you'd gotten out. Was that bloody contract voided?"

"Andrew, wonderful to see you." William called back, moving to the side of the floor, "No, I got the night off to escort my cousin about town. Esme, this is Andrew of Corinth."

"Delightful to meet you, Madame." He said with a roguish grin.

"How have things been since they conscripted me?" William asked, pulling Beryl to his side with a wink for Andrew.

"Dreadfully dull, nothing's been on for weeks. Have you heard of anything? Aren't you in the Palace now, surely you've heard of some good bashes?"

"I'm confined to quarters in the hovel on the edge of the grounds." William groaned, "Someone has to have something on. Serena's?"

"She's been cutting things off early most nights, the girls are wine and dining some group of nobles to bankroll her next project."

"What's she into now? Still painting?"

"Sculptures, I can't enjoy myself when she's got random nude guys standing about holding swords and such."

"Devon's, or didn't they get raided by the crown?"

"Yeah, stripped down to the wall tacks for missed tax payments. It's a damn shame. That was a fine place."

"What about Max? He's always got a crowd at his estate."

"A crowd of pickpockets," Andrew said with a snort, "I wouldn't be caught there. Last time I got dragged to Chambers-down, I barely made it home with my shoes."

"So we go to drink and ignore the tables, I've nothing left to spend, anyway. Is there anything else to do?"

"Nothing else is happening until after the Prince's masquerade, no one wants to be shown up by that extravaganza or to spend enough to manage it."

"Care to come along? You're welcome to mock me for the next month if it's a bore." William wheedled, "I'll even pay for the cab, I received my first wages for my apprenticeship. I might as well spend it on something fun."

"I came with a few lads." Andrew said with a wince, "I'll never hear the end of it if I ditch them."

"Invite them, but they have to find their own carriage." William said with a shrug, "We might as well make a party of it."

"All right, you're on. I'll see you at the door." He agreed, running off to gather his friends.

"All right with you, Cousin Esme?" William asked brightly, offering Beryl his arm.

"Perfect, thank you, Cousin William."

"Please tell me you weren't planning to bring Benjamin if I'd had to decline?" William asked as they worked their way to the door.

"People go out of their way to make him blush. The brothel I took him to declared him precious. I'd have played him off as my bumbling brother I was trying to force into having a good time. It works rather well."

"He is rather too polite for his own good." He mused, waving for their coach waiting down the street.

"You're in luck, Will!" Andrew called, half falling down the stairs to the street, "Everyone is in, they will be right behind us."

"Wonderful, we can watch them get fleeced and relax for a few hours before I have to return to my taskmaster." William said, giving Beryl a mocking grin.

"Surely it's not that bad. I mean, you are learning magic at least, right?"

"Oh, the lessons are wonderful," William agreed, handing her into the carriage where Argent was waiting, "it's the rules that are killing me. No drink allowed on the property at all, curfews when I go out."

"What a pity his poor cousin has kept him out much too late," Beryl said with a grin poking him in the side, "it will be all my fault this time, Cousin, consider it a gift."

"Good lord, that is a big dog. Is it yours?" Andrew asked slowly, easing into the seat and closing the door behind him wearily.

"Yes, don't worry. He's a big lamb." Beryl said, pressing a loud, smacking kiss to the top of the dog's head.

"She takes him everywhere, you get used to it." William huffed, rubbing one ear before pushing Argent into her lap with a huff to give the rest of them a little room, "So tell me what's been going on while I've been learning magic? Anything good?"

"It looks like Mathews might get married to that red head he's alway mooning about. Harrison got drunk, danced naked in a fountain in the square. His father took away his horses and is threatening to sell his share of the estate unless he gets his act together. Um, they arrested Blake for selling black market antiques. Not much has been going on for our group, just the usual parties and such." He offered with a shrug, "Are things any better with your father? I know you were worried about things last time we saw you."

"Not really, he's still refusing to discuss anything with me." William said fiddling with a tassel, "I'll probably find out the entire estate is bankrupt when he dies."

"It surely can't be that bad, he's still throwing those ridiculous parties for his cronies. Surely they would bail him out if things went that far downhill?"

"I can only hope." William shrugged, "I'm glad to be out and away from that at least. The apprenticeship should at least give me a paying occupation if things go bad."

"You're better than me, Will. My father has written me out of the will, no one will hire the youngest son of a minor nobleman with no marriage prospects and no inheritance."

"It can't be that bad, what skills could you offer?" Beryl asked, stoking the dog's head as the two men talked.

"That's the thing I have no idea. I received the same education Will did, but so did every other kid we grew up with. It means bugger all when it comes to practical skills. I'm not a good enough swordsman to teach, I've never worked anywhere, so I have no references. I tried writing poetry, but it's hopeless drivel. I'm at a loss, my friend, I will be living off my father until my sister kicks me out of the estate the second he dies."

"Perhaps you could get a contract like I have, learn a skill and get paid for the work you do?"

"No one does that anymore, it's archaic." Andrew huffed as the carriage bumped along, "It amazed me they offered you a contract like that."

"What about sailing? You could contract to a captain for a year of experience?" Beryl offered when the silence ran on for too long.

"My father would kill me if I did something like that."

"If he's already disowned you, what's to stop you?"

"I just, it's not done." He stuttered, frowning.

"Says who? It's common enough on the coast, it would get you out into the world for a few years. Maybe you'll do something else by then or come home and see how the estate suits you after some distance."

"You think I could?"

"You are your own man, Andrew. Your father doesn't have a final say in your life, he can offer guidance, but it's your choice."

"Huh," He hummed, blinking and turning to look out the window as the countryside rolled by.

"How far is Chambers-down?" she asked after another long pause in the conversation.

"Not too much farther, it's just outside of town." William said, gathering up his coat and gloves as Beryl adjusted her shawl, "We should turn down the lane any minute. Are we taking the mutt in?"

"No, he can stay in the carriage." Beryl said with an exaggerated sniff, "Along with you if you malign my pet anymore."

"I would never, he might maul me if I did." William said with a chuckle.

"I'm sorry if we've ruined the mood, Andrew." Beryl said, leaning forward to pat the young man's knee.

"Oh no, just given me something to think about. What did you do to snag such a good cousin, Will? I might have to steal her away for my own. My cousins are utter pigs who care for nothing but dresses and furs."

"Perhaps you can tell them of my business then," Beryl said, pulling out a card and handing it across, "I'm a seamstress and will open a shop on the coast sometime next year. I can always use the customers, or a letter if you find yourself in need of someone to rant to."

"Of course," he said with a grin, tucking the card away, "did you do an apprenticeship to sew?"

"No, I took lessons and do basic patch work for a while, but I started making dresses for myself. When everyone wanted to know where I found my amazing seamstress, I decided I might as well try to make a living off of it."

"So you're opening a dress shop?" William asked quietly as he helped her out of the carriage.

"No, Esme Reinald's is opening a dress shop. I'm opening a jeweler's shop." She murmured as they walked up the path to the doors, "It's a rather grand estate, a lovely drive in and only a hop from the town; How lovely."

The party was in full swing when they arrived, several carriages spilling out rowdy passengers already three cups to the wind. Someone was throwing up into the trees to one side and they had left the doors wide open, spilling raucous singing and brass instrumentals into the drive.

"You take me to all the best parties, William, dear." She purred, linking arms with both of the boys as they entered, making Andrew laugh helplessly as they dragged him along the long entryway and into the manor proper.

They passed several rooms branching off before William showed them into the massive ballroom with a deep bow, "My lady, shall I announce you?"

"Don't you dare, Will." She hissed, hitting him with her fan, "Be a darling and find your cousin a drink."

"As you wish, Cousin." He said tendering another bow and raising an eyebrow at Andrew.

"Just a punch or something;" He said with a shrug, "I'll show your cousin about."

"'Thank you, Andrew." She said happily, linking their arms again and letting him lead her towards one group hovering by a massive fire near the door.

"I don't believe we've been introduced before?" One of the dandies said offering her a bow as they walked up, "New to town?"

"I am visiting family and my cousin was kind enough to show me a night out on the town," Beryl said, offering her hand, "Esme Reinald."

"And your cousin?" he asked, looking Andrew up and down with a sniff as he released her with barely a touch.

"William of Westedge, he's gone to fetch drinks." She said airily, turning to watch the band playing rather badly to one side, noting how the man perked up at William's name.

"Ah, how wonderful for him;" He said taking a gulp from his own glass and ignoring them as he glanced over the crowd behind them, "Maximilian, at your service. Please feel free to wander about. I outfitted the entire estate for the evening."

"Thank you, it looks like a wonderful party." She said giving another curtsy.

"Please enjoy yourselves." He said waving them away as he turned back to his conversation.

"And that is how he treats everyone." Andrew huffed once they were out of earshot, "He's rich but has no title and no one will stoop to give him one outright. It's said that he has a finger in every deal that goes down in the country."

"Does he do legal business or is it fleecing the local aristocrats at the tables?" She murmured as they passed a gaming room full to bursting with young lads tossing markers out like they were nothing.

"He owns several ships and runs exotic goods through the markets around Orlean." Andrew said voice low as they walked, "It's said he's well acquainted with the more illicit side of the law."

"That is a risky undertaking."

"I believe that's how he likes it." Andrew huffed, "He gambles at everything, horses, business deals, it's how he's made his fortune."

"Shipping is a risky business, you have to have a deft mind to catch the markets in a favorable mood." She said pitching her voice to carry as they passed another small group.

"Are you interested in the such trivial things, madame?" One older gentleman asked from where he was leaning against an open window with his pipe.

"Several of my family are merchants and fishers, I've heard them talk enough about how hard it is to judge what will be valuable six months out before the ship arrives in port."

"Aye, it can be a tricky thing. It helps to have backers willing to buy at cost what you can't sell at market." He agreed puffing his pipe, "Not from around here I take it?"

"I would say the same to you," She offered with a bright grin, "how are the islands this time of year?"

"How on earth would you have guessed that?" He asked with a bark of laughter as William arrived with their drinks.

"Thank you, Cousin." She said taking a glass and turning back to the Captain.

"You are sea weathered in a room full of pale powdered dandies, your cuffs are salt stained," She said taking a tiny sip and trying not to wince, utter rot gut gin and fruit juice, "plus the shell bracelet you are wearing, my fishers cousins used to wear those for luck and favorable winds."

"Captain Justin Tennille," he said, offering a nod, "a pleasure to meet a lady with a mind in a den of depravity such as this."

"Esme Reinald," she said, giving a curtsy and gesturing to the others, "this is my cousin, William of Westedge and his friend Andrew, I'm afraid I wasn't told your surname."

"Andrew of Bryant Court," Andrew said with a quick bow, "I apologize, Lady, I left my manners in the carriage."

"Well, Lady Esme. You've exposed me for a sea captain. Care to take a whack at the other guests?" He asked with an innocent expression she didn't believe for a moment.

"What, as a game?" She asked blinking innocently as she took another sip of her drink and pulled out her fan one handed. Even with the windows open to the cool night breeze, it was stuffy inside with so many people wandering about.

"If you like, what would you say of the man over there?" he asked, gesturing to a dark-skinned man who was clinging to the wall like he hoped to disappear into the shadows.

Her immediate reaction was to note his training but she couldn't start listing out his knife skills, delaying with another sip she watched the firelight play over his clothes for a long moment. He was wearing custom fitted boots, but his brocade and shirt were loose, too loose to be fashionable, to hide the blades he wore under his coat. The man might even have a quilted bone vest under it to turn a blade if he was in a fight. He was waiting for some signal and was watching the room like a hawk, flickering his gaze back to Maximilian at the end of every circuit.

"He's not here to enjoy the party, he's not drinking, probably hasn't had a single glass tonight." She said with a shrug, "I'd say he's working, but he's not wait staff or a servant with what he's wearing."

"Then what do you think he's here for?" The captain pressed, puffing at his pipe with a wry smile.

"He's Maximilian's bodyguard." She sighed, gesturing to another woman slow dancing in place to one side with a frown, "I'd rather know who the woman wearing nothing but feathers is. That is a very daring creation. I wonder if I could recreate it with silks."

"You are wasted as a seamstress, Esme." Andrew laughed as William choked on his drink, "Will, can I steal your cousin away for the week? She would have my mother in hysterics."

"This has to be the worst swill I've ever had." William coughed, wiping at his chin.

"You haven't traveled enough, dear cousin." Beryl laughed, offering him a handkerchief.

"You've traveled a good bit with that sharp eye of yours," The captain said reaching in his coat and pulling out a pouch of tobacco to refill his pipe, "where did a young girl like you learn to tear a man down to his base parts so well?"

"Traveling with my drunkard of an uncle," Beryl said with a shrug and a tight smile as she finished her drink and set the cup on a passing server's tray without bothering to look, "You learn fast when everyone you meet is a stranger. Happily, I've improved my situation."

"I'm always happy to hear of someone who's pulled themselves out of the rough patches." The captain said giving her a salute with his pipe, "I'm off to Tigen on the late tide tomorrow or I'd invite you lot to dinner. You are wasted on Max and his guests."

"Drop me a note next time you are in harbor," Beryl offered handing him a card, "or pass me some work, I'm still trying to get my shop opened in the coming year."

"I shall do that, Lass, it's rare to meet such a sharp mind in a place like this. Take care of this one, boys, she's a rare bird." He huffed, standing and giving them a bow before taking his leave.

"You charm the strangest people," Andrew huffed, "why not turn some of that charm to our host?"

"Because he wouldn't have cared," Beryl sighed, "that kind of man only cares for money, nothing else will turn his head."

"Let's see who else we can charm," William said, offering her an arm, "the night is young yet."

"Lead on, dear cousin." Beryl laughed fanning herself and they wandered the mansion peeking into each room they passed.

It was nearly an hour later of wandering and playing random games before they found a young woman hanging off the arm of a gambler wearing grey crystals at her throat. Beryl steered William towards the game and they stood and watched until the current hand finished. She leaned in before they could deal the next hand.

"Madame, I must know where you acquired such unusual gems? They are lovely." She murmured, fiddling with her own thin strand of chain and inferior quality gems. Her cuffs and collar were well hidden under layers of cloth and lace.

"A gift," she chirped, "Max gave them to me himself. I had a bit of a cough and he insisted they could fix it, don't know if the stones helped, but they are beautiful."

"Lovely," Beryl agreed with a smile.

They watched part of the game before wandering away. It took another hour of wandering and idle conversation before a greasy-looking man finally approached them, offering them a drink that they declined, continuing to sip their still mostly full glasses.

"If I can't interest you in a libation, perhaps the lady would be interested in a few rare baubles? They are all the rage right now. I have a backroom set up as a small salon for those interested." The man offered with a slick smile.

"Well, you have me interested." Beryl said tugging at William's sleeve, "Let's go have a look, Cousin. I must have something to bring back from my trip."

"Very well, Cousin." William huff handing off his drink like it was empty and claiming another, "It's you money to waste."

"No less than you've wasted at the tables," She sniffed, offering the man her arm, "I would be delighted to view your wares, good sir."

"Wonderful, my lady; Let me show you the way." He said with a greedy smile leading them to a back room that had Beryl flinching before she'd even reached the door, the room was full of grey crystals, some shaded dark purple, blue, or red, but all of them pulling at her magic and strength.

She made a handful of random purchases before the drain overwhelmed her, "William, I'm feeling faint. Can we head on?"

"Of course, Cousin. Perhaps some air will help you." He said gathering up the bag with their purchases and leading her out with absent thanks to the dealer.

"Are you all right, you've gone very pale?" Andrew asked helping her as they stepped out into the drive and William went to collect the coach.

"Let me buy that necklace you bought, Andrew. I can't let you give that to your mother."

"What? Surely it's not that bad. It's gaudy, but my mother's a magpie, anything shiny is appreciated."

"Let's get you in the coach." William said, hurrying back and helping her up the steps, "I put the bags in the outside box. Andrew let me put your purchase out there too."

"Is there something wrong with the jewelry?" He asked reluctantly, handing it over.

"They make people sick," Beryl said with a sigh as Rune bounced down from his hiding spot and settled on her shoulders as Argent pressed close to her legs, "I friend of mine nearly died from wearing one and I've been determined to trace them back to the source so I can take proof to the King. Several people on the coast and around a friend's town in the mountains died from the crystals. People are claiming they heal you, but they are killing people instead."

"Why haven't I heard of this? This was the first time I'd seen crystals like that." Andrew asked, glancing at William in alarm as he returned to the coach and they headed out.

"They aren't flooding the market with them, there are only a few people selling them. No one is connecting the gems to the deaths because it's not everyone who gets sick. It's only if there is magic in your bloodline you fall ill, but anyone who comes near the gems with magic will fall ill if they are around them for long enough."

"Good heavens, I've never heard of such a thing. That is horrid."

"Especially since it mostly kills the old and sick or young children. Adults who aren't mages feel tired and ill, but it doesn't kill unless they pick up some other illness. It's assumed the second illness was the cause and they keep the crystals as keepsakes of the deceased making yet another person ill."

"The ones in this area all seem to be connected back to Max. Now that I have some proof, I can tell the King and have this place raided."

"It might not be that simple, Max has a lot of friends in high places. He'd probably get word of the raid before it ever happened." William sighed, "I've seen everyone from the local guard to the mayor in his halls from time to time."

"Which is why I will make sure they won't be using anyone local,

I'd advise your friends to stay home for a few weeks. There will be a lot of raids going on while they track down who is doing this."

"Frankly, if it messes them up in something like this, I hope they get caught." Andrew said rubbing his hands against his arms, "I might be off the party scene for a while anyway, you've given me some things to think about, Lady Esme."

"Let us drop you home, Andrew, it's not that far out of the way."

"Yeah, all right." He huffed, "Well, Will, I can't say your contract didn't make things more interesting. Are all your days like this now?"

"More often than you'd think," William laughed, "I can honestly say I'm never bored."

"My family hasn't a drop of magic or I might have approached your master for a contract right along with you. I'm not sure how long I will stomach staying at home much longer with how my family peeks and taunts. Perhaps sailing will suit me." He said with a huffed out laugh, "Think you could see me as a sailor?"

"It's hard work, but you've always had the adventurous streak in our group."

"I'm starting to think we were to two sane ones, I don't remember enjoying the nights out like I used to. Did you see them tonight? Not a word of greeting and all of them were drunk out of their minds. I doubt any of them will have a coin for the carriage in the morning."

"Yeah, amazing what happens when you stop blaming your parents for everything that happened to you." Beryl offered with a snort, "I never got the luxury of that growing up. I was my parent for much of my life, and any mistakes were mine to own. You two are just finally getting a taste of it."

"Terrifying, isn't it?" William offered with another laugh.

"Horrifying, more like." Andrew snorted, "It's my decision to destroy my life or change it and I've got no one to blame but myself if it goes wrong."

"One mistake doesn't ruin your entire life, you just pick yourself up and keep going." Beryl whispered, stroking her bond mates, "You don't have a choice but to keep trudging along most days."

"Life, the eternal trudge forward. That's depressing," Andrew sighed, "Can we change to a happier subject? Are you enjoying your new master, Will? You haven't been writing, and I was afraid they had you sequestered away somewhere."

"You know I've never been much of a letter writer, I'll try to do better." William sighed, "At first it was awful, I didn't realize how strung out on the drink I'd become and going from a constant supply to nothing was miserable. My master is a hard taskmaster and expects the best from me, but I think it's the first time anyone has expected something from me. It's hard work, but I'm enjoying it. I'm even training in weapons with her personal guard, up every morning at a gods awful hour, but I'm learning so much. I might even enter some of those weapons competitions by the time my contracts up."

"I thought you were learning magic, she has you enchanting swords or something?"

"Swords, daggers, random boxes that are lying about. I think I've tried to enchant half the kitchen at this rate, but it turns out my strength isn't in enchanting. I'm learning to heal which is twenty times harder than enchanting ever was but it's satisfying to know that someone is walking about healthy because you helped them."

"Wow, you're healing people? That is wonderful."

"Mostly bruises and cuts on the staff at the palace." William said with a glance at Beryl, "My master thinks I might even gain a mastery in healing."

"That is wonderful, I'm glad you found your place." Andrew said happy for his friend.

"You'll find yours. Maybe if seafaring doesn't work out you can work for Esme's shop or even for my master. She seems to collect people about her with unusual skills. You surely have something to offer."

"Everyone has a different strength, you just have to figure out how to make it compliment both your and their goals." Beryl hummed, exhausted, "Wake me when we reach the estate."

"Go to sleep, Cousin." William huffed with a laugh as he moved to the other side of the coach next to Andrew so Argent could climb up next to her.

"How in the world does your cousin travel with such a large dog? My father can't even travel with his hunting hounds without people complaining everywhere they go." He asked in a whisper to let the woman sleep.

"Would you have denied them?" he asked, gesturing at the tangle of limbs where the woman and hound curled against each other.

"My mother would have howled about the ruined dress, but no, I can't say I have an issue with it."

"There you go." William said with a shrug, "She makes people accept what would normally be impossible, I can't explain it."

* * *

The Prince eyed the crystals strewn across his desk with a frown. He seemed to have the same aversion to touching the crystals, but was poking at one with a stylus like it would react.

"You're asking us to use the palace guards to conduct raids across the country."

"Exactly."

"It can't be done." He huffed, falling into the chair behind his desk.

"These people have friends in the local guard. We would warn them of any upcoming raid before it could happen and destroy or move the crystals. It needs to be done quickly and as quietly as possible."

"I have no proof that these crystals do what you say, I need the royal advisers to examine these... things before we make any rash decisions."

"You asked me to find what was affecting your people, this is being used to destroy your magical protections and killing the magical children in your country. If you don't act more people will die."

"I only have your word that these crystals are making people sick, give me a few days to confirm that they absorb magic as you claim. If they do, I will send the guard to raid these properties and make arrests as needed, but I need more proof than a single mage telling me that my country is under attack!"

"I need to know what these people are hiding," Beryl snarled, "there are rumors of a temple in the mountains near here to Aedus. I should investigate that while you are rounding up the locations we know about."

"These things take time. Give me a few days to gather the evidence and put things in motion, I will keep the information as isolated as but I can't go running in making arrests without proof."

"Very well, I've given you the evidence you have. It's on the courts and the guard to act." Beryl sighed, standing and giving the Prince a curtsy, "I'll take my leave."

"Why the box?"

"Pardon?"

"Why a metal box to store the crystals, what's special about it?"

"It's lined in lead, it seems to slow the pull of magic into the stones or at least retard their function."

"Interesting," He sighed, "how is your apprentice doing? They have informed me that you've been teaching him weapons."

"He has an aptitude for the staff and long sword. My bodyguard has taken over his training at his request."

"And his magical studies?"

"He has a talent for healing and earth magics, I've asked the palace staff to send any minor injuries to the cottage for him to work on. So far he's been learning quickly, by next season he might need the tutelage of a more experienced healer."

"You aren't skilled as a healer?"

"I know war time triage, setting bones and stitching wounds until the soldier can be taken to a true healer. I can prevent infection in a wound and ease the pain, but I can't heal broken bones or massive injuries."

"It's refreshing to find out something that you can't do." He said with a laugh, "I'm glad that he seems to settle in. It worried me since he had the reputation of a bit of a rogue."

"His childhood seems to have been a lonely one, and it's taken a bit of adjustment on everyone's part, but he's doing well. He isn't suited for my runic approach to magic, but is slowly finding his strengths."

"That is good to hear, I was afraid we'd have to discipline him for public drunkenness or harassing the staff."

"He wasn't far off when he arrived, but adding the weapons training seems to have calmed him down."

"Good, good." He hummed slowly, moving each crystal into the lead-lined box using a cloth as they talked, "Are there any another topics you wish to discuss?"

"In the new year I'll be looking for an estate to purchase on the coast once the court returns to the palace there. I may need to travel a good bit to do so and would like to purchase and store a small couch at the cottage."

"That is fine as long as you keep your horses in the nearest stable as you have them now. I can't spend the funds to build you a personal stable at the moment."

"I wasn't planning to ask for one." Beryl sighed, "If my living on palace grounds is an issue, I can find a house to rent in town."

"Your staying on the grounds isn't an issue," The prince snapped rubbing at his eyes for a moment, "I'm not saying you are a hindrance, you are welcome at the palace or even in the royal quarters. At this point, you are one of three potential candidates for the position of court mage. You'd have rooms at the palace open to your use at all times if you are we give you the posting."

"And if I would rather live on my own?"

"Then you would have to travel to the palace for meetings and to attend any events that might need your input."

"I'm uncertain taking on the position of court mage would be beneficial to my work, if the King wishes me to continue to protect your family then it might be better for me to have a lesser position that would allow me to travel as needed instead of constantly being at the palace."

"If the crystals are the threat you believe, I could see where he might wish you to have more flexibility. You've mentioned opening a shop once you settle on the coast. Would this still be an option?"

"I doubt I would have the time if I took the position of court mage." She demurred, "I would much rather work in the shadows then be in such a prominent position with every eye on me. Would it be possible to be an adviser on foreign magic more than the court mage?"

"We would have to create a new position. What are you contemplating?"

"I know the King has his own intelligence gatherers that he employs however I've gained a rather unusual skill set in my travels that could work similarly. I have been building alliances and business deals with various people throughout your country and with my connections to Arden it would be easy enough to start a few minor business ventures that would bring in information and goods that the King has not previously considered."

"You wish to start a spy network."

"I wish to start a guild for people with broad skill sets that will bring information to the King and yourself, disguised as a merchant trading house."

"While that sounds worthwhile, I'm uncertain how ethical it would be for the crown to finance such a project."

"Which is why I would need a minor position at the court so that there are few connections between my business and the court."

"Has father agreed to this?"

"I have yet to ask for permission. He wished me to protect your family and Orlean from unknown threats. To do so, I had to reach out to the unsavory characters and businesses we would rather not see the court doing business with. In order to continue to provide the royal family with information, I need to at least have a reason to attend meetings or do business in the palace."

"I'm uncertain this is the best use for your skills, I will write to the King and see what his thoughts are on the matter. For now, you may continue on as you have been. Do what you must, and I will inform you when we are ready to move on to the known crystal merchants."

"Very well, thank you your royal highness." She said giving a final curtsy.

"I'm never certain what to do with you, Mage. You refuse to be slotted away tidily like most of the people I encounter."

"I will take that as a compliment, your royal highness." She said with a grin before turning and heading out the door, Jeremy stepped from the shadows to join her along with Argent.

"Where is the cat?" Jeremy huffed, glancing about for the missing bond mate.

"Exploring, he found another hallway not on our map. He'll return to the cottage on his own."

"Someone will take a boot to that beast one day," He huffed, "he's into more things than a rat in a cheese shop."

"Many people have tried, none have managed it yet." She singsonged with a grin as they exited the palace and headed out across the grounds to the cottage.

"What are your plans for the coming week? Will you need Benjamin or myself to accompany you anywhere?"

"I need to make another visit to Madame Lacene and while I love to see Benjamin blush, we need to talk business and I don't need him being a distraction."

"So you'll be taking William?"

"No, I'll be going alone. It's the only errand we have to run, so I shouldn't need an escort beyond your lovely presence."

"I shall try to wear my best and brightest for the occasion then." He chuckled, "Will you be giving the boy another project?"

"Yes, I haven't decided what to push him towards yet. I have a feeling a bond mate would ground him, but there aren't many animals at the palace to expose him to."

"Perhaps he can get some tracking training using his gift. Would he react badly to having animals hunted while he was there?"

"With the uncontrolled nature of his gifts at the moment I wouldn't want to find out, I think hunting is off the table for a time. Perhaps we can go tracking or ride the trails around the palace. The masquerade ball is at the end of the month and I got all but chased off the garden paths by the gardeners. I think it will limit us to the cottage and forest unless we want to head off the palace grounds."

* * *

"Master Rogen, a pleasure as always." Beryl hummed, keeping her eyes on the progress William was making with his greenhouse.

"I doubt that," he said with a sneer, "no one celebrates my arrival, Mistress Mage."

"Most people are too self absorbed to bother with most things outside of themselves."

"Most don't have the demands of an entire country placed on their shoulders."

"He isn't the only one to bear the burden, nor are you."

"Have the staff been spreading rumors again?" she asked, trying to sound lightly amused. She was sure it fell flat.

"A palace runs on rumor and speculation, even Orlean isn't immune to that. What rumors concern you?" He asked with a sigh, "It must weigh on your mind to seek me out."

"I'm hoping to sort fact from fiction."

"Let me see, there are so many." He offered with a sneer, "The prince has given me direct power over the country with the infirm king and its frivolous prince hunting and partying his life away, I have poisoned the king and hope to rule in his stead, or I am grooming an unknown heir to take the place of the prince after I engineer his death. Have I gotten close?"

"While I don't doubt you are capable of those, there is one thing you have left out."

"Do tell," He asked, raising one eyebrow like she was winding him up for a good joke.

"How would any of those rumors serve to better Orlean? For all the rumors and scandal behind you, your actions are always for the best outcome to Orlean." She said turning to meet his eyes, "You are loyal to your country. I may disagree with your methods, but you have protected Orlean and worked to ensure its advancement for your entire career while in the court."

"And yet you dislike my methods no matter the lives I've saved and the wealth I have funneled into Orlean."

"You see people as disposable. When someone has no more value to your schemes, you toss them aside."

"If they have served their purpose, then it was for the best. We must preserve Orlean at any cost."

"No matter the ruined lives you leave in your wake?"

"And which life am I supposed to have ruined? There are only so many you could have encountered in your short time in Orlean. I doubt my supposed rein of destruction could have reached Arden's shores."

"You employed a young maid on your northern estate." Beryl hissed, fighting to keep her temper in check and her face neutral, "You gifted her to a visiting noble for his stay."

"If it is the girl, we paid handsomely for her efforts."

"And released when she proved too damaged to continue work in your home. It has taken months for her to recover and she may never trust another man near her ever again."

"Your point?"

"She was a child who wasn't allowed to refuse. She was broken and discarded without a moment's thought because you needed to keep a potential ally happy."

"That ally saved Orlean from a trade war with Bastion. It was necessary to keep the country running. What does it matter?"

"People are not objects. They cannot be bought and sold without consequence."

"I agree, however, one maid versus the economic safety of Orlean? No one in his right mind would choose the maid."

"Sacrifices are always made, but we must account for the damage."

"We can argue about the morality of society until the end of time. What is it you wish from me? I will not apologize for a decision made months ago. She lived, that is enough."

"Mage Rogen,"

"I will not discuss this further, good day." He snapped, leaving Mage to watch as strode away.

Chapter 36

Prince's Birthday

The Prince's birthday party was as overblown affair as only a royal family could engineer. Exotic animals vied for space with acrobats and musicians wandering the garden and ballroom in twos and threes. Everyone was masked and costumed, making introductions redundant. There was no hope of keeping the guest lists straight with the entire inner garden and several halls being taken over by the sprawling extravagance.

Tables of every dish imaginable groaned in one room while the one next door contained boxes and bags of every shape possible as mounds of gifts for the Prince were opened and laid out for viewing by a team of servants.

A few visiting friends had dragged away William, and she was content to wander the room watching the population celebrate their prince and soon to be king's birthday. Arden had never openly celebrated the royal family's birthdays beyond the small seasonal festivals and a ball for the nobility. Here in Orlean it was a national holiday with all workers that were not essential given the day off and every town that could hold a festival.

The entire day had been devoted to various activities they

thought the prince to enjoy, though she'd noticed his absence for most of the morning. The princess however had enjoyed the constant tour of exotic animals and troops of entertainers at every corner. They had employed many of the mage apprentices for the day to cast small illusions and helpful enchantments to keep the wandering public entertained.

Beryl was more concerned with someone attempting to harm the guests or the royal family with so many being allowed onto the grounds. She wasn't sure to be relieved or annoyed that nothing had yet to trip the wards she'd layered throughout the palace and gardens. The royal guard had been pressed into patrolling the grounds and guards were posted throughout the palace, but it would be all too simple for someone to wander where they weren't supposed to be with the level of traffic through the halls.

The day hurried along and she returned to her rooms to change for the feast and ball to be held that night. The ball was a masquerade, and it was amusing to pull on the military uniform and tall riding boots. Being able to openly wear a short sword and a few other discrete weapons rounded out the outfit nicely.

She ignored the squeak from Olivia and Mary's shocked gasp as she gave them a mocking salute at the bottom of the stairs and pulled on her mask. With her hair piled under the dark grey cap and the padded shoulders, she looked the part of a young soldier. A plain black mask hid everything, but her amused eyes, leaving everyone wondering who the young man entering with the Apprentice Westedge was.

The ball was a confusion of masks, feathered headdresses, and exotic costumes. Few seemed to have twisted the norm as far as Beryl, sticking to their gendered roles however a few of the younger members of the crowd wore mocking masks that made them appear female. It seemed Orlean wasn't as embracing of the more relaxed roles that Arden and other countries tolerated.

She could only hope William was as accepting when his friend Andrew finally confessed his preferences to him. She honestly wasn't sure if William would be open to amorous advances from another man, even without the needs of his title pushing him towards a noble woman. Something to discuss with him at a later time.

Smirking at the simply dressed and masked man that offered her a bow, "Isn't it rude to hide at your own even, sir?"

"Considering I do it every year, I would think the nobility are used to it now." Prince Zyon said with a smirk, "It has become something of a game to try to spot the royalty, Noemi was rather put out she wasn't able to attend the dance."

"I'm sure she passed out as soon as they got her in bed, she's had a busy day."

"True, she enjoyed the animals in the gardens." He agreed with a nod, "Speaking of gardens, how goes the greenhouse?"

"Apprentice Westedge has it well in hand. It should be in full blood by late spring and the Princess' birthday."

"Wonderful, she's become enamored with the rose garden and bothering the staff there whenever she can catch them working."

"I must show her a few simple illusions and enchantments for scent. It may at least temper her affinity for perfume for a short while."

"If you can get her interested in the gentler scents, I would be indebted to you. Her current preference is eye watering."

"Viand would be a better tutor, perhaps a small gift of a few favored scents from her hand would be welcome?"

"That is a thought, I will speak with both of them later." Zyon agreed, "How are you enjoying the event? I know you tend to be anonymous, does it annoy you?"

"Only at times, I'm used to no one remembering my name." She said with a shrug, "At least I'm not disappearing completely,"

"True, that would be rather difficult to explain how Orlean lost one of the premier mages of the decade."

"Too much flattery is never done, good sir."

"Sadly, it isn't overdone. You show every chance of outdoing most of the Orlean mages in every way given a few years to learn our arts."

"Now I know you must need something. The royal prince does not flatter without reason."

"And you yourself said tonight I am just a common noble wandering the Prince's birthday event." He offered with a smirk, "Come dance, one dance so I won't have an excuse not to steal Viand for the next song."

"As the Prince orders, so I go." Beryl said with a mocking sniff, taking his hand and letting him lead the way to the floor, "In retaliation I promise not to abuse your toes."

"But not my ears?"

"I make no promises," she smirked as they took their places.

* * *

"Everyone, please enjoy the party. There is an issue I must tend to." Prince Zyon said, removing his mask and giving the room a wide smile. Moving quickly away, he gave Beryl a sharp glance as she followed him into the hallway and removed her own mask, "The King has fallen ill, they suspect poison. I will ride for the coast tonight."

"Would you like me to stay with Noemi?"

"Keep watch over her until she leaves the next day. She should be safe enough on the road, I'll send a squad of guards with her carriage."

"You don't want me to ride with her?"

"No, stay at the party. Keep the guests entertained if you are able." The Prince said waving for a page standing to one side, "I have that message stone you gave me, I'll send word if the situation changes."

"Very well, be safe Prince Zyon." Beryl murmured with a bow making him look at her with a frown as she turned away but didn't stop her as she made her way back into the party.

"William, watch the crowd and help with the illusion where you can. Keep everyone from panicking, I plan to pull everyone into the image."

"What? Mage,"

"Keep on your toes, Apprentice."

She gritted out a smile that was more a snarl of teeth than an expression of happiness, gods she hated being forced to play for a crowd. She searched and found Miss Viand and a few of the quieter women speaking with their masks lowered to one side. Argent was bristling at her side, making people give her a wider berth as she strode across the floor, glad for once to not be encumbered with skirts at a ball. Offering the group a bow, she fought back a snort as the women tittered over the unknown man approaching them.

"May I have this dance, Miss Viand?" Beryl asked, pitching her voice low.

"Are we acquainted with each other, sir?" She asked carefully, lowering her mask and eying the black mask covering most of Beryl's face with a frown.

"We are, I was hoping to exchange a few words while we danced."

"Very well." She agreed, taking Beryl's arm and allowing herself to be led to the dance floor, "How are we acquainted?"

"You know me as Mage, I am the foreign mage from Arden. Prince Zyon has asked me to mask his early absence with an illusion. Will you play piano while I cast?"

"I have never been one to entertain at such an enormous event, I do not play well enough."

"The Prince has requested it and he says you play very well. I need something to accompany the illusions and I can't play myself."

"Your apprentice,"

"William does not play, I need him in the crowd helping with the casting. Please, Lady Viand."

"Very well," Viand said, leading the dance toward the musicians stand and the waiting piano, "What am I to play?"

"Something the crowd can dance to as single pairs. Ignore the illusions if you are able. I will try to keep the stage from being included in the casting."

Viand quickly interrupted the conductor before they could start the next song. Rune and Argent hurried to William's side, herding him towards the wall and away from the worst of the crowd.

"Lords and Ladies, if I can have your attention, the prince has requested an entertainment from Lady Viand and Mistress Mage. Ladies, you have the stage."

"Thank you, Maestro." Viand announced, giving the crowded room a curtsy and taking her place at the piano, "Mistress Mage, whenever you are ready,"

"Lady Viand," Beryl said, giving the woman a courtly bow. She appreciated her costume all the more for the anonymity it had given her until now.

Raising her arms, she summoned the glyphs she had anchored in the wall and wards of the room. This was not how she'd planned to test them, but the Prince left her with little choice. The noise from the crowded room increases as the walls and floor glowed, enchanted fog rising to fill the room with a hazy mist. The piano continued behind her; the tone shifting as trees seemed to fill the walls, a starry night taking over the ceiling.

The room fell silent except for the piano as the trees swayed to an unfelt wind, the rustle of cloth and breath substituting for the swaying branches. The fog drifted through dappled light as small cool breezes caressed the waiting dancers.

Masked dancers stepped from the walls as the light pulsed in time with the music. Women found themselves faced with an unknown partner, hand extended to begin the dance dressed in dark military uniforms and animal masks while the men turned to find a flower masked woman draped in gauzy green or blue gowns that shifted and moved with the breeze.

Delighted cries rang out as the dancers formed opposing sides, and the other musicians took up the refrain as the dance began. Those at the edges of the room stood on the edge of a moonlit meadow, watching as masked dancers both real and illusionary met and parted, spinning through the forms of the dance.

Antlered masked men danced with the shocked woman while

pale women covered in glittering leaves and flowers danced the patterns with the men. The few who refused to partner with an illusion spun with their own partner amongst the fantastical illusionary dancers and steamers of sparkling mist that filled the moonlit scene.

Mage glanced behind her to see Viand gazing about her in wonder even while continuing to play. People would talk about this night for years to come. It would be hard to top if she was asked to do something for the next event. The dance continued for hours until Beryl was forced to plead for the band to take over to let both her and Viande rest.

Chapter 37

Traveling

Beryl arrived back at the cottage early the next morning and woke Mary and Olivia. They would need to have the cottage packed and luggage ready to go south as soon as possible. She would take William with her when the Princess left for the coast. Her magic was singing in her veins, pressing on her chest with every breath. Something big was coming, and she needed to be ready.

No one got much sleep that night. Beryl went to the Princesses rooms early the next morning to see if there was anything to help, but the maids and servants had the packing in hand. Noemi was waiting to one side, dressed in black with her ladies-in-waiting chatting about the ball the night before. Noemi immediately reached for Argent to her guard's disgust, curling against his enormous chest while he stood steady to take the small girl's hug.

"Will you be coming with us, Mage?" Noemi asked once she pulled away, pressing a kiss to Argent's muzzle.

"I'll be right behind you. It sounds like you might get underway before my carriage is ready. Yours are already outside being loaded." Beryl said, taking one hand and pressing a bit of magic into the girl's thin hand and letting it wash away some of her exhaustion and boost the protections woven into her gown and jewelry.

"I'm tired of traveling, will we be staying at the coast for the winter, do you think?" She asked glancing from Beryl to her ladies-in-waiting.

"I would hope so, but it depends on the King's health in the coming weeks." One lady-in-waiting responded, "If the Prince recalls the court, then everyone will travel for the next few weeks to move their households. It will be horrible traveling if the snows start soon."

"The roads are already a mess with the last storm, frozen at night and mud during the day." Another murmured with a sigh, glancing outside at the faint dawn light.

"I wish you could come with us, it will be so dull being in the carriage all day."

"Try to get some sleep on the drive," Beryl said, giving her hand a squeeze, "it will be a long couple weeks even once we arrive before things calm down. Maybe once everyone is settled, we can have a few lessons with my apprentice, he's learning a new magic you haven't seen yet."

"What is it?"

"He uses magic to make things grow, flowers, trees and every plant you can imagine."

"He can make anything bloom?" She asked bouncing before she recovered herself to the amusement of the other ladies.

"If it's meant to bloom, yes. He can't make trees that don't have blooms suddenly have them, but out of season roses can be coaxed to bloom like it's the middle of summer."

"Oh, that would be wonderful."

"When can I see?"

"Once everyone has arrived, I'll bring him to see you." Beryl said with a smile, it was nice to see the young girl so excited.

"Thank you, Mage. I can't wait to meet him." Princess Noemi said with a wide smile.

"Practice your magic once you arrive, I'd like to test you for what element you favor. I think you might favor earth like my apprentice."

"Then I could grow things?"

"Yes, once you learn to focus on your element, you can affect things that your element influences. If you don't favor earth, you might influence water or fire or air. We will have to see what you react to best."

"How do you find out?"

"No, I know you will try to cheat on the drive." Beryl chided, "I'll tell you once we are back at the coast and not a moment before."

"All right, but you promise to teach me?"

"I promise," Beryl agreed, "it looks like they may be ready for you. Give Argent a last hug so you won't be late for your carriage."

"They won't leave without me." She said even as she gave Argent a last kiss and stroked Rune once in goodbye.

"You don't wish to make them late either, no one likes to be kept waiting if they can help it." One lady murmured, helping the princess into her coat.

"Have a pleasant trip, be safe." Beryl said walking with the girl to the entrance to wave goodbye as the carriage slowly headed down the drive, a group of guards leading the way on horseback.

Going back to the cottage, she tried not to pace. Something was itching at her skin. Something was happening, and she needed to be moving. She tried to finish her errands, but by lunch times she'd had enough.

"William, are you packed?" she asked, ducking into the young man's room to check on him.

"Yes, everything is waiting to be loaded on the carriage except for what I'm taking with me."

"Put what you need in a saddlebag and wear your armor and sword. I will grab the horses."

"Are we in a rush?"

"We will ride ahead. Get your things together. I need to speak with the others before we leave."

"Jeremy isn't coming?" He asked, snatching his sword out of the pile of gear to one side.

"He doesn't have a horse, he'll be coming with the carriage. I'll bring the horses to the front." She said hurrying downstairs, "Mary? Is everything ready?"

"I just have the kitchen to clean out. We can't leave this food here to rot while the house sits empty." She said waving to the table covered in perishable items.

"Send Olivia to the palace kitchens for a cart to take everything there. They can use the food while everyone is back and forth." Beryl said filling a sack with a few staples for the road, "William and I will ride ahead, use the palace horses for the carriage and keep Jeremy in line."

"You know he will be sore at being left behind."

"I don't have a horse for him and his leg wouldn't stand up to the ride. I need him functional and not crippled by the end of the day if things go as I think they will. Make sure he wears his armor and all of you have at least the cuff and dagger I charmed for you."

"Should we be planning for the worst?" she asked, going still.

"I hope I'm wrong," Beryl said, moving forward and giving the older woman a hug, "I'll see you in a few days, Mary. Keep the household running until I get back. Benjamin is with his relatives, but I've sent off a message he'll be needed at the coast when he can get away."

"I'll keep an eye out for him." Mary huffed, taking the sack from Beryl and adding a few more items, "Make sure you and William come back in one piece, you hear?"

"I shall do my best." Beryl said giving her a last hug and pulling her great leather coat off the hook by the door. She needed a few things from the forge, "If you don't get the carriage out by this afternoon, go to the cellar and stay there. I'm not sure if the road is any safer than here, but I know the palace won't be safe by nightfall."

"I'll get the boys to hurry with the trunks." Mary said, hurrying back up the stairs to the front of the cottage.

Beryl paused at the lentil to pour as much magic as she dared spare into the cottage wards. It might stop a fire from spreading, but her vision kept superimposing with a cottage burned to the ground. Running to the forge, she grabbed up the two waiting bags and threw one to William as he hurried by. The stables were in an uproar, but the tack was where she'd left it after their last ride.

Sunny and her grey were fidgety with the commotion but let themselves be quickly tacked and loaded down without complaint. William would ride the grey while Beryl took the golden Sunny, she'd be able to spell the horse darker if it was needed but couldn't cast on a moving target or maintain a spell was out of sight if they got separated. It was just safer to ride the draft cross herself.

She mounted Sunny with the help of a passing stable hand and led the grey alongside on a long rein with Rune riding in the coat pocket. Argent was gamely waiting to one side. It was a given he would fall behind, but he would do his best. It was a brief trip back to the cottage with William taking the grey and quickly stuffing his bundles into saddlebags and strapping down things as securely as he could while Beryl adjusted her coat and gloves. The coat was too light for the cold weather but it would keep her dry and be easier to move in then the heavy wool one. William had changed into his chain mail shirt and wore his sword on his hip, tied so it wouldn't bounce as they rode. They were as ready as she could make them and once he was mounted, she set off at an easy trot, trying to warm up the mounts for the long ride.

"What are we riding into, Mage?" William asked as he drew even. They passed the long line of waiting carriages and carts being loaded along the palace drives, dodging servants and maids as they fought to get their master's possessions packed.

"I'm hoping nothing, but I'm guessing war."

"War?" he blurted, pushing his horse to keep pace after a shocked moment.

"What would the royal family do if they found out that the King was poisoned and they captured the Princess and is being ransomed?"

"They would raze the earth to find her, they would destroy every town in their way. They did it in the last war with Tigen, they burned every village they could reach until the country collapsed."

"We're hoping to get far enough ahead to prevent that. If we can get there first, then the war doesn't happen."

"So we're going in alone?"

"We're going to the one place no one would think to look for the princess, a temple of healers."

"Orlean doesn't have healers."

"Exactly, these aren't healers, but they are pretending to be to drain the magic out of the population and handicap the people of this world. Aedus wants there to be no magic on this world but his own, he's trying to make sure these of magic blood lines die out. In Arden he couldn't use the healer ruse since we already have healer guilds. Instead, they kidnapped children and drained them of magic before returning them to the family if they were able with no memory of the kidnapping."

"His followers are distributing the crystals?"

"Yes, and if we don't get there in time, they will do the same to the Princess and the rest of the royal family. No one with magic will be allowed to live if Aedus comes to power." She huffed, nudging her horse a hair faster.

"Should we be riding faster if it's that urgent?"

"I don't know when things will happen, I might be wrong that its today, but with the princess on the road it's when I would have tried it."

"Please tell me you didn't run a kidnapping gang in your youth." William quipped as they reached the road and cantered not pushing for speed with how sloppy the footing was but trying to lessen the distance between themselves and the royal carriages as much as possible.

* * *

It was dark by the time they caught up with the overturned carriages, one burning hotly while the others had black marks along the sides. It looked like the horses had bolted, but two lay dead in the mud, tangled in their harness. Another carriage had pulled up behind them, and the nobles were standing about in shock. Bodies lay strewn about the road, the guards that had accompanied the princess.

"Is the princess here?" Beryl barked, dismounting and running forward.

"I didn't see her," One man said, waving to one side where several bodies had been dragged, "my driver is tending to the wounded."

"William, check the coach." She said struggling through the thick mud to reach the driver the mess would have slowed the carriages to a crawl as they rounded the bend, a perfect place for an ambush, "I know some healing, do you need help?"

"The last one died just a few minutes ago," The driver said leaning back on his heels, "three were alive when we arrived but with no bandages and the cold they went into shock before we could do much."

"Did they say what happened to the princess?"

"One said she was taken by flaming men, but that's crazy." He said with a sigh, wiping at his face, "He was delirious with blood loss."

"Did he say what direction they went?"

"I think he pointed to the mountains, but like I said, he was in shock."

"Thank you," Beryl murmured, passing another servant who was dragging bodies to the side of the road on her way to meet William by the carriages, "find anything?"

"They didn't touch the trunks or possessions." William said standing and handing her a singed stuffed bear, the one she had gifted the princess, "Her ladies-in-waiting aren't here. It's just the guards and male servants."

"She traveled with two ladies-in-waiting and maybe one or two female servants, I didn't see who went in the carriage with her. The mud would have hindered the horses and any fighting, they had to be on foot." Beryl huffed, moving away to gather their horses with William trailing behind.

"Where next?" William asked as Argent ran up, his sides heaving, and started scenting the trail through the mud.

"They'll expect someone to track them, but not this soon, Argent will lead from here. Pull out your map, show me where we are." She asked, mentally scolding herself that she'd lost track of the direction they were headed in the headlong rush.

"We're half a day south of the winter palace, if we keep on this road it's a straight shot to the summer palace. They built it to suit the nobles traveling back and forth." He said pulling out his map and holding it against a tree to mark their location with one finger.

"If they are headed north, where is the nearest road they could take? We know they didn't backtrack on this road and if they are traveling with three women and a child, they need horses or a cart. I don't see cart tracks, but they could have hidden it further away and circled back."

"There is a side road ahead, but it doesn't go very far north, after that it's just farms and forest until you reach the northern passage along the mountains. I don't know the roads well there, many aren't on the official maps, its private roads and drives for each landowner."

"We must hope we don't lose the trail then. Our best guess for the temple is here." She said circling a spot near the foothills with one finger, "They have small niches in the mountain caves, but there is a private residence here that owns several entrances into a large cave system. They used it as catacombs for years before the land was sold and the locals barred from entering. They said the caves had become unsafe."

Chapter 38

Rescue

"**W**hy aren't there any guards?" William hissed as they eased down the tunnel. It seemed like they had been walking for hours with only quick searches of small storerooms to break the steady pace.

"The guards are at the main camp, they can see anyone exiting the mountain long before they reach them."

"Then why is no one here?"

"This is the back exit, the emergency exit in case of attack. Guarding it just points it out to attackers in a valley were there aren't supposed to be people. A large force couldn't come this way quickly or quietly. They would have to take the roads around the mountain, which gives them time to be spotted."

"Right,"

"Cast a glamor as we exit. Try to fade into the background and keep to the shadows like we practiced." She whispered as they approached the tunnel's exit.

"Hide or die, right?"

"Told you it would come in handy at some point." She whispered, gesturing for him to ease back as they neared the exit.

She hissed as the drained earth around the valley pulled at her magic. This was why no mage had sensed people in the valley, the drained, dead earth hid any magic and the forest and sprawling estate within hid anything but an extreme act. Even then, the soldiers and mages would have had to know exactly where to look to see anything.

They eased from the woods, blinking at the light spilling across the clearing. A massive party was being held with revelers wandering the lawn and around a central bonfire. The tracking spell was weak, but it pulled them on towards the manor house.

"Remember your lessons, we belong here." She said straightening her disheveled clothes and sauntering into the firelight.

"Hail Aedus!" A couple shouted, and she responded in kind with a drunken laugh, "Hail Aedus."

"We're covered in mud, we don't look like silk dressed courtiers." William hissed, hurrying to catch up.

"We took a quick tumble in the garden," She said, looping an arm through his and leaning into him as they strolled along, "we just need to get cleaned up."

The guard at the door frowned at their clothes, but she giggled drunkenly and complimented the man on his eyes, swaying so hard she almost made them both fall. "Doesn't he have beautiful eyes, Ronnie?" She asked breathlessly, giggling.

"Whatever you say, Moll." William huffed, rolling his eyes at the guard, "Let's go find you a glass of water."

"Rooms are on the second landing." The man said with a chuckle.

"Thanks, Mate." William sighed, manhandling her to the stairs, "One glass and she's off her feet."

* * *

They wandered down the main corridor once the door closed behind the amused guard. They passed a few other couples, but most were too interested in each other to notice. The sitting rooms were full of pipe smoke and raucous laughter. There was no sign of the princess or her maids. Any of the scattered men could have been someone who helped in the attack. A few sported injuries, but most were drunk.

The entrance when they found it was anything but hidden. Flickering mage lights and candles outlined the basement doorway. The drunken revel continued below and they kept up the charade, stumbling along waving half-empty bottles and crooning broken bits of song.

"Remind me never to ask you to sing again." William huffed, making Beryl snicker.

"There was a reason I learned the pipes, my boy. You, however are passable. Remind me to find you a wind magic teacher if we make it back. You could do well enough with some vocal lessons. Nearly there, just a bit further."

"How can you tell?" William asked, leaning against the wall and pretending to take a swig of his bottle.

"Have you seen any drunks in the last few hallways? This is where the serious work is done. Keep your eyes peeled and ready to cast a sleep spell if someone comes to see who is making all the noise."

"Right,"

"Remember your role, I'll deal with Delorean, you get the princess to safety."

"Yes, Mage."

The cavernous room at the end of the tunnel stripped the handful of enchantments from their clothes in a wash of broken magic. The walls and pillars were studded with dark grey and black crystals, pulsing softly as they consumed the energy and magic in the room. The princess and her two ladies-in-waiting cowered in a shadowed corner while a tall figure paced before the flame covered altar at the far wall.

Beryl strode forward without a hint of hesitation even as William slid along the outer wall towards the collapsed forms of the princess and her attendants. Delorean looked skeletal in the firelight, cheeks hollow and hair unwashed. Apparently being a god wasn't good for his health.

"Delorean, apologies for keeping you waiting," Beryl said with a wide grin, keeping her daggers at her side, hopefully hidden amidst the sleeves of her coat.

"Who speaks to Aedus so commonly? You will be punished for your insolence." The man sneered turning to face the room, the fire behind him should have sent his face into shadows but his very bones seemed to pulse with the same inner light as the crystals making Beryl lock her knees to keep from stepping back at the madness in his eyes.

"You were known as Count Delorean when I knew you, have you forgotten me already?" She asked in the same polite voice she'd have asked for a glass of water at the King's table, polite but without inflection.

"Delorean is dead, only Aedus remains. Leave me unless you wish to lose what little magic you have left." He said in a resonating voice, light catching the crystals imbedded in his skin and arms. The skin was edged in black and sickly looking, but he showed no signs of illness.

"So the man who attacked a child, trying to strip her magic and life away, doesn't remember his one failure?" She taunted, watching out of the corner of her eye as Rune and Argent darted from the shadow of one column to the next. She dared not look at the princess. Throwing the slowly widening connections between her bondmates and herself more magic, she braced for the first blow.

"Aedus does not fail!" He shouted, eyes and body glowing, magic infusing the sound and making the room ring with echoes, leaving her ears aching. The crystals were echoing every bit of magic he used out into the room.

"No, then why did you leave Arden? Why run like a beaten dog to Orlean if you weren't driven out, your plans thwarted and followers in disarray?" She snapped, tensing into a slight crouch. If he was going to break, it would need to be soon.

"Aedus is eternal, I have no reason to accept failure. All will bow to the cleansing flames." He said waving her away as insignificant and turning back to the flames, Beryl could feel the heat increasing, her skin tightening as she slowly crept closer.

"So you want the death of everything? All life to end?" She asked, praying he'd be distracted long enough to give William time to escape. It was like forcing herself to step into a magical furnace as she neared the altar.

"Everything returns to ash in the end, only fire is eternal." He crooned, reaching out to caress the flames like a doting parent, not flinching even as his skin split and burned.

"Even fire dies if there is nothing left to fuel it, what will you do once you have drained the magic from this region? Move to the next? What then? What will you do when there is no magic left?" She pressed, pulling all the magic she dared and forcing it along the bonds that bound her and her bondmates. No matter what happened, it would not be gentle.

"That will not happen, enough with these pointless questions. Aedus is all, and soon all will bow before me." He roared, turning back to find her only a few steps away.

"I will never bow. No mage who has ever practiced magic would bow before someone who believes in stealing magic from one to give to another." Beryl snapped, reaching for her magic. The entire walk down she'd pooled magic into the cuffs and collars that she and her bond mates wore, filling them until they felt ready to burst.

Lunging forward she buried a knife in his gut, Argent pulled him off balance by one arm, Rune screaming his challenge as he clawed at his back. The ground heaved as Aedus roared in pain and anger, snatching Beryl to him with inhuman strength. Smoke filled the air, the bond was wide open, every action tripled as they each fought.

Beryl/Argent/Rune screamed as their skin burned. Surging forward they threw everything into a last strike, Beryl feeling her stiletto slam hilt deep into the monster's face, plunging to the hilt in one eye. If he wanted magic, he would have it. He could take it all!

The monster that had been Delorean shrieked, magic pouring off of him. The gems in her cuffs cracked from the heat, giving the last of their magic as Beryl tore herself free. Delorean staggered and Beryl shoved, refusing to leave until he was dead, watching through the smoke and dust as he hit the flaming altar and was consumed in a wave of flames.

The ground heaved, fissures venting steam as the deep fire below the earth reached to reclaim what they had stolen from it. Snatching up Rune, she staggered toward the tunnels, praying to every god and goddess she could name that they would reach the exit before the caverns collapsed. She had no magic left to help. Her core felt as broken as the scorched and melted metal wrapping her arms and throat.

* * *

William clutched the princess tightly to his chest and ran. It was chaos in the garden when he emerged from the house. Soldiers and partiers ran in early direction, dodging the streaming cracks opening along the manicured paths. The ground shook hard, sending him sprawling, twisting as he fell to keep the child safe.

"Hold tight," he muttered, stumbling to his feet, eying a group of approaching soldiers before bolting for the trees. They just had to stay hidden until whatever this was calmed down enough to let them move. Instinct had him darting after the small fox that crossed his path. When they reached a creek he waded in, the fox leaping to join them on the other bank.

He collapsed into a small ditch when he couldn't run anymore. The fox curled against his side, hot against his ribs. He shifted the princess so she would get some warmth and she stared at the animal with wide eyes but didn't protest.

"Where are we going?" She whispered once the fox sat up and began washing its feet of the mud and ash that coated all of them.

"I have a horse near the mountain entrance. I will head there and then we are taking you home."

"Father is okay?"

"Yes, he sent Mage and I out after you." He said not knowing if it was true, but doubting it mattered now.

"I'm cold."

"I have another jacket in my pack," he said stripping out of his coat and wrapping it around her shoulders, "If we find the army first we can get you warmed up and some food before we go the rest of the way."

"Where is Mage? Is she alright?"

"Yes, she wanted me to get you somewhere safe. She will meet us at the palace."

"She won't get lost?"

"No, she tracked you all the way here. I don't think she can get lost." He said with a forced laugh as something rumbled in the distance, "Do you think you could ride on my back? We can go faster that way."

"Alright, is this your fox?" She asked as she slowly climbed up to wrap her arms around his neck.

"I think he just wants to get away from here as much as we do." He said making sure she was secure with her legs tucked into his arms, "Ready?"

"Yes,"

"Off we go then," he mumbled, heading out at a slow jog, the fox giving a rippling cry and bounding forward to join them.

"He's following us," she said.

"He can do as he likes, he's not a danger to us."

"But the man used magic. What if the fox is his?"

"I don't think it belongs to him. He didn't have any animals like Mage I saw and I doubt he could have. Mage said you have to have an open mind to find your animal bond, be a good person. He wasn't."

"No, he was a dangerous man."

"You don't have to worry about his, Mage will make sure he can't hurt you again."

"Yes, she promised." She agreed as he slowed to a walk. He eyed the sun and where the mountains sat on the edge of the trees and shifted to move parallel, "He said he wanted my magic, that it didn't belong to the royal family."

"Magic doesn't belong to anyone, you can't own something like that."

"He took another child's Magic to show me what would happen if Father didn't come for me. It was horrible."

"What he did was evil, no one can claim the magic of another without losing their own. There is a price for everything when you try to force magic to do things against its nature. He will be cursed for the rest of his life for taking it."

"Mage will make sure he can't do it again?"

"Yes, I'm certain of it;" he didn't mention that if Mage got the chance, then she'd kill the man in an instant, he'd heard enough of her nightmares over the months he'd lived with her to know the pain he'd caused her and countless others was extreme.

"Good," she said, smothering a yawn into his shoulder.

"Rest a bit, we still have a long way to go." He said with a huff, glaring at the fox that was pacing to his right.

They ran through the night, his steps guided by the silver pelt of the fox leading the way. He nearly collapsed when they reached the horses. He hated taking Mage's horse as well, but he couldn't leave it tied up with the ground still trembling.

They rode in silence, the princess asleep pressed against his chest. He'd tied them together with a stirrup leather when she first started nodding off. His muscled screamed for rest, but he pressed on. He did not understand how long they had been riding when the first scouts from the army found them and hustled them both back to the main force.

They hustled the princess back to the healer tent, and they questioned him for what felt like hours over where the estate was located and how many troops they might expect. The generals finally let him rest in the healer's tent when scouts arrived, reporting that they had found the cave entrance. A second force was being sent to the main entrance of the estate to block any attempts at retreat, but for now it was out of his hands. The Princess was safe and the army could clean up whatever mess Mage had left behind.

The fox peeked out from the edge of the tent, hidden under a low table. William was too tired to do more than curl against the animal's warmth when it joined him on his cot, pressed against his chest. It had helped keep them both safe, and that was worth anything the creature needed.

Chapter 39

Conversations

"Congratulations on saving the princess, Mistress Mage;"

"How do you make even the most pleasant statement an insult, Mage Rogen?" Beryl asked turning to watch the King's Advisor approach absently reaching to touch the bandages at her throat, she still wasn't used to not having the cuffs and collar she'd worn since childhood in place.

"It is a gift." He said with a mock sigh, "I have given some thought to our last conversation, I may have done the child a disservice in not keeping track of her. In my defense, I normally assign such tasks to others."

"Next time you sacrifice someone for the good of the country, send the damaged goods to me. Much of her pain and terror could have been avoided if someone had bothered to see to the child when it happened."

"So now you seek to right the wrongs of Orlean? Will you be our conquering hero marching to overthrow those in power who have abused the small peasants below them?"

"William will need to learn to heal" She said ignoring the jab,

"Having a small clinic where free care is offered in certain cases will assist in his education."

"I thought Arden was known for their magical subtlety. Your latest exploits haven't been without scrutiny. You will be a feared member of court once the rumors reach the general population." He said watching her closely.

"I've always been a person of action." She offered with a tired smile. Her magic was still recovering even more than a week later.

"As I am coming to see," He said with a grimace, watching her for a long moment, "I will arrange the purchase of a building near whichever coastal estate you decide upon and an allowance for staff. Hiring the healers and everything else will be in your hands."

"Thank you."

"Do not thank me, Mistress Mage. I am sure having a small private healer's clinic will come of use at some point."

"As ever, I strive to be useful to the Crown." She said giving a mock bow.

"Don't tempt me into charging you for the damages to the palace." He said with a sniff, "After all, only the things you warded were exempted from the damage, your cottage not withstanding. How did that burn down, anyway?"

"I designed it to withstand flames but not a concentrated magical attack considering it was so far from the actual palace."

"Something to consider for your next lodging."

"Very true, please let me know if there is anything particular you wish warded in the rebuilding. My apprentice will work in the healing halls while I concentrate on the grounds. I expect we will be busy for quite a while."

"I do not doubt the Prince is thinking of retiring to the coastal palace while the repairs continue. As a member of his court we will both be traveling with him should he leave."

"And if I think we would be more useful here?" She asked, feeling the need to press the issue.

"That would have to be decided at the Prince's discretion. There is still a royal funeral to plan which will require our presence."

"Ah, with everything going on, it had slipped my mind. I will speak to my staff. It might be better to move ahead of the mass resettlement if the court is moving."

"I will leave you to your preparations then. Have a pleasant afternoon, Mistress Mage." He said, giving her a curt bow.

"Good afternoon, Master Mage Rogen;" She said with a curtsy as he nodded and headed on his way, Argent wandered up from where he'd been waiting to press against her side for a long moment.

She glanced over the still smoldering ruin of the palace gardens with a sigh before turning to head back to the main hall that had been converted into an infirmary. Rune chirped from a bed as she entered with William's yet unnamed fox, watching the proceedings with interest.

William didn't glance up from his patient, too absorbed in the healing to notice her arrival. He had already far surpassed her in the healing arts and she was sure he would continue to heal where he could no matter what profession he settled on. It wasn't a gift you abandoned.

"Mage," He said with a flush, straightening and glancing for the Master Healer, "Do you need me?"

"Not yet, I just wanted to share some information that came my way. Do you have a moment?"

"Let me just let them know I'm taking a break." He said with a nod, hurrying over to where the other healers were tending to a badly burned soldier.

"You need to have a name," she told the black and silver-coated fox with a sigh, "everything needs a name."

"Where do you want to go? They have released me for my lunch break."

"Then let us go find some lunch, we can talk as we go." She said watching with a smothered chuckle as he packed up his things and plucked the fox up to ride in his arms like an enormous cat.

They walked through the destroyed lawn and gardens while she did her best not to look towards where the cottage used to stand. The kitchens laid out a massive lunch for the workers on tables to one side and they joined the line discussing the cleanup efforts and how different people they knew were doing as they collected thick sandwiches full of meat and cheese and a handful of fruit.

"What is happening, are we leaving?" He asked once they settled on a bench and distributed the extra to the animals.

"Have the rumors already hit? The Prince is considering moving to the coast for the rest of the year while the repairs continue. We still have the King's funeral to arrange and the Prince's coronation to plan. It needs to be done soon."

"When do we leave?"

"I need to speak with the Prince and see. For now, let the Healers know that you will help as long as able, but to not count on your continued presence." She said with a sigh, taking a bite of her sandwich while William fed a sliver of ham to his fox, "Your fox needs a name."

"I know, but we can't agree on anything." He huffed with a fond laugh, "How did you name your two?"

"They named themselves, Argent was already named when we bonded, and Rune insisted on his name when I compared his stripes to the runes I was studying. What does he think?"

"It's just pictures and images that make little sense, we don't talk like you do to Rune and Argent." He said in frustration.

"That comes with time, the bond has to strengthen. Talk things out, what does he show you?"

"Snow and fire, a warm den under a fir tree, something blue, something glittering in the dark? It makes little sense." He said with a sigh.

"Snow and fire can be dangers for a fox, but a den is safety. Safety and danger, warmth and ice, contradictions."

"Exactly," he said with a groan, resting his head in his hands only to chuckle as the fox wormed his way into his embrace.

"Chaos perhaps, he is showing you contradictions. Perhaps his name needs to have two meanings."

"Chaos is destruction. That's not a good name to give someone."

"It also means change, change is neither good or bad. The nature of change is what you give it, the meaning you take from it." She said with a tired smile, fighting the urge to scratch at her healing wrists.

"They said the mail finally arrived," He said setting down his food, "I need to get a letter to father at some point."

"Are you going to confront him?"

"No, I will leave things as they are for now. He can't use me if I know he's trying to. Even if he was forced to raise me, he still is the only father I know. Do you think the Prince knows we are related?"

"I don't know, it is something we will need to discuss. Do you want to be acknowledged?"

"Not really, I can't imagine trying to live like the princess with my life in danger and everyone trying to gain favor. I think I want to decide on my own life first before anything becomes public knowledge, if it ever does."

"You could do more to help the crown as you are." She offered, "Once they announce you as part of the royal line, there will never be a time you won't be under watch. Now you can do what you wish and being employed by the Prince isn't an inferior position to hold."

"What would I do?"

"It depends what you want to do. For now, you are my apprentice, you will assist me where you can in the projects I have for the crown but once you reach your mastery it will be up to you if you wish to change roles."

"You think I'll have a mastery soon?"

"The healers say you are ready for a full-time apprenticeship with their guild if you wish. You need at least a year as an apprentice before you can apply for a mastery in healing."

"And if I wanted to stay as your apprentice?"

"You are several years away from a mastery in magical studies but that could be put on hold if you wished to peruse an original line of study or you could suspend you apprenticeship at the end of the year and take a position in another household."

"What position? No one has offered me a position."

"The princess has offered for you to continue your swordsmanship training with the Royal guard."

"Oh,"

"It isn't something you have to decide now. I just want you aware of all your options."

"Too many options." William muttered with a groan.

"There always are, but only a few of them will make you happy, I think. Plus you have to option of going your own way if you wish at the end of the year. You don't have to stay here, William, if you have a better offer somewhere else."

"I want to stay, for now anyway." He offered with a small grin, "Will we be doing any more adventures for the Prince?"

"Next is getting settled at the new house and finding more staff. I have a feeling Mary will not approve of all of my choices, but we need a few people with skills hard to learn outside of a rough life."

"I thought Benjamin was joking when he said you were setting up a spy network."

"Less a spy network and more a group of individuals with skills that fill certain gaps in what we can offer the crown. We will be collectors of information and relationships. Knowing the right people and having the right connections can prevent things like this." She said with a sigh gesturing to the burned grounds around them before balling up the wax paper from her sandwich and stuffing it in her pocket, "Come, we both have a busy day ahead. Go learn more healing and try not to overdo it. I don't want to receive word that you are now in one bed."

"I won't, he won't let me anyhow." He said with a snort, scooping up the grinning fox as he stood.

Chapter 40

Epilogue

It was a month since the attack, and they were settling into the new house. She had sent word to her few friends and acquaintances with the new address and several long letters to Richard, but received few replies. The chaos and heavy snows had left the mail unreliable, so she did her best not to fret. He would come when he could, she was sure.

The new house was exactly what she had hoped for, if a good bit larger than the original plan. It was less cottage and more regal manor house, with several additional buildings scattered about the estate that could be converted in the coming years as the need arrived. For now, her main project was hiring the staff needed to run such an extensive property, not that she would go through the normal channels for most of them.

Mary just shook her head when she announced a former brothel worker who would work as a maid and teacher for any children the staff wished to bring when they arrived at the estate. Benjamin and Mary had refused to allow her to convert an entire wing of the house to servant quarters, and instead one of the smaller buildings was being used while they reworked the rooms upstairs.

"Madame, a rider is coming down the lane. Looks like a gentle-man." Sophea called down from her perch near the windows while they both sorted books. The estate had come partially furnished but would need a lot of updating given the state of the library.

"I'll go see, keep sorting. I don't know what kind of person leaves a library in such a state." Beryl huffed with a sigh, glancing at the disordered shelves.

"I doubt the last tenant was much of a reader, Madame." Sophea said with a snort, holding up a thin volume, "They haven't even cut the pages on some of these. They are just for show."

"Well, in this house books are to be read. Make sure the rest of the staff know that they are welcome to read any book as long as they return them. I'll be back in a minute." She said waiving Argent back to his spot by the small fireplace, Mary had found stacks of skins in the barn and every fireplace now had a fur or wool rug to one side for the animals.

Stepping outside she froze on the steps, John handed his gloves and hat to the stable boy before turning to see her waiting. He lunged forward, dragging her into a hard embrace.

"I'm so sorry, I just received your letters. We didn't hear about the attack until you wrote. It has snowed us in for weeks." He said into her hair, hands running up and down her back and shoulders like he was trying to memorize every inch.

"Are the horses alright? Your father and sister are okay?" She asked, making him laugh in giddy relief.

"Everyone is fine, the horses are going stir crazy and I may have pushed Remit too hard to get here but he will recover. Tell me you are alright." He said easing them apart just enough to see her face and press a chaste kiss to her lips.

"I am fine, none of us were hurt badly, even my burns are mostly healed. Everyone was just shaken and scared. The palace is a wreck, so the Prince moved everyone to the coast. The purchase went through on the estate so I moved what I could, the cottage burned down so I had little to move."

"Are you at liberty or do you need to head to the palace?" He asked, forcing himself to not cling as they discussed her duties.

"I have the next few weeks to deal with the new estate. Will you let me show you my new home?" She asked, leaning back against his chest and letting him fold her back into his embrace.

"Only if you allow me to hold you longer, I'm afraid I thought the worst the entire ride down." He murmured, pressing another kiss to her temple.

"I have no intention of letting you go, John." She said leaning back just enough to take his hand in hers, "Shall I show you our rooms?"

"Our rooms?" He repeated in surprise.

"I had hoped you intended to visit more than just the once." She whispered, afraid she had moved too quickly with things.

"I intended to propose in the spring, but I will take whatever you will give me, my lovely Beryl. I just wished to leave your reputation intact." He said pressing a kiss to her forehead.

"What?" She asked dazed, blinking at him in shock.

"I love you." He repeated with a small grin that faded as she watched him in shock, "Is something wrong?"

"You said my name."

"You told me it was Beryl, do you truly prefer Mage?"

"No one has called me Beryl since I was a child." She stuttered, clutching at him in shock.

"I won't if it bothers you," He said, pulling back to see her face in concern.

"Say it again," she sniffed, tears coursing down her cheeks.

"Beryl, I love you." He said stroking her cheek with a smile.

"I love you, John, now and forever." She said pulling him down for a kiss.

About the Author

Amelia G. Sides lives a double life in Columbia, SC. Quiet clinical information system programmer by day and daring fantasy writer by night. Amelia and her four legged companion, Reuben, can be found on most evenings sitting in front of her computer screen plotting out her next book.

The first in a new series, **"I don't want to fight!"**: A GameLit Novel, will become available the summer of 2024.

Check out her social media sites at the link below.

https://linktr.ee/asides3